AN
APPETITE
FOR
MURDER

A FRANCES DOUGHTY MYSTERY

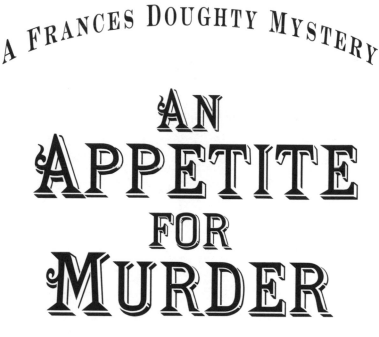

AN APPETITE FOR MURDER

LINDA STRATMANN

The Mystery Press

To Lyn Stratmann

First published 2014

The Mystery Press, an imprint of The History Press
The Mill, Brimscombe Port
Stroud, Gloucestershire, GL5 2QG
www.thehistorypress.co.uk

© Linda Stratmann, 2014

The right of Linda Stratmann to be identified as the Author
of this work has been asserted in accordance with the
Copyright, Designs and Patents Act 1988.

British Library Cataloguing in Publication Data.
A catalogue record for this book is available from the British Library.

ISBN 978 0 7509 5444 0

Typesetting and origination by The History Press
Printed in Great Britain

CHAPTER ONE

S

ometimes, thought Frances Doughty, with just a trace of irritation, the people of Bayswater had nothing better to do with themselves than quarrel. Even gentlemen of education and mature years, who really ought to know better, the very same gentlemen who addressed sensible ladies as if they had the intellect of small children, made themselves look ridiculous by puffing themselves up, pontificating about their erudition or their morals, and exchanging gibes and insults with other similarly stubborn and conceited gentlemen. They indulged in this sport not in decent privacy but in the public press, and these petty wars often ended up in a court of law or even in the street, where blows were exchanged, hats dented and noses pulled. Both participants then asserted, usually before a policeman, that the other had started it first, and both claimed to have won. The worst offenders, Frances observed, were politicians and medical men.

Take for example the furore that had erupted recently over the unfortunate death of Bayswater accountant Mr Thomas Whibley. Mr Whibley had been aged only forty-nine when he expired, but his death had not come as a great surprise. He was a wealthy gentleman who enjoyed the good things in life, and had enjoyed them all to excess. His pleasures were rich food, good wine and brandy, fat cigars, and beautiful women of high class and low morals. Such was his indulgence that it was the subject of some discussion, and not a few wagers, which species of gross intemperance would kill him first. Mr Whibley, although not quite a Daniel Lambert, had achieved monumental proportions of stoutness, weighing, although not a tall man, almost thirty stones. This, however, did not appear to have slowed him in his relentless pursuit of pleasure. In the event, he did not expire slumped across a table in his favourite restaurant, or in a cloud of cigar smoke at his club, or even in an actress' boudoir. He surprised everyone by being found dead one morning, in his own bed, quite alone. His heart, unable to maintain the task he had set it, had decided to stop beating.

There, with a few prayers over his extra wide coffin, the matter should have ended, and it only remained for his executors to dispose of his effects and distribute the proceeds between the four mistresses and twelve children mentioned in his will. Unfortunately someone calling him or herself 'Bainiardus' had written a letter to the *Bayswater Chronicle*, and even more unfortunately the *Chronicle*, which relished a good fight, published it. Bainiardus alleged that while Mr Whibley's heart had undoubtedly failed him, this was nothing to do with his dangerously imprudent mode of life, or even the strain of carrying so much weight about his person. Mr Whibley, the writer revealed, had been warned by his doctor that he must lose weight. For the last month, he had been on a reducing diet, and it had been no ordinary diet. Mr Whibley had been 'banting', and it was this harmful and ill-advised practice that had caused his death.

Mr William Banting, after whom the diet was named, was, Bainiardus explained, not even a medical man, but an undertaker, who had once been extremely corpulent. Some years previously he had advocated a dietary regime that consisted of nothing but meat, fruit, vegetables and dry wine. This had not been deleterious to Mr Banting's health; indeed, he had lost his excess weight and claimed that he had never felt better. Recent practitioners, however, had taken matters to hazardous extremes, and Mr Whibley had been living off nothing but broiled beefsteak and champagne for a fortnight before his death.

Further correspondence followed. Mr Whibley's doctor, who declined to give his name, stated that it would not be giving away too many secrets to reveal that he had been advising his patient to lose weight for the last ten years, although he had not recommended any particular regime, other than reducing intake of food, especially pastries and sweets, and taking exercise.

A Dr Adair, who practised in Bayswater and advocated the Banting diet, wrote to the *Chronicle* in warm support of it, saying that not only was it not dangerous to health, but it was a great boon to the corpulent who had been unable to reduce their girth in any other way.

Several other doctors took up the argument and they were soon joined by Mr Lathwal of the Bayswater Vegetarian Society, who abhorred the excessive consumption of meat advocated by Dr Adair, and Mr Rustrum of the Pure Food Society, who abhorred the excessive consumption of anything. Thus far, nothing being said or written was actually actionable, and while there was a certain amount of placard waving and pamphleteering on all sides, the excitement looked destined to die down, especially when the sudden advent of appalling weather in the middle part of January became the new topic of everyone's conversation.

After a balmy opening to the year 1881, which had led to optimistic forecasts of a mild winter, London was suddenly gripped by a cruel frost with temperatures dropping as low as fifteen Fahrenheit, while heavy snowfall was driven by gales into deep drifts, blocking windows and doorways, bringing the business of the capital to a halt and endangering deliveries of food, post and newspapers. Traffic in the streets was all but stopped and few pedestrians ventured out; clubs and places of entertainment were deserted, and communication between London and the rest of the country suspended. The enterprising carrier could make something of it, though at considerable risk to himself, charging double rates for the delivery of urgent messages, but for most, venturing onto the streets was a matter of necessity rather than choice. The few cabmen who still plied their trade were shrouded in veils and spectacles to protect their eyes, and on the Gray's Inn Road, a watchman froze to death.

For Frances, the weather was not only inconvenient for the essentials of food and laundry, it also prevented the arrival of new custom for her business of private detective, and was the perfect excuse for existing clients to delay paying their bills. When a small improvement in conditions later in the month brought new clients, not all of them were welcome, but by then she felt she had little choice in the matter.

A correspondent of the *Chronicle* signing him or herself 'Sanitas' had resurrected the argument that had begun with Mr Whibley's death, introducing a new and worrying tone. The Pure Food Society, claimed Sanitas, was a dangerous movement, and its chairman, Mr Rustrum, had no right to criticise either Dr Adair or anyone else. The Society advocated regular fasting, had undoubtedly been responsible for a number of deaths, and its practitioners were guilty of criminal negligence or worse. The Vegetarian Society, Sanitas hinted, was not a great deal better. Sanitas had struck a nerve, and undoubtedly meant to do so. Many people thought that the letter emanated from a medical man, not a few supposed that Sanitas was actually Dr Adair, and several were unwise enough to say so.

Frances, who had rather hoped that her services would not be required to settle this particular squabble, received three letters on the issue, one from Dr Adair who said he was being libelled and that he was not Sanitas and did not know who was, one from Mr Rustrum and one from Mr Lathwal. These three gentlemen, while deeply divided on the subject of correct diet, were united in one respect; they all wanted to know who Sanitas was, and they wanted the letters stopped. Frances wrote to all three to make appointments, and found, with some difficulty, a cab which proceeded cautiously along the still largely snow-obstructed streets to the offices of the *Bayswater Chronicle* on Westbourne Grove.

Her appearance at that establishment often occasioned excited anticipation amongst the employees who assumed, always correctly, that she was there because she was working on a case. 'Has there been murder done?' she would be asked, rather too eagerly, and the reply that there had not was greeted with disappointment. Frances, whose activities had provided the *Chronicle* with some of its more sensational stories, was readily granted permission to look at the folder of letters that had arrived following the death of Mr Whibley, and took it to a desk in a corner where she would not be overlooked. She also carried with her the letters that she had received from Dr Adair, Mr Rustrum and Mr Lathwal, and was quickly able to determine from comparison of handwriting and notepaper that neither the Bainiardus nor the Sanitas letters had been written by any of those gentlemen.

The *Chronicle* had only printed extracts of the letters and their full content made interesting reading. Bainiardus had claimed to be a personal friend and business associate of the late Mr Whibley. 'While it must be admitted that he exhibited a degree of corpulence that many another man might have found restricting,' he had written, 'this was not the case with Mr Whibley. He bore his weight well; indeed, he was remarkably active and light on his feet for a man of his dimensions. He often observed to me that much of what others thought to be fat was in actuality sturdy muscle and the weight of extra-large bones, and his size was in no way detrimental to his health. Imagine therefore my concern when he informed me that a medical man had advised him to take up the practice generally known as "banting". Over the next few weeks I was distressed to see my friend grow slowly weaker and more miserable under this dangerous regime, and begged him to stop.'

The whole blame for Whibley's death should, felt Bainiardus, be laid at the door of 'the man who advised him to take up the pernicious practice of "banting".'

Several letters had followed, several condemning the practice of banting as unnatural, while others, including one from Dr Adair, declared that it was safe and beneficial provided it was conducted under the supervision of a medical man.

Then Sanitas had entered the fray, commenting, 'While the practice of banting may be beneficial in some cases of corpulence, there are others in which it is highly injurious. We must not submit men and women to these extremes simply because it is fashionable, but only in cases of necessity, otherwise we may, as undoubtedly occurred in the case of Mr Whibley, do great harm. Banting is only safe where it is actually required. We have heard from Bainiardus, a friend of Mr Whibley, who tells us that Mr Whibley was not in any way inconvenienced by his girth. Why then was there any necessity for him to try and shed flesh at all?'

While most correspondents believed that excess weight was always harmful, Sanitas clearly did not. 'What is not generally known is that excessive leanness may be as injurious to health as excessive fatness, and lead to decline and an early death,' he continued. 'In times of grave illness it is the fat man who has the better chance of life, since he may lose flesh with impunity, whereas the lean man may quickly wither away and die.'

Thus far the letter had been merely an expression of opinion, refraining from personal insult, but then the writer, perhaps in a burst of emotion, had added:

'These men of the so-called Pure Food movement walk amongst us like so many horrible skeletons and tell us we are better to eat almost nothing, and on some days actually nothing, while the vegetarians would have us renounce the most nutritious and healthful food we have. And, what is most dangerous, this is actually advocated as a life-long practice, so their foolish followers suffer great inconvenience and misery. These men are not doctors, and have no right to criticise qualified medical men. How many members of the Pure Food and vegetarian movements have gone to an early grave? Should there be charges made of criminal negligence or still worse, manslaughter?'

Frances could not help wondering if Sanitas was a corpulent individual who, not wishing to undertake the restrictions necessary for the reduction in his weight, had decided to make it a virtue. She asked the editor if she might be allowed to borrow the folder for further study, and permission was granted with the stipulation that the letters must be preserved with great care, and returned at once if they ever became the subject of legal action, something he hoped her intervention might avoid.

Frances thought it would be useful to learn as much as she could about what diet was recommended by doctors, both for reduction of corpulence and general health, and on her return home, she delved into the collection of medical texts that had been left to her by her late father. Mr William Doughty had once been the proprietor of a chemists shop on Westbourne Grove, and had liked to read about the diseases of his customers to give him better authority when selling remedies. Irregularities of the digestive system along the whole of its turbulent, troubled and lengthy tract had often been discussed with much relish at the Doughty dinner table.

There was however, as Frances discovered, a considerable difference between the opinions of pharmacists, who were in general agreement as to which draught or powder best suited their customers, and doctors, who could agree on nothing at all, and her studies only served to increase her mystification on the subject. Frances' companion, Sarah, who had once been the Doughty family's servant and was now a no less indispensable assistant detective, arrived home from an errand to find her employer throwing down pamphlets onto the table in despair.

Frances and Sarah had only been detectives for a year, and both, though they would not have admitted it to their clients, had been obliged to learn the art as they practised it. At first, Sarah had acted only as directed, but the former maid of all work, with more insight and initiative than anyone other than Frances gave her credit for, had a hard cynical view of the world and soon showed that she could see to the heart of problems and determine a course of action on her own account.

'There is almost no article of food or drink,' exclaimed Frances, 'that has not been both denounced as the cause of fatness and praised as the natural food of man. Here we have a doctor who tells us that we are made fat by drinking pure water, and others who urge us to drink nothing else. Meat is of course either the best food of all, or a snare for the unholy. One man says that butter is to be avoided at all costs by those wishing to lose excess weight, but another declares that it cannot make us fat at all. It seems he tested his theory by feeding doves on nothing but butter and found that they grew very thin and died.'

'Do doves eat butter?' queried Sarah, looking dubious.

'They do not, I am sure of it,' said Frances, 'but this gentleman, while a person of education, seemed not to know that.'

'I am not considered fat, am I?' asked Sarah, suddenly. She was a woman constructed on generous principles, large in every part of her person, especially about the waist, shoulders and forearms.

'You are exactly as you should be,' Frances reassured her firmly. She had read a great many opinions, all of them expressed by gentlemen, as to the correct amount of fat a woman should carry on her person, and there was considerable disagreement on that too, leading to pages of animated exposition on the subject of bosoms and hips and abdomens and how full and rounded and soft they should be. Frances was tall and thin and wanting fat on every part of her form, and it was no comfort to have it confirmed in medical prose, that sometimes approached indecency, just how far she deviated from the most admired female proportions.

That evening, as Frances and Sarah enjoyed a hearty supper of mutton stew followed by a pie made from the best bottled gooseberries, Frances wondered how it was possible for so many persons to disagree on the diet that was best for health. Surely if one simply ate wholesome, nourishing and digestible food, neither too much nor too little, that ought to be enough?

As they ate, another letter arrived, hand delivered, which was, thankfully, nothing to do with diet, and which Frances discussed with Sarah. A Mr Hubert Sweetman, who revealed that he had not long emerged from a term in prison, wanted to trace his estranged family; a wife, son and daughter from whom he had heard nothing since his conviction in the autumn of 1866. A man who had been in prison for over fourteen years, and who might well have originally been sentenced to twenty and granted an early release, had clearly not committed a trivial offence. 'He might be a murderer,' observed Sarah with a thrust of her lower lip. Frances agreed, pointing out that she had interviewed murderers before, although admittedly she had not known them to be murderers at the time.

It was, thought Frances, an unusual proceeding for two single ladies to consider allowing a potentially dangerous convict into their home without at least securing the protection of a man. Fortunately, one of the two single ladies concerned was Sarah, whose powerful hands were equally well adapted to kneading pastry or knocking a man unconscious. She could show a fearsome aspect in times of danger, and had learned the secrets of personal combat from her eight brothers, one of whom, Jeb Smith, was, when in the roped ring, known professionally as the Wapping Walloper.

For the last two months, Sarah had been 'walking out' with Professor Pounder, proprietor of a gentlemen's sparring and self-defence academy. While the Professor was good-looking, modest, kind and respectful, Sarah had made it very clear to Frances that no tender words had been exchanged, were expected, or wanted, and that the friendship made no difference to her steadfast allegiance to her employer. Frances felt sure that had Professor Pounder attempted to introduce a little romance into the association, the result would have been bare-knuckle fisticuffs, with no guarantees as to which of the pair would be able to come up to the scratch after the first round.

Since Frances had been a child of six when Mr Sweetman entered prison, and Sarah had then been living in Wapping in conditions that had given her little leisure for reading, neither recalled Mr Sweetman's crime, and both felt that more information was required before deciding how to reply to the letter. After supper Frances and Sarah went down to the kitchen to make tea, and shared an amiable cup with their landlady, Mrs Embleton. That lady's generosity in allowing them to remain in the house even after discovering their profession was something for which Frances was constantly grateful, and she tried, not always successfully, to do nothing that might alarm either her landlady or the other tenants. Admitting a hardened criminal to her apartments was, she thought, most probably beyond what Mrs Embleton might deem acceptable behaviour.

'I do recall the event,' she said, when Frances broached the subject of Mr Sweetman. 'It was all the talk of Bayswater at the time, a man who had never given any trouble before, but brought low by debt. He robbed a safe, and used great violence to an unfortunate old man, who nearly died.'

'He is out of prison now and has asked me to find his family, from whom he has heard nothing since his conviction,' said Frances.

Mrs Embleton was usually a very calm lady, but even she drew a sharp little breath. 'If they have not visited or written to him in all that time he must be a very abandoned character,' she said.

'I think,' said Frances, 'you would prefer it if I did not accept him as a client. I will abide by your wishes, of course.'

'You have not yet seen him?'

'No.'

Mrs Embleton sipped her tea thoughtfully. 'Perhaps we should not judge him. He was by all accounts once considered respectable, and even the worst of men might be reclaimed. He may be truly penitent. I think he should be allowed the chance to prove that he has seen the error of his ways and wishes to lead a useful and honest life.'

'Then you would not object to him coming here?'

'I would object to your going to meet him anywhere else,' said Mrs Embleton. 'I am glad that you are so confiding as to ask. See him, and use your judgement. You will know very soon if he is fit company.' She glanced at Sarah. 'I am sure he will give you no trouble.'

Later, Frances re-read Mr Sweetman's letter but it offered no further clues as to the man and his intentions. She was not so optimistic as Mrs Embleton. Many of her clients came to her with a sincere and candid manner and a simple request but really wanted something else far less creditable that they were unwilling to reveal. So it might prove with Mr Sweetman, and if he did call, she must make it very clear to him from the outset that she wanted no dissembling. Sweetman, as a convicted felon, would have emerged from prison destitute and might want to find his family only in order to live off them. Or worse – perhaps he blamed them in some way for his predicament and was seeking revenge. His wife could well have very good reason to want to have nothing to do with him, and if necessary Frances might have to take Mrs Sweetman's part against her husband. It was a potentially dangerous situation, but the more Frances thought about it the more she felt obliged to take the case, since if she declined, Mr Sweetman might go to another detective less concerned for the safety of his wife. If she heard no more from him, which given the fact that he was probably unable to afford her services, she would have a word with Inspector Sharrock of Paddington Green, who might be interested in the recent arrival in Bayswater.

Frances duly replied to Mr Sweetman, who was lodging in Moscow Road, advising him of her fees and adding that she would be able to see him at any suitable time on the following day.

CHAPTER TWO

At an early hour the next morning, Frances unexpectedly received a hand-delivered reply from Mr Sweetman, saying that he would call that evening at seven o'clock. The time of both delivery and meeting suggested to Frances that Mr Sweetman had some occupation that commanded his day, and she wondered what it might be. She spent much of the intervening time composing reports on her investigations, and dealing with correspondence, a significant portion of which she noted unhappily was directed to those clients who had failed to settle their accounts in over a month. One lady, a customer of the carriage class, who were the worst payers of all, had actually favoured Frances with a request to perform a second task before she had paid for the first. Doughty's chemist shop had never supplied goods on credit, but this client, with a wide circle of acquaintances, all of whom she heartily detested, seemed to think that Frances was a gossip-collection agency, and was therefore too valuable to lose. It was one instance when Sarah's undoubted skills in the task of extracting payment were best not employed.

Her correspondence done, Frances read the obituary and letters of tribute to Mr Whibley in recent copies of the *Chronicle*, then opened the folder of letters on the subject of his demise, laid the papers on the table in front of her, and studied them carefully.

Mr Sweetman arrived promptly at the appointed hour, a little ruffled by the gales that still swept the streets, and spattered with fresh sleet. He was something over fifty years of age, with the sallow yet barely lined face of a man who had not been burned by the sun for many a year. Other than that he bore no resemblance to the dangerous felon Frances had been expecting. Altogether he looked well set-up and respectable, and was, under his greatcoat, clad in a suit of clothes which, while obviously made for another man some years previously, was clean and well brushed. He sat at the little table across which Frances met all her clients, and removed his hat, carefully wiping away spots of moisture from the crown with a pocket handkerchief. His hair was trim and quite grey.

Frances introduced Sarah, who sat knitting a woollen shawl with a pair of long steel needles that gleamed in the firelight, and it was to Mr Sweetman's credit that he did not find the sight especially alarming, something that suggested to Frances that he did not have a guilty conscience.

'It is very kind of you to see me,' he said, gratefully, his expression speaking more of unhappiness than anxiety.

'Have you consulted any other detectives?' asked Frances, suspecting from his tone that she was not the first.

'I – yes – I have spoken to two but I took the decision not to employ their services,' said Sweetman, with an air of distaste. 'They did not seem trustworthy. You, on the other hand, have been recommended to me as both honest and efficient. I have been told many stories of your successes which I can scarcely credit in one so young.'

'They are all true,' declared Frances, not without some apprehension as she knew that the stories of her exploits published in the *Chronicle* were highly exaggerated, and did not know which ones he had read, 'and you will find me trustworthy, but I expect my clients to be the same, although I am too often disappointed. You must tell me the truth, and you must not conceal anything of importance.'

He nodded. 'I will be perfectly frank and open with you, Miss Doughty. In the year 1866, I counted myself as a contented man. I was employed as office manager of J. Finn Insurance, a trusted position I had held for three years, with a salary sufficient for my needs. Susan, my dear wife, and I had been married for nearly fifteen years and we had two children in good health. My only unhappiness concerned my sister, Jane, a widow, who was very ill and lacked means. I assisted her out of my earnings, but later I was obliged to borrow funds both to pay for her care and also to secure the education of her son, a youth of considerable promise. But, I was more than able, with a little economy, to repay the interest on the loan, and Edward – my nephew – promised me that he would repay the capital as soon as he was able. In August that year I arrived at the office one morning to find the safe had been opened and emptied, and one of the clerks, Mr Gibson, who had been working late, had been violently attacked and was hovering between life and death. It was a very shocking thing, of course, and I never imagined for a minute that I might be suspected, but then the police came to know that I was in debt, and also it was clear that the safe had not been forced but opened with a key. Only two men apart from myself had a key to the safe, and they were dining at a club that evening in full view of a large company. I, too, had an alibi; I had been visiting my sister and the police interviewed her, but she was too frail and confused to give a certain reply, and when they looked in my house they found Mr Gibson's pocket book, which I had never seen before. I had hoped that when Mr Gibson came to his senses he would be able to say that I had not been his attacker, but unfortunately although he recovered, he remembered nothing of the circumstances.' Sweetman shook his head with regret. 'Mr Finn, the director, actually came to court and was a character witness for me, but to no avail. One of the other clerks, Mr Browne, had been passing by the office that night and actually saw the thief at the door, but they tried to make out it was me he saw.'

'Who do you think the thief was?' asked Frances.

He gestured helplessly. 'I really don't know. The police insisted that it must have been someone who worked in the office, and who had tried to make it look as if a thief had broken in but had made a poor job of it. Myself, I think it could just as well have been a burglar, who had stolen the keys to the office and the safe, and had them copied.'

'What was in the safe?'

'Three hundred pounds and more,' replied Sweetman. 'It was never found. Even now I worry that there are people watching me, thinking I have it hidden somewhere and am about to retrieve it.' He glanced about, nervously, as if afraid that there were watchers lurking in the shadowed corners of Frances' parlour. 'I never took that money, Miss Doughty,' he pleaded earnestly, 'and even if I was to find it by some chance, I could not keep it because it is not mine.'

'How do you think Mr Gibson's pocket book came to be in your house?' asked Frances.

'He had called on me a few days before the robbery and might have dropped it by accident, but of course he could not remember having missed it,' said Sweetman. He paused. 'Mr Gibson was not known as a gentleman who opened his pocket book very frequently.'

'Where was it found?'

'In a drawer. I always thought the maid had picked it up and put it away thinking it was mine, but she denied it.'

'And now, as you say in your letter, you would like to be reunited with your family? What was the last occasion on which you saw them?'

He gave a deep shuddering sigh. 'Oh, Miss Doughty, I never saw or spoke to them after my arrest! That was only a week after the robbery.'

'Your wife did not visit you in the police cells or in prison?' Frances asked, in some surprise. 'She did not appear in court? You had no message from her?'

He shook his head miserably. 'All I received very shortly after I was arrested was a note from her solicitor saying that she was terribly distressed by what I had done and wanted nothing more to do with me. I wrote, begging to see her, to be allowed at least to see the children, but received no reply.'

'Why do you think she believed you to be guilty?' questioned Frances. 'Many a man who has committed far worse crimes is forgiven by his wife and allowed to see his family.'

'I wish I could say,' he murmured pathetically. 'How could she have known me so little? Perhaps it was because the police thought that I had committed the crime; maybe to her mind that settled the matter. And I am afraid, very afraid, that she has convinced my children of the same.'

'Did you learn anything of her circumstances after your arrest?'

'No. Nothing at all.' There was a damp glimmer in his eyes.

He looked so desperately unhappy that Frances almost sent for tea. She glanced at Sarah, who was watching their visitor carefully. If Sarah had suspected Sweetman of being a clever liar it would have shown in her face, but there was no trace of suspicion there. Could they accept his story after all?

'Who was your solicitor?' asked Frances.

'Mr Manley. I think he is dead now.'

'Yes, his junior Mr Rawsthorne took over the practice.' Frances reflected that a great deal of the information she needed to help Mr Sweetman might well have gone into the grave during the intervening years. Rawsthorne, however, was her own family solicitor and a friend, and might be willing to offer some insights, or even have retained some documentation relating to the case. 'Tell me about your family,' she asked.

'Susan is fifty years of age – three years younger than I,' said Sweetman, his voice gentle with fond memories, 'and she has not sought a legal separation from me, or I would surely have known of it. She was once Susan Porter, and her father was a clerk. We were married in October 1851, and there are two children: Benjamin, our eldest, will be twenty-eight now, and Mary twenty-six. I miss them so much – I –' he was suddenly so overcome with emotion it choked in his throat, and he was briefly unable to speak. Frances offered him a glass of water, which he took, gratefully. 'I am sorry, but this is such a grief to me. From the moment I was accused of that terrible crime, I have seen nothing of my wife and nothing of my children. Benjamin and Mary might be married by now – I might even be a grandfather! What a joy it would be to know that they are well and happy!'

'How do you make your living now, Mr Sweetman?' asked Frances with a stern edge to her voice.

He wiped his eyes, gave a wry smile and nodded. 'Ah, I understand you. You are wondering if I want to find my family so that I can demand money from them, or live off them like a leech. No, I will make no demands; they have suffered so much that even though it is no fault of mine I do not think I have any claim on them. But just to see them, to know that they are in health and provided for, even if I cannot speak to them or make myself known, that will be sufficient. I work for my nephew Edward, my sister's boy, as a clerk and general factotum. He is now a dental surgeon, and very successful. He believes in my innocence. He even thought to offer me lodgings in his home, but his wife – she has daughters by a previous marriage and not knowing me, she was nervous to have me in the house. I live simply, I need very little, and yes, with his assistance I can pay your fee.'

Sarah had stopped knitting and was staring at Frances very keenly. She was strongly aware of how much Frances wanted to find her own mother, whom she had not seen since she was three years old, and yet at the same time feared to find her, feared so much that she had not dared to look. Sometimes Frances felt certain that her mother wanted to see her, but that she too was afraid of a meeting. Perhaps her mother had read about her achievements in the newspapers, especially the *Bayswater Chronicle*, which represented the intrepid lady detective as a towering champion of justice, or even in the halfpenny illustrated stories that were in wide circulation about the exploits of the daring 'Miss Dauntless', who, it could not be doubted, was intended to represent Frances. It would surely warm her mother's heart to know that Frances was well and a success, but it might also deter her from confronting a daughter who she might believe would not want to know her. Frances often liked to imagine that ladies who passed her in the street with a polite greeting and a smile were her own parent. If that was the case, she must have a hundred of them.

'I expect you have already tried to find your family,' said Frances.

'Oh, since I came out of prison last month I have thought of little else,' said her client with some feeling. 'I have spoken to everyone who might know where they are, but have learned nothing.'

'Can you describe to me what you have done so far, and also let me have details of all Mrs Sweetman's relatives and friends? I will need names and any addresses you can remember.' Frances poised a freshly sharpened pencil over her notebook.

'Of course, I will tell you everything I know. Unfortunately, Susan has no brothers or sisters living, and her parents were deceased long ago. My own dear sister died while I was in prison and left no message for me to suggest that she knew what had become of Susan and my children. My nephew, likewise, knows nothing. He was away at school when the catastrophe occurred. I went to our old home in Garway Road, but Susan was not there and the neighbours, all of whom were unknown to me as they had lived there under ten years, could tell me nothing. I have no way of finding our maid, Betty — I never even knew her surname. I went to the school that my children attended, but the building was gone — all knocked down and a furniture warehouse where it once stood, and I was told that the headmistress had retired to the country many years ago. I placed an advertisement in the newspaper but there was no reply. I thought then to go to the offices of J. Finn Insurance, as Susan did very occasionally come there when she had a message for me. The company is still in the same building, but old Mr Finn died some years ago, as did Mr Browne, and all the others I knew when I worked there have left. Gibson — well he was sixty-five at the time of the robbery and I was told that he was never well enough to come back to work, so he can scarcely be alive now. Of the other three clerks, Minster left to become a publican, and Elliott and Whibley went to join an accountancy firm, Anderson and Walsh. Anderson was Whibley's uncle.'

'Whibley?' said Frances, startled at the familiar name. 'Is that the Thomas Whibley who died recently?'

'Yes, and that was rather upsetting because I went there and spoke to him only two days before he died.'

Frances paused to consider this unexpected development. She always entertained a suspicion of coincidences, but in the busy world of Bayswater finance it was perhaps not too surprising when two individuals were acquainted. There seemed to be no obvious connection between a fourteen-year-old robbery and the controversy surrounding the reasons for Mr Whibley's recent death, but the opportunity to interview someone who had recently spoken to the deceased man was too good to miss. 'Tell me about your visit to Mr Whibley,' she requested.

'I went to see him because out of all the people at J. Finn Insurance, only he and Mr Finn knew Susan at all well. We had sometimes dined together. I hoped he had heard from her or knew something of what she did after I was convicted, but he was unable to help me.'

'Did he seem unwell to you?' asked Frances. 'I appreciate that you could not have been aware of any recent deterioration in his health, but in view of the allegations that have been made about him in the press I would value your observations.'

'Oh, are you enquiring into that?' he exclaimed. 'The most terrible things have been said!'

'I like to keep informed of all matters of current interest in Bayswater,' replied Frances, evenly.

Sweetman nodded. 'Of course. Well, I can tell you that I was very shocked by his appearance. He was always rather portly, but since I last saw him he had become enormously fat and looked quite aged, although he was not yet fifty. He did not look like a man destined to live long, although of course I could not have anticipated ...' he sighed.

'So,' said Frances, looking at her notes, 'of the employees of J. Finn Insurance who might have known or heard about Mrs Sweetman; Mr Finn, Mr Whibley and Mr Browne are deceased, and in all probability Mr Gibson is too. Did Mr Browne have any family?'

'No, he was a bachelor and lived alone.'

'And was Mr Whibley able to tell you where the others were to be found?'

'Yes, Minster is now the landlord of the Cooper's Arms, a small beer house on the corner of Bott's Mews, a very low establishment. He inherited some money and used it to start the business. I did try to see him, but he made it very plain that he thought I was a criminal and told me to leave. He was never a very pleasant individual and the years have not improved him.'

Frances raised her eyebrows. 'Mr Minster inherited money? From whom, and how much?'

'Yes,' said Sweetman, 'I had thought of that, too. Even at the time I wondered if it was he who stole the money. Whibley also suspected him, but I suppose Minster was able to account for his movements, for there was never any suggestion of his being arrested. I don't know about the inheritance and Whibley couldn't tell me any more, but it does appear that out of all the employees of the company Minster is the only man to have suddenly acquired any wealth shortly after the robbery. Elliott went to work for Anderson and Walsh as a clerk. Whibley started as a junior accountant and eventually became a partner. Later, when his uncle, Mr Anderson, died, he inherited the business. Elliott married the widow who was a great deal younger than Anderson and not only left well provided for, but is very beautiful so I am told. The only person at J. Finn Insurance I haven't been able to find is the messenger boy, Timmy, but he was scarcely nine years old at the time.'

'But, to clarify, you are not asking me to prove you innocent of the crime, or find the real thief or the stolen money,' Frances established.

He looked surprised. 'No, I can hardly think that would be possible, after so long.'

'All the same,' said Frances, 'I imagine that if you were to find your family you would like to be able to offer them proof of your innocence.'

'They are my family,' said Sweetman, with some dignity, 'not a jury. What proof should they need?'

Frances questioned him closely and made a note of the full names and last known addresses of everyone who she might need to interview, including the unfortunate clerk, Arthur Gibson, in the faint hope that he was still alive and had recovered a memory that could exonerate Mr Sweetman. 'The two other men who had keys, the ones who had alibis for the robbery — who were they?'

'Mr Finn, and Whibley,' said Sweetman. 'But really I can't believe that either would have been capable of such a crime. Both of them I remember were horribly shocked by what happened.'

'Do you have a portrait of your family?' asked Frances.

He shook his head. 'No, that is a great regret to me.'

'Then I would like a description.'

He nodded, and a wistful smile spread across his features. 'Susan is about the same height as myself, about five feet and seven inches, so a little above what is common for a woman, and very pretty with light brown hair. Benjamin resembles me; I think once grown he would be a little taller, and his hair is brown, as mine once was. Mary ...' he sighed, 'such a pretty thing, the image of her mother, hair like spun gold.'

'They were not portrayed in the illustrated papers at the time of the trial?'

'No, and I was glad of it,' Sweetman said with some feeling.

Frances was completing her notes when there was a loud rapping at the front door. She exchanged glances with Sarah, since the insistent quality of the knock had already told them whom they might expect to see very soon. Sarah rose and went to look out of the window. Their rooms were on the first floor and afforded a good view of who stood on the doorstep. It was not a feature that had especially recommended the apartment when Frances had first seen it, but since moving there it had proved to be very useful. Sarah gave a grunt. 'Inspector Sharrock,' she said, 'and he's got a constable with him.'

Given that the only other residents of the house were Mrs Embleton, the Allaby sisters, who occupied the ground floor apartments and never went out except to church, and Mrs Parmiter on the second floor, who thought of nothing but her charity work, it was almost certain that the Inspector had come to see Frances, though why he had felt the need to bring a constable with him was a mystery. 'It seems I have visitors,' she told Mr Sweetman, 'but I believe our business is done for today. I will take the case.'

Sweetman heaved a sigh of relief, and handed her a small envelope. 'The advance payment you require,' he said. 'And may I expect a weekly report?'

'Of course,' said Frances.

There was a loud thumping sound as two pairs of heavily booted feet advanced rapidly up the staircase, but no sooner had the housemaid's knock sounded at the apartment door when it burst open, and the policemen entered. Their caped figures were smudged with sleet, and Sharrock's coarse red face glowed like a beacon.

It was a year since Frances had first met Inspector Sharrock, and he had made a very poor initial impression since he had attempted to bully her father into admitting that he had accidentally poisoned a customer of his chemists shop. The bullying and blustering were, she now knew, the Inspector's normal mode of address, which he rarely varied and were necessary tactics when dealing with some of the rougher criminal elements of Paddington. In his world, doors were there to be pounded with fists, stairs to be mounted at the double, and rooms to be invaded.

He came boldly to the front of Bayswater homes minding nothing about the quality of the residents, and brushing aside any suggestion that he should go humbly to the tradesman's entrance. Frances had learned to do a little of that herself. During that eventful year, Sharrock, while still remaining convinced that detective work was an unsuitable occupation for females, had grudgingly come to accept that Frances was adept at untangling the knottier problems that he had no leisure to attempt, while she had come to see him as a sound and hardworking policeman, even if he did have the untidiest desk she had ever seen. Sharrock worked long hours either at the station or out on cases, usually pleading that his home, where Mrs Sharrock was busy with the needs of six children under the age of nine, was a domestic pandemonium which he preferred to avoid. Frances happened to know that Mrs Sharrock was in the habit of asking a married but childless sister to look after her noisy offspring while she attended meetings of the Bayswater Women's Suffrage Society, but had decided not to mention this to the Inspector.

'Inspector Sharrock,' said Frances, rising to her feet, 'if you would grant me a few moments, my client is just leaving.'

'I don't think so,' announced Sharrock, slapping moisture from his cape, 'or at least, he isn't leaving alone.' He fixed Sweetman with a sharp look and gestured to the constable to stand guard by the door.

'What do you mean?' asked Sweetman apprehensively, starting to rise from his chair.

'You are Hubert Sweetman?' said the Inspector.

'I am.'

'Your nephew said you would be here. You're to come to the station, now.'

'But I was released – I have all the papers!' Sweetman exclaimed, delving into his pocket with trembling fingers. 'Here, I can show you.'

'Never mind that now,' said Sharrock brusquely. 'Hubert Sweetman, I am arresting you on suspicion of murder.' He nodded to the constable who stepped forward and secured the astonished man. 'And you, Miss Doughty, should be more careful about who you allow in here.'

'I don't understand!' exclaimed Sweetman. 'Who am I supposed to have killed? And when? I have been working for my nephew all day and came straight here.'

'You're not going to cut up rough, are you?' warned Sharrock, although nothing looked less likely.

'No, of course not, I will come with you, but this is all a mistake!' Sweetman was hustled towards the door, and as he reached it he turned and cried, 'Miss Doughty, you must help me!' before he was taken downstairs.

'I suppose,' said Frances, 'it is too much to hope that you will tell me what all this is about?' She showed Sharrock the envelope. 'Mr Sweetman's advance payment,' she said. 'He is my client.'

Sharrock raised his eyebrows. 'Oh? And what did he want you to do?'

'He is hoping to find his family. He became estranged from them after his conviction for robbery in 1866.'

'Well, if I was you, I would hand him his money back,' said Sharrock with a sarcastic grin. 'He's using you as a smokescreen. He's already found his wife, and he's killed her.'

CHAPTER THREE

When Sharrock had gone, Sarah, with silent disapproval marked deeply in every line of her face, quickly cleaned the scattered mud spots from the carpet, then went down to the kitchen and made cocoa. All they had succeeded in learning from the Inspector before he departed with his prisoner to Paddington Green police station was that Mrs Susan Sweetman had been found dead at her home, where she lived alone.

As the two women sat thoughtfully before the fire and sipped their drinks, Frances commented, 'Inspector Sharrock was noticeably reticent about what evidence he has against Mr Sweetman. I am inclined to think that there is none, and all he actually has is suspicion and a likely man near to hand. When hard-pressed, as is usual with him, he will take the easy way, and for the most part he gets good results from this principle. But for all we know Mr Sweetman's hours of work will give him an alibi for the time of the murder, and come tomorrow he will have been released.'

'You'll want to find the son and daughter in any case,' said Sarah, 'if only so they can go to their mother's funeral.'

'They must surely have been in touch with her,' said Frances, with a little sigh as she thought of her own absent mother. 'They will have called on her and the neighbours might know something, or if not they will hear of her death soon enough through the newspapers. Then they will attend the funeral and I will speak to them. But if they had reason not to wish to see their father before, they are unlikely to change their minds now, unless he can be cleared of the murder. I'll send a note to Mr Gillan so he can place a report in the *Chronicle*.' Max Gillan was a newspaper correspondent who sometimes supplied Frances with intelligence he obtained from what he called his 'secret sources', whom Frances suspected were policemen.

The police were officially prohibited from supplying informa-tion to the press, but unofficially all pressmen cultivated those officers who appreciated that newspaper reports published during the course of their enquiries might bring in important witnesses. In return, Frances gave Mr Gillan material for his columns, which gave him priority over his rivals. He wrote a regular piece for the *Chronicle* about Frances' adventures, although he firmly denied being the author of the Miss Dauntless detective stories.

'They might have gone away, and not get here in time,' worried Sarah.

'True,' said Frances, 'and I have thought of another difficulty. Benjamin and Mary Sweetman might be so ashamed of their father's crime that they will not want their connection with him known. They could be living under other names to conceal their identity and decide not to attend their mother's funeral but pay their respects privately at a later date.'

'They might come in disguise,' Sarah mused, with a smile at the prospect of a dramatic unmasking.

'Well,' said Frances, 'Mr Sweetman has paid me a fee and while I wait for his son and daughter to appear I will start the work.'

'They could have married, or died,' said Sarah. 'I'll go to Somerset House; see what's in the registers.'

'And Mrs Sweetman might have made a bigamous marriage,' Frances observed. 'A woman in that position might risk discovery to secure a better future. If she used her maiden name of Porter that will cause us some difficulty, as there will be dozens to choose from. I shall go to see Inspector Sharrock tomorrow. We should at least find out when the police think Mrs Sweetman died and when the inquest is to open. Once I know her address we can make enquiries there.'

After composing a note to Mr Gillan, Frances wrote a letter to her solicitor, Mr Rawsthorne, hoping that he might still have his predecessor's papers relating to Mr Sweetman's convic-tion and would be willing to discuss them with her. She then studied the list of people Mr Sweetman had already visited. Any or all of them, she thought, might conceivably know where Mrs Sweetman had recently lived and where her son and daughter were, but had perhaps been unwilling to reveal what they knew to Mr Sweetman. With the death of Mrs Sweetman and the arrest of her husband, they might now speak to Frances.

'Where will you go first?' asked Sarah.

'I think,' decided Frances, as she sealed the letters, 'I will start at the beginning.'

Early the next morning, Frances braved gales and cold drizzle to visit the Sweetman family's old home. The damp air held the promise of a lasting thaw. Everywhere windows were sparkling with a steel-blue frost that she hoped would disperse as the temperature struggled to rise during the day. Walking was difficult, even for someone with Frances' long stride. The snow that had once lain inches deep had been churned by carriage wheels into dirty brown ridges speckled with soot and tiny ice jewels of yesterday's refrozen sleet. She was grateful to secure a cab, which crunched its way over the brittle surface. Her destination, Garway Road, ran south from Westbourne Grove, and its houses were neat and plain with two storeys and a basement – the homes of senior clerks, company secretaries and comfortable though not wealthy annuitants.

As Frances had anticipated, Mr Sweetman's earlier visits had helped prepare the ground for her arrival and the name on her card, which was fast becoming notorious in Bayswater, was enough to ensure her admission to the homes she wished to enter and agreement to interviews.

Frances also carried with her the shocking news of Mrs Sweetman's murder and the fact that the police were questioning her husband, which was enough to arouse anyone's interest. She discovered that Mr Sweetman had been painfully honest in revealing the full circumstances of his absence from home for so many years, albeit with earnest assurances that he was an innocent man. In all cases he had been seen by the gentlemen of the house, none of whom had wanted to submit their wives, sisters or servants to the presence of a convicted criminal, however respectful his manners.

The family currently living in the Sweetmans' old home had been there for eight years and had never met them, neither did they know anyone who might have lived in Garway Road in 1866. Sweetman had spoken to a Mr Willis, a youthful solicitor still making his way up in the world, and his wife now informed Frances that while naturally suspicious of their visitor's motives, her husband had told him nothing because he had nothing to tell. Frances asked about the previous occupier, but Mrs Willis said that when they had first rented the house – the owner being a gentleman who lived abroad and acted through an agent – it had been empty. The property agent was long since retired.

The neighbours on either side were similarly unhelpful, and none could give any information about the current address of the persons who had previously occupied their properties. Frances, thankful to find that the rain had stopped and detecting a watery glisten on the surface of the melting snow, was just descending the steps of the third house she had visited, and wondering if she might have to call on every one of them in the street, when a figure in a heavy dark servant's gown, her head and shoulders wound about with shawls, ran down the steps of the Willis house.

'Miss Doughty! Might I have a word?'

'Certainly,' said Frances, pausing to allow the woman to approach.

Close up, it could be seen that the figure was a person of middle years. Her mittened hands smelt as if they had been rubbed with lemon and her cheeks were lined and reddened by frequent closeness to fire.

'I'm Mr Willis' cook,' said the woman, breathlessly, 'and the maid just told me you were asking after the Sweetmans. I'd been wondering if I ought to write to Mr Sweetman after he came asking questions last time, and then I thought better of it in case – well – I just now heard that Mrs Sweetman is dead and he is suspected so it looks like I was right not to.'

'That remains to be seen,' said Frances. 'Were you living here in 1866?'

'No, but my father used to deliver fish all round these parts. He's old now, and his head isn't what it was, but he might remember something.' She handed Frances a scrap of wrapping paper with an address. 'Say that Eliza sent you. My sister Nora looks after him, but he doesn't get many visitors now, and I'm sure he'd like to talk to you.'

Frances thanked her, and the woman turned and ran back through the snowy puddles, her heels kicking up little spurts of icy liquid. The paper gave the name Jack Jennings and the address of a lodging house in Newton Road, which was just a short walk away. Frances pulled her mantle tightly about her and set off.

A small, thin girl of about thirteen with a face like smudged paper and a ragged excuse for a cap opened the door, and on being told Frances' business admitted her and asked her to wait while she took her card and the message up to Miss Jennings. There was nowhere to wait except the hall, so Frances stayed there. It was a narrow space innocent of paint or paper, and rarely swept, with a single unlit candle on an iron holder sagging dangerously from the wall. The air was damp, and although the floor was just bare boards, there was a smell of rotting carpets, while a bitter draught under the front door made it seem colder inside than out. After a few minutes, the maid returned saying that Frances could go up to the third floor, and should knock at the door with a number eight chalked on it.

Frances clambered up the wooden stairs, which gave under her feet rather more than they ought, and was admitted to the Jennings apartments by a lady of about fifty. At first glance, Frances wondered if she had seen Miss Jennings before, but then realised that she was experiencing recognition of another kind. Miss Jennings, a plain single lady, her life devoted to the care of an elderly parent, was the future that Frances would have had if her father had lived. She was the woman that Frances might be in thirty years' time; neat, quiet, uncomplaining and unloved.

Jack Jennings was in his seventies, his head and cheeks powdered with white hairs like the snow. He sat in an easy chair in front of a fire, where a large well-blackened kettle stood on the hearth. He was wrapped in shawls, puffing at a pipe, and in front of him was a stool on which rested a mug of tea and a plate with two thick slices of bread and dripping. His expression was amiable, and he looked peacefully content with his lot.

The room was clean and tidy, and though small, escaped clutter by being furnished with only the simplest necessities. A narrow dresser was sufficient for the Jennings' crockery and linen, and there was a bed with folded blankets in one corner, a washbasin and jug on a table and drying laundry on a wooden clotheshorse. Another door suggested the existence of a second room, a smaller one in all probability, where Miss Jennings could have some measure of personal privacy. Frances hoped so.

'You have spoken to my sister?' asked Miss Jennings, offering Frances a chair before the fire. 'Is she well?'

'Oh yes, she is very well,' said Frances. 'My enquiries concern a Mr Sweetman, who used to live in Garway Road, and has been trying to trace his family.' She glanced at Mr Jennings who sucked at his pipe, smiled, and nodded to himself.

Nora Jennings brought cups and poured tea from a brown pot of commendable size, and fetched a small jug of milk with a muslin cover from its perch on the chilly window ledge. 'Yes, father used to make deliveries in Garway Road, but I am sorry to say his memory is very poor nowadays, although he remembers the old times better than he does last week. He did tell me about the robbery and that poor man who was hurt. He said Mr Sweetman was a very quiet gentleman and he would never have believed that he could do such a thing.'

'He is out of prison now, and called on me yesterday asking if I could find his family, and I agreed to do so,' said Frances. 'He has not seen them in over fourteen years. But Mrs Sweetman has just been found dead and the police came to my house and arrested him. It seems she was murdered.'

Nora was astonished and appalled. 'Oh what a dreadful thing to happen! Do you suspect Mr Sweetman?'

'No, neither of the murder nor the robbery. I am hoping that his son and daughter may be able to help him, and in any case they will want to attend their mother's funeral.'

Jack Jennings puffed a small cloud of pungent smoke and chuckled. It was such an inappropriate response that Frances could only assume he was unable either to hear her or understand what she said.

Miss Jennings saw her dilemma. 'Tell me what it is you need to know,' she said, kindly.

'I wondered,' Frances went on, although not with a great deal of hope, 'if you might know anything about where the family went after Mr Sweetman was convicted.'

Miss Jennings shook her head. 'I am afraid not. I do recall father telling me after the robbery that he felt sorry for Mrs Sweetman and the children, although she had good friends who called on her and saw that she had everything she needed.'

'Did he say who these friends were?'

'No, and I don't think he knew, but Mrs Sweetman did once say how grateful she was to the people her husband had worked with for helping her, so I suppose it must have been them. But that all changed after the trial. In those days, but I expect you already know this, if someone was found guilty of a serious crime, the Crown took all their property away, whether it was stolen or not, and that was what happened to Mrs Sweetman. The poor woman had to give up the house and go away.' She turned to her father, who had taken his pipe from his mouth long enough to gulp tea. 'Father, do you remember Mrs Sweetman?'

Mr Jennings, who had seemed blithely indifferent to Frances' presence, responded without difficulty to his daughter's voice, with a broad smile and a nod. 'Mrs Sweetman?' he said in a surprisingly strong voice. 'Oh yes!'

'Do you know where she went?' asked Frances. 'After her husband was put in prison?'

He gave her a sly sideways glance as if to say that he was not as absent as he looked and she had discovered his secret. 'No, no, but she did go away.' He paused. 'Oh yes. Yes, she went away all right.'

'But do you know where?' Frances persisted.

He puffed at his pipe, but made no reply.

'The boy and girl, Benjamin and Mary,' urged Frances. 'Do you remember them? Did they find some occupation?'

He chuckled again.

'I'm afraid father has this idea in his head that he once saw the Sweetman boy and girl at the music hall, actually on the stage, but that can hardly be the case,' said Miss Jennings, with a smile.

'I can't imagine that their mother would have approved,' said Frances.

'I am sure of it,' agreed Nora.

'I suppose,' said Frances, 'that as the children of a convict they might not have had their choice of employment, but it does seem unlikely. Perhaps they went into service.'

Jack Jennings took his pipe out of his mouth and started to whistle. A little light danced in his eyes that had not been there before.

'Please, father,' said Nora, gently. 'Not in company.'

'That was what *he* did!' said Jennings. 'Harold Froy the Jaunty Boy, 'cos he couldn't sing, not for nothing he couldn't sing, so he *had* to whistle. That was his turn. Whistling.' He took another copious gulp of tea. 'He was terrible.'

'Was Harold Froy really Benjamin Sweetman?' asked Frances.

'Yes,' said Jennings, further enlivened by the conversation. 'The lad Sweetman, only he was calling himself Froy.'

'What about his sister, Mary?' asked Frances.

Jennings grinned. 'Oh, yes, he had a sister. *She* was a pretty thing.' He puffed vigorously on his pipe.

'And she was on the stage, too?'

The old man took the pipe from his mouth reflectively and to Frances' surprise, he began to sing. 'I don't know how to milk a cow, oh please take pity on me!' He laughed and stuffed a piece of bread and dripping into his mouth.

Frances waited until he stopped chewing which was quite a while. 'Was that the song Miss Sweetman sang?'

He nodded and sang the line again.

'Was she a milkmaid? Was that her "turn"?'

'No! *Course* she wasn't a milkmaid!' he said scornfully. 'She couldn't be, could she? She dressed like one, she wanted to be one, but she couldn't on account of how she didn't know how to milk the cow!'

'I don't think you can place much reliance on what he says,' said Nora, sadly. 'He has a lot of memories but they only come out every so often and sometimes they can mix themselves up. I am sure he must have seen these things but whether they were the Sweetman boy and girl must be doubted.'

'I don't know how to milk a cow!' warbled Mr Jennings happily.

'Which theatre did your father visit?' Frances asked.

'It was the Bijou in Archer Street, but that's all closed up now.'

Frances sighed inwardly. So far everything and everyone who might have helped her was closed, gone away, demolished or dead. She left Miss Jennings with her address and asked her to write if her father should remember anything more, but felt, as her boots carved a path through the slush, that she had merely succeeded in lighting a small torch in Jack Jennings' mind that had flared brightly for a moment only to vanish forever.

CHAPTER FOUR

rances' next call was at the Westbourne Grove office of the accountancy firm of Anderson, Walsh and Whibley. She knew from newspaper reports that the business was in the process of being sold, and thought it as well to make this one of her earliest appointments in case it was about to close its doors. She found, however, that the sudden death of the sole owner had not curtailed its activities in any way. A senior clerk called Richardson was busy meeting prospective buyers but while that matter remained to be settled, business went on. Frances spoke to a junior clerk, introducing herself and explaining the reason for her visit. She was asked to wait while Mr Richardson completed his interview and eventually she was conducted into an office that still had Mr Whibley's name on the doorplate.

It did not look like the office of a dedicated sybarite. The only female portrait on the wall was of the queen, and while the chair behind the desk was wide and comfortably upholstered this had more to do with the occupant's weight and girth than his love of luxury. There was an impressive library on the subject of taxation, handsome leather-bound volumes with gold-stamped spines, and on a side table there were bundles of papers tied up with string and piled up in good order, waiting for attention.

'Ah yes, the unhappy Mr Sweetman,' said Richardson, taking his late employer's chair and ushering Frances to the seat facing him. A discreet man of business, he was aged about fifty-five, immaculately dressed with well-trimmed hair and beard, once black but now well-salted with grey. 'His visit was unannounced,' he continued, with an acid hint of disapproval in his tone, which Frances ignored, 'and took place just two days before Mr Whibley died.'

'Mr Whibley,' said Frances, examining her notebook, 'was found dead in bed on the morning of Thursday the thirteenth of January, so Mr Sweetman must have called on the Tuesday.'

'He did,' said Richardson.

'Do you know what was said at that meeting?' asked Frances.

'No, I was not present, and Mr Whibley did not discuss it with me afterwards.' He closed his mouth, like an oyster snapping shut, and waited for the next question.

Frances felt that Mr Richardson was a man who knew exactly what he ought and ought not to know. She was also sure that he must have similar opinions on what she ought and ought not to know, opinions with which she might not concur.

'How long have you worked for the partnership?' she asked.

'Twenty-seven years,' he said, as if announcing it to a meeting, with a proud tilt of the chin.

'It would have been just Anderson and Walsh then?'

'Yes, it was.'

'Mr Anderson was Mr Whibley's uncle, I believe?'

'That is the case.'

'And Mr Walsh? Was Mr Whibley related to him?'

'He was not.' Richardson looked quite at his ease, and there was no hesitation in making his replies.

'Do you recall the robbery that took place at J. Finn Insurance where Mr Whibley once worked? It was in 1866.'

'I do. It was in all the newspapers,' said Richardson, his tone implying that this was his sole source of information on the subject.

'How long after the robbery did Mr Whibley come to work here?'

'Not long afterwards. Six months, perhaps.'

'And Mr Elliott, who had also worked there, he came here too. Was that at about the same time?'

'I think it was a little after.'

'So the robbery and Mr Sweetman's trial would still have been very fresh in people's memories,' said Frances. 'I am sure that Mr Whibley and Mr Elliott would have been asked about them.'

'That is only human nature, of course. People like to pry.' His lip curled in distaste. Clearly prying was a contemptible activity and something he never did.

'Did Mr Whibley say who he thought was guilty? I know he didn't think it was Mr Sweetman.'

'I'm afraid I don't recall. In fact, I don't believe I ever discussed it with him.' Richardson paused. 'If you don't mind my asking,

Miss Doughty, are you trying to prove that Mr Sweetman was innocent of the crime?'

'He has not asked me to do so,' said Frances, 'although he has assured me of his innocence, but he did come to me yesterday and engaged me to find his family from whom he had become estranged. I am interviewing everyone he knew in case they have heard anything of them.'

'I don't believe anyone currently working here had ever encountered Mr Sweetman before his recent visit,' said Richardson, 'and no one will know his family.'

'I came here in the hope that Mr Whibley might have said something about them after he saw Mr Sweetman,' said Frances. 'Perhaps he did have some information but for some reason of which I am unaware, did not wish to reveal it. I should tell you that while Mr Sweetman was in my home, he was arrested on suspicion of murder. It appears that Mrs Sweetman has been killed. At present I know no further details.' She watched Mr Richardson carefully, and it was clear even through his shell of carefully studied calm that the news had astounded him.

'I think …' he said, after taking a few moments to absorb the information, 'that had Mr Whibley been alive to hear this, he would have been very distressed.'

'Then he did speak of the Sweetmans?'

Richardson hesitated, and it was clear that he thought he had said too much. 'He might have done, it was a long time ago, but he knew the family and I believe he had a good opinion of them.'

'And had he mentioned them recently?'

There was another thoughtful silence, and then he took a deep breath. 'No. As I have said, I know nothing of the interview that took place between Mr Whibley and Mr Sweetman, but I do think it is possible that it may indirectly have led to Mr Whibley's death.'

'In what way?' asked Frances, both surprised and dubious at this extraordinary allegation. 'I had understood that he suffered from a weak heart due to his unusual size.'

'There are a number of things that have been said about Mr Whibley in the press and not all of them are true,' said Richardson, severely. 'He is represented as a gourmand and a libertine. That is a cruel distortion of the truth. Of course, he enjoyed the good things his wealth brought him, but he was also a generous man who would never do an unkind thing, knowledgeable in his profession and diligent in his work. We mourn his death, and we also appreciate his life and dedication, which has left the business in such a thriving and well-ordered state.'

He spoke with all the confidence of an advertisement for the issue of shares, and Frances could not help wondering what interests Mr Richardson had in the business, and how important it was to him that his former employer's reputation and that of Anderson, Walsh and Whibley should be protected.

'Had he been trying to lose weight, as has been suggested in the newspapers?' she asked.

Richardson had recovered his earlier composure. 'I did not observe his dining habits and he never discussed them with me.'

'Mr Sweetman told me that when he spoke to Mr Whibley recently he thought him a considerably changed man,' said Frances, 'chiefly, I think, due to his increase in weight. Of course he had not seen him in many years, but even allowing for that, he thought the change quite shocking.'

'Mr Whibley was never a slender man,' Richardson admitted, 'but his size in recent years was not entirely his fault. About eight years ago, he suffered a bad accident on the railway and he was never quite the same afterwards. His leg was broken in two places and he was unable to leave his bed for several weeks. He made a good recovery and it did not affect his work, but it was as a result of that period of enforced inactivity that his girth underwent a considerable increase. Yes, I can see that his weight might have affected the action of his heart, but I had never seen him actually ill until after Mr Sweetman called.'

'And you believe that it was the interview with Mr Sweetman that made him ill?' queried Frances, realising that her incredulity must be apparent in her voice. Whatever the effect of the meeting on Mr Whibley, it was apparent that something had been said which could be of vital significance to her enquiries. 'Did you see him immediately afterwards? What was his manner? Please,' she urged, 'try and remember anything he said to you, however trivial it might seem.'

Richardson looked less sure of himself. 'It was either the interview itself or something else that occurred soon afterwards. I did not see him again that day. Mr Whibley went out directly after Mr Sweetman left, and did not advise anyone of where he was going. There was no appointment in his book, and it was unlike him to leave the office in the middle of the day without prior arrangement, or any warning. The following morning he came to the office at his usual time, but he was clearly unwell; his face was almost grey. I advised him to go home at once and rest, and he did. Later that night, he died. I can tell you nothing more.' The oyster snapped shut again.

'His doctor wrote to the *Chronicle* but declined to sign his name,' said Frances. 'Do you know who he consulted?'

'No, of course not.'

'I take it you don't know the identity of the recent correspondents in the *Chronicle*, Bainiardus and Sanitas, who wrote on the subject of Mr Whibley's death and diet?'

'I do not. And before you enquire, I can assure you that neither I nor any person here employed would under any circumstances write to the newspapers about a private matter that concerned Mr Whibley.'

'Perhaps you are acquainted with the handwriting of Mr Whibley's friends?' asked Frances. She opened the folder of letters and showed the Bainiardus and Sanitas letters to Mr Richardson. He gazed at them, but his expression did not change. 'I am afraid I cannot help you with that.'

'If either of these should look familiar to you and you do not wish to mention the names of the authors for the sake of confidentiality, then might I suggest that you speak to the person or persons concerned, and ask them to write to me?' Frances presented her card. 'I have no wish to expose them; I only wish to reassure my clients that the letters will cease.'

He stared at the card on the table but did not pick it up. 'As I have said, I cannot help you with that.'

'Do you happen to know what became of Mr Sweetman's son and daughter? They were called Benjamin and Mary.'

'No. Mr Whibley never mentioned them to me.'

'What family did Mr Whibley have? The obituaries said that he was unmarried.'

'I knew of none, other than his late uncle Mr Anderson. He lived alone, apart from servants. I was at his funeral, which was well attended by business associates and friends.'

'I am wondering if there is any person he might have spoken to after seeing Mr Sweetman.' Frances waited hopefully for a response, but Mr Richardson did not feel any need to assist her. 'I assume that his house has been sold and the servants dispersed?'

'That is correct.'

'Do you know the names of his servants or his intimate friends?'

'They were mentioned in his will.'

'Who were his executors?'

'Mr Elliott and myself, although Mr Elliott did the bulk of the work.'

'What position did Mr Elliott hold when he was employed here?'

'Junior clerk.'

'But he married Mr Anderson's widow?'

'He did.'

'And does he still work here?'

'No, he has his own interests now.'

'I would like to speak to Mr Elliott. I am sure you would be able to provide me with his address. I would also like to see a copy of Mr Whibley's will.'

Richardson smiled thinly. 'I will arrange for a note to be delivered to that effect.'

'There was a messenger boy at J. Finn Insurance called Timmy. Did he come to work here?'

'No.'

Frances decided not to ask Mr Richardson how familiar he was with the music hall.

❧

When Frances returned home, she found that Sarah had already made enquiries at the coroner's court and attended the brief opening of the inquest on Mrs Sweetman. The body had been discovered at her home in Redan Place by a neighbour, who claimed that she had called to see if there was anything Mrs Sweetman needed, but who, Sarah thought, was actually hoping to borrow something. Apart from the neighbour, who had identified the body, and Mr Gillan of the *Chronicle*, the only other people in attendance at the inquest were Mr Sweetman's nephew, Edward Curtis, and his solicitor Mr Marsden. Despite hopes that Benjamin and Mary Sweetman might attend if only incognito; there was a notable absence of heavily veiled ladies and men with suspicious looking moustaches. No medical evidence had been taken and the inquiry had been adjourned for a week. Since the proceedings had taken barely fifteen minutes, Sarah had gone on from there to Somerset House, where she had been unable to find any marriages or deaths relating to the Sweetman family, although ledgers were unfortunately only available up to 1878. She had, on her own initiative, also looked for the death of Mr Arthur Gibson, the clerk injured in the robbery, but no one of that name and the right age had died in London, which suggested either that he had moved away, died recently or, less likely, that he was still alive.

Sarah had never been a frequenter of the music halls and had never heard of either the whistling boy or the singing would-be milkmaid, but she promised to look into it.

Frances had also received a letter from Dr Adair, who enclosed a copy of Mr William Banting's acclaimed pamphlet on diet, another from Mr Lathwal, who supplied an application form to join the Vegetarian Society together with a leaflet about the immorality of eating meat, and one from Mr Rustrum of the Pure Food Society, who enclosed a paper on the pleasures of self-denial. All three confirmed their appointments to see Frances.

'I am hoping,' said Frances, 'that this will prove to be a simple matter, and we will soon have Sanitas unmasked and apologetic.'

'Well, we haven't been so lucky on finding out who writes the Miss Dauntless books,' said Sarah. 'Don't tell me you don't want to know.'

The stories had been published locally under the obvious pseudonym W. Grove, and showed, so Sarah believed, a sincere and ardent admiration for the lady detective. The books had caused some disquiet to Mrs Embleton, since one illustration had clearly shown the front of the property in Westbourne Park Road where Frances and Sarah lived, and frightened the other tenants. Frances had written to the author through the publisher and an apology and flowers had smoothed over the trouble. In the next story, it was made plain that Miss Dauntless and her associate, Sally, had moved their home from Bayswater to Hyde Park, but Sarah only commented that if that was the case then Hyde Park had moved and was now a part of Bayswater. 'I am sure I could find out the author if I wanted to,' said Frances, 'but I have no reason to. If Mr Grove wants to make himself known, he knows where I am to be found. Now, I must take a cab to Paddington Green, where I very much hope that Inspector Sharrock will have established that there is no case against Mr Sweetman and has subsequently released him. I am not engaged to discover the murderer of Mrs Sweetman, that is a police matter and I may safely leave it to them.'

'What if Mr Sweetman asks you to find his wife's murderer?' asked Sarah. 'He might do.'

'I do not take murder cases,' replied Frances firmly.

'No,' said Sarah, 'you take cases that turn into murder.'

This, thought Frances, was unfortunately very true.

❧

When Frances arrived at Paddington Green police station, she saw a respectable and rather good-looking gentleman of about thirty in earnest and agitated conversation with the sour-faced Mr Marsden, Bayswater solicitor and bitter professional rival of the far more amiable Mr Rawsthorne. The young gentleman seemed a little startled as she walked up to him; understandably, since a lone woman in a police station who approached men, even if plain and sombrely clad like Frances, was assumed to be of a certain class. Mr Marsden, however, knew Frances by sight having encountered her at inquests and in courtrooms, not that he approved of her any the better for that.

'Miss Doughty,' said the solicitor, wrinkling his nose in disdain, 'you seem to be everywhere. I cannot imagine what legitimate business you might have here.'

'Oh!' exclaimed his client, throwing up his hands with an expression of relief. 'Pardon me; if you are Miss Doughty then you will be helping my unfortunate uncle, Mr Hubert Sweetman. I am Edward Curtis. It is my honour to make your acquaintance.'

Frances acknowledged the warm greeting, ignoring not only Mr Marsden's gibe but Mr Marsden himself. 'I hope I may be of service, but still more I was hoping that my services would no longer be required. Is Mr Sweetman still here? I had expected him to have been released by now.'

'I am sorry to say that not only is he still here, but he has actually been charged with the murder of my aunt,' explained Curtis, despairingly.

'On what grounds?' asked Frances.

'The police believe,' he said, with some effort, 'that they argued over my aunt not allowing him to see the children, and he strangled her in his rage. From the nature of the crime and the strength employed it was undoubtedly the work of a man, but anyone who imagines that my uncle is capable of such a thing does not know him!'

'Does he have no alibi?' asked Frances. 'Do we know when the murder took place?'

Curtis shook his head. 'Her body was found only yesterday but she had been dead for some time. Unfortunately, what with the dreadful weather we have had over the last two weeks, so few people have been about and no one was seen going into her house. And, of course, there were the cold conditions and no fire in the house for some time …' He left the implications unspoken and ended on a groan. 'It is impossible even to know the day she died, and therefore quite useless to look for an alibi.'

'Then they have no proof,' declared Frances. 'Neither can they show that your aunt and uncle had had any communication since his release from prison.'

'Ah, well, as to that,' Curtis admitted, 'my uncle put an advertisement in the newspaper, asking if Aunt Susan would write to him via Mr Marsden and a copy of the paper was found in her house with the advertisement circled in pencil. Although no letter was sent, the police think that they might have encountered each other by chance in the street – since their homes are not far distant – and agreed to meet, although uncle denies this. He says he did not know aunt's address until after she died.'

'And that is all their evidence?' exclaimed Frances. 'Why, it is nothing at all!'

'It is, although the previous conviction will tell against him, and suggest to the police that my uncle is a man of violence, which he is not. It cannot be brought in evidence against him if he comes to trial, but by the time the newspapers have finished with him everyone will know of it and he will not get a fair hearing. If it had not been for the weather!' Curtis cried. 'The police say that uncle might easily have walked to Redan Place from Moscow Road and not been seen or recognised, what with the blizzards and everyone muffled against the cold.'

'That is also true of the real murderer,' said Frances.

'Then you believe in him?' said Curtis excitedly. 'Oh please say that you do!' His plaintive appeal was for a moment quite disarming, and he looked almost boyish in his eagerness.

'I try not to be swayed by fancy,' said Frances, 'but on my initial meeting with Mr Sweetman he did impress me as sincere. I have in the course of my enquiries met a number of criminals. I have met people who seemed at first to be honest but who disappointed me. So I can be mistaken. All I can say at present, is that the case against your uncle is a poor one, and I would not wish to see him convicted out of prejudice on such slender evidence.'

'I thank you for your honesty,' said Curtis, who was clearly an emotional gentleman but not unbecomingly so.

'And you must be honest with me,' said Frances, 'whatever you imagine the consequences to be. Do you know where Benjamin and Mary Sweetman are living?'

He shook his head. 'No, Miss Doughty, I do not. If I did then I can assure you that I would already have gone to them and told them that their mother had died.'

'Mr Marsden?' asked Frances, turning to the solicitor. 'I do not expect you to reveal the confidences of clients, but can you say if Mr Sweetman's son and daughter have approached you?'

'I have nothing to tell,' said Marsden, stiffly. 'If they do approach me I will respect their wishes whatever they may be.'

'Please help my uncle!' Curtis entreated Frances. 'I have heard so much of your successes in the past. You may name your fee!'

'Mr Curtis,' Marsden warned, 'it is hardly appropriate to ask a young woman to become involved in a case of murder, or indeed, in my opinion, any criminal matter. I appreciate that Miss Doughty has, largely through sensational stories which I am convinced she writes herself, acquired the reputation of a detective amongst the uninformed masses. True, she has been known to stumble across the solutions to a few trifling mysteries, but she would, in my opinion, be better occupied in looking for a husband, unless of course,' he added with a cold smile, 'that quest is beyond her skills.'

'I will help you,' Frances assured Mr Curtis, passing him her card and receiving his in return. 'I will find your uncle's son and daughter and I will find your aunt's murderer. Mr Marsden, I suggest you try and locate your manners, but that, I fear, may be beyond *your* skills.' She turned and walked out.

Chapter Five

All the way home, Frances berated herself for her impulsive and unwise behaviour, and determined to write to Mr Curtis without delay expressing her sincere regrets at having made such an ill-judged promise to him and withdrawing from the case, regarding the murder, at least. She started to compose the letter in her imagination, but by the time she had completed her journey calmer thoughts prevailed. She had after all, she reminded herself, deliberately set out to investigate a murder once before, although that had been before she was a detective by profession and the adventure had been prompted by grave personal necessity. It had been her first triumph. Since then she had solved a number of murders, not by accident, as Mr Marsden had insultingly suggested, but by the exercise of her brain. Clearly this was not a skill confined solely to the male sex.

When she reached her apartments, she found a gentleman waiting to see her. He had been admitted by Sarah who had ordered him to be seated and was regarding him with the kind of deeply suspicious and hostile glare she reserved for most men. He rose to his feet at once, and introduced himself to Frances as James Elliott, producing a business card that showed him to be the proprietor of Elliott Properties of Bayswater. He was a tall man, and the smiling creases about his eyes announced him to be about forty, although he gave an impression of youthfulness and energy. Judging by the quality and style of his clothing his business was doing well.

'I received a message from Mr Richardson,' said Elliott, 'and of course I came at once. Is it true? Has Mrs Sweetman been killed?'

'I am afraid it is true,' said Frances, 'and Mr Sweetman has just been charged with her murder.'

'Oh surely not!' said Elliott in amazement. 'Why, the man could not harm a fly! Really, what can the police be thinking of!'

'At present he is the only suspect, and of course there is his earlier conviction, although he denies responsibility for that crime also,' said Frances. 'Since the police feel they have their man they will not look further, but I have just been engaged by Mr Sweetman's nephew to make enquiries.'

Sarah greeted this revelation with a sharp stare, which Frances knew was the harbinger of some close questioning once their visitor had gone.

'You may be able to assist me if you would answer some questions,' she continued.

'Of course,' said Elliott readily. 'I will do whatever I can.'

They sat facing each other across the little table. The visitor did not require the water carafe, and appeared to be at his ease and eager to help, although not, thought Frances, who had seen this fault before in others, over-eager. 'I understand you were working for J. Finn Insurance at the time of the robbery in 1866?' she asked.

'Yes, I was a junior clerk, back then. I remember the day very well, of course. I came into work that morning and found the police already there. I think it was poor Whibley who was first in as usual and found the door forced and Mr Gibson lying on the floor terribly injured. I must say it was a great shock to all of us when Sweetman was arrested. We thought it must have been a burglar who had somehow got hold of the key to the safe and managed to break open the front door, but the police said that the office door had only been damaged to make it *look* as if someone had broken in.'

'Did you know Mrs Sweetman?'

'I had met her a number of times, but I cannot say that we were well acquainted. She sometimes came to the office during the day if she wanted to see her husband. And after he was arrested, I carried letters to her from Mr Finn.'

'Did she ever bring the children to the office with her?'

'No, they must have been at school, I have never seen them.'

'What can you tell me about Mrs Sweetman? What impression did she give you of her character and manners? Was she on good terms with her husband?'

Elliott looked thoughtful as if conjuring up a portrait. 'She was a quiet lady, modest and good-natured. From the little I was able to observe she seemed to be on the best of terms with her husband. He always seemed pleased to see her when she called. After his arrest, she was very upset, of course, but I thought she bore her trouble with great dignity. I should mention that Mr Finn, the director, was quite convinced that Sweetman would be acquitted and even continued to pay a portion of his salary; he said he could have his position back when he was freed. He and Whibley used to visit Mrs Sweetman often to reassure her that they were doing all they could for her husband.'

'What happened after Mr Sweetman was convicted? Do you know where Mrs Sweetman and her children went?'

'I wish I could help you,' he said with regret, 'but as a junior in the company there were many things I was not privy to. We started a little subscription for Mrs Sweetman in the office, and I believe that Mr Finn sometimes supplied the poor lady with funds. After all, her plight was none of her own fault. I was told that the children had been removed from school and sent out to work, and Mrs Sweetman took in needlework and washing to live. Then Mr Finn said she had moved away, but he didn't say where. I never saw her again.'

'Mr Sweetman said that after he was arrested his wife refused to see him or allow him to see his children,' said Frances. 'Do you know why that was?'

Elliott looked mystified. 'I really couldn't say. Perhaps she was a sensitive lady, or knew something that everyone else did not.'

Frances glanced at her notes. 'Mr Finn has passed away, I believe.'

'Yes, about three or four years ago, I was told. And Browne, one of the other clerks, he too has gone. You will have heard about Whibley, of course.'

'How soon after the robbery did Mr Whibley go to work for his uncle?'

'A few months afterwards, I think. He had been studying accountancy in his own time, and Mr Anderson said he could come and work for him as soon as he had completed his studies, which he did. Then one of Mr Anderson's clerks retired and Whibley was kind enough to recommend me for the position. You will know, I expect, that some years later I married my dear Emily, who was Mr Anderson's widow.'

'And now you are in the property business?'

'Yes,' he said cheerfully. 'I purchase dilapidated houses and restore them or convert them to commercial use. That is a good business to get into in Bayswater.'

'And Mr Minster, he is a publican now?'

'Oh, I remember Minster,' said Elliott and from his change of tone and expression, the memory did not give him pleasure. 'He was not suited to the clerking business. He always said that if he ever came into money he would be a publican. And then it so happened that he did.'

'You don't recall when he came into that money?'

'No, but it would have been some months after the robbery.'

'Do you remember a messenger boy called Timmy?'

'I do.' Clearly he thought even less of Timmy than Mr Minster. 'He was a dishonest, lazy and untruthful boy and I can't imagine why Mr Finn employed him, unless it was out of charity to some relative. I don't know what became of him, and never thought to enquire. I doubt that it was anything good.'

'Why do you think Mr Finn chose to send you, a clerk, with letters to Mrs Sweetman and not the messenger boy?' asked Frances.

He smiled. 'It was not my position to ask, but if you would like me to guess I would say that the letters contained money.'

Frances nodded, any comment being superfluous. 'I am told that after the robbery Mr Gibson was never well enough to return to his employment. Did you go to see him? I was wondering if he recovered any of his memory. Perhaps he said something of significance?'

Elliott appeared somewhat embarrassed. 'I am very ashamed to say that I did not call on him. He was an active man for his age and I did not like to see him suddenly so weakened and failed. I know that Mr Finn and Mr Whibley did see him, and they said he could recall nothing of what happened that night.'

'Did he have any family?'

'I think there was a brother, who was older, and he enjoyed a little private income so the family was not left destitute. Both gone now, I expect.'

'You are not a devotee of the theatre?' asked Frances, abruptly.

'I do beg your pardon,' said Elliott. 'Did I hear you correctly? The theatre?'

'Mr Sweetman initially came to me asking if I could locate his family for him, and I believe that he genuinely did not know their whereabouts. The only clue I have as to his son and daughter is that they might have gone on the stage. The girl sang a song about not being able to milk a cow, and the boy whistled, although the witness is not reliable.'

'I can only hope your witness was mistaken,' said Elliott. 'It would be a sad fate if they came to that. Mr Finn said that they were very intelligent and showed promise if they could only be allowed to continue their education, but it was not to be.'

'When did you last see Mr Whibley?' asked Frances.

'Oh!' said Elliott, surprised. 'Is that important?'

'It could be. Mr Sweetman called on him at his office very shortly before he died, and asked if he knew anything about his son and daughter. He said he did not, but left the office soon afterwards without saying where he was going. I am wondering if he knew where they were and went to warn them. Or he may have spoken to another person about Mr Sweetman's visit.'

Elliott rubbed his chin, frowning with thought.

'When a friend or relative dies suddenly it is usual to remember very clearly one's last meeting with them,' said Frances.

'So it is,' said Elliott. 'And it is always a memory that brings sadness. I do believe that I may have been one of the last of Whibley's friends to speak to him, if not actually the last. It was the afternoon two days before he died. I received a message from him, asking me to call on him at his home. I thought it strange since he was always to be found at his office at that time of day and I did wonder if he had been taken ill.'

'Had he?' asked Frances, realising that this must have been the eleventh of January, immediately following Whibley's meeting with Mr Sweetman.

'He did not appear to be unwell, but he was very worried about something. Perhaps –' he shook his head wistfully, 'Poor fellow! You have made me wonder about this now – he may have had a premonition of his death. He said he was establishing a charitable foundation that would bear his name, a hospital for the aged poor, and he asked my advice about a suitable property to purchase in Bayswater. I said that I would look into it, and I made some enquiries the following day, but when I called to see him at the office the next morning I was told the terrible news.'

'And he said nothing to you about Mr Sweetman or his children?'

'No, he never mentioned them at all.'

'What was the name of his doctor?'

'I'm afraid I don't know. It may seem unlikely but until shortly before his death I had never known him complain of any illness.'

'You were his main executor, were you not?'

'I was.'

'The newspapers reported he left over twenty thousand pounds.'

'Indeed, and it would have been far more had he not been the most generous of men. You know of course of –' he hesitated.

'Yes, that although he had never been a married man he was the father of a number of children.'

'All well-cared for, all educated, and destined for good positions in life.' He handed a folded paper to Frances. 'A copy of Mr Whibley's will, as you have requested.'

There were minor bequests to Whibley's servants, and annuities to four women specifically named while Mr Elliott had been left three hundred pounds. The residuary legatee was the Paddington Orphan School and Foundling Hospital. Frances had a curious and ridiculously amusing thought that the beneficiaries of his favoured institution were all Mr Whibley's natural offspring. 'I wish to locate anyone he might have spoken to after seeing Mr Sweetman,' she said. 'He was alone at his home when you saw him?'

'Yes, apart from the servants, of course.'

'And after his death you examined all his papers and found nothing to suggest that he had any special knowledge of where the Sweetman children went?'

'If I knew that, I would tell you. I have no reason to conceal such information.'

'Was there a trusted servant he might have confided in?'

'There was a valet, Mr Pennyforth, who had been with him five years.'

'Do you have his address?'

'I am afraid not. He was entitled to one hundred pounds under the will, but I have never been able to find him to hand him what he was due. When I went to Whibley's house on that sad morning, I found that Pennyforth had already departed and left no message or forwarding address. I placed an advertisement in the newspapers but received no reply. I retain the money safely for him still, in case he should reappear.'

'Could you describe him to me?'

Elliott looked surprised, as might any man asked to describe a servant. 'Er – he was quite young, about thirty or possibly a little less, nothing very remarkable about his appearance. Middling height, hair dark, I think. That is really all I can remember.'

Frances passed a sheet of paper and a pencil to him. 'Please could you write the valet's name so I can be sure of how it is spelled,' she said.

'Yes, of course,' he said, without demur. He was obliged, while writing with his right hand to steady the paper with his left, and Frances observed that he had some difficulty in moving his left arm into place, and there were the marks of an old scar down the back of his hand. He wrote the valet's name unhesitatingly in a neat, clear and perfectly even script, and passed the paper back. Frances quickly saw that Mr Elliott was neither Bainiardus nor Sanitas.

Frances hoped she would not find it necessary to call upon all Mr Whibley's past friends and their offspring in the faint hope that he might have said something to them about the Sweetman family. It would be better, she thought, to begin by tracing Mr Pennyforth, who might be the one person who could reveal if there was anyone other than Mr Elliott who Mr Whibley had spoken to shortly before he died.

Frances showed Elliott a portion of the Bainiardus letter. 'This is a letter received from a gentlemen saying that he was an intimate friend of Mr Whibley's for some years,' she said. 'Do you recognise either the hand or the paper?'

'I am afraid not.'

She then presented the Sanitas letter, which received the same response.

'Do you still have Mr Whibley's correspondence?'

'No, he was, like so many gentlemen, in the habit of destroying letters that he felt he no longer needed. He liked everything about him very tidily arranged.'

'Did the housemaid or the cook mention him receiving any callers on the day before his death?'

'It was not something I thought to ask them,' he said reasonably.

Frances could think of nothing more to ask, and Mr Elliott, promising that he would advise Frances if he thought of anything new that was relevant to Mr Sweetman, departed.

Frances completed her notes without glancing at Sarah, who she knew would be giving her a very hard look. 'So it's murder cases now?' said Sarah, at last. 'And from the outset; not just ones that happen to fall on you by chance.'

'Mr Curtis asked me to help his uncle,' said Frances, 'which I am already doing. I am sure it would have come to this eventually, and if I am to take a case of murder I might as well be paid for it from the start.'

'This Mr Curtis, is he one of those handsome types?' asked Sarah, suspiciously.

'He is married with a family, and his looks, whatever they may be, are of interest only to his lady wife,' said Frances, although she thought that Mr Curtis could well be considered handsome. 'Now then, we have a lot to do and must make plans.'

Frances was far too busy to think of eating supper. She had been perusing Mr Rustrum's slim booklet entitled *Healthful Living*, which advocated a breakfast consisting of dry brown bread, fruit and tea taken in the Russian style with lemon. Dinner was the same, with the addition of no more than four ounces of poached white fish or lean meat with vegetables, and supper was the same as breakfast. Frances looked in vain for a mention of a nice pot of tea made properly with milk, and cake or buns in the afternoon, but this seemed to have been omitted.

Missing a meal entirely was, according to Mr Rustrum, better than eating to excess. He declared that he sometimes went for a whole day without food and felt better and stronger for it and claimed that his system of eating, allied to fresh air and exercise, was bound to lead to a long and active life. It certainly sounded economical, and Frances thought that if her clients continued to delay payment she might be obliged to follow Mr Rustrum's advice out of necessity. Mr Lathwal had also provided a treatise on the vegetarian diet, explaining how it was both approved by science and calming to the spirit, including instructions for the preparation of lentils — something that Frances had never eaten — dishes of rice and vegetables and various combinations of the three with some interesting sounding spices. There was no suggestion that any of these foodstuffs should be restricted in quantity. The consumption of flesh food was denounced as both unnecessary and harmful, clogging the body with poisons and making the eater dull and heavy, not to mention tainted by the horrible cruelty involved in its production.

'Supper!' announced Sarah, putting a jug of milk, some thick slices of bread and butter and a corner of ham on the table. Frances put the booklets aside and began to eat.

'If only I could find someone who was a patron of the Bijou Theatre and remembers what happened to the boy and girl!' she exclaimed. 'Sarah, could you go to Redan Place tomorrow and find out as much as you can about Mrs Sweetman; when she was last seen and if she had any visitors. Of course, if she did they would all have been dressed like Esquimaux, and we could scarcely tell if they were men or women, but at least we would know the day they called. And ask if anyone ever went to the Bijou Theatre or knows someone who was once employed there.'

'Then I'll go to some agencies to see if they know where Mr Pennyforth is,' said Sarah. 'If he had a good place with Mr Whibley he ought to have found a new situation by now.'

'So he ought,' agreed Frances, 'but only if he had a good character from his employer. If Mr Whibley's death was unexpected, he should have stayed on to receive a character from a family friend or executor. Perhaps Mr Whibley dismissed him? Well, the agencies will know. If you can find Mr Whibley's housemaid and cook I will need to know if any visitors were admitted between Mr Elliott's visit on the eleventh of January and the morning of the thirteenth, when Mr Whibley was found dead. Then could you call on Mr Knight and Mr Taylor for their usual services regarding both J. Finn Insurance and Anderson, Walsh and Whibley.'

Charles Knight and Sebastian Taylor, generally known as 'Chas' and 'Barstie', were two businessmen – proprietors of the impressive sounding Bayswater Display and Advertising Company, which they ran from a single attic room above a watchmaker's shop on the Grove, a room which was also, although they did not care to admit it, their living accommodation. Their long association with some of the more unconventional elements of Bayswater business life had given them useful insights into local companies, and they were often able to supply Frances with information unknown to the press or indeed the police.

Ignoring Sarah's grimace at this prospect, Frances went on, 'I shall visit J. Finn Insurance where I already have an appointment with the present manager, Mr Finn the younger, who may recall something his father said. After that, I will go to see Mr Minster, the gentleman who unexpectedly came into money after the robbery. And then –' she sighed, 'I am sorry to say I will be seeing Dr Adair, Mr Lathwal and Mr Rustrum, those keen rivals in the question of diet and joint enemies of Sanitas.'

'Not all of them at once?' queried Sarah, bringing a jam tart to round off the meal.

'Yes, although they do not yet know it.'

Sarah nodded. 'Interesting. Do you want me here in case a fight breaks out?'

'They should be ashamed of themselves if it does, and Mr Gillan will get to hear of it the same day,' said Frances. 'I have no patience with such pretensions. These men all claim to have the interests of society at heart, yet it seems that all they can do is stand by their beliefs for reasons of reputation. Surely the general good is more important than their personal fame?'

Supper over, Frances sent a note to Mr Sweetman's undeniably handsome nephew confirming that she would be helping his uncle, and asking for an early meeting.

CHAPTER SIX

The office of J. Finn Insurance, scene of the 1866 robbery and attack on the unfortunate Mr Gibson, was situated near where Westbourne Grove met Chepstow Road, and was flanked by an auctioneer on one side and a seller of sweets on the other. Frances observed that the door to the main office, while fashioned to look invitingly solid and reliable in its own right, was also furnished with a number of heavy security locks. There was a narrow vestibule which opened into a main office closely crowded with desks, the clerks who manned them bent over their work in attitudes calculated to suggest to the eye of their employer both enthusiasm and industry. Frances, who had written a preliminary letter explaining her business, was shown at once into the presence of the manager.

Mr Finn junior had a room of his own and, thought Frances, needed one. He was younger than the late Mr Thomas Whibley probably by some twenty years, but was heading towards that gentlemen's appearance and, in all probability, his fate.

He reposed at his ease behind a desk piled high on either side with papers, crossing his hands over a bulging stomach. His face was pink and pulpy, the skin with a freshly groomed shine, and a thick roll of fat around the neck and throat lapped over his collar. His auburn hair was trimmed very short, and a narrow clipped beard dotted pale bristles about the line of his jaw.

On the wall behind the desk beside the portrait of the queen, there was a picture of a venerable and dignified looking gentleman with an abundance of white whiskers bearing the legend 'John Finn 1804–1877'. A decorative silver photograph frame sat on the desk, tilted so that only Finn could see the subject. There was nothing on open display that would enable Frances to easily see Mr Finn's handwriting, although there were a few sheets of paper with jotted notes and a bundle of sealed letters, which she could not examine closely without it causing some comment.

He rose to greet her and it was an effort for him to do so. Although young, he did not carry his weight well, as some men did, and there was a cushion on his chair of a kind that gave support to an overworked spine.

Young Mr Finn had Frances' letter lying open on the desk before him. Once he had ushered her to a chair and sat down again, tucking the cushion into the small of his back, he rested his fingertips on the paper and tapped it gently.

'Miss Doughty,' he said softly, 'I will do whatever I can to help you, but I fear that may be very little. I was not working here at the time of the robbery; I was a mere schoolboy then.'

'Did you attend the same school as Benjamin Sweetman?' asked Frances, hopefully.

'No, I was born in Cambridgeshire and schooled there. I did not come to London until I was sixteen; that was two years after the robbery.'

'I had thought, perhaps, your father might have spoken of it,' said Frances, glancing at the portrait of the elder Finn.

Mr Finn placed his fingertips together, producing the effect of linked pork sausages hanging in the window of a butcher's shop. 'Ah, a great many people make that assumption,' he said. 'No, Mr Finn senior was not my father, he was my great-uncle. Of course, he did sometimes allude to the crime, which grieved him deeply. It was not so much the theft of the money, but the violent assault on Mr Gibson, who was a trusted employee of many years standing, and of course, the terrible betrayal by Mr Sweetman.'

'He thought Mr Sweetman to be guilty?' said Frances, surprised. 'I had heard otherwise.'

'Yes, I am sure you have. My uncle was a good, charitable man, who liked to think the best of everyone, and right up to the trial he believed Sweetman's protestations of innocence, and did everything he could for him, but he admitted to me later in confidence that once he had heard the evidence there seemed to be no other conclusion.'

'Did he ever tell you what became of Mrs Sweetman and the children after the trial?' asked Frances. 'Mr Sweetman is very anxious to find his family, and I do not, as the police do, believe he had any hand in the death of his wife.'

Finn sighed and, young as he was, he looked for a few moments almost aged as his heavy features sagged into deep crevices. 'That is a horrible business. We heard of it only yesterday and could scarcely believe it. How can such tragedy strike a respectable family twice? All I know,' he went on, 'and all that my uncle ever knew is that after Sweetman was found guilty the family went away. I expect they did not like to be pointed out in the street as the wife and children of a criminal.'

'They might have changed their names,' suggested Frances.

'It would not surprise me to learn that they had, but if they did my uncle was not told what it was.'

'Did he offer Mrs Sweetman any monetary assistance after she left Garway Road? He cannot have done so without knowing her new address.'

'My understanding,' said Finn, carefully, 'and this is only from small comments that were dropped into conversation and never elaborated upon, is that she found some other means of financial support. In those circumstances my uncle might well have ceased to assist her.'

'A man, do you think?' said Frances, drawing the inevitable conclusion from his delicacy of expression.

Finn bent his head over Frances' letter, although he hardly seemed to be looking at it. 'I think nothing,' he said after a few moments, glancing up again. 'It is all story and rumour and very unpleasant and may not even be true, and I was far too young to know more. Even that much I was probably not intended to hear.'

There was a smart double rap on the door of the office and a gentleman was admitted. He was neither tall nor short nor was he plump or slender, but compensated for this lack of distinction in his form by sporting a beautifully groomed beard of horticultural proportions, tinged at the margins with a less than natural red. He was neatly attired after the manner of a clerk, with a large leather document case tucked under his arm, from which he extracted some invoices, laying them on the desk.

Although from Frances' point of view they were upside down, the printed illustrations announced them to be more related to gentleman's attire than business matters.

'Thank you Yeldon,' said Finn, picking up the packet of letters from the desk and handing them to the new arrival. 'Could you deliver these and also arrange for two bottles of Apollinaris Water to be sent tomorrow?'

'At once, sir,' said Mr Yeldon, casting a look of intense curiosity at Frances, then, turning swiftly on his heel, he departed.

Frances, from her days as her father's assistant in the chemists shop, was familiar with Apollinaris Water; a naturally sparkling table water from a German spa, noted for its healthful digestive properties. She could not help but wonder what young Mr Finn ate to make him so large. It was a condition one saw all too often in middle aged and less active persons, but more rarely in the young. Did he gorge himself on beefsteaks and bonbons and then resort to digestives to repair what he had done? Or was the medical man who declared that water made one fat actually correct? It was all very puzzling.

Frances examined the list of names in her notebook. 'By the time you joined your uncle's company Mr Whibley and Mr Elliott had left,' she said. 'Did you ever meet them?'

'No, although I knew of them, of course, as men who had once been employed here and had moved up in the world. And now poor Whibley is gone.' He shook his head. 'He was a great smoker, I understand. Cigars – they were the death of him in my opinion. I could never abide the smell of them, something for which my dear wife is very grateful, as she cannot endure them either.' He gave an affectionate glance at the portrait on his desk, and touched the scrollwork on the frame with gentle fingertips. 'Oh I know there are those who say he died from excessive corpulence, but I do not agree; a good round belly on a man can be a fine thing if it does not weigh him down.' He patted his stomach. 'I shall certainly not be "banting",' he added with a smile, 'that seems a most unwise proceeding.'

Seeing Frances eyeing the back of the picture frame, he turned it towards her. The portrait was of a pretty, young, bright-eyed woman of slender build, with a chubby child on one knee and a chubby baby in the crook of her arm. 'My dear girl Alice and the children,' said Finn, with evident pride.

'How delightful,' said Frances, with more enthusiasm than she actually felt, 'may I see?' As she reached out for the portrait, she grasped, as if by chance, one of Mr Finn's jotted notes, and quickly apologised and returned it to him. The handwriting, she observed, was quite unlike that of any of the letters written to the *Chronicle*.

She permitted the doting husband and father a few moments to replace the picture at the correct angle before she went on. 'Can you tell me anything about Mr Minster, who was once employed here and left to become a publican?'

'I have never met him.'

'And Mr Browne?'

'Poor Browne, yes. He retired with failing health not long after I arrived. He was not an old man, only about fifty, I believe, but he was found to have a cancer of the stomach and wasted away to nothing before he died.'

'I don't suppose you know what became of the unfortunate Mr Gibson?'

'My uncle only said that he was an invalid in the care of relatives. He must be dead by now.'

'And Timmy the messenger boy?'

Finn shook his head. 'I can't say. I don't believe there was a boy of that name when I first came here.'

Frances produced her folder of letters. 'I must ask you to look at some letters now and tell me if you can identify the writer, they are the originals of some correspondence sent to the *Chronicle* after Mr Whibley's death.'

'People are so exercised on the question of diet, a matter which I feel should be left to a man's common sense,' said Mr Finn, as he looked through the letters with no trace of recognition on his face. 'And whatever one might believe about organisations like the Pure Food Society, and the vegetarians, who seem to be well-meaning if a little eccentric, it is no reason to descend into personal insult and unfounded accusations which can only cheapen the argument. Sometimes even clever men can be like children squabbling at play.' He handed back the folder. 'No, I can't say I know who wrote any of these.'

'So do you dissociate yourself from the sentiments in the letter written by Sanitas?' asked Frances.

'I do indeed,' he assured her. 'I suppose you might imagine that I am the very man to have written such a letter, but I did not and would never have done so.'

Frances had been careful to make no allusion to young Mr Finn's size, but it appeared, as he rubbed his belly almost affectionately, that he was rather proud of it.

※

'Look here,' said Fred Minster, aggressively, 'I know what you're after, and it's not as if there wasn't any whispering going on at the time, but I'll show you the papers and then you can see for yourself. Do I *look* like a rich man?'

He did not, but Frances felt that it would not be polite to say so, and thus said nothing. The Cooper's Arms was a small establishment that had once been a private house. Downstairs the front and back parlours had been combined by the expedient of knocking down most of the intervening wall into a long taproom with tables placed almost edge-to-edge where thirty or forty people might crowd together over their beer and pies. Mr Minster and his wife, when not dispensing refreshment, lived in the rooms above.

No one who met Mr Minster would imagine that he had ever been a clerk. There was no sign of it in either his dress or his manner, both of which were coarser than necessary. He looked like a labourer who had just downed tools for the day and gone for a foaming glass to wet his throat. Perhaps, thought Frances, Mr Minster had deliberately cultivated this appearance to make his particular class of customers feel at home. They would not appreciate being served their beer by someone who looked as though he could manage a good copperplate. The Cooper's Arms was not a salubrious establishment, and Frances would not have gone there without both an appointment and the assurance that Mrs Minster would personally admit her and take her straight up to the parlour. Even passing quickly through the taproom, she found the smell of stale beer, cheap pastry, and unwashed clothes and bodies almost overpowering. There were women there too, in dresses unsuited to the daytime, and they did not look content.

The upper apartments were better kept, showing that Mrs Minster had not entirely relinquished her status as the wife of a man who once wore a suit and clean collar to work.

'I've got all the papers and that can be an end of it,' said Minster, opening a drawer and pulling out a bundle of documents bound about with string. He untied the string and threw the bundle defiantly on the table. 'See there!'

Frances felt from his manner that she was not the first person he had had to convince in this way. She examined the papers, which showed that in January 1867 the will of John Jones of Chippenham in Wiltshire, who had passed away the previous November, had been proved. All his estate – amounting in value to some two hundred pounds – had been left to his only grandchild Ann Minster, previously Jones. A Wiltshire solicitor had acted as executor, and there was correspondence relating to the payment of the sum. For all his coarse appearance and manners, Mr Minster, true to his earlier profession, wrote a neat and very clear hand.

'So you see I didn't rob the safe, and anyone who says I did is a liar!' said Minster. 'I've already got damages and an apology off someone who flapped his mouth when he shouldn't have done, and I can do it again if need be!'

'Thank you for showing me these,' said Frances, politely.

'No, it was Sweetman who took the money and half-killed poor old Gibson.'

'What makes you so sure of it?' asked Frances. 'I have met Mr Sweetman and he does not appear to be the violent type.'

'Who knows what a man might be driven to if he needs money?' said Minster, flinging himself into a chair. 'Oh I don't deny I would have liked the money, we all would, but that's not the same as *needing* it, is it? Needing it enough to go against your own nature and steal it. No, I knew he was in trouble when I saw him talking to old Sidebottom the moneylender, and only a desperate man ever did that.'

'Are you sure he actually borrowed money from Mr Sidebottom?'

'Oh yes, he admitted it. Said something about his sister and her doctor's bills. I think Sweetman paid off Sidebottom with the stolen money. That's why it was never found.'

'And what did Mr Sidebottom have to say for himself?'

Minster gave a short bark of a laugh. 'Nothing. Someone stuck him with a knife just after Sweetman was arrested. At least Sweetman can't have done it, as he was in the cells, but then half of Bayswater wanted rid of *that* pestilence. Sidebottom had a nasty little book he kept in his coat pocket with notes of all the money going back and forth, but when they found him, it was gone. So it was one of his debtors who done him. Never did find out which one.'

'I must agree,' said Frances carefully, 'that it would appear that Mr Sweetman could be seen as having a motive to commit the robbery, and also he had the means, since he held the key to the safe, but that is not proof, and I am surprised that the verdict went against him. Unless of course there is some other fact of which I am unaware. Why was he found guilty, Mr Minster? Why did his wife turn against him?'

Minster seemed calmer now that Frances was asking his opinion rather than challenging him. She suspected that his customers were very well behaved.

'As to his wife, I don't know. Perhaps he raised his hand to her and the children a bit too often, and she was pleased to be free of him. Now, I'm not averse to a man correcting his wife when she needs it – a little tap now and again is a husband's privilege – but there are limits to how hard he ought to be. Maybe Sweetman stepped over the line.' He gave a swift grin. 'Maybe he stepped over it – *well* over it – just the other day. But the robbery; well first of all he had no alibi – concocted some story about being with his sister and she tried to lie for him, but got it all mixed up so it didn't wash. It was Browne that done for him, though.'

'Mr Browne, his colleague?'

'That's right. Browne was walking down the Grove that night. He saw the light was on in the office, and at first he didn't think anything of it as he knew Gibson was working late. Then he saw a man standing at the outer door of the office, a man who looked at him and then ducked back in again. It was Sweetman.'

'Perhaps he saw the real thief,' said Frances. 'That's what Mr Sweetman thinks.'

'That was what the defence tried to show, but the jury believed Browne. If I were you, Miss Doughty, I wouldn't let myself be alone with Mr Sweetman in case he took against you. It's the quiet ones you have to be worried about.'

'He came to me a few days ago asking if I would look for his family,' said Frances.

'Yes, well he found his wife, didn't he?' Minster gave another little bark.

'Do you happen to know where his son and daughter went? The only information I have is that they performed on the stage at the Bijou Theatre.'

'Oh, I remember the old Bijou,' said Minster. 'All kinds of things there; plays, concerts, varieties.'

'Do you recall Harold Froy the Jaunty Boy? He used to whistle.'

'No. Is this some sort of a joke?'

'Not at all. I was told that Benjamin Sweetman performed under that name.'

He pulled a face. 'There was any number of acts, some of them you only ever saw the once, because if they were no good they didn't get asked again. Can't say as I remember any whistling boy.'

'And a girl who sang of wanting to be a milkmaid?'

'Oh *they* were a penny a dozen, if you get my meaning.' He sniggered.

Frances did get his meaning and did not ask him to elaborate. As she left the Cooper's Arms she could not help but wonder about Mr Minster's views on maintaining domestic harmony. Judging by the appearance of Mrs Minster, a sturdy grim-faced woman with hands reddened by hard work, the publican's opinions on the question were more likely to be theoretical than practical. Frances did not expect to marry, having neither beauty nor fortune, but she still entertained the occasional idle thought as to the manner of man she might choose if it was ever to prove possible. One of the Miss Dauntless adventures included an incident where a gallant gentleman rescued the heroine from certain death and claimed a kiss as his reward. It was a disturbing story and Frances tried not to read it too often.

CHAPTER SEVEN

Everyone Frances had questioned about the robbery had slightly differing opinions, but that was only to be expected. It was probable to the point of certainty that the intervening years had affected memories, altering not only the witnesses' perceptions of what had actually happened and been said, but also of how the events should be interpreted.

Even though it was not part of Frances' remit, from either her agreement with Mr Sweetman or his nephew, to prove him innocent of the 1866 burglary and wounding of Mr Gibson, she could not help thinking that only by extracting the truth about that crime from the tangle of rumour and supposition would she know precisely why Mr Sweetman's family had deserted him, and thus have a better chance of finding his son and daughter. Why had Mrs Sweetman found her husband's position so heinous as to refuse to see him again, when other wives had forgiven far worse? Or was Mr Sweetman guilty of other crimes, unknown to the police, of which he was so ashamed that he had failed to mention them at their interview? Even if Mr Sweetman had not murdered his wife, was it a coincidence that Mrs Sweetman had been killed so soon after his release? Frances could hardly imagine that someone might hate Mr Sweetman so much that they would murder his wife for the sole purpose of having him hanged. Evil of that kind did, she thought sadly, probably exist in the world, but if that had been the plan some more incriminating clue than a newspaper would have been placed at the scene, something like Mr Gibson's pocket book which had been such strong evidence in 1866. Perhaps Mrs Sweetman had information that, with her husband recently out of prison, it had become necessary to suppress. Or perhaps, thought Frances, it was, as so many things were, far simpler. Mrs Sweetman had fallen on hard times, got into bad company, strayed from the path of honesty and been killed, either for debt or informing on her criminal friends.

Frances decided on an early return to the *Chronicle* offices, this time to study the bound copies of the 1866 newspapers, and read for herself what evidence was given at the trial. She might even find out something about productions at the Bijou Theatre, and the careers of a whistling boy and a forlorn milkmaid.

She was preparing for her interview with the three enemies of Sanitas when Sarah returned from her visits with a catalogue of disappointing news. Mrs Sweetman, she had found, had only been living in Redan Place for a few months and had not made any close friends in the neighbourhood. No one knew her previous address, and neither was anyone able to say if she had received any visitors other than ladies who brought her needle-work or washing. As far as anyone knew she had had no callers at all during the great frost, not that anyone Sarah had interviewed had lingered on the streets during that time. Most, if they had ventured out at all, had been closely muffled with heads down so as not to face the bite of the icy wind. The upper floor of the house was let to an elderly lady who was deaf, and whose grandson called once a week to see that she had everything she needed, but he had his own key and neither of them had thought to look in on Mrs Sweetman. The last certain sighting of her alive was on Sunday, 16 January, in church. The body had been found on 26 January, the day before Mr Sweetman had been arrested. Between those two dates, the freezing weather meant that it was very much a matter of guesswork as to when she had been killed.

It was now, thought Frances, more than ever important that she question Edward Curtis closely about his family. Fortunately, a note arrived saying that he would call upon her that evening if convenient, after he had seen the last patient of the day, and she sent a reply to the effect that this would be very convenient indeed.

Sarah had also visited all the agencies for the supply of servants in the vicinity of Westbourne Grove, but none of them knew anything of Mr Pennyforth. She had left them with Frances' card in case he should call on them in future. There was better news about Mr Whibley's cook and housemaid, both of whom were still employed in Bayswater. Sarah had spoken to them and they agreed that after Mr Elliott's last visit to Mr Whibley on 11 January their employer had looked decidedly unwell. The cook was unable to say if Mr Whibley had received any further visitors, but the housemaid recalled that on the following day Mr Whibley had come home from his office very much earlier than expected, saying that he felt tired. That afternoon Mr Pennyforth had gone out on an errand, and she felt sure that when he returned he was accompanied by another gentleman.

Sarah's next task was to scale the narrow stairs to the offices of the Bayswater Display and Advertising Co. Ltd, which occupied a single room above Mr Beccles' watchmaker's shop. She was surprised to find not only that the proprietors, Chas and Barstie, were not there, but her young relative, Tom, was effectively using the office for his own enterprise, running a busy team of messenger boys.

Tom, though hardly more than twelve, was a businessman in the making, always looking for an opportunity of making money. He had once been the delivery boy for William Doughty, but had quickly developed a sideline in transporting messages and parcels for anyone who would pay him. He was fast and trustworthy and knew every street in Paddington. More recently he had worn the uniform provided by the Doughtys' successor at the chemists shop, Mr Jacobs, and still worked for him on busy days as he liked the smart cap and shiny buttons, but in recent months most of his time was spent directing others. Several businesses in the Grove now used his services exclusively.

During the worst of the January weather, Tom's band of 'men' as he called them had kept the wheels of Bayswater commerce turning by dashing about with improvised snowshoes made from the soles of discarded boots lashed to their feet with string. Fragments of broken carriages and packing cases had provided them with enough kindling to keep a fire burning, so they could come up to the office for a warm and a pint of tea and slice of bread. Tom was a regular caller at Frances' apartments, and rarely left without scrounging half a cake or some cold pudding and crumbs of cheese, which she could hardly begrudge him. His ability through the agency of his numerous and well-drilled subordinates to have sharp eyes all over Bayswater at once had solved many a tricky case for her.

Sarah found him sitting behind the desk in the chair usually occupied by Chas, his face alight with energy, hair in spiky disarray, handing out a parcel of leaflets to his best 'man', who went by the name of Ratty. This youth, who was about the same age as Tom, resembled a bundle of clothing of all sizes and conditions of wear that had by some magical spell become animated and moved about of its own accord. He had not long ago been bought a new suit of clothes by Frances as a reward for supplying useful information, but he had probably pawned them in favour of his customary ill-fitting rags. 'It weren't me,' said Ratty to Sarah, and dashed downstairs before she could open her mouth.

'What's the job, then?' asked Tom, leaning back in his chair, with an air of authority that would have sat well on a company director three times his age.

'Information,' said Sarah. 'Where are the other two? Miss Doughty has some work for them.'

'Oh I 'aven't seen 'em for a day or two, now. They got a letter and off they went, said they was goin' to Afriky where the weather was warmer, and would I look after the bus'ness till they come back.'

'It's not that Filleter up to his tricks, is it?' said Sarah, with a scowl.

She was referring to the repellent young man, so called because of the thin sharp knife he carried, whose mere presence in Bayswater had once been enough to frighten Chas and Barstie away for weeks. He had recently given them to understand that he had no further designs upon their safety, although they felt that this might only be a temporary situation.

'Nah, 'e's not been seen round 'ere for a month at least,' said Tom, airily, 'an' I don't give 'im no mind, in any case! *I'm* not afraid of 'im! No, the gents 'ave got bus'ness elsewhere – not Afriky, that was jus' a joke, though I think Ratty believed 'em. They've gone east.'

'What? China?' Sarah exclaimed.

'Nah – Essex. Mr Knight, 'e's a sharp cove and no mistake, 'e sez it's a good place to go when you want do somethin' quiet where you won't get bothered, 'n put things where they won't get found.' He tapped the side of his nose with a grubby forefinger. ''Nuff said if you know what I mean.'

'Well, when they come back, tell them Miss Doughty wants to see them,' said Sarah. 'It's not your line of work.'

''ow much for the message?' Tom demanded.

'It's just telling them, there's no work in that!'

'I c'd choose not to if I want! 'Ow much?'

She snorted. 'No result, no money!'

'No money, no work!' retorted Tom.

'No work and a clip round the ear!' Sarah gave an angry growl and stamped downstairs.

🌸

'That is a disappointment,' said Frances, when Sarah reported back. 'Mr Knight and Mr Taylor would have known every underhand thing happening in both businesses, or at least know where to find it out.'

She had no time to devise further plans because the arrival of the three warring gentlemen was imminently expected.

Frances had read the letters sent to the *Chronicle* several times and had made a close examination of their appearance. The Sanitas letter was written on plain, pale blue notepaper of a very common type; a foolscap sheet, folded in half in the usual way. The hand was firm and legible, but was not that of an individual occupied in any profession where superior clarity and neatness of script was essential. The last paragraph, while undoubtedly in the same hand, seemed to have been written in a faster, more flowing manner than the earlier part, perhaps expressing its more emotional content. The letter from Mr Whibley's medical man was a thready scrawl, which looked as though it had been done by someone careless of appearances. Little spots of ink suggested an indifferent pen, and the pressure on the paper expressed irritation. The paper was good quality and plain white, slightly smaller than foolscap, and the upper right corner of the top fold had been torn away, indicating that it had been printed with the sender's address, which he had decided to conceal. The Bainiardus letter was neatly written, in a rounded hand, its execution slow and studied. If, as the writer claimed, he had suffered distress at the illness and death of a friend, it was not apparent in his handwriting. It was on a small, plain unfolded sheet, the paper inferior in type to the two others, and imperfectly cut on one edge. All three letters used standard black ink. None had any notable scent.

Dr Adair was the first to arrive. He was a vigorous looking man of forty-five, who, if the size of his moustache and length of his stride were anything to judge by, liked to cultivate an air of authority. There was a rounded bulge about his belly, causing noticeable strain to his waistcoat buttons, which he seemed quite proud of and he had no hesitation about thrusting it forward to lend weight to his words. Frances could not help wondering if he was one of those medical men, of a type she knew to be all too common, who was very free with his advice to others, but disdained to take that good advice himself. He was followed almost at once by Mr Lathwal, a slender and very young man of Indian extraction, who, as he had already advised Frances in his letter, was lodging in Bayswater while studying the law. The two were understandably astonished to see each other.

'There must be some error!' exclaimed Dr Adair in a voice altogether too loud for the small parlour. 'I had not expected to see Mr Lathwal here, especially in view of our dispute!'

'I too am somewhat mystified,' Mr Lathwal admitted.

'There is no error,' Frances assured them. 'Please be seated gentlemen, we are awaiting a third party.'

Adair was lowering himself into a chair with very ill-grace when Frances' words made him leap to his feet. 'That wouldn't be that dangerous lunatic Rustrum, would it?' he said. 'If so, I shall depart at once!'

'It is Mr Rustrum, and you may do as you please,' said Frances, coolly.

'The impudence!' boomed Adair.

Frances remained uncowed. 'Please moderate your voice, sir, there are ladies of a nervous disposition in the house and I do not wish them to be disturbed.'

At that moment Mr Rustrum arrived, a tall, spare gentleman with a lively gait. Contrary to the popular prejudice that those who restrained themselves from excess at the dinner table must therefore be unhappy individuals, he was abundantly cheerful in demeanour, indeed his smile seemed to be permanently fixed to his face. His initial letter to Frances, in which he advised her that he was an architect by profession although retired for many years, had made a great point of stating his age, which was seventy-four, and on meeting him she could see why he chose to mention it, since he looked about twenty years younger, and clearly knew it. His present occupation was writing books and pamphlets about the Pure Food diet and promoting them by travelling about the country and lecturing on the subject to anyone willing to listen, and most probably to a great many more who were not. 'How extraordinary!' he said, with an expression of great pleasure, on seeing the other two gentlemen. 'That is very clever of you Miss Doughty. At last we might get something done.' He sat down. The other two men, Dr Adair with a scowl and Mr Lathwal with a bland expression, did the same.

'Now gentlemen,' Frances began, 'I have called you all together not because of your differences, which I realise are substantial, but because you are all concerned in the same question: the identity and activities of the person calling him or herself "Sanitas". This, I must warn you, is not the time or the place to argue about diet. I have read many books on the subject and find that there are hardly any principles on which all are agreed, apart from the fact that excess corpulence may in some cases be deleterious to health. As to how it comes about and how it may be cured there are as many opinions as there are authors. So, we will leave that aside for today. Do you agree?'

They all looked surprised and not a little disappointed, but they agreed.

'Your letters conveniently supplied me with examples of your handwriting, and when I visited the offices of the *Bayswater Chronicle* I was able to compare them with the letters written during the correspondence that followed the death of Mr Thomas Whibley. I observed that all three of you wrote to the *Chronicle* under your own names, none of you wrote under the name Bainiardus, and neither is any one of you Sanitas.'

The men glanced at each other. 'But it is possible,' said Adair, 'that this Sanitas fellow, being a conniving underhand type, might have disguised his hand.'

'I have given that some consideration,' said Frances, 'but the Sanitas correspondence is written with an ease that does not suggest disguise, and is consistent in form, though not speed, throughout the letter. I am inclined to believe that it is that person's natural hand.'

'If you have the letter in your possession, I insist on seeing it,' Adair demanded.

'You will all have that opportunity, I promise,' said Frances. 'May I take it, gentlemen, that you are now able to accept that whoever it is you are in dispute with over the letter from Sanitas, it is not each other?'

There was something of a pause and then, with a small measure of reluctance, they assented.

'The editor of the *Chronicle* has told me that correspondence on the subject is now closed, so even if further letters should arrive at his office, he will not publish them,' said Frances. 'Before we continue, I would like an assurance from all of you that while I am engaged by yourselves to look into this matter, you will refrain from taking any legal action which might complicate my investigation?'

Adair looked disgruntled, but joined the other two men in granting that assurance.

'One of the correspondents was Mr Whibley's doctor, who declined to give his name,' said Frances. 'If any of you know his name, I should like to know it, as I would very much like to interview him.'

'Well, I was not Whibley's doctor, although there were many who suggested I was,' said Adair. 'I do not think I ever met the man, neither do I know who advised him.'

Mr Lathwal and Mr Rustrum similarly did not have the information and said that they had never met Mr Whibley.

Frances gave a clean sheet of paper and a pencil to each of the men. 'Kindly write your names at the top of the sheet,' she said. 'When you have done so I will ask you to look at some correspondence and make a note of your conclusions.'

While her visitors were thus occupied, looking comically like a row of overgrown schoolboys at their lessons, Frances took a letter from the folder and laid it on the table in front of her, the salutation and signature concealed by pieces of card. It was a test, since the document was not a letter that the *Chronicle* had chosen to publish, probably because it was wholly innocuous in content. The writer stated only that the sad demise of Mr Whibley must serve as a warning that any course of weight reduction should be undertaken very gradually. Frances simply wanted to see how the three gentlemen reacted to an item of neutral import so that she might compare this to their later behaviour.

'I am going to ask you to examine a number of letters. In each case, I wish you to come forward one by one and view but do not touch what is on the table. Say nothing, but if you recognise the writing or the notepaper, or anything that tells you who the author might be, please record the name of that person. If you do not know, then write down that fact.'

Each of the men came to look at the first letter, and as they did so, Frances studied their expressions. Only Mr Rustrum seemed to show any sign of recognition. There was no displeasure on his face, just a small tilt of the eyebrow.

The next letter Frances showed them was written by Mr Whibley's medical man. She did not wish to give her visitors any clues by showing them text that had already appeared in the newspapers, but fortunately, the correspondence had been so extensive that the *Chronicle* had been obliged to edit some of the duller passages and Frances was able to select for viewing a few lines that had not been printed.

This time a brief change in Dr Adair's expression told her that he had seen something with which he was familiar.

The next letter was by Bainiardus. Frances felt sure that none of the three men recognised the hand, although once they had returned to their seats, Mr Lathwal returned to the table for a second glance.

There followed another test, a letter written to Frances by her own doctor, Dr Collin, and finally there was the letter from Sanitas.

Frances closed the folder and addressed her visitors. 'Please consider what you have seen and written, and if you wish to see any of these letters again, you need only ask,' she said. 'When you have written all that you can, please hand me your papers.'

The gentlemen had gone very quiet and meek, as if they enjoyed being lined up and treated as scholars and were sorry that it would have to end. One by one they delivered their papers to Frances, who took them without examining them and slipped them into the folder.

'The third letter,' said Mr Lathwal, hesitantly.

'Yes,' said Frances, opening the folder and looking at the item signed 'Bainiardus'. The other two visitors leaned forward and stared at Mr Lathwal expectantly.

'I do not know the hand, but I would observe that the paper is of a kind very similar to, although not the same, as that which you have given us to write upon. It is not letter-writing paper, but small cut sheets which are sold in bulk, the kind lawyers use to make notes.'

Frances took one of the sheets written on by her visitors and compared it with the paper of the Bainiardus letter. 'Yes, it is very like,' she said. 'Thank you, Mr Lathwal.'

With instructions that all three were to inform her at once should they learn anything of relevance, she dismissed the visitors so that she could examine their papers at leisure and promised to send a weekly report on her findings.

Mr Rustrum, with great good humour, complimented Frances on her sagacity, and said before he departed that he hoped he might see her in future at meetings of the Pure Food Society. Frances realised that he had mistakenly assumed from her appearance that she was a devotee of restraint in her dining habits. She was glad that he could not see the cheese tart and apple pudding that were to be her supper. Dr Adair only gave a formal, somewhat curtly spoken valediction, and Mr Lathwal took the opportunity to mention that he must hurry away to organise a vegetarian funeral breakfast for a gentleman who was to be buried on Monday. Seeing Dr Adair's look of disdain he only smiled and added with quiet pride that the gentleman concerned, Mr Outram, a confirmed vegetarian for the last forty years, had passed away peacefully at the age of ninety-two.

When Frances read the notes she saw that the first letter had not been recognised by either Dr Adair or Mr Lathwal, but Mr Rustrum believed it had been written by a friend of his, a fellow member of the Pure Food Society, who had stated only what was eminent good sense.

Neither Mr Lathwal nor Mr Rustrum could identify Mr Whibley's doctor, but Dr Adair had written 'I know the hand and will advise the writer of your enquiries.'

Unfortunately, none of the three had recognised the hand-writing of Sanitas.

Frances was writing an account of the interview for her records when she received a letter, hand-delivered by a neat, quiet maid who stood in a corner and waited politely to bear back her reply.

The missive was in a dainty little envelope, the kind often used for invitations to a tea party. The ink was a delicate shade of violet, the script much decorated with artistic embellishments, as if the writer had more time on her hands than she knew what to do with and so employed her idle moments in taking five times as long as was really necessary to write a letter. The paper hinted at scent, not the romantic libations of a lover but the faint waft exuded by someone who wore sweet perfumes as a matter of habit. The author was Alice Finn, wife of Mr Finn the younger, and she asked if she might call on Frances the following day regarding a matter that required the utmost discretion.

CHAPTER EIGHT

Before Mr Curtis arrived, Frances refreshed herself with a cup of tea, and spent a few minutes with the fount of so much that was useful, the Bayswater street directory. The young dentist had more than realised all his uncle's hopes, doing very well for himself in a remarkably short time, for his home and practice were in fashionably expensive Elgin Crescent. Earlier editions of the directory showed that the address had previously been the practice of a Mr Cowan, a long established and well-respected resident of Bayswater who, she recalled, had passed away about two years previously. In view of the straitened finances of the Curtis family during her client's education, she wondered how he had been able to acquire such a lucrative practice so early in his career. She then recalled that Mrs Curtis had been a widow with two daughters by her previous marriage, and therein must lie the answer. His looks, good manners and excellent prospects had secured a wealthy wife whose fortune had made the purchase.

While she mused on the way of the world, a message was delivered from her solicitor, Mr Rawsthorne, saying that he doubted very much that he could assist her concerning Mr Sweetman's history, nevertheless he would examine his papers and would be delighted to see her on Monday morning.

❧

At their first brief meeting at Paddington Green police station, Edward Curtis, an excitable young man not given to concealing his emotions, had been visibly distressed at the plight of his uncle. On a second meeting, he was calmer, but still strained and anxious. He sat shifting in his chair as if it lacked comfort and he needed to constantly change his position to achieve anything like repose. Frances offered him water from the carafe on the table and he gulped down a glassful rather too quickly and coughed, pressing a handkerchief to his mouth.

When he was sufficiently recovered, Frances reported her failure to learn anything from his aunt's neighbours in Redan Place, observing that he was at present the only person she knew who might be able to offer a clue as to Mrs Sweetman's movements after she left the family home. He looked less than confident about his ability to help, and she suggested that he should begin by telling her his history.

'I will do my best,' he responded, somewhat surprised at the request. 'Where should I start?'

'Tell me about your parents,' she advised.

He assented, and the nervous attitude of his body eased a little. Whether or not she would learn anything of value from Mr Curtis talking about his parents, Frances did not know, but by persuading him to start gently she hoped he would feel able to let his thoughts flow more freely into subjects of greater importance.

'My father was a senior medical orderly,' he said. 'He died when I was twelve, and we were left in greatly reduced circumstances, but my mother was determined to ensure that I completed my education, and worked long hours and went without comforts and even necessities to achieve this. She was the kindest, sweetest tempered lady I have ever known, and the most devoted mother imaginable, and I have always striven to be a credit to her. When she became very ill, I thought I would never be able to qualify, but my uncle was kind enough to assist by paying our doctors' bills, and supplying my wants. My gratitude to him knows no bounds.' He paused. 'This is hard for me to say, but I always felt that Aunt Susan was unhappy that uncle had placed himself in debt to help my mother and me, but she never said so openly, at least she never did so in my hearing. I promised uncle that I would repay his generosity as soon as I was able, and I would have done so, but then of course he was arrested for that horrible robbery. I was only fifteen and still at school – there was nothing I could do. I know that uncle's employers gave my aunt some assistance, and he wrote to her asking if she could help us, but we received nothing. Somehow, we managed, but it was very hard for us. Later I made a little income assisting a dentist, but that was all. Then when my mother died a small insurance policy enabled me to finally complete my studies.'

'And you have established a thriving practice in a very short time,' said Frances.

'I worked every hour there was, and qualified first in my year,' Curtis said modestly. 'As a result I was recommended to Mr Cowan, who was kind enough to employ me as his junior in the practice. He was a fine gentleman, with an impeccable reputation and great skill and knowledge, but of advanced years, and his grip was not so strong as it used to be. There are some procedures where a younger more vigorous man is needed.'

Frances touched her tongue to her wisdom teeth, which had, fortunately for her, grown in without trouble. Mr Curtis was not a man of great bulk but she could easily imagine his strong hands on a pair of dental forceps.

'The late Mrs Cowan had been an invalid for many years and they had no children, so when Mr Cowan died, he left the practice to me. Yes, I am a man of some substance, now, but I have never forgotten what it is to be poor.' He smiled, but it was a curiously thin smile, tired and drawn out, with hollow eyes.

'What can you tell me about your uncle's arrest for the robbery?' asked Frances.

'Only that it was a terrible shock when I heard of it, and I did not and have never believed him to be guilty. A less violent man could not be imagined.'

'But he was in want of money,' observed Frances, 'and that told against him. The stolen funds were never found, and the police believe he used it to repay his creditor. Did you ever discover more about that?'

'No, never. I was granted leave of absence from school to be with my mother, whose illness was made still worse by events. She never believed in uncle's guilt. I found myself suddenly obliged, as a mere schoolboy, to try and assume the role of the man of the family, a role for which I was ill-equipped. I went with uncle's solicitor to see him while he was awaiting trial, and he told me that aunt had refused to see him, and he missed her and his children very much. I knew that he had been constrained to borrow in order to help us, but, strangely enough, there were never any documents to show that the loan even existed. I can't believe that he obtained the money dishonestly, so I assume that he fell victim to a private lender who demanded an exorbitant rate of interest.'

'Did you see your aunt and cousins during that time?'

'I went to visit Aunt Susan once, but she was not very cordial. I think she held me partly to blame for what had happened – uncle putting my ambitions ahead of his own children's education. She said that she had never seen a penny of what she believed he had stolen.'

'Were your cousins there?'

'No, they had gone to seek employment.'

'What was the nature of the employment?'

Curtis considered this for a moment. 'I don't think aunt told me. I was left with the impression that it must have been domestic service, but now that I think about it, she didn't say. I only gathered from her manner that it was not something she would have wished for her children, but that pressing need had driven them. She did her best to make me feel very guilty about that, and I believe she succeeded,' he added despondently.

'Why do you think she was so certain that your uncle was guilty? Did she say anything which suggested that she had any information on the matter?'

'No,' he sighed, in a tone of great melancholy. 'That was the hardest thing. It was all statements without explanation. She was adamant about it, but when I asked her for reasons, she just said that I was too young to understand. She only said that he had betrayed her in a way that she could never forgive, and she did not want to see him again. I went back to school and the next thing I heard was that uncle had been convicted and my aunt had gone away. We heard nothing more from her. I was terribly shocked, not only by her death, but finding out that she had been living in such poverty. I was unable to do anything for her while I was a student, but once I was earning a salary, I could have helped her. Perhaps she thought, as she had been less than kind to me, that I would turn her away, but I would never have done such a thing.'

'Even though she did not help you when you were in need?' asked Frances.

'I would have done it for the sake of my uncle if nothing else.'

'And all these years you knew nothing of how she lived? I ask because it is possible that whoever murdered her might be someone she met during that time. If I can find out where she was and who her associates were then I might be able to discover the guilty person.'

An expression very like pain passed across her visitor's face and he glanced at the carafe. Frances gestured for him to help himself to more water, which he did. 'There were rumours, of course …' he said, awkwardly.

'What rumours were they?'

'Oh,' he gave a mirthless little laugh of embarrassment, 'some of them very indelicate.'

'We must forget delicacy if I am to help you,' said Frances. 'There are places where delicacy is a hindrance to progress such as a doctor's surgery, or a court of law. This is such a place.'

'But there are some things it is hardly proper to speak of before an unmarried lady, or any respectable lady for that matter,' he protested.

'Then kindly forget my sex,' she instructed, with a little dash of impatience.

'Oh, I fear that would be most difficult,' he assured her.

'Try harder, Mr Curtis, or we will get nowhere,' said Frances, inserting a thin sliver of steel into her voice.

There was a short silence. 'I heard several rumours,' he said at last, 'but of such a nature that they could not all be true at once. Perhaps none of them were true and in any case it was beyond our resources to pursue them. The mystery only seemed to encourage ill-natured persons to invent vile stories for their own amusement. What pleasure it gives these people to say such cruel things is beyond my understanding. We were told that she was living as the mistress of a robber, that she had been seen in prison, or in the workhouse, or – walking along a street in Whitechapel. One person actually came up to us and whispered that he had learned that she was living in a house of a certain nature, a house to which no gentleman who valued his reputation should go. Another told us that she had been found dead in the gutter.'

'You are certain, are you not, that your uncle is innocent of any crime?'

'I am, although my wife, who does not know his nature as I do, is less sanguine.' He gave a little grimace.

Frances recalled how, when a well-respected Bayswater gentleman had died of poisoning just over a year ago, the blame had seemed to fall on a prescription her father had composed, and valued customers whom he had served impeccably for many years had immediately deserted the business for a rival chemist. She wondered if Mr Curtis, in addition to his undeniably genuine concern for his uncle, was suffering professionally as a result of the connection with a sordid crime, and was having his ear burned by the observations of his disapproving wife.

'I am very anxious to trace your cousins, who may know something that could assist my enquiries,' said Frances. 'Even if they cannot help me, it would be a great comfort to your uncle to see them again. I recently spoke to a man who recalled seeing them on stage at the Bijou Theatre. That would have been many years ago. I was told that Mary sang a song about wanting to be a milkmaid, and Benjamin, who could not sing, whistled. Do you recall ever going to the Bijou Theatre or hearing it mentioned? Did your cousins ever show any inclination to sing or whistle?'

'What a curious question! When I was very young we did sometimes go as a family to the charity performances, but the theatre was never something any of us ever considered as a way of life. I have heard Mary sing, and she had a sweet voice, but Benjamin, as you say, had no talent for music.'

'When was the last time you saw them?'

'Before uncle was arrested. It was during a school holiday and we all dined together, and …' his voice drifted away.

'Yes?'

'It is strange how memories lie buried, and only come back when a comment brings them to the front of the mind. I recall now that Mary sang for us that day, after we had dined. She talked about the pretty dresses of the ladies at the Bijou. I can see her now, she wore a scarf as if it was an evening wrapper and put a paper flower in her hair. I remember thinking that she was more beautiful and charming than any of the ladies at the Bijou.' He sighed. 'I hope, I do so hope that she has led an honest life and not fallen into bad ways.'

'Do you remember what songs she sang?' asked Frances.

'No, it was so long ago. But she had a talent for music and rhymes, so I think she may have made them up herself.'

'Anything you can tell me about your cousins would be very useful,' said Frances.

He nodded. 'I do have a portrait,' he said. 'I was going through my aunt's papers and discovered this.'

He reached into his pocket and took out a card-mounted photograph. 'I remember this being taken,' he said. 'I am not sure if there was any particular occasion, but my uncle mentioned his new position so it must have been when he was appointed manager at the insurance company. This lady in mourning is my late mother, before her last illness bore her down. You will recognise my uncle, of course, and the lady beside him is my late aunt. This serious looking boy is myself in my Sunday best suit, and beside me are Benjamin and Mary. They would have been about eleven and nine, I suppose.'

Frances gazed at the picture, of a kind that had been common when sitters had been obliged to remain perfectly still for several minutes at a time. Understandably, all the persons depicted looked unnaturally rigid, but she could see that Susan Sweetman had been a woman of considerable personal attractiveness, with the kind of buxom rounded figure that men seemed to admire so much. Mary, with a small face and delicate chin, more closely resembled her mother than her father and might grow to look like her. Benjamin, although two years older than Mary, was the same height, with darker hair, and his father's features.

'Were brother and sister close?' asked Frances. 'If I was to find one, would I thereby find the other?'

Curtis considered the question carefully. 'Benjamin and Mary were different in character,' he said at last. 'Mary seemed to have more energy, and did better at school than her brother; in fact, she did better than him at almost anything she tried. But she was very kind to him, and there were no jealousies that I could perceive. They were extremely fond of one another, I am sure of it. I think that if you found one, then even if they were not actually residing together, he or she would be sure to know where to find the other.'

*

The next day was Sunday. Frances and Sarah attended St Stephen's church, where she had learned long ago to ignore the whispers of gossips and commune only with her own private thoughts. The Sabbath was meant to be a day of rest, so why was it that her busy mind could find no peace? Every hymn she sang, every nuance of the sermon, which appealed for charitable assistance for victims of the recent cold weather, seemed to harbour a meaning that kept her turning again and again to the mysteries she had been asked to solve. Although the weather was becoming milder, there was still considerable distress in London caused by the freezing conditions earlier in the month, not the least, thought Frances, the misery caused to Mr Sweetman by obscuring the time and even the day of his wife's death.

She wondered where the Sweetman children might be, and prayed that she might find them; alive and healthy and happy and forgiving. Tomorrow morning, Mrs Sweetman would be buried at All Souls' Kensal Green, and Sarah was to attend and take careful notice of who appeared. Tom and Ratty would wait nearby for her signal, and any person of the right age and appearance to be either Benjamin or Mary would be stealthily followed home.

*

Frances had advised Mrs Finn that she would be available to interview her at three o'clock on Monday afternoon, and that morning received, again from the hand of the discreet maidservant, a little note confirming that her new client would call at the appointed time.

It was all very elegant and tasteful, like an arrangement for two chattering ladies to meet for tea and sugar-topped biscuits, to exchange views on the latest fashions and disseminate scandal. Mrs Finn had thus far given no hint as to why she wished to consult a detective, but Frances' experience told her that when a married lady sent letters via a trusted maid, and asked for a private interview without mentioning the subject to be discussed, there was usually only one reason.

CHAPTER NINE

With Sarah on her way to Kensal Green, Frances' first call of the day was to the offices of the *Bayswater Chronicle*. Seeing the busy clerks bent over their desks, working, it seemed, in a disorganised litter, she was reminded of Mr Lathwal's comment about the paper used to write the Bainiardus letter. She went to examine the blocks of cheap paper on the clerks' desks, and a young man offered her some with a smile. Being plain bulk paper it naturally had some similarity to that used for the Bainiardus letter, but it was not the same; being smaller and more neatly cut.

The storeroom where bound copies were kept of earlier editions was a quiet place of deep shadow, the huge leather-bound volumes on their shelves insulating the student of the past from the bustle and chatter of the main office. Frances was left to her own devices, a chair and a table being left free for her use, and there was a tall, sloping wooden stand on which she could place the heavy book she needed to examine. Even stored in semi-darkness and kept closed, the pages of newspapers more than fourteen years old were already starting to dry with age, and smelled not like fresh newsprint but old paper. Frances took great care when turning the pages, wondering how much longer they could exist before they crumbled away and all their information was lost forever. Thousands of copies were made every day and on the morrow used to light fires, but these relics were valuable histories, and held, she felt sure, precious clues to events that many a criminal might have hoped had been forgotten. Perhaps buried amongst the pages was evidence – a line here, a paragraph there – that would, if she could find it, tell her what Mrs Sweetman had been doing in the years between her husband's arrest and her death. If only, thought Frances, she could hire an army of readers willing to scour tirelessly, minutely and accurately fourteen years of weekly newspapers, she might have the answer. But even if she could, where would such an army sit? There was only one chair in the room.

The trial of Hubert Sweetman on charges of burglary and attempted murder had taken place in October 1866 at the Old Bailey. Due to the extensive local interest in the case, it had been reported in great detail, even *The Times* could not have carried a better account, since the bare facts revealed by the hearing, which were available to every newsman, had been supplemented in the *Chronicle* by interviews with Bayswater residents. The general flavour of opinion was sympathy for the victim, Mr Arthur Gibson, a blameless and hardworking clerk, and the director, old Mr Finn, a gentleman in the very best sense of the word who commanded universal respect in the neighbourhood, and shock at the terrible disloyalty of Mr Sweetman. The public, Frances observed, could be fickle and often made a hero into a villain in a great wash of emotion that sometimes defied the facts. Once made into a villain, it was, however, far harder to reverse the process.

The chief witness for the defence was Mr Finn senior, who testified as to the good character of the accused; however, he was obliged to admit under questioning that he, Sweetman and Whibley were the only holders of a key to the safe, and that he and Whibley had been dining at his club a mile from the office that night. His own keys, he told the court, pressing his hand flat to his breast in a gesture that inspired trust, never left his person and it was impossible for anyone to have stolen or copied them. He was aware that Mr Sweetman had been very anxious about the expense of the care of his sister, who was gravely ill, and the education of his nephew, a promising boy who was hoping to qualify in dentistry. Mr Sweetman, he revealed, had recently asked for an increase in salary, a request he had agreed to consider, though without the promise of any immediate result. On the morning after he had dined with Mr Whibley, he had arrived at the office to a scene so distressing he could hardly bear to think about it much less describe it. Later, at the request of the police, he had examined the empty safe and provided a list of its former contents.

Mr Whibley had then given evidence to confirm that he had dined with Mr Finn on the night of the robbery. He too testified warmly to the excellent character of the accused man. Like Mr Finn, he kept his office and safe keys always upon his person and they had never been missing for an instant. The gentlemen had arrived at the club together at half past seven, started to dine in the well-attended restaurant at eight and departed at half past ten. Since neither Mr Finn nor Mr Whibley was under suspicion, no witnesses were brought to support their alibis but Frances assumed that the police had already satisfied themselves that there was no reason to doubt them. Whibley said that he had been first to arrive at the business premises the following morning. The front door had been unlocked, from which he had simply assumed that someone else, in all probability Mr Finn, had preceded him. As he closed the door, however, he noticed some deep gouges in the wood and scratches on the metal lock plate, which had at once aroused his suspicion. On entering the premises, he had been shocked to find Mr Gibson lying on the floor unconscious and bleeding from a wound to his head. He had dashed out into the street and found a messenger boy to send for the police and a doctor, after which he had done his best to tend the injured man until help arrived.

Mr Elliott also appeared for the defence, stating that he had the highest opinion of Hubert Sweetman's character and believed him to be incapable of the crime with which he had been charged. The prosecution made a great deal of Elliott's junior position in the company, and the fact that he had not known Sweetman for very long.

Mrs Curtis, Hubert Sweetman's sister, had had to be carried in and specially accommodated in an invalid chair in the body of the court. During her testimony, she had wept a great deal, and since her voice was so quiet as to be on occasion inaudible, little could be determined of what she said. The general impression was that she felt sure her brother must have been in her company for the whole of the evening on which the robbery took place, but even the sympathetic questioning of the prosecution made it apparent that the frail woman could not be sure of the date. Mrs Sweetman, the *Chronicle's* reporter took particular care to mention, was not in court, and it was nowhere suggested that she was unable to attend due to illness.

The first policeman on the scene of the robbery was, Frances noted with some interest, a Constable Sharrock of Paddington Green, who testified that by the time he arrived, a doctor was already tending Mr Gibson and most of the office staff were there. Mr Gibson was still unconscious, and a great quantity of blood had dripped from the wound to his head, much of which had been smeared and trampled through the office by multiple feet. If the robber had left any footprints in Mr Gibson's blood, observed the constable rather pointedly, they had been obliterated and there was, therefore, nothing which the police might use as evidence. Even when some slight measure of consciousness returned to the stricken man before he was carried away, no one that morning heard Gibson utter any intelligible words. Constable Sharrock had also been present when a search was made of Mr Sweetman's home, and he had found Mr Gibson's pocket book hidden at the back of a drawer.

Dr Collin testified that he had been brought to the scene of the crime to see Mr Gibson. He had later visited his patient at home, and while the unfortunate man later regained full consciousness, he had retained no memory of the robbery. The doctor had no doubts that the wounds to Mr Gibson's head, which were caused by impact with an item of furniture, were the result not of a fall, but a violent and potentially fatal assault.

Mr Gibson, who walked with the aid of a stick, the scars of his injuries clearly visible, was brought into court leaning on the arm of his brother Matthew, amidst audible expressions of sympathy. He remembered that he had intended to remain in the office until at least nine that night, and earlier that day he had told his fellow clerk, Mr Browne, of his decision. Unfortunately, he was still unable to recall the robbery and could provide the court with no clue as to the identity of his attacker. In the last weeks, however, his memory had cleared a little and he had recalled something new. He now felt sure that he had looked at his watch during the course of the evening and seen that it was half past eight. The watch kept excellent time. Importantly, he also recalled thinking at the time that the work he needed to do was well advanced, and was confident that he would be able to leave and lock up the office promptly at nine o'clock. After that his memory was a blank until he found himself at home in bed. The implication of his testimony was clear, the robbery had taken place between half past eight and nine.

Mr Browne's testimony was of especial interest. Browne, who said he was feeling unwell and asked to be seated in the witness box, had left the office at seven on the night of the robbery. Sweetman, saying that he was going to see his sister, had left at half past six. Just before Browne went home, at which time only he and Gibson remained on the premises, Gibson had told him that he intended to work until late that night, as there were a number of urgent letters and telegrams to be sent. He would consequently be in at a later hour than usual the next morning, and asked Browne to inform Mr Finn of this change in his plans. It followed, and the prosecution made much of this, that out of all the staff of J. Finn Insurance only one man, Mr Browne, knew that there would be someone still in the office after half past eight.

Browne had dined with a friend that evening, but his stomach had been troubling him and he had decided to leave early, hoping that a walk in the fresh air would do him good. He had adjusted his watch by a chiming clock when it struck nine, and departed about ten minutes later. On his way home he passed the office, which was barely five minutes' walk from his friend's house, and saw that a light was on. Since he knew of Gibson's plan to work late, he had not thought this to be strange.

As he walked past, however, the outer door of the office had opened, and he saw a man standing in the entrance hall that led to the main office. At first he thought the figure was Gibson, but this was only because that was the man he would have expected to see. He had then realised that it was not Gibson at all, but Sweetman. He had not been inclined to stop and talk as he was still feeling unwell and wanted to hurry home, so he simply nodded an acknowledgement. The man had neither nodded nor spoken, but withdrew back into the building.

Browne's identification of Sweetman was the crucial piece of evidence on which the trial turned. The defence tried to suggest that he was mistaken, that the lighting was poor, as it was after sunset, that the figure in the doorway was standing with the light behind him and would, therefore, have been no more than a silhouette, but Browne said that the gas lamp in the street provided more than adequate light to recognise a man whom he had known personally for some years. He was questioned about his eyesight and asked to read a poster from across the court, which he successfully did. He was questioned about his original belief that the man had been Gibson, since Gibson and Sweetman did not resemble each other, the one being twenty-five years senior to the other. He said that it was a thought that had crossed his mind for an instant only, as the two men were of similar height and build, and he had expected to see Gibson there, but the very next moment he had realised his mistake.

Mr Browne, his evidence unshaken, stepped from the witness box, his former colleague's fate sealed. It was hardly necessary, but the friend with whom Browne had dined that evening came forward to confirm that his guest had adjusted his watch as the clock, which kept perfect time, chimed nine and left about ten minutes later. There was no argument about the time required to walk from his home to the office of J. Finn Insurance, it was almost exactly five minutes. He was a customer, and he had done it himself.

The judge in his summing up had made sure to instruct the jury that they were not entitled to draw any conclusions about Mrs Sweetman's absence from the courtroom, nevertheless, thought Frances, they cannot have failed to ponder on the reasons she had not been there to demonstrate her belief in her husband's innocence.

Frances did not wish Mr Gibson any ill, but she knew that had the man died there would have been an inquest, and the evidence given there, probably before any criminal charges had been laid, would have been the best and the freshest there could be. What a man might or might not have seen or done, ruminated upon and agonised over for two months might emerge quite differently at a trial.

Frances turned back through the pages to find the initial reports of the robbery, which had mainly focused on the condition of the injured man and old Mr Finn's distress. Two weeks later the *Chronicle* described the appearance of Hubert Sweetman at the first police court hearing, which added nothing to the story. The adjourned hearing a week later was the first proceeding to take detailed evidence. Mr Gibson had been too ill to attend, and it was stated that his memory of events was still very cloudy, although he was starting to recall a few details.

On this occasion, Mr Minster, who, Frances noticed, had not been called to give evidence at the subsequent trial, had testified that he had been walking down Westbourne Grove at half past nine and seen a light on in the office. Browne also gave his account of the evening, and the timings, confirmed by his friend, were identical to those later described at the trial, but his identification of the man he had seen at the door was far shakier. The difference, Frances realised, was that Gibson's memory of looking at his watch had yet to emerge. It was not until a month later that it became known that the robbery had taken place before nine o'clock and that the man Browne had seen at the door after that hour could not, as he had at first thought, been Gibson, who was then lying unconscious in the office.

When Browne had given evidence before the magistrates, however, he had still thought it possible that he might have seen Gibson, which meant that the robbery would have taken place after a quarter past nine. Gibson and Sweetman, he pointed out, although different in age, were of very similar build, both had trim beards, and Gibson, while older, had been vain enough to dye his whiskers. He had certainly felt that the man at the door had been someone he knew and not a stranger, or he would not have walked on believing nothing to be the matter. The defence tried to show that Browne had, as he supposed, seen Gibson, either that or he had seen a stranger and only imagined he had seen someone he knew. The hearing had then been adjourned for another week as Mr Gibson's doctor thought his patient might soon be recovered enough to testify. A week later, Mr Gibson was carried into the court, and here for the first time said that he could recall looking at his watch, thus placing the time of robbery in the half hour leading up to nine o'clock. It was put to Mr Browne that he could not therefore have seen Gibson after nine, and he accepted that this was not possible. He was adamant, however, that the man in the doorway was not a stranger otherwise he would certainly have alerted the police. He now thought it very likely that the man he had seen was Hubert Sweetman. No one else in the office matched the description of the figure he had seen, since Mr Finn and Mr Elliott were taller, Mr Minster broader and with large side-whiskers, Timmy much shorter, and Mr Whibley both shorter and more rotund.

What was anyone to make of Mr Minster's evidence, thought Frances? He had not been called at the trial and she could see why, since according to his earlier testimony he had been in the Grove fifteen minutes after Browne. The prosecution must have decided not to muddy the waters with conflicting evidence. All that Minster had seen was a light, which proved nothing, and Browne's evidence was far stronger. Also, Minster's timing suggested that the robber, having already been spotted in the doorway by Browne, had then remained on the premises for another fifteen minutes, which made no sense at all. Surely after being seen he would have escaped almost immediately? Or had he already fled the scene leaving the light on – careless, but not impossible. Frances re-read Whibley's testimony but found no mention of him finding a light on when he arrived. It seemed probable that Minster, who had not, as Browne had done, checked his watch against a reliable timepiece, had simply made a mistake about the time.

Following the magistrates' hearing, old Mr Finn had spoken to a reporter from the *Chronicle*, saying that he fully believed in the innocence of Mr Sweetman and deplored the action of counsel in bullying Mr Browne, who was not a well man, into saying something he had in all probability not intended. To Frances the conclusion was obvious. Mr Browne had not initially been at all certain that the man in the doorway was Sweetman, in fact, he had been inclined to think the man was Gibson until it had been demonstrated that this was not possible. Over the next few weeks he had persuaded himself, or perhaps been persuaded, that he had seen Sweetman and by the time the case came to trial he was certain and Mr Sweetman was duly condemned.

CHAPTER TEN

rances was digesting the information when Mr Gillan came in and leaned a little too intrusively over the pages she was studying. 'What are you busy with today, Miss Doughty?' he asked, although his casual manner was only a thin veneer over his professional interest.

'I am reading about Mr Hubert Sweetman's trial for robbery in 1866,' she said. 'I don't suppose you know what became of Mr Gibson, the clerk who was attacked?'

'No, only that he left Bayswater. I think he took a little cottage somewhere on the coast and lived quietly there. He'd be eighty now if he was alive. The papers have commented on the old case, of course, but do you think you can squeeze some fresh interest out of it? Is there a story in it for me?'

'Not at present, no.'

'That was a good tip you gave me about his wife's murder,' said Gillan with great satisfaction. 'We were first with it out of all the papers. It seems like Sweetman is a dangerous sort of gent, though I must admit he doesn't look it.'

'My hope, when I gave you that story,' said Frances, 'was that your article would bring in new information about the case, but so far it has not, unless there is something you have to tell me?'

'Well, I have heard rumours that you are trying to clear Sweetman of murdering his wife,' he said with a grin. 'It seems his solicitor, Mr Marsden, has made very merry on that story. That can't be true, can it?'

'Mr Marsden is not a merry fellow, but he was present when I agreed to take the case. I must ask for your discretion on that point, and your help, on the understanding that you will be the only correspondent who will receive my secrets.'

Gillan nodded. 'That seems fair, but I expect that by now most of Bayswater will know you are working on Mr Sweetman's behalf.'

'I have been making enquiries to discover where Mrs Susan Sweetman lived and who her associates were between leaving the family home in Garway Road after her husband's conviction and taking up residence in Redan Place. If Mr Sweetman is not guilty of her murder, the secret may lie in what she did during those years. When one considers the weather conditions at the time of her murder, it is obvious that her killer was not an idle caller but someone who came there for a very particular purpose.'

'Yes, I see what you mean. But tell me, do you really think Mr Sweetman didn't do it, or is that just his nephew's money talking? Have you seen Curtis' wife, by the way? I saw her coming out of the house once.' He puffed out his cheeks. 'Makes me glad I'm single! I'd not want to come home to that face!'

Frances ignored the last observation. 'I believed Mr Sweetman to be innocent before I was engaged on the case,' she said, a little stung by the suggestion that her opinions could be bought, 'and it is not and never will be my business to prove a man innocent when I think him guilty, not for any sum.'

'It's a good thing ladies don't study to be lawyers then,' said Gillan, with a laugh. 'You'd never make a penny with that way of thinking.'

Frances did not see the humour in his comment. 'I take it you have no information about Mrs Sweetman.'

'No, none, but I'll keep my eyes and ears open.' He put his hands in his pockets and showed no sign of leaving her to her work. 'I was told you had borrowed the folder of letters that came in after Mr Whibley died,' he said casually. 'All that arguing about diets. Funny business.'

'I did, do you need them returned?'

'No, I was just curious as to your interest. You know that your adventures are followed with great attention by my readers.'

Frances had long given up trying to persuade him to write more truthfully about her investigations, especially as her embellished reputation brought her new clients and opened a number of doors that might otherwise have been closed.

'I have been approached by some gentlemen who are very displeased with some of the allegations made in the letters, and in particular they would like to know the identity of the person who signed him or herself Sanitas.'

'Not thinking of going to the law, are they?' he said with a frown. 'We've had enough of that round here what with that libel case last year. I know we won, but it still cost us a pretty penny.'

'I am hoping that if I am able to settle things amicably they will decide against it,' said Frances. 'There are altogether too many cases of that nature troubling the courts. Do you know who Sanitas is? Have you received any other letters in the same hand?'

'No, that is as much a mystery to me as it is you. But if we do receive any more letters from him, whatever the subject, I will let you know. I'm sure you'll find him out.'

Frances turned a page, and found some advertisements for performances at the Bijou Theatre. They were, she noticed, all for amateur troupes, performing plays and operettas in order to raise funds for worthy causes. A memory suddenly bloomed in her mind, clear and colourful and fresh as if it had been yesterday. She had been ten years old, and her dear brother Frederick, whose loss just over a year ago was a pain in her heart that would never ease, had been fifteen. Their uncle Cornelius, whose many acts of kindness had been the only real paternal warmth she had known as a child, had taken them to the theatre. It had been hard to persuade her father to permit this seemingly innocent amusement, but he had eventually capitulated on the understanding that the works exhibited would be of a morally improving nature, the money contributed being devoted to the restoration of a church roof. The journey there had been brief, and she was sure that they had not left Bayswater, so their destination could only have been the Bijou Theatre. On a stage with brightly painted scenery representing a garden bower, ladies in pretty dresses had sung sweetly about the joys of springtime, and gentlemen with flowers in their buttonholes had carolled on similar themes, while a small orchestra played with energy and determination. No one had whistled, and neither, as far as Frances could recall, had a young girl bemoaned her inability to milk a cow.

'I am also trying to trace two people who were said to have appeared at the Bijou in 1866,' said Frances.

'Oh, what company were they with?'

'I don't know. I was told there was a girl who performed songs and a boy who gave a demonstration of whistling. This would seem more suitable for the music hall than the kind of entertainment described here. I had been given to understand that the people I am looking for were hoping for a career on the professional stage, but as far as I can see the Bijou was hired only by amateur companies for charity performances.'

'Oh there used to be these variety nights,' said Gillan. 'Some years back, now. Anyone who could put on a turn was welcome to come and try, and you could get in for a shilling or even less. There was a rumour, and who knows if it was true or not, that people from the big London halls used to come and watch, and if they liked you, they'd offer you a season. I never heard of anyone from round here going on the stage so it might just have been a way of putting on a cheap show. The producer took his cut and the rest was said to go to charity, though it was never said which. I seem to remember one of the managers ran off with the funds and that put a stop to it.'

'When was that?'

'I'm not sure, but it'll be in the papers.'

Frances looked through the pages until she came across an advertisement for 'Varieties' in October of 1866. It was the only such evening in the latter part of that year. None of the turns was named, however the evening's entertainment was made up with a *comedietta*, a play in one act called 'The Happy Sisters', performed by members of the Bayswater Ladies' Society, which was devoted to collecting funds for distressed females. Nothing in the newspaper suggested who the leading lights of this society might be, and the later review of the actual performance was very brief and gave no names.

'The Bijou has been through several hands since then,' added Gillan. 'I doubt the current owners will be able to advise you. In fact, I don't think there have been any performances there for some time. Weren't they trying to turn it into a skating rink? So who are you searching for?'

'This is confidential,' said Frances, 'but I am trying to find Benjamin and Mary Sweetman, Mr Hubert Sweetman's son and daughter. I was told that when they were very young they went on stage at the Bijou.'

'When Sweetman came out of prison last month he advertised in the paper for his family to write to him,' responded Gillan. 'So he's got you on the case, has he?'

'Either Benjamin and Mary have not heard of recent events or, as seems very possible, they prefer not to come forward,' replied Frances. 'When the advertisement was unsuccessful Mr Sweetman came to me. In fact he was arrested at my home.'

'Was he now?' Gillan replied, his eyes lighting up. 'Now that must have been a drama!'

'He is very anxious to find his children. But please be discreet. I fear that advertising for them openly may only make them withdraw further into obscurity and then he will never find them, and you will lose your story.'

Gillan nodded, but drew out his notebook and jotted down some lines in his usual shorthand. Frances had never taken any particular notice before, but observed that his name was written in normal script on the cover of the notebook, and was thus able to satisfy herself that he was neither Bainiardus nor Sanitas.

She turned another page and saw a column headed 'Horrible Murder in Notting Hill' in November 1866. It was reporting that Jack Sidebottom, the moneylender to whom Mr Sweetman had been indebted, a man whose financial dealings had grown like a strangling weed through all of Paddington, had been found dead with his throat cut in a narrow alley leading to Ledbury Mews. Ledbury Road, which ran from north to south across Westbourne Grove, was a busy commercial and residential street, the area close to the Mews a noisy cluster of carpenters, goldbeaters, butchers and dairymen. The Mews itself was mainly given over to stabling and the homes of cabmen, who, so Frances had gleaned from her regular perusal of the newspapers, were more inclined to settle their financial and domestic differences with fists than knives. Assaults were common, murders were not.

'You're not interested in that, are you?' said Gillan.

'No, not at all,' said Frances, although it was natural for her mind to retain any item which was out of the common way.

She paused at another page. In December, Mr Edward Hatfield, who had been the sole producer of the varieties at the Bijou Theatre, had appeared before the magistrates at Marylebone police court charged with stealing funds from his employer, a manufacturer of gentlemen's shirts. He had made a tearful confession of guilt; pleading straitened financial circumstances and was sent for trial. It was believed that as a consequence, the varieties would be discontinued. If this was true, thought Frances hopefully, it meant that if the Sweetman children had ever been on stage at the Bijou, there was only one variety performance when it could have occurred, the one in October.

'Now, I know that look,' said Gillan. 'You're like a blood-hound who's caught the scent.'

'Oh, it seems I can hide nothing from you,' said Frances, who could and did as a matter of necessity hide a great deal from Mr Gillan. 'No, I have just discovered the little scandal you mentioned – Mr Hatfield the producer of the varieties being tried for embezzlement. I assume he lost his theatrical employment thereafter. Do you know if anyone else replaced him as producer of the variety evenings?'

'I don't believe they did,' said Gillan. 'I was a very young fellow then and they sometimes sent me to report at the Bijou, but I don't remember any varieties being put on after that.'

'Can you tell me anything about the Bayswater Ladies' Society, who produced a *comedietta* on the same day as the last variety performance?'

He shrugged. 'Oh, just one of a number of charitable societies.'

'To keep idle ladies amused,' said Frances, 'and therefore of no note?'

He opened his mouth to reply, then hesitated and gave a quick laugh. 'Oh that may have been the view of the editor, when deciding what to print, but of course *I* would not dare underestimate the efforts of dedicated ladies.'

Frances could not recall seeing anything about a Bayswater Ladies' Society in recent editions of the *Chronicle* and assumed that it had disbanded or changed its name, however she felt sure she knew some 'dedicated ladies' who might be able to advise her. Once home, she wrote a letter to Miss Gilbert and Miss John of the Bayswater Women's Suffrage Society. Ardent admirers of Frances' abilities to a degree that sometimes veered towards suffocating excess, they enjoyed a wide circle of female acquaintances in Bayswater, and conducted meetings at which hundreds of interested parties attended. Frances felt confident that with a single-minded application that would put any mere bloodhound to shame, they would soon discover a friend who could tell her all about the Bayswater Ladies' Society.

❀

Frances' next call was to keep the appointment with her solicitor, Mr Rawsthorne. That gentleman was both astute and good-natured, and had acted for the Doughty family for many years during which he and Frances' father had grown from terms of solicitor and client to mutual respect, trust and friendship. It was, Frances reflected ruefully, her father's failure to take the good advice of his old friend that had led him to make the unwise investments that had all but ruined the family, and had after his death obliged her to sell the business to settle their debts and seek a new profession. She sometimes dwelled on how different her life would have been had she been able to retain the chemists shop, complete her studies and qualify as a pharmacist. More settled, more certain, more profitable, and very much less interesting.

Mr Rawsthorne was, as ever, attended by his clerk, Mr Wheelock, whose resemblance to a pantomime droll only increased with acquaintance. Mr Wheelock liked ink, he liked the look and the smell and the taste of it. He sucked pens as if they gave him nourishment, and was never to be seen without streaks of black and blue, and sometimes red, on his lips, chin and cheeks. A smile from Mr Wheelock, never a friendly one, was a thing of horror. Why Mr Rawsthorne should wish to employ Mr Wheelock had always been a great mystery to Frances. Did he, like Uriah Heep, exert some diabolical hold over his master, or did he have some extraordinary talent in the matter of numbers or understanding the law?

Mr Rawsthorne was a married man with two daughters who had once been pupils of the ill-fated Bayswater Academy for the Education of Young Ladies, an establishment that had not survived Frances' recent investigation into its affairs. The girls had since been removed to a fashionable boarding school out of London, and while they were far from being of marriageable age, Frances could not help wondering if by this expedient they had also been secured a long way from Mr Wheelock's ambitious eye.

'Oh,' said the young clerk with an insolent grin, throwing a folder of papers down on his employer's desk. 'If it isn't the famous Miss Dauntless, the terror of all Bayswater! I read how you chased a gang of robbers down the Grove in a hansom cab, sitting up top and whipping the horses yourself. That must have been a sight to see!'

'It was,' said Frances. 'I have a firm hand with a whip and my valiant assistant cracked a great many skulls that night.' She smiled as if she would have liked to see Mr Wheelock soundly whipped and his skull cracked. The clerk sneered at her, stuck two pens in his mouth, and shuffled off to do whatever it was he did.

'Miss Doughty,' said Rawsthorne, whose friendly manner more than compensated for the rudeness of Mr Wheelock, 'it is always a pleasure to see you. Tales of your successes continue to excite us all. I am sure your poor late father would have been very proud of you.'

'I would like to think so,' said Frances, knowing that her father, looking down on her from his seat in Heaven, would be deeply ashamed of her activities and quite certain that she would never join him in the afterlife, being consigned to quite another place.

'It seems that you cannot fail to uncover crime and misdeeds wherever you go.'

'I have not yet been defeated,' Frances said, 'but that day may come.' Whenever Frances met Mr Rawsthorne she was obliged to reflect that a past enquiry of hers had provoked a bank failure that had all but ruined him, something to which he never alluded. Even though Frances could never have anticipated this consequence of her actions, another man might have harboured a deep resentment, but Mr Rawsthorne had generously not allowed the incident to cloud his admiration and friendship.

'Please let me know how I may help you and I promise I will do whatever I can,' he said.

'I have asked for this interview because I have been trying to locate the two children of Mr Hubert Sweetman who was released from prison very recently and then, unfortunately, arrested for the murder of his wife. He told me that Mr Manley acted for him after his arrest in 1866 and I was hoping that you still retain the papers.'

'There are a few remaining, yes,' said Rawsthorne, 'but the correspondence only mentions the children when Mr Sweetman wrote to his wife asking to be allowed to see them. I am afraid his wife did not comply.'

'Did she give any reason for this?'

Rawsthorne extracted a letter from the folder, and passed it to Frances. 'This was her reply.'

Frances perused the letter, which was cruelly brief:

Dear Mr Manley,
Please inform my husband that what he asks is impossible.
He has forfeited the right to my affection and that of the children. I do not wish to see or speak to him again.
Susan Sweetman

'Is that all she says?'

'Yes, that is all.'

Frances glanced at the letter, which was written a week after Sweetman's arrest. There was, she felt sure now, some other circumstance, something Mr Sweetman had not told her, something else he had done that had led to this terrible letter. Something that might even have led to the murder of his wife.

CHAPTER ELEVEN

rue to the appointed hour, Alice Finn arrived by closed
carriage, her features softly veiled. Frances, looking out
of the window, saw a slight form step lightly to her door,
and thought of how many other blameless ladies had trodden
the same path for the same reason, and the sorrow she had
brought them. Domestic difficulties, or affairs of the heart,
which were the daily bread of Frances' profession, were also the
hardest to resolve. So many of her clients, their settled happy
worlds breaking up around them, still clung to the love that had
been betrayed, and hoped for the impossible.

As Mrs Finn took her seat across the small table in the parlour,
she lifted her veil, to reveal that the portrait placed so reverently
on her husband's desk had failed to do her full justice. A portrait
is a still, quiet thing and the subject no more than a statue, guided
into a position determined by the photographic artist. It shows
only what a cold image can show. It cannot convey grace of
movement, or colour, or the play of emotions across a face. Alice
Finn in the flesh was a pretty, delicate-looking girl in her twenties,
very slender, like the branch of a sapling made of sweet-scented
wood. Her skin was creamy and unblemished, with a natural
blush, her hair, its curls escaping artlessly from a lace-edged
bonnet, was fine and fair and made even prettier, if that were
possible, by being dressed with sprays of blue silk flowers.

Frances had met many women whose whole appearance
was intended to demonstrate the status of a husband or father.
These poor creatures were loaded with heavy garments that did
not display their figures well but seemed to have been designed
as something on which to hang ornaments, or ugly velvet
bows or deep frills, and their wearers were doomed to parade
around like so many Christmas trees, wanting only an array
of flickering candles to make the effect complete. By contrast,

Alice's costume had been chosen to show the woman, in an unassuming and flattering yet modest way.

Frances hoped, even more than she usually did in such cases, that the lady was mistaken in her suspicions, that Mr Finn's look of pleasure as he had gazed at the portrait of his wife and children had showed a genuine affection and was not feigned in order to conceal a disreputable secret. Despite the gentleman's lack of personal attraction they should have been a contented, even a model family. Mrs Finn's letter had not supplied her address, but the street directory had revealed that they lived on Hereford Road, a row of clean, smart family villas. This location afforded the gentleman of the house a convenient journey every weekday to his office, and the lady her choice of Bayswater's fashionable shops or healthful open spaces. Truly, thought Frances, it was a place in which to be happy. From Paddington Station in the east to Ladbroke Grove in the west, from the thundering railway line in the north to the cheerful boundary of Hyde Park and Kensington Gardens in the south, all the world was there, and for the most part it was good.

Alice Finn, although clearly labouring under a great anxiety that chiefly showed in the tense attitude of her shoulders, looked determined to be as natural as possible, and greeted Frances with unforced friendliness. 'Miss Doughty, it is such a pleasure to meet you,' she said. 'I have to admit that when John told me about his interview with you, I was overcome with curiosity and excitement, and questioned him very closely. You are all the talk of Bayswater. I know that gentlemen often do not give ladies the credit they deserve, but even some of them are obliged to admit that you have more than ordinary ability.'

Frances had once been in the habit of denying any fame, or even skill beyond what any sensible person might have, but there were, she realised, situations where modesty was not the best demeanour, and most of those she encountered when engaged in her profession. 'So I am given to understand,' she said, adding in a confidential tone, 'and if I chose to tell all the truth of my adventures, it would be even more startling than the stories you read in the newspapers!'

Alice gave a little gasp, and her eyes sparkled as blue as the flowers in her hair.

'Of course, I do not broadcast the details of my cases, or tell my secrets,' Frances continued. 'I am no gossip, I can assure you of that. My watchwords are care and discretion. You may have complete confidence in me in that respect, especially where the matter is, as I judge it may be in this instance, a question of husband and wife.'

There was a brief silence as a cloud settled across Alice's youthful face.

'Many of my clients are married ladies,' Frances reassured her, 'and I am very familiar with the sorrows and disappointments that stem entirely from their husbands' lack of proper consideration, and failure to adhere to the promises made at the altar. You need not hesitate to tell me all.'

'Oh, I shall be very open with you, Miss Doughty,' said Alice, wholeheartedly. 'It would be of no benefit to engage you and then not give you the means of doing what is needful.' She uttered a deep sigh. 'And you judge correctly, as it is my husband about whom I must speak. It is very unfortunate but I see no other way to alleviate my terrible anxiety.'

'How long have you been married?' Frances asked.

'Almost five years, and we have two beautiful children. John is a good, kind man, a most affectionate husband, and my happiness would be complete if it were not that I am convinced –' she gave a little gasp '– that he is deceiving me.' There was a pause and her eyes were bright with emotion. She took a kerchief from her reticule, a lacy wisp of nothingness, that she held briefly to her face. 'You have never been married, Miss Doughty, but I am sure you understand that the greatest happiness of a wife should be when her husband is at home, with his family, showing in every way that it is there and only there that his true contentment lies. I try to be everything to him that a good wife should be, but it seems –' she dabbed at her eyes again, 'that I have failed.'

'I assume,' said Frances, pouring a glass of water and pushing it across the table, 'that all you have at present are suspicions, and what you wish me to do is provide you with the proof you require.'

'Thank you, you are very kind,' said Alice, sipping the water gratefully and making an effort to compose herself. 'Yes,' she admitted, 'you are correct in your assumption, and I regret — and how disloyal it makes me feel — that I must ask you to arrange for some competent person to follow my husband and discover where he goes on those evenings when he is not at home. He may even, for all I know, sometimes be absent from his office during the daytime.'

'Before we begin,' said Frances, 'may I ask the purpose for which you require this information?' She did not think, from her client's demeanour, that Alice was hoping for a divorce, which was as well, since infidelity unless compounded with some other terrible crime was insufficient grounds for a woman to procure one. Frances appreciated the biological and inheritance reasons why a wife's disloyalty was alone enough for her husband to discard her, but it was, as Miss Gilbert had often said, an unequal law that forced many a woman to stay with a husband she hated. 'Is it simply in order that you might advise your husband that you know his secret and thus persuade him to amend his ways?'

'Yes, that is exactly the purpose.'

Frances opened her notebook and selected a fresh pencil. 'Do you have any suspicions as to where he goes and the person or persons he meets there?'

Alice shook her head, helplessly. 'No, not at all, it may be many places, every kind of establishment or the homes of his friends. He may even indulge himself in his own office.'

'Surely not,' said Frances, with a frown. 'That would be very shocking and unpleasant. I cannot think he would dare.'

'Oh a man who is driven, as I fear he is, may dare anything,' said Alice.

'Does he often work late hours?'

'Yes, and when he returns he is very weary, and his manner is heavy and dull. Also, I sometimes wonder if in our own home ...'

'What, in the family home?' exclaimed Frances. 'That would be too cruel.' Cruel, yes, but she had uncovered cases before of supposedly respectable men who had committed acts that ought by rights to have been confined to the marital bed in the most unsuitable places, and in the wrong company. These men, even when found out, were not drummed out of their clubs or shunned by society, but considered in some circles to be swaggering roguish types and were even sometimes envied by those who were less adventurous. She thought of young Mr Finn and his lumbering walk and painful back, and she could not think of a man less designed to be a rake. A worrying thought suddenly presented itself. Suppose that Mr Finn was an innocent man after all, and his wife was a sensitive lady, who was allowing her fears to become suspicions, such that she saw infidelity everywhere, even where it did not exist.

'John's study is always locked, as I understand is the habit of many gentlemen of business,' said Alice. 'I never trouble myself about business matters so it is of no moment to me, but I am sure that if he has any secrets they are there. The only person who has free entry to the study is his valet, Mr Yeldon, who he trusts in everything. He may collude with my husband, but I have been unable to prove it.'

'Mrs Finn,' said Frances carefully, 'can you be quite certain that you are correct in your suppositions? It seems that you have never actually been a witness to anything that might cause you disquiet. Is it possible that your husband may, after all, be blameless?'

'But it really cannot be denied, Miss Doughty,' said Alice with some surprise, 'after all, you have met him and the situation is quite plain for all to see. Why, all my friends comment on it.'

'They do? What do they say?' asked Frances, mystified.

'They tell me that I must speak to him and make him stop. And I have done so, many times, but he denies everything. That is why I have come to you. I must have proof.'

'Very well,' said Frances, wondering what it was in Mr Finn's demeanour that had escaped her notice. 'I will see what can be done. First of all, I will employ my agents to follow your husband and discover where he goes and whom he meets. They will be able to do so very discreetly and he will never suspect that he is being watched. Since you think that Mr Yeldon is somehow complicit in the matter, and that your husband has polluted your home, he too will be followed. I will receive daily reports on both their activities. In addition, I suggest introducing an agent into your home in the guise of a daily cleaner, a lady who assists me in many cases of a domestic nature and who will make careful observations. Do you have any thoughts about the methods of deception employed by Mr Yeldon? How is he able to satisfy your husband's requirements without anyone else in the house seeing what is transpiring?'

'I really can't say for certain,' said Mrs Finn, thoughtfully, 'but I assume that John supplies him with the necessary funds, and he purchases what is needed and brings it to him in his document case.'

Frances paused. She was either about to be subjected to a horror she had never previously known existed or something quite different. 'Mrs Finn,' she said carefully, 'please could you describe to me exactly and very precisely what it is you believe your husband has been doing in secret.'

'Why, eating of course, what else?' said Alice, innocently.

'I see,' said Frances. She re-read her notes and made a pencil mark through most of them, relieved that Alice appeared to be unaware of her mistake.

'Does Mr Finn usually take his meals at home, or does he dine out with friends and business associates?'

'He breakfasts at home, every day, and luncheon also. Usually he dines at home, but there are occasions when he dines with friends. He has always had a hearty appetite, and I fear, takes too little exercise, but in the last few months I have become very concerned for his health and taken a firmer hand in the matter. I know that there are men and women who carry excess fat on their persons without it affecting their comfort and wellbeing, but my husband is not so fortunate, and I have noticed that he moves with less agility than is usual for such a young man. He is only twenty-eight, Miss Doughty, but men more than twice that age are lighter on their feet and more vigorous. Sometimes his digestion is upset and his back gives him pain. Two months ago I instructed cook that henceforward she should only provide light and wholesome food and not too much. He is not allowed the fat of meat, and very little butter. Bread and potatoes are also restricted, and if he is hungry, he is offered vegetables and fruit. Pastry and sweets are never on our table. He has always been moderate in his consumption of wine and I think it does no harm to allow him one glass a day. But he has still failed to reduce his weight and may even have gained a little. I am led to the conclusion that while complying with my wishes when in my company, he makes other arrangements in secret. He may call at the pastrycook's, or the confectioner's, or send Mr Yeldon there. Miss Doughty, I love my husband dearly, he is the very best husband any woman could wish for and I do not want him to die as Mr Whibley did, still in the prime of his life. I do not wish to be a widow and the sole guide of two fatherless children.'

'Does Mr Finn belong to any clubs?' asked Frances. 'I understand that many of these establishments pride themselves on providing a generous table.'

'Not so far as I am aware. In fact, he has never shown any inclination to join a club. He always says they are full of cigar smoke, the smell of which disgusts him, and men drinking to excess, which he never does. He was invited to join the Literati, the Freemasons Lodge, which is very well thought of, and a number of his friends are members, but he declined.'

'When you task him on the subject of his diet, does he deny that he is eating to excess?'

'Yes, I am afraid he does,' replied Alice, unhappily. 'And that cannot be true. I do not think he means to deceive me, rather I think he may be deceiving himself.'

'Does he provide an explanation for his corpulence?' questioned Frances. 'He commented to me that a little fat does a man no harm, but privately, does he admit to being dangerously overweight?'

'He admits to being a little plump but he sees nothing wrong in it. He thinks he was just born to be that way and nothing can be done to change it. I have begged him many times to take a cure for my sake, and he has done so, but with very great reluctance. He went to Harrogate once, and another time to Brighton. There was no doubt that it benefitted him, but he said afterwards that he did not enjoy himself and felt faint when he did not have proper food. I doubt that he would be willing to try it again. More recently, I suggested he try banting, but when Mr Whibley died John said that he would not do it, as it would be dangerous. He says it is more healthful to be too fat than too lean.'

'Mrs Finn,' said Frances, carefully, 'I am going to ask you a very impertinent question. It is, I fear, something I am often obliged to do, and I do hope that you will not be offended. Please understand that it is necessary.'

'Of course,' said Alice, sitting a little straighter in preparation. 'What is your question?'

'You have told me that you suspect you husband of eating more than the meals he receives at home, which is affecting his weight and his health. You would like him to be observed, and that I can do. Can you assure me that this is indeed your only motive for consulting me? I ask this because in the past whenever a wife has asked me to have her husband followed it was never in order to supervise his diet. Bluntly – do you believe that your husband may have a mistress?'

Mrs Finn gasped. 'Miss Doughty, I am very shocked indeed. I find it hard to believe that respectable Bayswater ladies have any need of the services you describe. Supposing anyone was to suspect that I have come here for that purpose – what might they think? Oh, it is too horrible!' She put her hands to her cheeks, which had gone pink with shame.

'I regret,' said Frances, 'that as a detective I encounter as a part of my daily work situations that respectable persons would consider to be inconceivable, even impossible. But sadly, they are fact. However, you need not worry about any misunderstanding as regards yourself. Ladies of the most impeccable character often consult me about servant problems, and missing pets, although in such instances they will always mention in their letters what it is that concerns them.'

Alice gazed at her with a new expression, the admiration and wonder replaced by discomfort.

'You have nothing to fear,' said Frances. 'I am not tainted by my profession. Virtue is stronger than wickedness, and most of those who commit crimes are either foolish or arrogant, and so I find them out.'

'But as a weak woman …' Alice protested.

'That is my strength,' smiled Frances.

The usual arrangements having been decided upon, it was agreed that Sarah would shortly present herself at the Finns' home and acquaint herself with the domestic arrangements, bringing any messages from Frances directly to Mrs Finn by word of mouth. Fortunately, Alice had sway over all the household arrangements, her husband being very under- standing and compliant on the matter.

❧

When Sarah returned, she reported on the funeral of Mrs Sweetman, which through the agency of her nephew had taken place in the main part of All Souls and not where the paupers were usually interred. The only other mourners were Inspector Sharrock, hoping perhaps that the murderer would come to gloat over his work, and Edward Curtis. 'How dreadful to die so friend- less,' said Frances, 'and so neglected by her own children.'

'They might be dead,' said Sarah, 'or in America, or in prison,' her voice holding no hint as to which of these fates she consid- ered to be the worst.

This sombre mood was enlivened soon afterwards. When Frances told Sarah about the interview with Mrs Finn, and the initial confusion as to its subject, she thought her assistant would never stop laughing.

CHAPTER TWELVE

arah's capacity for hard work, carried out thoroughly and without complaint, always excited both wonder and gratitude in Frances. During her day spent under the direction of Mrs Finn, Sarah was to undertake all the heavy cleaning tasks, which would by their nature give her free access to most of the house. As she did so, she was to watch for evidence of food smuggling and secret feasting, make a note of what provisions were ordered, cooked, served and eaten as part of the normal family meals, to see if Mrs Finn's estimation of her husband's restraint when eating at home was correct. Frances had also requested that she gain the trust of the other servants and, if at all possible, see inside the study. It was, Frances realised when she had outlined the plan, far more than even Sarah could achieve in a single day. Nevertheless, Sarah departed early with an expression of determination that had rattled many a would-be dissembler.

A letter arrived for Frances from a Dr Jilks of Kensington advising her that he was the medical man who had been attending Mr Whibley, and he had received a note from his friend Dr Adair saying that she wished to speak with him. He was, with some reservations about confidentiality, willing to see her that afternoon. Frances sent a reply confirming the appointment.

Her first call of the day was the offices of the Bayswater Display and Advertising Co. Ltd, where, disappointingly, the proprietors had still failed to reappear. 'Off makin' their fortunes,' said Tom, who, judging from his activity as he marshalled his band of scurrying 'men', was already half way to making his own. 'Oh, Miss Doughty, I did see a sight yesterday!' he exclaimed suddenly. 'I was down at Mr Jacobs', doin' a job, and I saw such a peach, such a little pearl as I have never seen before in all my life. An' she is called Pearl which is jus' the right

name an' all. Turns out she is Mr Jacobs' niece.' An expression of
bliss passed across his face, which Frances had only previously
seen when he was drinking cocoa.

'How old is the lady?' asked Frances.

'She is six,' said Tom, 'so she is not growed into a lady yet, but
she will do. I don't mind waitin', and it's all to the good really,
as when she is old enough to marry I will be a rich man and
will deserve her.'

'You are very ambitious, Tom,' said Frances.

'Don' get nowhere without ambition,' said Tom.

'Well, I have a job for you, which will earn you something to
take you further on your way.' Frances described both Mr Finn
and Mr Yeldon, and where they were to be found, explaining
how they were both to be followed, the former for evidence
that he indulged in secret suppers and extra luncheons,
and both in case their perambulations involved purchases of
pastry and bonbons.

Her next visit of the day was Paddington Green police
station. The unfortunate Mr Sweetman was still in the cells,
where Edward Curtis and Mr Marsden visited him daily. There
had been no further developments, and would be none until the
resumed inquest and hearing before the magistrates; however,
Frances thought that she might extract useful information from
Inspector Sharrock. She also wanted to confront Mr Sweetman
about the letter his wife had written to Mr Manley and her
thoughts on its implications. Even though her client had
impressed her as an honest and truthful man, there might still
be actions of which he was ashamed and which he had not
therefore described to her. She would also ask if there was
anything further he could recall about his conversation with
Mr Whibley. Perhaps Whibley had known something about
Benjamin and Mary after all, and had hurried away on some
errand that was a consequence of that conversation.

At the police station, Frances, who was confident that she and
Inspector Sharrock had in the last year achieved an uneasy understanding, was astonished to receive an openly hostile reception.
He must have heard her voice when she asked for him at the
desk, and came storming out of his office with a face of fury.

'Miss Doughty, have you taken leave of your senses?' he thundered. When this produced no response other than a look of surprise, he gestured angrily. 'You're to come into my office! Now!'

Frances stared at him, but kept her dignity and refused to be unnerved by his manner. Ignoring the smirk of the desk sergeant, who seemed unable to view her as anything other than a comical eccentric, she squared her shoulders and followed Sharrock into his office.

Instead of throwing himself into the scarred and creaking chair behind the mountain of papers on his desk, as he usually did, Sharrock strode up and down the room barely able to contain himself. 'I have stood by for too long,' he said at last, 'watching you walk blindly into any danger you can find. If you were my daughter, I would lock you up and not let you out of the house! I'd see you married off to the first man insane enough to ask for you and that would be an end to all these goings on!'

Frances said nothing, seeing that he had more to express, and waited for him to finish. He was obliged to stop for a moment and breathe heavily to enable himself to continue.

'That business with your father, all right, I can understand why you meddled in that – family feeling and so on, but then to offer yourself as a detective, I could hardly believe it when I heard. I have told you a dozen times, this is not women's work! Can you imagine women dressed up as policemen parading about the streets and chasing criminals? Of course not! Missing pets, thieving maidservants, scandalous letters, perhaps – I was prepared to ignore that and hope that you would find yourself some more suitable employment before too long. I thought you might do all right at that school but no, as soon as you step into any establishment, there's an end to it! You closed the school, bankrupted the Bayswater Bank, and I suppose you have seen the pile of rubble where the mortuary once was. And now I have been told that you are offering to look into a murder, and a nasty, brutal one at that.' He glared at her and pointed a thick finger with an angry stabbing motion. 'Don't deny it; Mr Marsden has told me that you have agreed to act for Mr Sweetman.'

'I deny nothing,' replied Frances, calmly, 'but please do tell me the reason for your agitation. I am not seeking to undermine your work. After all, we both have the same object; we wish to see justice done.'

'*Police* work, Miss Doughty,' he insisted. '*Men's* work. Hard and dangerous. I have spoken to Mr Curtis about it but he is obstinate.'

'I act for him, too,' Frances reminded the Inspector. 'I hope you have not been trying to persuade him to dismiss me.'

Sharrock scowled, folded his arms and paced up and down again. Clearly, that was precisely what he had been doing.

'Obviously he has *not* dismissed me,' said Frances. 'So now I wish to see Mr Sweetman.'

'Well you can't!' snapped Sharrock, turning on her petulantly.

'He is my client.'

'That gives you no rights round here!'

This, unfortunately, was true. It was clear to Frances, annoyed and frustrated as she was, that she would have to remain calm if she was to make any progress. 'Inspector, you know me by now,' she said gently, 'and I will see Mr Sweetman either sooner or later. It would avoid trouble and delay if you were simply to permit me to speak to him today.'

Sharrock, however, was determined to be obstinate. 'It's no trouble or delay to me. The answer is no and it will stay no.'

Frances decided to try a different argument. 'But why are you so anxious about my safety in taking this case?' she asked. 'You have in your cells the man who you believe to be the killer of Mrs Sweetman. You assume it to be solely a domestic matter, and there has never been any suggestion that Mr Sweetman might have dangerous associates. So where is the risk to me in taking the case, or indeed to anyone else if the right man is in custody? Unless,' she went on, seeing that her words were finding their mark, 'you have changed your mind and now suspect that Mr Sweetman is, after all, innocent.'

'It was a good arrest,' he asserted, 'and I stand by it. Whether or not he is guilty is for the courts to decide. I've done my job.'

'But now that you have had a chance to know the man better you do not see him as a murderer,' said Frances. 'And this despite his previous record.'

'Well if you are right, Miss Clever, and I don't say you are,' he said belligerently, 'all the more reason for you to have nothing to do with the case!'

Frances could see that he would not be persuaded and she would have to be patient and try other means. Nevertheless, she was determined not to have had a wasted journey.

'Very well, I must abide by your decision,' she said, 'but since I am here I wish to discuss the crime for which Mr Sweetman was convicted in 1866.'

Sharrock opened his mouth to protest.

'You were the first policeman at the scene, were you not?'

Sharrock's mouth snapped shut and he raked his fingers through his thick brush of hair. 'You are a very annoying young woman!' he said. 'Two minutes and not a moment more!' He moved a pile of papers from the visitors' chair, throwing it on top of a lopsided heap on his desk where it threatened to slither to the floor, and gestured her to be seated before taking his place opposite. Frances could not resist straightening the unruly heap of documents before it collapsed, and noticed that it included the file on the 1866 robbery, its dusty surface streaked with fingermarks.

'What was your impression of Mr Sweetman when you first encountered him?'

Sharrock grunted. 'He wasn't a serious suspect at first, not the right type, not until we found out about his money troubles. But I could see from the start that I wouldn't have to look far. My old Inspector, he used to say, when a safe gets emptied, start with the company staff. They know what was in it, and they'll have been tempted by it every day. There was never any doubt that the thief was an amateur. He'd used a company key to unlock the safe, and then tried to make it look like someone had broken in by damaging the door. But it was obvious that the door had been damaged *after* it was opened, and from the inside, and he'd used old Mr Finn's brass inkstand to do it, which was dented, and it wasn't the day before. So it didn't take a Miss Doughty or even a Miss Dauntless to solve *that* one.'

'So you suspected Sweetman because he had the key to the safe and no reliable alibi, and was in debt.'

'You would have done the same,' Sharrock protested. 'When his colleague identified him as the man he saw in the doorway we had our case.'

'Tell me about that morning,' said Frances. 'What was the first thing you saw when you walked in?'

He grunted again. 'Blood on the floor, all trodden about, people dashing here and there in a panic, and the man lying on his face.'

'Whereabouts? In the main office?'

'Yes, though it turned out he hadn't been attacked there.'

'No? Where was he attacked?'

'In Mr Finn's office. He must have staggered or crawled out, and collapsed where he was found.'

'You surprise me,' said Frances. 'Why was he working there and not at his own desk?' She thought for a moment. 'Surely anyone who intended to enter the premises and rob the safe would have chosen a time when the office was empty. Any robber would have seen the light in Mr Finn's office from the street as Mr Browne and Mr Minster did, and known that someone was there. Why would they have taken the risk?'

'Ah, but Gibson *wasn't* working in Mr Finn's office, or at his own desk. He'd been working in a room at the back where the customer files were stored. We found some papers on a table there, letters he'd written that evening. His lamp couldn't be seen by someone passing by in the street, so from the outside the office would have looked unoccupied. Sweetman must have let himself in, not realising that Gibson was there, and lit the gas in Mr Finn's office so he could see to open the safe. There was no risk about that; enough men work late at their desks so a light on in an office wouldn't attract attention. Finn was in the habit of doing that himself, and any police patrol would have known it. That night, however, Mr Finn had already told Sweetman that he wouldn't be working late, he'd be dining at his club with Mr Whibley.

'When Gibson finished his work, he would have left the storeroom, and walked across the main office to reach the outer door. On his way, he had to pass the door to Mr Finn's room. We think that he saw the light on in the room, which it hadn't been before, and heard movement, but of course he knew that Mr Finn had already left for the night, so he walked in to investigate and interrupted Sweetman while he was emptying the safe. There was a struggle, and Gibson hit his head on the edge of the desk. We found blood and hair there.'

'So his injuries were accidental?' said Frances. 'Dr Collin thought otherwise.'

'Oh, it was no accident; the doctor thought Gibson had had his head smashed against the desk more than once.'

'A brutal crime,' agreed Frances, 'and you thought that Mr Sweetman was capable of that? Pounding another man's head against a desk?'

'He was a desperate man. Who knows what a desperate man might do on the spur of the moment?'

'Did Mr Whibley say when he arrived the next morning whether the light was still on?'

Sharrock grabbed the file from the desk and examined it. 'I don't know why I'm helping you,' he growled. Frances smiled as he studied the written statements. 'He arrived at half past seven o'clock, but didn't notice whether the light had been left burning. We think that was because the gas was on very low in Mr Finn's room and it was already bright daylight. It wasn't until I examined the room that I saw that the gas was still on.'

'Would the door have appeared to be tampered with or unlocked from the outside?'

'No, it would not.'

'Was there a light on in the main office?'

'No, but the light coming through the windows was enough for Whibley to see Gibson on the floor.'

The light coming from Mr Finn's room together with the light of the street lamps had also been enough the night before, thought Frances, for Mr Browne to recognise someone he already knew.

'What can you tell me about the murder of Mrs Sweetman?'

Sharrock threw the file down on the desk. 'Now you don't expect me to encourage you in this madness, do you?'

'I will discover what I need to know at the inquest in any case. You can't stop me going there.'

'Oh, can't I? Just give me one reason and I'll do it.' He stared at her aggressively then gave in. 'Well, it's best you know the kind of man you are dealing with. Then you might see some sense. She was hit on the head with a bottle, and then strangled. It was a savage attack and he meant to kill.'

'Was she hit from behind or the front?'

'She was hit on the side of the head so it could have been either. It wasn't enough to kill her, but she would have fallen. Then he knelt on her and strangled her.'

'Were there any other injuries? Did she put up her hands to defend herself?'

'No. But it was a brandy bottle, and there were two glasses on the table. We don't know for sure yet, but she may have been part drunk when she died.'

'Do you think the visitor came with the intention of killing? Perhaps the brandy was a part of the plan, to make her less able to defend herself.'

'That's possible, or maybe it was a peace offering in a reconciliation that went wrong. We think they argued, and it got violent. And Sweetman and his wife had any number of things to argue about.'

'But there could be many other suspects apart from Mr Sweetman,' said Frances. 'After all, we know nothing of Mrs Sweetman's life between her leaving the family home in 1866 and taking up residence in Redan Place. Unless *you* know something you are not telling me.'

'Even if I did, which I do not, I would make sure not to tell you, Miss Doughty. I won't have you go chasing after dangerous men.'

'I could set Sarah on them,' said Frances with a smile.

'No thank you – she's not a woman, she's an army. She'll tear someone's head off one of these days.'

'And what of Mrs Sweetman's children? Have they not appeared? Surely you can tell me that.'

'They have not,' Sharrock answered firmly.

'If it is of any help, I heard a rumour that when they were very young they were seen on stage at a variety night at the Bijou Theatre, but no one seems to have seen them since.'

'Well it's not my business to find them. They might have gone abroad, a lot of these theatrical types do. And now I've given you far too much of my time, so if you could go home where you rightly belong, I shall get some *proper* police work done.'

Frances could see that she was not going to get any more out of Inspector Sharrock on that visit, but she did not go home – instead she went to see Dr Jilks.

❧

The late Mr Whibley's doctor was a gentleman in his fifties who was a rare example of a medical man that took his own advice. His complexion was fresh, without a trace of the ravages of alcohol, his figure was neither too fat nor too thin, and his room did not reek of tobacco. He looked like a man who would prefer a brisk walk in the open air to a cigar. He readily admitted to being the author of the letter to the *Chronicle* concerning Mr Whibley, in which he had said that he had advocated a reducing diet and exercise to his patient for many years.

'I am afraid he failed to follow my recommendations, which became more urgent with the passage of time, and his death was therefore not a surprise to me. There are some people who cannot or will not be helped. He was a pleasant and courteous man, and his business acumen was a great boon to his clients. I regret his loss.'

'How long had he been your patient?'

'About twelve years.'

Frances opened her folder. 'There are two letters I would like you to look at. Both these persons adopted pen names when writing to the *Chronicle*, but is there anything in the handwriting or the content or the paper or the ink that looks at all familiar?'

Jilks studied the Bainiardus and the Sanitas letters carefully but shook his head. 'I am sorry, but I see nothing which suggests to me who the authors might be.'

'I have spoken to Mr Whibley's chief clerk, Mr Richardson, and he was extremely annoyed about this correspondence and would not hear a word against his employer. He suggested that Mr Whibley's weight had nothing to do with his mode of life but was the result of an accident he had suffered. Do you think that is the case?'

Jilks chuckled. 'Mr Richardson is a loyal servant who will protect the business by exonerating Mr Whibley, especially now it is about to be sold. In my experience, corpulent people blame their condition upon everything and everyone except for the real cause – their own excesses at the table and idleness when away from it. It is true that, after Mr Whibley's accident, the injury to his leg meant that he was unable to move about for some time and he did, as a consequence, gain weight – and he was far from being a slender man before – but it is possible to adjust one's intake of nourishment to suit one's activity and he should have done so, but he did not. Curiously, the accident was the sole occasion on which his weight benefitted him.'

'Oh? How come?'

'His fat was like a cushion against the worst of the impact, and he lived while others did not. Even so, he suffered a bad head injury and was unconscious for a day afterwards, although he did make a full recovery with all his faculties intact. He was lucky to have survived.'

'I had no idea it was such a serious matter,' said Frances. 'Was it in London?'

'No, it was in Sussex, somewhere on the Brighton line I believe, about eight or maybe nine years ago. I think it was an excursion to mark an anniversary of the founding of the company, and most, if not all, of the employees were included. Mr Anderson and Mr Walsh were both killed – a very great tragedy.'

'Neither Mr Richardson nor Mr Elliott told me as much,' said Frances, with some surprise, although now she thought about it, Mr Richardson had been careful to say nothing that might detract from Mr Whibley's reputation as an astute man of business, and a blow to the head, even if it was one from which he had recovered, was not something he would have wanted to draw to anyone's attention. She wondered if Mr Elliott's arm injury had resulted from the accident.

'Ah well, it is better not to dwell on the past,' said Dr Jilks cheerfully. 'I tell all my patients that. Accidents do happen, and most of the time they are nobody's fault. I think this one was something to do with the weather. There is nothing to be done except look to the future.'

'Do you remember the last time you saw Mr Whibley alive?' asked Frances.

He nodded. 'Yes I do. It was probably only a few hours before he died. His valet called asking if I might come at once as his master was very unwell, and I complied. I could see immediately that Whibley was extremely ill. I thought that his heart was labouring under the strain he had imposed upon it for so many years, and advised him to rest, and prescribed heart stimulants. He was very agitated – I have seen this before, as a man's life draws to a close, the mind senses that the body is about to expire, even if he does not consciously know it, and things come crowding upon him, the guilt of the past, of things done or left undone. I suggested he arrange for a nurse to attend him, but he said that his valet could do all that was required.'

'Mr Pennyforth?'

'Yes, I believe that was his name.'

'Do you know where he is now?'

'I am afraid not.'

'Did Mr Whibley mention his meeting with Mr Sweetman? Was that one of the things worrying him?'

Jilks paused, thoughtfully. 'Yes, as it happens it was. Whibley said he had spoken to the man very recently and felt sorry for him.'

'Did he say anything else? Did he mention Mr Sweetman's son and daughter?'

'No, that was all he said. He also felt guilty over the death of his uncle.'

'Mr Anderson?' Frances was surprised. 'I thought you said he died in the railway accident. Why did Mr Whibley feel guilty?'

'Ah, well, you see Mr Whibley had been seated facing Mr Anderson in the railway carriage. It was only later at the inquest that he learned that the impact had thrown him on top of his uncle, who was more slight of form, and by the time they were brought from the wreckage the poor man had suffocated.'

'He could hardly be blamed for that,' said Frances.

'No, but it was because of Mr Anderson's untimely death that Whibley inherited the business,' said Jilks. 'There were some malicious whispers at the time. All quite unfounded.'

Frances glanced at her notes again. 'What is your opinion of the Vegetarian Society and the Pure Food Society?' she asked.

Jilks shrugged. 'I think they do little harm if not taken to extremes. Their members are all very earnest people who believe they are acting for the benefit of mankind, and who knows, one day their critics may be confounded. Did you know that Mrs Anderson — Mrs Elliott as she is now — is a great exponent of the Pure Food movement? Mr Elliott, in common with a number of my patients, became very anxious about his wife's interest when he read the letter in the *Chronicle* from that Sanitas fellow. He came to ask my advice, but I was able to reassure him that as long as she includes a variety of wholesome foodstuffs in her diet, she will remain in good health.'

'Is it possible,' asked Frances, 'for a person to be moderate in his or her diet, and yet still gain weight?'

'Hmm,' said Jilks, 'that is an interesting question. You should read my publication on the subject of corpulence.' He opened a drawer of his desk and extracted a slim pamphlet, which he handed to Frances. '*The Cause of Fatness and its Treatment*,' he said, 'I think that will answer most of your questions. My opinion is that in almost all cases, excessive weight is a result of too much food and too little activity. There are exceptions, however, as I have very occasionally met individuals labouring under some disease, which causes them to gain weight even when they curtail their intake of food. But these are rare.'

'Can anything be done for these people?' asked Frances, wondering if this nameless disease could be the cause of Mr Finn's inability to lose fat.

'I regret that is one of those mysteries that medical science has as yet been unable to solve,' said Dr Jilks with all the equanimity of a man content in the knowledge that whatever the shortcomings of the situation they were not of his making.

CHAPTER THIRTEEN

Frances agreed with Dr Jilks' observation that a man in his last moments will often be assailed with guilt, and try to make amends for the offences and neglects of the past, although she also reflected that the last days of Mr Whibley's life had immediately followed his interview with Mr Sweetman. Supposing, she thought, he had not felt guilty because he was dying, but it was the other way about; the visit from Sweetman had led to his state of agitation and guilt about past wrongdoings and provoked his fatal collapse.

She was not sure if there was anything more to learn, but determined to place an advertisement in the *Chronicle* to see if she could discover the elusive Mr Pennyforth. Once this had been arranged, she decided to see Mr Elliott once more.

Elliott was in his office but he was happy to allow Frances a few minutes of his time. He was just conducting a lady client to the door. She was aged about seventy, and resplendent in the deepest mourning glittering with Whitby jet. Though recently widowed, she looked positively cheerful; in fact, Frances thought the cheerfulness was rather overdone. The lady was not so much putting a brave face on her bereavement as enjoying it. She might have been assisted in this by Mr Elliott's gallant attentiveness, which was a balm and a comfort to the elderly, especially those who had valuable property to sell. Once the lady had departed, Elliott gave instructions to a clerk for some papers to be drawn up, and from a little of the conversation that Frances was able to overhear, she realised that the lady client was the relict of the virtuous vegetarian Mr Outram, whose demise at the commendable age of ninety-two had been mentioned by Mr Lathwal.

Unlike the offices of J. Finn Insurance and Anderson, Walsh and Whibley, Mr Elliott's domain was bright and cheerful with no hint that his clerks were hard pressed. One of them, Frances saw with approval, was a lady clerk, and he had a brief word with her before he ushered Frances into a private office.

His room was well set up and very neat, with a small desk, and comfortable chairs. There were no books and very few papers. Frances had once visited the offices of a land agent which had been a whirlwind of paperwork, and was surprised to see everything so quiet, calm and uncluttered, but reflected that the nature of Mr Elliott's business must be very different. If all his clients were as wealthy as Mrs Outram then he needed very few of them.

'How may I help you?' asked Elliott. 'Is there further news of Sweetman? If so, I hope it is favourable.'

'He still awaits the outcome of the inquest and magistrates' hearing,' said Frances. 'I hope to visit him soon. But I would like, if I may, to ask you some further questions about the last time you saw Mr Whibley. I have just spoken to his doctor who told me that shortly before he died, Mr Whibley, who was feeling unwell and might have had a premonition of his death, expressed his contrition for certain actions, or possibly omissions, in his past. I was wondering if some of his unhappiness arose from his interview with Mr Sweetman and could furnish me with a clue as to the whereabouts of the children, and even throw some light on the fate of Mrs Sweetman. Is there anything you can remember which might help me?'

'As you can imagine,' said Elliott, 'I have been giving the matter a great deal of thought since we last spoke, and I would really help if I could, but unfortunately, I can recall nothing further.'

'Amongst other things it seems that he was dwelling on the railway accident.' Frances paused significantly, since he had failed to mention this incident at all in their earlier interview. 'The one in which Mr Walsh and Mr Anderson were both killed,' she added, as if to jog his memory. 'It appears that he felt some responsibility for the death of his uncle, although it can hardly have been his fault.'

'No, indeed,' said Elliott, his expression speaking of a painful recollection. 'Miss Doughty – this is not a pleasant subject for me to discuss, and brings back some very upsetting memories, but if it is of interest and can assist your enquiries, I will tell you more.'

'I am sorry to distress you,' said Frances, 'but the more I know of what was pressing on Mr Whibley's mind the clearer the situation will be.'

The door opened and the lady clerk entered bearing a tray of tea things, which she set down on the desk. There was the inevitable delay occasioned by the management of tea, sugar, milk and biscuits, then the lady clerk departed.

'I was in the same carriage as Whibley,' said Elliott. 'In fact I was sitting next to him. When the carriage was struck, the side on which I sat took the worst of the damage. I suffered a dislocation of the shoulder which was crushed under the weight of the falling roof, while my arm and wrist were broken by the impact.' His right hand moved up to touch his left shoulder and travelled down the arm to rest on the scars on the back of his hand. 'There was some talk of amputation, though thankfully I was spared that. Afterwards I had several operations and it was many weeks before I was able to resume my duties. Even now, the adhesions in the shoulder joint still trouble me. But I do remember, since I retained consciousness the whole of the time, seeing that Whibley had been thrown out of his seat on top of Anderson, who had been facing him, and of course since I was pinned to the spot and had only one arm free, I was quite unable to do anything about it. Emily, who was then Mrs Anderson, as you know, was very distressed and desperately tried to save her husband, but it was beyond her strength to do so.'

There were a few moments of tea sipping and unhappy thoughts.

'What was the cause of the accident?' asked Frances.

'A heavy mist near Keymer that meant the train was obliged to slow down to enable the driver to see the signal. For some reason the fast train behind us wasn't warned and went into our carriage, which was the last one. It came off the rails and slid down an embankment. It was a nasty business.'

'Mr Walsh was killed as well?'

'Yes, but he was very much older than Anderson. Emily was shaken by the impact but apart from some superficial bruising she was mercifully unharmed.'

'Who else was on this excursion?'

'Mr Walsh's elderly sister, who suffered very severe injuries. I sat facing her, and saw that the roof had crushed her chest. She never really recovered and died about a year later. The carriage in front of ours was far less damaged.'

'Were any of the company employees in it?' asked Frances, her biscuit losing its savour as she pictured the collapsed carriage and broken bodies.

'Mr Richardson, the chief clerk, and his wife and son, and there were some ladies who were not of our party. I am glad to say their injuries were of a trifling nature.'

'Do *you* think Mr Whibley blamed himself for his uncle's death? Did he ever talk to you about it?'

'It was not a subject he alluded to,' said Elliott. 'Of course at the time I was merely a junior clerk, it was only much later, after Emily and I were married, that we became better acquainted, but I think it did weigh on his mind, although he was of course quite blameless. It was through Mr Anderson's death that Whibley inherited the business. I suppose it was only natural that he should feel guilty.'

'Please think very carefully about everything he said to you in his final days, however slight and unimportant it might seem,' Frances urged.

Elliott smiled suddenly. 'Well of course I was acting for him in the capacity of executor, and he spoke a great deal about the ladies in his life for whom he entertained a genuine regard, and also their children, who were generously provided for. He said – I don't know if this has any relevance – he said that it was his pleasure and privilege to take care of his dependents and how sorry he felt for any woman who found herself alone in the world with no man to take care of her, and who might be tempted to dishonesty.'

'Do you think that was a general observation or was he describing one lady in particular? Mrs Sweetman, perhaps?'

He gave a little shrug of his right shoulder only. 'Who can say? I suppose it is just possible that –' he shook his head, 'but no!'

'What is possible?' asked Frances.

'I just wondered, and this is only a supposition, if Sweetman had found his wife living in disgrace and killed her in a temper.

But from the little I know of the man, I find that hard to believe. How was she killed? The newspapers said it was very violent.'

'Oh I am not privy to information of that nature,' said Frances.

That evening Frances wrote a letter regarding her wish to pay a visit to Mr Sweetman. Inspector Sharrock did not know it, in fact very few people did, but there was another aspect to Frances' work, one for which she received a small monthly fee to secure her services, on the understanding that she would always be available to meet the very discreet and hidden requirements of some of the most exalted names in the land. No word of this would ever escape her lips, any papers on such cases were always destroyed and it was understood that she would never include these adventures in her memoirs, should she ever decide to write them. The work was in itself of a very dull nature, and no doubt other things occurred which she was never told of and might have made a more exciting story. For her part, she delivered notes or passed on information by word of mouth, or went to an appointed location and made observations. Her youth, her sex, her quiet self-composure, and her drab clothing were all the essentials she needed. There was a gentleman in an office, who received her messages, and it was to him that she now wrote to ask for a small favour.

While she waited for Sarah's return, she took out the folder of letters sent to the *Chronicle* on the subject of Mr Whibley's demise, and studied them again. Someone in Bayswater she felt sure must know the handwriting of Sanitas. A wife, a brother, an employer perhaps. She could scarcely show the letter to every person in the district, and a notice in the newspapers would only cause alarm and lead to precisely the kind of legal tangle that Dr Adair, Mr Rustrum and Mr Lathwal wanted to avoid. It then occurred to her that Tom and his band of 'men', who handled dozens of messages every day and therefore saw the handwriting of a great many individuals, might be able to help, and it would be better still if they could have a copy of the letter constantly to hand for comparison. She took a sheet of notepaper and her best pen, and struggled for a while to make a good enough facsimile of the handwriting for the purpose, as she could hardly entrust the original to them, but the task was beyond her capabilities. She then thought about having an engraving made, although that in itself relied on the skill of an artist to reproduce the writing exactly. Then another thought sprang to mind. Only a few weeks ago she had read an article in the newspapers about the advances made in the science of photography. There had been a recent exhibition in Pall Mall displaying a photograph in which a train travelling at sixty miles per hour had been captured with the most astonishing sharpness. Surely, even though the Westbourne Grove photographic studio was not yet in possession of the most modern equipment, it ought to be possible to obtain a good enough image of the letter?

Sarah returned from her day at the Finn household with a very thorough report, which she delivered across the supper table, which Frances, exhausting the limits of her culinary expertise, had laid ready with cold pie, cheese, pickles, bread and stewed apples.

Frances already partly knew Hereford Road, which ran parallel to Garway Road where the Sweetmans had once lived, and was not far from Chepstow Place, where, as Inspector Sharrock had been at some pains to remind her, the Bayswater Academy for the Education of Young Ladies had once, before her involvement in its affairs, been an ornament to the neighbourhood. The Finns' home had met with Sarah's warmest approval, from which Frances gathered it was an immaculately kept property, clean and well appointed with everything arranged in good taste and for the pleasure and comfort of the family. 'None of them showy ornaments with gold painted on and lots of old pots full of dust,' said Sarah.

'If the home reflects the wife,' said Frances, 'then would you say she is a wife who is very fond of her husband?'

'Well, I don't know much about these things,' said Sarah, 'but it's a home where anyone would be pleased to live. If she wants him to stay away then she is going about it wrong.'

'Tell me about the other servants.'

'There's a cook-housekeeper, Mrs Goswell, who knows her business very thoroughly, and Mary Ann, who looks after the children and is lady's maid to Mrs Finn, though Mrs Finn is not one of those women who has no time for her own children – she likes to amuse them as well. There's also the housemaid, Lizzie, a young girl but strong, reliable and willing. Mrs Finn sees the housekeeper in the morning and gives the orders for the day. Mrs Goswell writes out the lists for the tradesmen and checks deliveries when they come in. She does most of the cooking but she's training up the maid. And the economy is good, there's no waste in that kitchen, all leftovers turned to another use.'

'What of Mr Yeldon?'

Sarah wrinkled her nose. 'He's one of those dandified types, who thinks he's more important than he is. He sees to Mr Finn's shaving and dressing in the morning and supervises his wardrobe, gives orders for mending and cleaning. He went into Mr Finn's private office once, but he was only in there a few minutes. All he took in was some bottles of mineral water and he took nothing away. Then he went out, and Tom had Ratty follow him. He went to see Mr Finn's tailor, and was in there for an hour, then he went to see Mr Finn with what looked like samples of gentlemen's suitings. No pastries, no eatables of any kind. Then at dinner, Mr Yeldon acted as butler and footman, saw to the silver and glass, and poured the wine.'

'What was served?'

'Vegetable soup, fish, roast mutton with gravy, cabbage, leeks, and currant jelly. Luncheon was a vegetable salad with cheese and brown bread.'

'Of course you would not have seen how much was eaten by the two parties, but we can assume that Mrs Finn does not eat as much as her husband.'

'I only know what was sent up and came back. They ate well, but it wasn't a feast. There was only one bottle of wine opened for dinner, and from what I saw, they had a glass each. No wine for the luncheon. They drank water.'

'What was the order for breakfast?'

'Coffee, oranges, toast and an egg. I don't believe there is enough there to keep a man as fat as her husband is.'

'Neither do I,' agreed Frances, 'but if doctors cannot agree on the best diet for reducing corpulence, how may we judge as to whether they followed the best arrangement?' She had read the pamphlet supplied by Dr Jilks which was a very long winded way of talking common sense, however, she supposed that he would not have felt able to charge sixpence for a publication consisting of just four words, 'Eat less, work more'. 'What about the servants? They cannot be similarly restricted.'

Sarah grinned. 'Oh, they do very well! I gave Mrs Goswell my recipe for pound cake and she said it was the best she had ever tasted. And she gave me her recipe for fig tart.'

'I assume that Mrs Finn would not have pound cake or fig tart served to her husband,' said Frances with a smile.

'No, I am told that when he is home for tea he has meat sandwiches cut very thin, and little dry rusks, and not too many of those.'

'But there is more substantial fare in the larder,' said Frances. 'Did Mr Finn go into the kitchen? Perhaps he crept in and helped himself?'

'He could have done, but I didn't see him. Mr Yeldon did go in when he was making the dinner arrangements but I didn't see him take anything. Mrs Goswell didn't go into the other rooms in the house but of course the maid did.'

'That is just one day's evidence,' said Frances, 'and we may find another day is different. Do you think we need to look as far as the shops for the cause of Mr Finn's girth? If Mrs Finn keeps a careful eye on the accounts then could additional deliveries, presumably financed by Mr Finn, be coming in either in the form of prepared foods or as materials to be converted into cakes and pastries and brought to him secretly?' She shook her head. 'No, that is altogether too complicated. I really cannot believe that the entire household is united in both serving Mr Finn and deceiving his wife. If he is eating too heartily then he is doing it on his own account or with one accomplice he can trust.'

'Mr Yeldon,' said Sarah. 'He is the only man allowed in the study. And if he brought no food in today he might do tomorrow.'

'I agree. You seem to be on good terms with Mrs Goswell, perhaps you could give her some assistance and see what she thinks of Mr Finn's diet. If she trusts you and is in some way complicit in his excessive eating, she might even engage you in the deception. Is Mrs Goswell a large lady?'

'No more than middling, but she's a youngish person with a good hand for pastry so she might go that way.'

'Then she might sympathise with Mr Finn and be willing to help him obtain the sweet things he craves,' said Frances. 'There is another possibility, which has suggested itself following my conversation with Dr Jilks. Mr Finn's weight may be nothing at all to do with his consumption of food but the result of disease. There are such cases, although they are rare. I would like you to carry a note from me to Mrs Finn asking for the name of her husband's doctor and if he has ever consulted him about his weight.'

A letter arrived which, from the specially embellished envelope, was from that energetic *doyenne* of the Bayswater Women's Suffrage Society, Miss Gilbert. Frances opened it with some anticipation, and was not disappointed. Miss Gilbert's great talent was language, and she both spoke and wrote in the same tone of breathless enthusiasm, so the missive, which ran to four pages of script, commenced with her deep gratitude and almost unbearable excitement at being asked to assist Frances. This overflowed without restraint into her curiosity as to the reason for the enquiry, but was subsequently modified by her appreciation of the need for great secrecy. It ended, at last, with the news that if she and her devoted companion, Miss John, without whom no enterprise could or should be undertaken, could call the next morning, they would introduce Frances to a Miss Rose, a lady who had once been a member of the Bayswater Ladies' Society and who had, in her day, been a leading light of the theatrical company that had performed at the Bijou Theatre.

CHAPTER FOURTEEN

Next morning, after Sarah had departed for her second day at the Finns, Frances attended to her correspondence, of which there were four items. The milder weather had thawed the temporary freeze of crime and dissatisfaction in Bayswater into a rivulet of new clients, and while not every case was of interest or every task to her taste, she was obliged to appreciate the way in which they transformed themselves into her bread and butter.

On opening the first letter she acknowledged with weary dismay that since last year's incident with the parrot, she was somehow expected to find every lost pet in the vicinity. Fortunately this was the kind of commission she could always turn over to young Tom and his 'men'. The distressed owner in this instance was missing a monkey. Quite what anyone would want with a monkey in the house Frances did not know, as this hardly seemed to be the best place for such a creature, which according to its description and pedigree ought by rights to have been living somewhere in the East Indies. She would have thought that anyone having purchased such an expensive pet should have taken the trouble to ensure that it did not escape into the cold, which would not suit the animal at all. She composed a note to Tom and a letter to the client, but it was a sorrowful task, since she felt certain that the unfortunate creature was very unlikely to be found alive.

The next letter was from a young lady entreating Frances to discover if the gentleman she loved and who declared that he loved her in return, was true or not. Her account of him, which was clearly intended to demonstrate the noble nature of her beloved's character, made him an even greater object of suspicion in Frances' eyes. If he was such a paragon, she wondered, why did the lady doubt him? The letter contained no clue. Frances received many such enquiries, and the result was usually the same.

If this had been a storybook romance, the young man would be true to his love, and behaving in a manner that aroused suspicion only to keep secret his efforts to acquire some wonderful gift with which to surprise the lady. In the world that Frances knew, he was visiting a mistress or a wife or seeking a cure for an unmentionable disease, or quite possibly all three. Reflecting on how rarely those who came to her for this particular kind of help were actually content with the outcome, she wrote a letter inviting the new client for an interview.

The third letter she opened with more pleasure and smiled as she read it. She had been assigned a small task to be performed on behalf of Her Majesty's Government, which would require her absence for a day, but she would be well rewarded. Not only would it pay her rent for the month, but directions had already been sent to Inspector Sharrock of Paddington Green that she was to be permitted to interview Mr Sweetman whenever she pleased. Frances could not help wondering about the expression on the Inspector's face when he received his instructions, and was glad that she had not been there to overhear his comments.

The fourth letter, in a delicate web-like hand that spoke of the concentrated care of extreme age, was from an address in Shoreham:

Dear Miss Doughty

I have been most terribly upset to learn that Hubert Sweetman, the man who killed my poor brother and destroyed the happiness of our family, has been freed from prison only to kill again, and that this time his victim was the unfortunate Mrs Sweetman. The newspapers have been very quick not only to report this horrible crime, but suggest that you are in some way acting in his interests. I cannot begin to imagine what might have persuaded you to do such a thing. Perhaps he has told you some tale that has convinced you of his innocence. If he has, I must disabuse you of that false impression. Hubert Sweetman is a man of low cunning and habitual mendacity. His poor late wife – a most ill-used woman and an unhappy creature – was kind enough to visit my brother soon after the attack that rendered him an invalid for the rest of his life, and revealed to us, with many bitter tears, the kind of man her husband was. I could say much more, but her account would fill a volume.

I will shortly be paying a visit to London to attend to some business matters, and would be happy to meet you there in order to enlighten you as to the true nature of Hubert Sweetman.

Yours truly,

Matthew Gibson

Frances read this surprising letter several times.

Occasionally she received correspondence giving supposedly valuable information and accusing a named individual of a crime. These letters, which were usually either unsigned, or signed with an obvious pseudonym, were often littered with exclamation marks and capital letters, and sometimes written in red ink. They invariably revealed a great deal more about the writers than their subjects. Frances presumed that the authors entertained some hope that she would, out of nothing more than curiosity or public spiritedness and certainly not for any fee, act upon the information received. She had never done so. Such correspondents were, she suspected, only attempting to use her as an instrument of their jealousy to carry out a wholly unwarranted and possibly criminal harassment of an innocent individual, something they were too cowardly to attempt themselves. She hesitated to show such letters to the police, although in all probability they had received them too, neither did she have the leisure to spare to discover the identity of the writers. Such unpleasant missives were lodged in a drawer of her desk, where one day they might prove to be valuable evidence of malice.

This one, had it been unattributed, would have aroused her suspicion, but its very openness declared it to be sincere. It was a truly damning assault on the character of Hubert Sweetman, and for the first time caused Frances to hesitate and wonder if she had after all been wrong about a man with whom she had such a brief acquaintance. She found herself wishing that

Sarah was there to be consulted, as her assistant's rude common sense was often the best antidote to her own hesitant musings when her confidence ebbed. Opinions were so divided on the question of Mr Sweetman's guilt or innocence of the 1866 crime that Frances decided to take a sheet of plain notepaper, rule a line down its centre and place on one side the names of all those people who believed Sweetman to be innocent and on the other, those who thought him guilty. Perhaps, she hoped, some pattern might emerge from the lists. She decided to restrict the names to those persons who knew Sweetman well, either family or colleagues.

The result was that the persons who had stated their firm belief that Hubert Sweetman was innocent were his nephew, Edward Curtis, colleagues James Elliott and Thomas Whibley, the delivery man Jack Jennings and old Mr Finn, whose certainty had later been shaken by the trial. Those who believed him to be guilty were Mrs Sweetman, Matthew Gibson, brother of the victim, and the coarse and unpleasant Mr Minster. Frances dismissed consideration of Mr Minster, who she believed was the kind of man who judged others by his own standards and therefore always thought the worst of everyone. She was left with Mrs Sweetman, who clearly had some very profound but, as yet, unknown reasons to believe her husband guilty, and Matthew Gibson, who had either formed his opinion based solely on what Mrs Sweetman had told him, or perhaps something he had heard from his brother, or even both.

Frances wrote at once to Matthew Gibson saying that she regarded his observations as being of very great importance and would like to see him as soon as was convenient. It was all she could do not to take the next train to Shoreham.

There was just time for Frances to visit the photographer's studio on Westbourne Grove and explain very carefully what it was she required, before she returned home to make preparations for her visitors. This necessitated not only the provision of refreshments, but putting in place all the generous gifts produced by the busy fingers of Miss John, a needlewoman of great accomplishment, who made all the Suffrage Society's banners. Frances told herself that these gifts – the gold-fringed cushions embellished with the figures of Britannia and Boadicea, the richly embroidered anti-macassars and the crocheted d'oyleys almost as large as tablecloths – were all far too precious for everyday use and needed to be stored away almost all the time to protect them from dust and soiling, only to be brought out to honour her guests.

Miss Gilbert was a buxom lady approaching her middle years, but with all the energy and spirit of a young girl. She viewed Frances as the epitome of what womanhood should be; bold, intelligent, and unencumbered by inconvenient men. Both Frances and Sarah had joined the Suffrage Society, and Frances, after some initial diffidence on the issue, had been persuaded to take a place on the platform at meetings and, later, to give lectures about her career to a polite and patient audience, while Sarah stood guard at the door to keep out undesirables.

Miss John, Miss Gilbert's inseparable and essential companion, was a small, very quiet lady, her hair a cloud of grey curls. She rarely spoke, but when she did it was to the point, and though her customary expression was timid, her eyes could sometimes display a most mischievous sparkle.

The ladies arrived; Miss Gilbert as usual like a volcano bubbling with the heat of her enthusiasm, and she at once embraced Frances as a beloved sister. 'My dear,' she exclaimed, standing back to gaze on Frances, her clasped hands pressed to her bosom, as if to curtail an explosion of feeling, 'it is the most wonderful adventure to be, as it were, a helpmeet to such a renowned detective! Long may that continue! To know that I am the humble instrument of solving some great mystery is the most inexpressible delight! Allow me to introduce my very good friend Miss Rose, who has been an ornament to womanhood in Bayswater since she was just a girl.'

Miss Rose was a tall lady, like a silver birch, with pale hair and eyes and a suspicion of powder on her face. She wore layers of violet lace, a necklace of glittering crystals, and carried a grey silk scarf in her hand, which seemed to have no other function than to add drama to her gestures. She smiled prettily at Frances, but there was also a cold sly glance of evaluation before the smile warmed again. Miss Rose, who was sixty if she was a day, had summed up the plain drab awkward girl of twenty who stood before her and reassured herself that she was still, despite the march of time, the fairest of them all.

Frances fetched the tea things while Miss Gilbert patted the cushions admiringly, Miss John sat and clutched a large fabric bag, her fingers moving compulsively as if missing the touch of her needle, and Miss Rose draped her scarf, her gown and herself on an easy chair.

'So, can you tell us at last what the conundrum is?' asked Miss Gilbert eagerly, 'I know we are all bursting to hear! You know of course that none of us would breathe a word if the matter is to be regarded as confidential!'

Frances poured the tea. 'Miss Gilbert, you and your friends are very dear to me and I would do anything rather than place you in danger. There are times when my profession makes me privy to certain facts which, were it known that I was in possession of them, would put me at some risk. I would not dream of sharing that risk with others.'

Miss Gilbert looked disappointed, but was not in a position to protest. 'I understand,' she said, with a deep sigh of regret. 'Oh, what a very dangerous and exciting life you lead, Miss Doughty!'

'I do indeed,' said Frances, deciding not to mention lovelorn girls and missing monkeys.

'But does that not make you nervous?' asked Miss Rose, drawing her scarf through her fingers. 'Or do you perchance carry a little gun about your person? I was once in a play where a lady had a gun and used it to dispatch the villain. It was very effective.'

'Oh, Miss Doughty has a constant companion who is a veritable Car of Juggernaut who will demolish all opposition,' declared Miss Gilbert. 'Miss Smith. You may have seen her at our meetings dealing with rowdy intruders intent on disrupting our proceedings. They do not attempt it a second time.'

From her expression, Miss Rose had observed Sarah performing that role.

'And where is your very special friend today?' asked Miss Gilbert, with a teasing smile.

'I couldn't possibly reveal that,' said Frances.

'A secret mission!' exclaimed Miss Gilbert, so excited that she sipped her tea a little too quickly and coughed, which allowed the conversation to progress.

'I am very interested,' said Frances, as she offered a plate of biscuits to Miss Rose, 'to hear of your theatrical experiences, particularly as they related to the Bayswater Ladies' Society and the Bijou Theatre. Do you recall a *comedietta* called "The Happy Sisters" which was performed there in October 1866?'

'I remember it very well,' said Miss Rose, declining a biscuit with an elegant gesture suggestive of virtue and self-denial. 'It was a pretty piece, very amusing, about the rivalry between the three daughters of a duke. The comedy came, as you might have guessed, from the fact that the sisters were not happy at all.'

Frances had not guessed, or even thought to try. 'But I assume, indeed I hope, that they were all happy by the end of the piece?'

'Of course,' said Miss Rose, 'or it would not have been a comedy but a tragedy.' She waved her scarf in a silvery cascade. 'But people did not come to the Bijou to see tragedies. They came for an evening's diversion. The play was very light, and the discomfiture of the girls, which centred about the fact that there were three of them but only two eligible suitors, achieved a wonderful comic effect. The sisters were noted for accomplishment, good manners and beauty, but, to the regret of their parents, each girl had been granted only one of these virtues.' She paused. Frances decided it would be impolite to ask which part Miss Rose had played and was silent. 'I was the youngest sister, the beauty,' Miss Rose continued, as if that was self-evident.

'I was sure that was the case,' Frances declared.

'Of course you will want to know how the dilemma was resolved.'

'Naturally,' responded Frances.

'It was resolved,' said Miss Rose, with calm deliberation, 'by the arrival in the neighbourhood of a third gentleman.'

'Well, how very clever!' exclaimed Miss Gilbert. 'I would never have thought of that. Were the ladies obliged to engage a gentleman to play the role?'

'Or was he played by a lady *en travesti*?' said Miss John, softly.

'No, that was quite unnecessary, his arrival was by repute only; the news was brought by a maid,' said Miss Rose. 'I recall it particularly because the lady who was to have played the part of the maid had been taken ill and could not perform the role. There were only two lines to learn and a young girl who was appearing that same night as a songstress agreed to take her place.'

Frances understood now that Miss Rose had been reserving this information all along. 'The young girl, she was Mary Sweetman, wasn't she?'

Miss Rose fluttered her scarf. 'I didn't know her name. She sang a vulgar song about farm animals, and her brother whistled popular tunes. It was a very low kind of entertainment. But later, when I saw them together, I could see that they were devoted to each other, and very unhappy. The boy, although he was the elder of the two, was the more despondent, and his sister was comforting him. I asked if there was anything I could do, but they only said that they had suffered a great disappointment and could not go back to their family but were obliged, young as they were, to make their own way in the world.'

Frances showed Miss Rose the portrait that Edward Curtis had provided and she declared that while it had been many years since she had seen the pair, it depicted nothing to suggest that the boy and girl she had encountered at the Bijou were not Benjamin and Mary Sweetman.

'Did no one try to help them?' asked Frances. 'Surely the charitable ladies could have done something?'

'I offered to make enquiries on their behalf, to see if there was some respectable occupation that could be found for them, but I was assured that they had both obtained suitable means of earning their bread. The girl had some talent in song, and might have done well in that line, but she could not endure the unsavoury persons who sometimes frequented the theatre and paid her unwanted attention, and had determined to give it up. I assumed that she was to go into service. The brother had no talent at all, or if he did, it was not apparent on the stage. But he was a well-looking and active boy, and the theatre had offered to employ him in selling tickets and distributing notices. He could earn sufficient to keep himself, but not both, and so they were obliged to part, which was a great source of distress to them, that and the fact that their family had once been respectable and their present situation was a great fall in their expectations.'

'Did you ever see either of them again?' asked Frances, hopefully. She offered the biscuits again and Miss Rose absent-mindedly took one and nibbled it.

'I did not see the girl, but from time to time I saw the boy going about his business. He was there for six or seven years. I don't know what became of him after that.'

'Did he ever say what had become of his sister?'

'I did enquire after her once and he said she had found a good situation and was happy.'

Frances questioned Miss Rose further, but she knew of no one living in Bayswater who had been associated with the Bijou Theatre at the time that Benjamin Sweetman had worked there. Still, she had made some progress.

'I believe that the variety nights were discontinued in 1866,' said Frances.

'Oh dear me, yes,' said Miss Rose, throatily. 'Did you know about the scandal concerning that despicable creature Mr Hatfield who produced the varieties?'

Frances pretended ignorance and Miss Gilbert and Miss John leaned forward and breathed a little faster in anticipation. 'A scandal, how exciting!' said Miss Gilbert, with a little squeal.

'It transpired,' confided Miss Rose, warming to her audience, 'that the profits from the variety nights were going in his pocket and not to charity as he claimed. Gambling debts. I once saw him in conversation with that coarse moneylender person, the one who —' she pressed the back of her hand to her forehead. 'Well, it was all rather horrid.'

'He had his throat cut,' said Miss John, with relish, and Frances half expected her to take a scissors from her bag to demonstrate. 'Perhaps Mr Hatfield did it?'

'I don't believe so,' said Miss Rose, 'because the moneylender was a tall man and Mr Hatfield was very short.' The ladies spent a few moments pondering the practicalities of throat cutting. 'Someone said the murderer must be a cabdriver, because it happened near a mews and the police questioned all the men who lived nearby, but nothing ever came of it.'

'Oh, Miss Doughty, here is a fine mystery,' exclaimed Miss Gilbert. 'I am sure that if you were to look into it, with your wonderful brain, you could easily find out the murderer.'

'Is there a reward offered?' asked Frances, not because she thought there was one, but to make a point of the fact that she rarely gave her services gratis.

Miss Gilbert was unsure.

'And think of the *danger!*' said Miss John, although her tone suggested that this was not a bad thing, indeed both ladies appeared to be of the opinion that Frances pursued criminals not as a profession but for amusement, in the same way as Miss Rose offered her services as an actress.

'I would very much like it,' said Miss Gilbert, 'if you were to address the society next Monday. We have some very distinguished gentlemen visitors, who I know will be impressed with you and this will add to our campaign to convince them that we women can manage our own affairs as well as or better than men. One day, Miss Doughty, ladies will enter parliament – not just to watch men making such turmoil in the world, as they do now, but actually putting their mistakes right. If women ruled, then I am convinced we would have no conflicts and no wars, and how wonderful that would be!'

'What subject do you wish me to choose for my address?' asked Frances.

'Oh, anything you please! I know it will be interesting.'

While Frances considered this, the conversation turned to the drama, in which Miss Rose was still active, being a leading member of the Bayswater Ladies' Artistic Society, who often performed interludes at Westbourne Hall. There was even talk of reviving 'The Happy Sisters', and Miss Rose revealed that this time the Society had asked her to portray the oldest, most accomplished sister, because with her experience of the stage she now merited a larger role than before.

CHAPTER FIFTEEN

As Frances bid farewell to her guests and tidied away the tea things, her ruminations on the subject of Matthew Gibson's letter promoted another thought. She opened the drawer of her desk and extracted the folder of anonymous letters that had been sent to her over the course of the last year. Jealous wives and cast-off mistresses, rival businessmen, unhappy servants, vengeful employees; they were all here in moods of various shades of green and purple. The first trial at which she had appeared as a witness and which had established her reputation as a discoverer of hidden crime, had resulted in a small deluge of letters, the contents of which varied from proposals of marriage to insults, while a few correspondents simply expressed their undying admiration and said that if they ever wanted a murder investigating they would call on her at once, all of which she found equally disturbing. As she sifted through the rest, her mind was telling her that the idea that had suddenly come to her was the result of pure confusion, and that she had examined so many letters and notes that they had somehow all started to look the same, but she persevered and finally lighted on a letter she had received some eight months previously:

Dear Miss Doughty

You are a very clever detective and I know the newspapers cannot be lying when they say how you have caught so many murderers and helped ladies who have been cruelly ill-used. I am sure that if you were to look into the affairs of Alfred Thorpe who works at the Westminster Bank, you would find something to his detriment.

Yours faithfully

A sincere friend

Three things were very apparent to Frances on reading this letter. Firstly, whoever the writer was a sincere friend of, it was not Alfred Thorpe. Secondly, the author was in all probability female, and had been passed over in romance by Mr Thorpe, but, most importantly, the writer was none other than that supposed friend of the late Mr Whibley – Bainiardus. The paper, while of a common type, had the same irregularity on one edge as the Bainiardus letter, showing that not only was it the same paper, but it had been cut at the same time and was part of the same batch. The writing was identical.

This information placed Frances in something of a quandary. She had not been engaged to find Bainiardus but Sanitas, and there was no suggestion that by identifying one she would thereby unmask the other. Showing Mr Thorpe the letter and asking if he knew the writing might well result in the exposure of Bainiardus, but also distress to the gentleman and his family, the prosecution of Bainiardus and painful scenes in a public court. She could show him the opening lines of the letter, or even just the envelope, but on what pretext might she do so?

For some months Frances been in the habit of retaining copies of the *Chronicle* for professional purposes and she now consulted her collection, and very quickly found what she was looking for. The letter was, inconveniently, undated, but she felt certain that she had received it last May. In that same month, Mr Alfred Thorpe had announced his engagement to a Miss Lambert.

Frances looked through all the other letters in her folder of anonymous missives, and found to her relief that there were none others from 'a sincere friend', nor any on the subject of Mr Thorpe. The newspapers also told her that Mr Thorpe had conferred marital happiness on Miss Lambert last September. The fact that this event had not provoked another letter on that gentleman's supposed defects suggested that the lady he had either jilted or ignored had recovered from her disappointment. No one would wish the distasteful incident to be exposed, and worse still, supposing Bainiardus was actually Miss Lambert, who had dashed off a bitter missive in the heat of a quarrel that had been quickly made up to end with a joyous result?

Mr Thorpe would know his wife's handwriting at once and the consequences would be terrible indeed. Frances could do no more than note the discovery before she set off for Paddington Green.

Inspector Sharrock's expression when he saw her was at first, unreadable. He did not lose his temper, or order her to leave, which was a promising start, but neither did he speak to her, he simply went to get a bunch of keys and returned. Standing before her, with a belligerent twist of the mouth, he rattled the keys with a jerky movement indicating insufficiently suppressed anger and frustration.

'So now I am to do your bidding,' he blurted out at last. 'Here's a fine thing. I suppose you will be lady commissioner next and command the police force.'

'I am sorry if you have been offended,' said Frances, 'but I do hope we can resolve our differences. We both act in the interests of justice, and if we could work in harmony that would be so much the better for everyone. I would never have chosen to be a detective; it was circumstances that made it my profession.'

'Humph!' Sharrock snorted.

'Now then, before we proceed to the cells, I wish to show you two letters and ask if you can identify the writers.'

'Libel, is it now?' said Sharrock. 'Oh well, at least that's better than murder. But we get hundreds of letters here. Most of the writers want locking up.'

Frances showed him the Sanitas and Bainiardus letters and he nodded. 'Oh I know what these are, they're the ones sent to the *Chronicle* after that Whibley died. What a lot of rumpus about nothing!'

'Do you know the hand?' asked Frances.

He shook his head. 'No, but that's not to say these aren't from the regular types who make it their business to complain about everything.'

'I don't suppose you keep letters of this kind?'

'We might if they're of any interest and not obviously from a lunatic.' He paused and tapped the Bainiardus letter. 'Now you come to mention it, this one does look like something I've seen. There was more than one as well, about a Mr …' he scratched his head. 'No, I can't think of the name, and I wouldn't know where to find them, even if we still had them, which I doubt.'

Frances decided not to prompt him by naming Mr Thorpe. 'I have seen something similar concerning a bank,' she suggested.

'Yes, that's right,' said Sharrock, 'I remember now, he was a bank clerk. He'd been getting letters threatening to expose him for some crime, and we got sent them, too. In view of the seriousness of the allegations, and the prospect of a criminal charge, we showed the letters to him.'

'Did he know who the writer was?' asked Frances.

'He said he did, it was a lady who had taken a fancy to him and mistaken a kindness for something more and wanted to get back at him when she found out he was to be married. He didn't want to press charges, and offered to speak to her about it. The letters stopped.' He shook his head. 'The trouble is, there are too many single ladies about with nothing to keep them busy. These ladies ought to find husbands, and then they'd not be idle and get silly ideas in their heads, or involve themselves in things they ought to leave alone.' He gave Frances a meaningful stare.

'Well, that is very helpful, thank you,' said Frances. 'And now, if you please, I would like to see Mr Sweetman.'

'That nephew of his seems like an eligible type,' hinted Sharrock.

'He has a wife,' said Frances.

'My brother doesn't. You could meet him if you like.'

'The cells, Inspector, please.'

He gave up and signalled to a constable to accompany them. They marched along a narrow, cold corridor of white-washed brick, towards a stout iron gate. 'Constable Mayberry will be your guardian,' said Sharrock. 'I am not going to leave you alone with a murder suspect without an order from the Queen herself, and even you, Miss Doughty, might find that difficult to obtain.'

Frances glanced at Mayberry who looked too young to be a policeman and rather nervous. His face was blotched with red spots, and his efforts to grow a moustache had not to date been very successful. Sarah could probably snap him in half with one hand.

The gate was unlocked and swung open with a screech and a bang that for so many had spelled the end of their freedom, possibly forever. Beyond this point were hardened murderers, desperate women, and frightened children. The odour was apparent very soon, the smell of unwashed bodies, filthy clothes and the contents of earth closets. The Inspector looked at her. 'Well, it isn't a hotel,' he said, dryly. 'If it's too much for you, I'll have the constable conduct you home.'

'Thank you,' said Frances, recalling the time she had discovered a rotting corpse buried in mud and the dreadful decay in the mortuary near Kensal Green. 'I have experienced worse and will continue.'

'If you insist, but you must allow us to walk ahead of you. I can't protect you from the smell but there are sights you should not see.' Sharrock strode on, and Mayberry, after a moment's hesitation, followed, with Frances uncomplainingly bringing up the rear.

The tiny lockups boasted few amenities; a bed made of wooden planks with a straw mattress and coarse blanket, a jug of water, and an earth box with a rudimentary seat in one corner. As Frances walked past the gated cells, she saw miserable huddled figures within. The faces that looked up at her, hopeful at first then bowed again as she passed them by, were not vicious or even dissolute. They were faces starved of hope and nourishment and affection, the faces of people who were there not because they were born to be wicked, but because they had been born with very little alternative.

'Are the prisoners not accorded even the most basic privacy?' Frances asked, realising that Sharrock had walked ahead to protect her from the sight of someone using the necessary.

'They are not,' said Sharrock. 'Who knows what they would do with it?'

Frances wondered what horrors Mr Sweetman had been enduring in the last week. For fourteen years he had suffered not only the privations of prison but the infamy of being branded a violent criminal, and had hardly won his freedom when he had been plunged once again into the nightmare.

'How is Mr Sweetman faring?' asked Frances.

'Well, he hasn't given us any trouble, he's been very quiet, but then his sort usually are.'

'His sort?'

'Respectable, then brought low. His nephew has paid for a few comforts, so he's better off than most, but he doesn't take much notice of that. Says he didn't kill his wife.'

'If you believe he didn't then you should be looking for the man who did,' said Frances.

Sharrock grunted and said nothing, but she knew what his reply would be, that he had enough on his plate without chasing murderers when he already had a man under arrest.

Hubert Sweetman was sitting dejectedly on his plank bed. He had been brought a pillow and a warm coverlet and there was a towel draped over the convenient item in the corner so as to conceal as far as possible its true purpose.

'Visitor for Sweetman!' said Sharrock and the prisoner looked up. He was haggard, like a man who had scarcely eaten and slept for some while, but his expression brightened when he saw Frances and he lurched stiffly to his feet. She was ushered into the cell and Mayberry accompanied her and stood silently by.

'Oh Miss Doughty, I have been asking for you and they said you would not be permitted to visit,' exclaimed Sweetman.

'That is all resolved now,' said Frances, and they both sat. Sharrock walked away, but she felt sure he had not gone far.

'Do you have any news for me about my children?' he asked. Frances was touched that even in his terrible predicament he was not thinking of himself. Either he was an innocent man, or a very skilled dissembler.

'I have discovered that they both left home to try and find employment,' said Frances. 'Benjamin worked for several years at the Bijou Theatre selling tickets and giving out notices, and then he left. Mary found a respectable situation. Further than that I have no information.'

'They could do no better without schooling,' said Mr Sweetman with a little wail of dismay. 'Benjamin might have gone into business and Mary would have married well. Oh, this is all my fault! I was so determined to see that Edward's education was not lost that I neglected my own children and made them poor.'

'You could hardly have known that you would be accused of robbery,' said Frances. 'On that subject, I have recently received a letter from Mr Gibson's brother, Matthew, who said that after the robbery your wife visited him and that she was convinced of your guilt. Do you know why that should have been?'

Sweetman looked confused. 'I can't imagine.'

'I will be interviewing him soon and perhaps he will provide more information. But tell me, Mr Sweetman, and you must be open with me even if you think it will lower you in my opinion, is there a transgression of any kind that you have committed that you have not mentioned to me? Was there a disagreement between you and your wife that could have led to her lack of confidence in you?'

'Our only point of dispute was my borrowing to help Edward, but while Susan made her disapproval known we never actually quarrelled about it,' he said. 'As for transgressions, I do not believe I have ever knowingly done a dishonest thing in my life.' A small darkness passed across his face. There was something else, Frances was sure of it, and she allowed him time to think. 'Susan would not have known about company matters, would she?' he said at last.

'While you were in custody she did receive visits from old Mr Finn, and Mr Whibley and Mr Elliott, so I suppose they might have spoken about that, but I doubt it. They were mainly there to ensure that she was not in want. They were all convinced that you were innocent.'

'Were they?' he said wistfully.

'Old Mr Finn was very much in your favour, although the trial verdict did shake his certainty, and as you know, Mr Whibley gave evidence as to your good character. Mr Elliott believes you innocent to this day.'

'I am not so sure of Mr Finn's confidence,' said Sweetman. 'How terrible it would be to admit on a public platform that someone to whom you had given your trust could be such a villain?'

'I recently saw a letter your wife wrote to your solicitor shortly after you were arrested,' said Frances. 'She was most insistent that she did not want to see you again and did not wish the children to see you either. I am sorry, but I must ask you again – is there any reason other than your arrest for the robbery that might have influenced her?'

'No, none.'

'I am hoping that Mr Matthew Gibson will be able to tell me something about your wife's circumstances after the trial. The key to her murder may lie in those years. Do you know anything of her movements or her associates during that time?'

'I heard rumours, of course,' he said, 'many of them. Some were quite disgusting. Other prisoners used to delight in tormenting me with the most horrible stories. Susan was a beautiful woman – anyone might think …' he gave a little gasp and for a moment he seemed to be choking, almost unable to breathe for emotion. 'She came into the office to see me sometimes and I could see the way Whibley looked at her. And you know his reputation with women. He did once comment to me that I had a very pretty wife. I thought nothing of it at the time, but since then, I have wondered …'

Frances thought back to the list of mistresses in Whibley's will. Could one of them have been Mrs Sweetman under another name? But if she had been, why had Elliott as executor not known this? Or had he only communicated with them by letter?

Sweetman suddenly leaned forward and clutched at his hair with both fists. 'Oh, Miss Doughty,' he groaned, 'I would never have harmed her, whatever she did! Even if there was another, she must have been driven to it by circumstances and I would have forgiven her! When I learned of the way she was leading her life at the last, I only wished that I could have seen her and perhaps helped her in some small way. But if she truly believed that I was a heartless criminal she would never have agreed to see me.' He sat up and wiped his face with a handkerchief. 'Miss Doughty, there is one thing I must tell you which I have never revealed to another soul!'

So here it was. Frances waited and said nothing, not wishing to interrupt either his thoughts or his resolve.

'Not long before the robbery I was preparing a report on the company accounts and discovered to my horror that I had made a mistake, a terrible mistake. And almost certainly more than one, perhaps several. Of course I was very distracted at the time, what with my own financial worries and my sister's grave illness, but I had not thought it would affect my concentration or my work.' He paused. 'I assume, Miss Doughty, that you are not familiar with the practice of double-entry bookkeeping?'

'I used to maintain the accounts of my father's shop, so I do know something of the principles.'

'Ah, then my explanation will be simpler. You will know, therefore, that for the most part mistakes in a set of accounts are those of addition only, although sometimes entries can be made mistakenly on the wrong side of the sheet. Even the most meticulous bookkeeper may commit that act on occasion, though it is rare. Unfortunately, once an error is made it is like a stone thrown into a pond, it sends ripples through the books so that when it is finally discovered it is very hard to find its origin. When the accounts do not balance and it is simply a matter of arithmetic – a mistake in adding a long column of figures – one will usually see a difference of a pound, or ten pounds or even a hundred, depending on the column in which the error lies. It is harder when the sum is, for example, ninety pounds, for then you fear that two mistakes have been made, a hundred on one side and ten on the other, so you see only the net result. And of course as soon you see any such thing appearing it is imperative to search out and find the errors immediately and correct them before going any further.'

'How much was the error in the accounts of the company?'

'It was,' and he gave a little whimper, as if the horror was fresh with him still, 'one thousand, five hundred and twenty five pounds, seven shillings and sixpence.' His very precision spoke of something that had tormented him for all the intervening fourteen years, and Frances could imagine him lying awake during the long nights of darkness in his cell, exploring the figures in his mind. 'Imagine, Miss Doughty, multiple errors and no clue as to where they might be! It so appalled me that I thought at first it could not be true, but I checked again and again, and there it was, to the penny!'

'And you told no one of this? Not even Mr Finn?'

'No! I dared not! I was afraid of dismissal or demotion, and then where would I have been? How could I have repaid my debts or helped my sister? No, there was only one thing to do; I set to at once to find where the mistakes were so I could correct them before my report was due.'

'I assume from your distress that you did not find them,' said Frances.

'No. The more I looked the more confused I became. And then came the robbery and my arrest. The company must have employed another man to take my place, and then, I fear, the mistakes would have been found and laid at my door. They might even have suspected that I had been taking money from the company and altering the books to cover my thefts. Supposing they had intimated as much to Susan? She knew nothing of business affairs and would have believed them.'

'But you were never charged with this?'

He shook his head.

'So it is possible that your successor simply found the errors and corrected them. And if it was merely a matter of number work then no actual money was missing.'

'Yes,' he admitted.

'Could anyone else in the company have been responsible for either the errors or possibly any misappropriations?'

'Only old Mr Finn was skilled in accounts, and I cannot imagine him doing such a thing.'

'But Mr Whibley was studying accountancy at the time?'

'Yes, he was.'

'And Mr Elliott?'

'Oh no, he was simply a copy clerk, as was Mr Minster. Mr Browne was engaged in sales, he visited clients. None of those three had any knowledge of bookkeeping.'

Frances considered this new information. 'Mr Sweetman, we know that the robber let himself in with a key and he also had the key to the safe. Mr Finn and Mr Whibley were both dining at a club that night, and both said they had their keys on their persons. Where were yours?'

'I had them with me at all times.'

'Do you think there has ever been an opportunity for someone to take them and have copies made?'

'I don't believe so. We were all very careful.'

'And yet if someone had, the result was that you were the only man suspected,' said Frances. 'Every circumstance of the case pointed to you and only you. Why should that be?'

Mr Sweetman, deflated and miserable, had no answer, but Frances thought she knew.

CHAPTER SIXTEEN

Frances was beginning to see the events of the robbery in a different and far more worrying light. Supposing the arrest of Mr Sweetman had not simply been the unfortunate consequence of his being by chance the only man who had a key and no reliable alibi, but the result of a deliberate act to remove him? What if the errors in the accounts had not been errors at all, but the attempts of another person to cover up acts of embezzlement? Sweetman was adamant that he had told no one of his discovery and had bent his efforts to finding what he imagined to be his mistakes and putting them right, but it was possible that he had revealed by his demeanour that he had noticed something amiss. The guilty party, almost certainly a colleague, would have seen him perspiring over the ledgers, suspected what was afoot, and been prompted to action. The theft from the safe would have thrown matters into further confusion, especially if the amount thought to have been there was incorrect. Any discrepancies would have made it appear that Sweetman had extracted funds from the company, and led to the suspicion that he had carried out the robbery in order to conceal his earlier crimes. Once again, Frances found that her enquiries were being hindered by all the most probable suspects being dead.

It was curious, however, that no one she had interviewed to date had mentioned any concern regarding the accounts after Sweetman's arrest, so the possibility remained that no suspicion had ever been aroused. In order to alleviate her client's anxiety on that point, Frances felt she should at least broach the subject with the two former copy clerks, Minster and Elliott, who might have heard some gossip in the office, while young Mr Finn, although not actually there, might, through his uncle, have been made privy to what had occurred, if only to serve as a warning for the future. She wrote to all three requesting another interview.

Sarah was home in time for supper, with a further report on the Finn household. With her duties at the house completed, it was decided that she should not return to work there unless called for, although Tom and Ratty would remain available to follow Mr Finn and Mr Yeldon. Sarah had by now established a firm friendship with the cook, young Mrs Goswell, whose title was only a courtesy one, as she was single and hoped to remain so as men were too much trouble, and had an open invitation to come to the kitchen for some refreshment whenever she had a minute. After a long discussion with Mrs Goswell, over buns and tea, on the subject of men and their faults, Sarah had established that Mr Finn, while occasionally begging for more food as his wife had become adamant that he reduce his weight, had been, on Mrs Finn's express command, permitted no more than extra salad, vegetables and fruit prepared without sugar. Mr Finn was very partial to fruit, and consumed it often. He usually adhered to his wife's wishes, but Mrs Goswell confessed that she had once caught him in the larder eating sponge cake, cheese and sweet pickles straight from the jar and had had to shoo him out. The maid had been warned that she was not to give in to any entreaties to bring him any other food on pain of dismissal, and Mr Yeldon had also been spoken to on the subject. As far as the cook could tell, they had both obeyed these instructions. The nursemaid never went into the kitchen except to dine. Mrs Goswell kept a close watch on the food that came in and what was prepared, as well as the economical use of leftovers. Had food been unaccounted for, she would have known.

Frances' note to Mrs Finn had been delivered and the reply was that she believed her husband did have a medical man, but she had never learned his name. He had refused to see a doctor about his weight, as he had not thought it to be necessary.

In the last day, Mr Yeldon had attended to his normal duties but he had also paid a visit to Dr Collin, who was Frances' own general practitioner. He had then gone to Mr Jacobs' chemist shop on Westbourne Grove and purchased two bottles of Apollinaris mineral water and a proprietary antacid mixture. After posting some letters, he had made some enquiries at Paddington Station, purchased a basket of Spanish oranges, and then visited the offices of J. Finn Insurance. He returned home without the water or the oranges and presumably without the antacid.

'And Mr Yeldon bought nothing else? No pastries or sweets?'

'Nothing else.'

'I cannot help wondering if Mrs Finn, on the understanding that fruit is a healthful foodstuff, which I believe it is, has therefore permitted her husband to eat it in any quantity he desires, thinking it will do him no harm, and there we may have some of the reason why he is unable to reduce his weight. Fruit without sugar taken in moderation has never been cited as a cause of fatness, but there must be a limit to the quantity even a man the size of Mr Finn can consume.'

Frances sent a note to Tom with the names and addresses of Mr Whibley's four mistresses, asking him to observe them and report back to her with a description. If one of the four had been Mrs Sweetman under an alias there should now only be three to be found. She also asked Sarah to collect the photographic prints of the Sanitas letter from the studio and hand them to Tom with instructions.

Frances had received a letter from Matthew Gibson who would be coming up from Shoreham on the following Monday, and would be pleased to entertain her to tea at his hotel. She replied confirming the appointment, and then, taking a small leather travelling bag, departed for her secret mission on behalf of Her Majesty's Government. On the way, she stopped at an office to receive a sealed letter, a letter that she was forbidden to open or to make enquiries as to what it contained. The letter was to be handed to a lady, and she was to ensure that she was present when the lady read it, so as to observe her responses in the minutest detail, not only remembering what the lady said, but also the tone of her voice, the attitude of her body and any change in her expression or the colouring of her face. Should the lady offer to show her the letter she must refuse to see it, and should the lady offer to reveal or discuss what was in the letter she must refuse to hear it. She was to carry back a reply that was to consist of only one word, either 'yes' or 'no'. Frances should have been curious as to the nature of her mission and what the letter contained, but knew that it was her duty not to be curious, and therefore she was not.

✿

Frances returned late and very tired to find Sarah still waiting up for her. Her assistant's expression suggested at once that any protest that this duty was unnecessary would be quickly dismissed. Frances was happy to be wrapped in warm shawls and fed cocoa until she relaxed into sleep. 'Is there any news?' she asked as she drifted into slumber, with Sarah drawing the blankets over her before creeping away, but she was asleep before she heard the answer.

✿

Next morning Frances awoke bone-weary from travel, but stretched and emerged from her bed to the scent of hot coffee and toasted muffins. Sarah liked the ones with raisins in, which lent a charred bitter sweetness to the aroma and held the promise of long mornings and conversation. Frances had not had the opportunity to read the most recent edition of the *Chronicle*, but she studied it now. The only item that caught her interest was the extensive obituary of the vegetarian Mr Outram, a gentleman who had devoted his life and fortune to good works.

During Frances' absence, Sarah had been deputed to call on Mr Sweetman's nephew and tell him of what had so far been discovered. 'And that is not a happy household,' she said, 'for all that it's in Elgin Crescent and a very handsome place. It's clean enough, and the brass plate gets shone every day, but for the rest of it, I think Mrs Curtis cares about nothing except show, and certainly not about her husband, but he defers to her in everything without a word. At least, no words that are spoken aloud, but you can see they are in his head. And Mrs Curtis is old enough to be his mother, and the housekeeper and maids are even older.'

'Did he recall his uncle saying anything about mistakes in the accounts?' asked Frances, telling herself that this picture of domestic discontent should be of no importance.

'Nothing at all.'

'I think I can accept Mr Sweetman's statement that he told no one of it at the time, and it does appear that I am the only person to whom he has made this confession,' mused Frances.

Sarah reported that she had also called on Mrs Goswell for a cup of tea and some gossip and exchange of recipes. She confirmed Frances' suspicions that Mrs Finn, having been told by her doctor that fruit was a very healthful foodstuff and ideal for the man who wished to reduce his weight, had been happy to allow her husband to eat as much as he wanted of the fresh or dried article, or cooked without pastry or sugar. She had also permitted him unlimited nuts as this, she believed, was merely a species of fruit.

'Nuts are said to contain fat, in the form of oil,' said Frances, 'but the question is, does fat in the diet become fat on the body? There are doctors who believe that the fat we eat, ready-formed either in animal or vegetable foodstuffs, is deposited directly onto our – ' she clasped her palms to her hips, and finding very little in the way of illustration, went on to say, 'well, everywhere, I suppose, with little or no change, and they advise, indeed command, that fatty meat and butter should never be on the table of the man who desires to reduce his weight.'

Sarah pushed the plate of liberally buttered muffins across the table and Frances helped herself to another.

'But there are others who say that the fat we consume does not increase weight, and reassure their corpulent patients that they might feed on the fat of meat and butter with impunity. Indeed, they say it will help them to reduce their girth by increasing satiety. If doctors cannot agree with each other I am certainly not able to form an opinion on the matter, neither can I advise Mrs Finn as to what she should do.'

There was good news, however, as Mrs Goswell had told Sarah a story she had heard from a neighbour, that a lady had recently complained of being bitten by a monkey at a nearby cookshop, an event which everyone had attributed more to her imagination than anything else. All the talk had been of whether the animal in question had really been a dog, a cat or a giant rat. Sarah had duly notified Tom and as a result, the animal, which was as she had surmised the missing monkey, was found sheltering in the shop's storeroom, where it had been basking in the warmth of the adjoining bakehouse. Tom had recovered the animal, overcoming its objections and an inclination to bite by wrapping it in a cloth, and returned it to the grateful and relieved owner for a suitable fee.

A further fee arrived that morning in the shape of a plain envelope, delivered by hand and containing a number of banknotes and no message.

'That's your secret work,' said Sarah.

'It is,' said Frances, 'and I would gladly tell you all about it if I was permitted. But if I ever require a strong and loyal second I will look no further.'

Sarah had supplied Tom with the photographs of the Sanitas letter, which was being compared to every message his enterprise received, and he reported that he had arranged for observation of the four ladies mentioned in Mr Whibley's will and discovered that all were very much alive and under the age of thirty. If there had been a liaison between Whibley and Mrs Sweetman he had not chosen to recognise it financially.

There were four letters of importance. The young lady who had entertained doubts about the affections of her gentleman admirer had written to advise Frances that she no longer had any doubts, as he had made her an offer of marriage. He had relieved her anxieties about his absences from home by explaining that he went to visit an elderly aunt of whom he was sole heir, who was residing in a sanitarium. He thought it best that she did not accompany him, as she would find it too distressing. Frances had no doubts that the lady would find any visits to the aunt very distressing indeed, and put the letter away in the full expectation of her being a future client in an action for legal separation.

In the same post was a neat little note from Mr Elliott, saying that Frances could call at any time convenient that very day. She received a similar note from Mr Finn, and a grubby missive from Mr Minster saying that she could call if she liked, but he didn't have anything to say, and if he did, he wanted a guinea for it or he wouldn't be troubled.

'And on Monday I see Mr Gibson,' said Frances. 'I know I have made no progress at all in finding out who killed

Mrs Sweetman, but I am hopeful that he may have some information about her.'

'If she was Mr Whibley's fancy woman,' said Sarah, 'perhaps she had a child by him that he left out of his will, and got herself killed when she asked for her cut?'

'Perhaps,' said Frances. 'But why leave her out of the will when he had provided for all the others? Mr Whibley was found dead on the morning of the thirteenth of January, which was a Thursday. Mrs Sweetman was seen alive at church on the following Sunday. She might well have lived long enough to learn that he had died, and made enquiries to see if she was to benefit under the will. But neither of the executors has mentioned this. Even if she found that she was not a beneficiary, what could she have done about it? She had no means to pursue the matter, and no legal right. Mr Whibley's proclivities were well known so she could hardly have damaged his reputation, and a woman in her position would not have been believed whatever she said. I'm sure if she had been offered five pounds to hold her tongue that would have been an end to the matter.'

'Where did she get the brandy?' asked Sarah. 'That's a fancy drink for a poor woman.'

'It is, and I think Inspector Sharrock was right, the visitor brought it with him.'

'So she'd be sure to let him in,' said Sarah.

'Yes, so it was either a stranger or someone she knew and didn't trust. Whatever the motive, I think this murder was done on the spur of the moment. They drank, they talked, perhaps they quarrelled, and then she was killed. If we could discover when the murder took place I could find out the location of the people who I know were acquainted with her, if only to eliminate them as suspects, but at present everyone and no one has an alibi.'

❧

The Cooper's Arms, where Frances went to meet Mr Minster once more, was as salubrious as she remembered it, and so discomfited was she by the surroundings that she even imagined for a moment that a thin dark figure hunched over a glass of ale and a hunk of bread in one corner was the Filleter, come back to Bayswater to do whatever distasteful things he did there. She turned away in case he should see her, then steadied herself and looked back again, but when she did, the man had gone. She was not, she told herself, afraid of him, rather he represented something that was unpleasant and beyond any redemption other than that of the scaffold and the hereafter.

Mrs Minster, who was at the door to meet her and conduct her upstairs, wore a scowl, and there was an angry red mark on her cheek. There was a glowing pinkness about her knuckles too. She conducted Frances to the door of the parlour and walked away with a quick and overly heavy stride. Mr Minster wore a similar scowl and a purple eyelid. Frances was curious about the topic of their discussion, but thought it best not to enquire or mention the external signs.

'Well then, where's the guinea?' said Minster, stretching his legs under the parlour table and tapping its scrubbed surface with his fingernails.

'I won't know until the end of our conversation whether what you say is worth a whole guinea,' said Frances.

'Oh, well, we'll say good day, then,' he said, but made no move to show her out. He had the superior look of a man with something to sell that he knew his buyer very much wanted.

Frances took a half guinea from her purse and laid it on the table. 'This is yours in any case,' she said, 'and I will see about the rest.'

He snatched up the coin with a sweep of his fist. 'Go on.'

'After Mr Sweetman was arrested, did Mr Finn senior appoint another manager to take his place? I mean immediately afterwards?'

Minster chewed his lip and winced. It looked like the eyelid was not the only part of his face to receive the benefits of Mrs Minster's reprimand. 'No,' he said, 'not straight off. I remember he said that he believed Sweetman was innocent and would be set free, and then he could come back to his old position, so he took on some of Sweetman's duties and Whibley attended to the rest.'

'Was Mr Whibley mainly concerned with finance?'

'Yes, he was. Arranging contracts, seeing to payments, issuing bills, chasing debts and so on.'

'And you were a copy clerk, so I suppose you were not involved in that area of work?'

'No, that wasn't my line.'

'But old Mr Finn lost some of his faith in Mr Sweetman, didn't he?'

'Yes, after the trial.'

'Not before?'

'No. Should he have done?'

'Do you know whether before the trial, while Mr Sweetman was in custody, old Mr Finn found anything on the premises – documents, or financial records – that suggested something other than the robbery was a matter of concern? I'm not necessarily saying that Mr Sweetman was involved, but what with the arrest he might have been suspected if anything else was found amiss.'

'There was nothing of that sort that I know of. But Finn and Whibley used to talk in his office a lot. Who knows what they talked about? *I* didn't. Why, what do you know?'

'Not nearly enough, I'm afraid. After Mr Sweetman was convicted was a new manager appointed?'

'Whibley took over right up until he left to work for his uncle. I don't know what happened after that because I left at about the same time.'

'And you heard no gossip or whispers?'

'I'm not one for gossip. That's women's business, wasting time talking about nothing. What's all this about then?'

'All I can say is that Mr Sweetman is fretting because he thinks he may have made some mistakes in the books, which might have been found after his arrest and added to the suspicion against him. But if, as it seems, all was calm in the office, it may have been that he had not made any mistakes at all, or that they were found by Mr Whibley and corrected.' Frances paused. 'On another subject – please do not misunderstand me, but I need to ask this – do you think Mrs Sweetman to have been a woman of great personal attraction?'

Minster threw back his head and laughed. 'Oh, she was that! Not a young woman by any means, but tasty as plum cake. I don't think Sweetman knew how lucky he was.'

'I know she used to come to the office sometimes when her husband worked there but did she ever visit after he was arrested?'

'No, as far as I know she never set foot there again.'

'Did Mr Whibley admire her?'

'She was a pretty woman, of course he did. We all knew what he was like.'

'But could there have been more than just a visual appreciation? What I am asking is whether, after Mr Sweetman was arrested, Mrs Sweetman and Mr Whibley commenced an inappropriate association.'

Minster pretended to be shocked. 'I'd like to know where you was brought up, Miss Doughty, to have thoughts like that and say such things,' he said.

'Please answer the question,' said Frances.

'Well, I think he would have, given a chance, or even half of a chance, and she was on her own, and so there might have been a good chance, but if he did he kept it quiet.'

'I know that Mr Whibley had a number of female friends, and these friends had children, and they were all provided for in his will, but Mrs Sweetman was not mentioned. So either there was no association, or they quarrelled, or else she was omitted in error.'

Minster smiled. 'Oh, Whibley wasn't a man to make a mistake about a will, he knew all about wills and what they could do.'

'Did he? Oh, you mean about his inheriting the business of Anderson and Walsh from his uncle?'

Minster leaned forward. 'Do you know,' he said, 'that Whibley killed his uncle?'

'I know that there was a railway accident,' said Frances, 'and surely Mr Anderson's death was unintentional, or Mr Whibley could never have inherited from him.'

'Well, as to that, I suppose so,' said Minster grudgingly, sitting back in his chair again. 'Funny things wills, though, you never know what might happen.' He paused meaningfully and glanced at Frances' purse.

'It would not cost me a guinea or even half a guinea to discover that,' said Frances.

'Well, I'll tell you, and *you* judge what it's worth. Some of it was in the papers and some of it I heard later. Old Mr Walsh, who died in the accident, he was the original founder of the business, and Anderson joined as a junior and worked his way up. Got taken on as a partner with a small share, and then later Whibley came along, and he worked his way up and then he became a partner too, also with a small share. I don't know how much, but I doubt it was more than about ten per cent apiece, perhaps less. Mr Walsh might have been an old man, but he kept charge of everything and he had the biggest piece of the business. So Mr Walsh and Mr Anderson both made wills. Mr Walsh was a single man, with a sister in her dotage and a few distant relatives. So what does he do? He leaves the family enough to keep them happy and he leaves the business to Mr Anderson.'

'That seems fair,' said Frances.

'Now Mr Anderson has a nice new little wife so he wants to see her comfortable. She's Mrs Elliott now, I suppose you know that. Elliott saw his chance and took it, and I don't blame him. Anderson leaves his house and movables and an annuity to Mrs Anderson, and all the rest of his property, which includes his little bit of the business, to his nephew Mr Whibley.'

'What were the ages of the gentlemen?' asked Frances.

'Mr Walsh was well over seventy and Mr Anderson not much more than fifty.'

'So in the usual course of events,' Frances reflected, 'one would expect that Mr Walsh would pass away first and then the bulk of the business would pass from Mr Walsh to Mr Anderson, who would probably still be alive today had it not been for the accident.'

'Normally, yes, except that Mr Walsh was one of these old gents who look like they've been dried like a herring, and will last forever, while Mr Anderson had a weak chest. He almost croaked the previous winter and wasn't expected to last through the next. No, if it hadn't been for the accident, Anderson would have gone first.'

Frances frowned with thought, then drew some diagrams in her notebook. 'Supposing Mr Anderson *had* died before the accident, then under his will Mr Whibley would only have got his uncle's small share of the business. But if that had happened, Mr Walsh, who sounds like a prudent man, would surely have changed his will.'

'Even if he hadn't,' said Minster, 'with Anderson not alive to inherit, if Mr Walsh had died the very next day, the business would have been divided between his relatives. If he *had* changed the will, though, I don't think he'd had left the business to Whibley; he was making plans to bring a cousin into the business and train him up to replace Mr Anderson.' Minster chuckled. 'You know that old chief clerk Mr Richardson?'

'I have met him,' said Frances, recalling the oyster-mouthed gentleman she had interviewed.

'Well, I heard that he was *very* unhappy about that. Seems that he had his own candidate for that position – his son. No, if Anderson had died before Mr Walsh, Whibley would stayed very small, so to speak. But what they couldn't have guessed was that they would both die at once. And that was where the law came in. The law is a funny thing and it doesn't take any note of some things and too much note of others. It turned out that no doctor could say whether it was Walsh or Anderson who had died first. So the law had to rule and it said that it should be taken that Mr Walsh died first because he was older. So the business went to Mr Anderson, who, for the last few moments of his life owned all except Whibley's share.'

'And then it passed straight to Mr Whibley, who found he owned it all,' said Frances. 'He could hardly have expected such a thing.'

'He didn't,' said Minster.

Frances had no idea whether this curious turn of events was of any importance, but it was at any rate very interesting. She took another half guinea out of her purse and laid it on the table.

On her way out, Mrs Minster avoided her gaze and made only those remarks that were absolutely necessary, but at the door, she suddenly paused. 'Miss Doughty,' she said, and then stopped.

'Yes,' said Frances hopefully.

Mrs Minster shook her head. 'Nothing,' she said. 'Good day.'

Frances gave her one of her little business cards. 'If that nothing should ever become something, let me know,' she said.

Mrs Minster thrust the card quickly into the pocket of her apron and hurried away.

CHAPTER SEVENTEEN

On the way to Mr Elliott's office Frances tried the puzzle in her mind from every possible angle. It could not be doubted that the railway accident was anything other than a wholly unforeseen tragedy, but supposing it had offered a valuable opportunity to a quick-thinking person? Had someone in the carriage that day hurried Mr Walsh to his death? Whatever way she looked at it, however, there was only one person present who had stood to gain from the situation and that was Mr Whibley, who was unconscious and immobile from injury. Perhaps, she thought, she was developing the kind of mind that saw evil everywhere, and expected that anyone exposed to temptation would fall.

Mr Elliott looked like a man who could not be troubled by very much for long. He was constantly optimistic, and sociable without being overly familiar. He had been in conference with old Mrs Outram again, and looked well pleased with the new business she had brought him. Mrs Outram, finding the flattery of a man of forty rather pleasanter than the company of her husband of ninety-two, was like a giggling girl with a new suitor. She departed reluctantly, patting her grey hair which Frances felt sure would darken in time.

Frances' questions about the books of J. Finn Insurance only made Mr Elliott smile. 'Number work was never my strong point, Miss Doughty. Clerking was better as I have a neat and steady hand, but my best work is done with people, buying and selling. Bookkeeping has always been a mystery I have never attempted to solve. It's like watching a conjuror putting a silk scarf up one sleeve and then pulling it out of his hat. It's the same scarf but you can't for the life of you see how it got from one place to the other. At least, I never could.'

'Do you remember anything being said in the office shortly after Mr Sweetman's arrest about problems with the ledgers?'

'I wouldn't have been included in professional conversations of that nature. After Sweetman was arrested there was, of course, idle speculation about the consequences. Whibley took over a lot of Sweetman's work, and he and Finn spent many an hour poring over the books together. Old Mr Finn was dreadfully despondent.'

'It has been suggested,' said Frances, 'that Mr Whibley found Mrs Sweetman a most charming and attractive lady. Do you know if he took advantage of her husband's absence?'

Elliott smiled. 'I would not have been surprised to learn that that was the case, but Mr Whibley, for all his reputation, always took care never to allow his private affairs to intrude into the office.'

'Did Mrs Sweetman ever come to you concerning any possible benefit from Mr Whibley's will?'

'Mrs Sweetman?' he said, puzzled. 'No, there was no reason for it, she was not mentioned in the will and as far as I know there was no reason she should have been. Ah, I see what you are suggesting, that had she been his mistress or even the mother of a child, she might have expected something from him. He was a generous man, and the fact that he left her nothing is in my opinion, the strongest evidence that there was no association. No, I don't believe Whibley ever mentioned her to me, and I have not seen the lady or heard anything from her since her husband's conviction.'

☙

Mr Finn, who seemed if anything a little larger and a little less comfortable than he had been at their last meeting, was unable to assist Frances in her enquiries about the books. 'My uncle said nothing to me about it, and I heard no rumours. And you know what offices can be like, there are always a dozen or so stories going about, so if there had been anything discovered I would have known about it. I could hire a team of specialist accountants to go back through the books, if you were prepared to finance the operation,' he added.

'That will not be necessary at this point,' said Frances, although she thought it might come to that. If it did, she had just the persons in mind.

❦

At home, she wrote a brief reassuring note to Mr Sweetman, wondering if she would still be as reassuring after her interview with Mr Matthew Gibson.

Sarah had been out on her own errands that day, since there were a number of cases Frances turned over to her sole discretion as being particularly suitable to her talents. Not a few ladies of the Bayswater Women's Suffrage Society, having reason to complain of their husbands, had received a visit from Sarah and some sound advice. She also, on her return, revealed that her good friend Professor Pounder, encouraged by the great success of his Sparring Academy for Gentlemen, had agreed that an establishment for the healthful exercise of the female sex would be of great benefit. There was to be one day a week when only ladies would be admitted and only ladies in charge, and Sarah was to supervise. 'I'll have them swinging clubs,' she said, with an expression of great satisfaction. 'All ladies ought to know how to swing a club.'

As they were finishing supper, Tom arrived, and Frances entertained some hope that he might have found the author of the Sanitas letter, but so far he had not, although every message he had been asked to run had been compared to the photograph Frances had provided. While Sarah was no longer acting as cleaner to the Finn residence, he and his team had continued to keep a watch on both Mr Finn and Mr Yeldon to identify outbreaks of secret eating and the purchase of extra comestibles, so far without success. That evening, however, Mr Finn, after leaving the office, had gone straight from there to another residence he had not previously visited, and Tom had hurried to Frances with the address.

Frances was not sure how many industrious 'men' Tom was now harbouring and feeding, but on receiving the note, she handed him a bag of buns, a pot of jam and some cheese. He seemed happy enough although she sensed that he felt curiously cheated at not being obliged to employ his skills in abstracting items of food. He looked about him, saw that Sarah was munching raisins from a dish and his eyes lit up.

Frances frowned at the address on the paper, since she had seen it very recently. 'Surely not!' she said, and went to get her directory. When she returned, both Tom and the raisins had disappeared. Studying the directory, she found that her initial impression had been correct. 'Well,' she exclaimed in amazement, 'that would have been the very last person I would have expected him to be visiting.' The address was that of Mr Rustrum, Chairman of the Bayswater Pure Food Society and advocate of abstemious living for good health. 'Now why should Mr Finn be visiting Mr Rustrum?' said Frances. 'I had no idea that the two gentlemen even knew each other.'

'He certainly hasn't been going there to get fed,' said Sarah, looking about for the missing raisins.

'No indeed,' said Frances thoughtfully. 'But I believe that Mr Finn, for all his many protestations that fat is good for a man and that he does not need to shed weight, is secretly worried about his health. He has been in a great deal of pain from his back, and that may have changed his mind. He will have read about the Pure Food Society in the newspapers and I know that Mr Rustrum is very free with his pamphlets and lectures. Perhaps Mr Finn made an appointment with him to seek advice. When you next go to take tea with Mrs Goswell, could you take a note for Mrs Finn? I will tell her that her husband has been consulting an expert on diet about his weight. That will certainly please her and she may decide that she no longer requires my services. We don't know of course how long Mr Finn has been consulting Mr Rustrum, or why he chooses not to tell his wife of it.'

'That last bit's easy enough,' said Sarah. 'He's been so sure of his opinion he doesn't like to admit he was wrong, so he's doing it on the quiet. That's true of all men.'

'And it may explain why Mr Finn was so critical of the Sanitas letter, as it was attacking a friend of his.'

Frances composed the note and handed it to Sarah. 'I am only pleased that the matter has been resolved without pain to either party,' she said, with satisfaction. 'If only all my cases could end so.'

❧

Frances had barely commenced breakfast the following morning when a banging at the door and a shrill shouting announced that there was a visitor with a very urgent errand. She peered out of the window, with the uncomfortable feeling that a stern rebuke from her landlady would inevitably follow this disturbance. She was in time to see the housemaid waving her arms in despair after being thwarted in the middle of her indignation and the flapping tails of some rags scurrying into the house. Moments later, young Ratty was at her door in a breathless state.

'Miss Doughterey!' he gasped. Ratty had a tendency to add extra syllables to words, especially when he was agitated. 'Y' got t' come quick! Right now! It's Mr Finn, y'know Fatty Finn, he's been burglered. All the coppers'r there and the Grove is in a state, and y' got t' come.'

Frances threw on her cloak. 'I'll get a cab and you can tell me all about it on the way. It's the office, yes, not the house?'

They dashed downstairs. 'Yer, the door's all broke, n' that, an' 'spector Sharrock is there, 'n they got Mr Finn ter come, n' 'e don't look good. Man with a belly bigger'n me, that in't right!' He shook his head. 'Oh, an' Tom says to say that the two fly gents came back from Afriky this mornin', lookin' very dapper, so gawd only knows what *they've* been up to.'

They left the house at a run. Frances waved at the first cab she saw, and they leaped in. Ratty, for whom this must have been his first time in a cab, stared about him, open-mouthed, and prodded the seats with an inquisitive finger.

'I hope no one is injured?' asked Frances, anxiously.

'No, 'cos they don' think the burglerer got in, but 'e'd bin 'avin' a good go at the locks on the door.'

'I suppose it was last night,' said Frances. 'But whoever did it hadn't reckoned with the stout locks they had put in after the previous robbery. I wonder,' she thought aloud, 'what they have got in there that a robber might want and easily take?'

'Munny, 'n gold, 'n all sorts,' said Ratty, excitedly. 'Jools, 'n munny 'n treasure n' important things …' he ran out of ideas.

'Hmm, well what they have and what a robber might *think* they have could be very different,' said Frances. 'But even when the office was robbed a long time ago, everything of value was kept in the safe, and on that occasion the thief had a key. I very much doubt that that situation has changed.' She could not help wondering if this development had anything to do with her recent enquiries, and the more she thought about it the more certain she became.

'This bein' a 'tective, y' need to be clever 'n think 'n that,' said Ratty, twisting his grubby face into a serious little knot.

'Yes,' agreed Frances. 'Thinking is very important. It's –' she paused. 'It's the most important thing there is.'

Ratty opened his eyes wide in wonder. 'C'n I be a 'tective?' he asked suddenly. 'I c'd; I c'd do all sorts 'v things – 'n I c'd learn about thinkin' 'n all that.'

Frances stared at him. 'How old are you, Ratty?'

'D'no.'

'What's your real name?'

'D'no.'

'Well, you are quite the man of mystery, which is a very good start. Here we are!'

The excitement in the Grove had drawn the usual idlers, who had gathered in the street around the front door of J. Finn Insurance in the hope of seeing something sensational. Really, thought Frances, if people were so desperate for a little novelty in their lives they should all become detectives and then their passion for the unusual would be satisfied every day. She and Ratty jumped down from the cab and hurried to where Constable Mayberry was standing guard at the office door.

'You can't come in here!' said Mayberry, stretching out his arm, palm forward.

'Nonsense!' said Frances impatiently, and swept past him before he knew what had happened.

The office interior was crowded with worried-looking clerks, and Mr Finn was sitting at a desk looking crumpled, like a hot-air balloon that had come to earth and was in the process of deflating.

'How did *you* get in?' demanded Sharrock as Frances appeared.

'Through the door,' said Frances. 'Can you tell me what has occurred?'

'If I do, will you go away?' said Sharrock. 'And what's *that*?' he added pointing at Ratty, who had somehow managed to slip past Mayberry in the confusion and was gazing about very intently looking for clues, rubbing his forehead as if that might stimulate his brain.

'My special assistant,' said Frances.

Ratty grinned and squared his shoulders. 'I'm a 'tective!' he said, '"n I'm learnin' how t' think!'

'It's not even human!' said Sharrock. 'Mayberry!' he bellowed, 'when I get you back to the station I shall skin you alive! You're turning this place into a menagerie!'

'I am sorry to have caused trouble for your constable,' placated Frances.

'Oh he can get into trouble without any help from you. Now tell me what you want and then clear off.'

'Inspector,' said Frances, 'I think you will agree that I have had some interest in this establishment in the last week or two and I might be able to advise you. I am told that an attempt was made to break into the premises last night but it was unsuccessful. Is that correct?'

'It is, but I don't want you or *that* touching anything. There's toolmarks on the door that might be helpful.'

'Was it a serious attempt do you think?'

'I would say so, yes. And not an inside man trying to make it look like an outside job. Not this time. If the door hadn't had special locks they would have got in.'

'Even if they had,' interrupted Mr Finn, his voice cracking with the strain, his face shiny with nervous sweat, 'what would they have achieved? The safe is secure and they could hardly have carried it out of the door. There is nothing else in here to tempt a thief.'

'Perhaps it wasn't the safe they wanted,' said Frances. 'The company books are still on the premises are they not?'

'Yes, they are in the storeroom,' said Finn.

'But who would want the books?' said Sharrock. 'You can't sell books!'

'Someone who knows what is in them and doesn't want it to be found,' replied Frances.

Sharrock grasped her meaning at once. 'Oh, I see; financial hanky-panky conjuring tricks,' he said, nodding. 'What do you have to say about *that*, Mr Finn?'

'There is nothing untoward in the books,' said Finn indignantly, '—unless —' he looked at Frances. 'Surely you can't mean —'

'I fear this may have something to do with some questions I have been asking very recently,' said Frances, 'but concerning events that took place in 1866, long before Mr Finn was manager here. The company was then owned by his great-uncle Mr Finn senior, who passed away in 1877.'

'Oh, so this is all down to you, is it?' exclaimed Sharrock. 'Why am I not surprised?'

'Let us take a look,' said Frances, marching into the storeroom with the Inspector hurrying at her heels. The ledgers were arranged on deep shelves, and each leather-bound volume bore a neat label on the spine showing to which year it referred. As she walked along the row, she saw a thin film of dust on the outer leather of the older volumes. It took only moments for her to find the ledger for 1866, which, like the others, had not been disturbed for some years. Frances brought it out and laid it on a desk, with Sharrock peering over her shoulder. She opened the book, seeing that the records commenced on the first of January, and were written up by Mr Sweetman. 'Here we are,' she said, after turning through the pages, 'these are the entries made up to the date of Mr Sweetman's arrest and they are in his hand, which I recognise. Mr Finn, can you identify whose writing this is in the book after Mr Sweetman's?'

Finn rose wearily from his chair, knuckling the small of his back and wincing in discomfort. He looked like a man just about to faint, which was a worrying prospect, for if he was to do so, it would be some trouble to tend to someone of his bulk. He studied the book. 'That is my uncle's hand; I would know it at once. I can find numerous examples of his writing if you wish to compare them.'

'Is that what you were expecting?' asked Sharrock.

'It is,' said Frances. 'I know that Mr Finn senior did not appoint a new manager when Mr Sweetman was arrested in the hope that he would soon be released, and took on some of his duties while he waited for his return. But there may be something else here that only an expert would be able to find. Mr Sweetman told me that just before the robbery he thought he had found some errors in the accounts and was trying to trace their origin. But perhaps they weren't errors, perhaps what he had found was evidence of criminality. I think that this is what the robber was hoping to take away. It might not be only in this book, but earlier ones also. He wanted them removed and destroyed before anyone with expertise in accounts had the chance to examine them for fraud.'

'I don't suppose you have the name and address of the robber, Miss Doughty?' said Sharrock, sarcastically. 'If you do, would you be so kind as to let me know, as it would save me so much time and trouble.'

'I am afraid I can't tell you that,' said Frances. 'But there were only three people working at this office at the time with the skill to alter the books, and two of them, Mr Finn senior and Mr Whibley, are deceased.'

'The other being Mr Sweetman, I suppose?'

'Yes. And he is hardly in a position to commit robbery at present.'

'Anyone can have a confederate,' said Sharrock, dubiously.

'As far as I know the only persons Mr Sweetman has communicated with since his arrest, apart from myself, are his solicitor Mr Marsden and his nephew Mr Curtis, who is a highly respectable dentist. Do you suspect any of us?'

'No, of course not, but it's very suspicious that this should happen just after you poked your nose in.'

'Miss Doughty did come and ask me about the books,' said Finn. 'I said she could see them if she could pay for an expert to examine them, but she declined. Given that if there were any mistakes they were made many years ago, I did not trouble myself to look for them.'

'I also made enquiries of Mr Elliott and Mr Minster,' said Frances, 'both of whom were copy clerks here at the time of the 1866 robbery. I see neither of their hands here and would not expect to. Now, Inspector, I suggest that you take this book, and several earlier ones too, and place them in safekeeping, and if there is a man you usually consult in cases of fraud, he should be employed to look at them.'

'Well, of course Miss Doughty, as you know I have a hundred special city gentlemen, all tip-top financial experts from the very best houses, just waiting for a note from me to do my bidding gratis,' said Sharrock dryly. 'I'll send a telegram to Mr Rothschild this very morning and he'll be right along.'

'But if he should be otherwise occupied, I might be able to suggest a Bayswater firm which specialises in commercial fraud and could well be a little cheaper,' said Frances. She took one of her cards from her pocket and wrote the address of Chas and Barstie's office. 'Just say that I sent you.'

'And what are they supposed to be looking for?' asked Sharrock, staring at the card.

'One thousand, five hundred and twenty-five pounds, seven shillings and sixpence,' responded Frances.

'That's a lot!' said Ratty. 'I'd be rich if I 'ad that!'

'You'd be in prison if you had that,' said Sharrock. 'Now scarper, the both of you!'

CHAPTER EIGHTEEN

Frances and Ratty walked the short distance up the Grove to the offices of the Bayswater Display & Advertising Company, where they found Chas and Barstie in great good humour. Their moods tended to vary with the quality of their clothing, and on that day Chas was resplendently attired in a dashing jacket of the sporting type, mustard-coloured trousers, and a handsome waistcoat to match, embellished with a watch and chain, while Barstie, sitting at a desk heaped with papers, was more sombrely but still freshly suited and dusting off a brand new hat.

'A coup!' said Chas, a wide beam of pleasure on his pink face, 'a veritable coup! I always knew we would do it and we have! You just watch and see, Miss Doughty, we are making our way up in the world. We are thinking of moving to bigger premises already.' He strode excitedly back and forth, which, given that the office was very small and almost filled with the desk, two lopsided chairs and a pagoda-like edifice made of boxes of papers, was a very short journey.

'In the City, perhaps?' asked Frances.

'Oh no,' he said, shaking his head very emphatically, 'there are too many sharks in the City, all fighting for food. We are not sharks, and may never be, but neither are we minnows, not any more. Here is where we will stay, and here is where our interests lie. *All* our interests,' he added with a significant wink, as if to convey that his ambitions concerning Frances were undiminished. Frances, aware that Chas was more attracted to her financial acumen then either her person or character, hoped that they would remain platonic associates, and that the inevitable rebuff she would have to deliver when he decided it was time to make his formal declaration would not harm their friendship.

Barstie laid aside his hat and gazed at it hopefully. For the last few months, he had been paying his addresses to a young lady of fortune, and his chances of success depended on his position in life. He had not yet attained that measure of either respectability or wealth which was required, but the hat clearly held promise.

'I think I should mention,' said Frances, 'that I have been instrumental in bringing you a very special commission which will, unless I advise you of it now, come as a surprise, and therefore I am here to give you notice. Your new employers will be ones with whom you may not previously have dealt – the Paddington police.'

Both men paled noticeably. 'What have you done, Miss Doughty?' exclaimed Barstie, sweeping a pile of letters into a drawer and turning a key in the lock.

'Please don't be alarmed,' said Frances. 'The exercise can only enhance your reputation in Bayswater.' She explained the nature of the problem with the books of J. Finn Insurance, and as she proceeded, the two men breathed more easily.

'Hmm …' said Chas, thoughtfully, pushing his thumbs into his waistcoat pockets. 'Special consultants to the police. Not much money involved, but a bundle of respectability, which has its own value and can bring in more business. Yes, I can see how that would benefit us.'

Barstie shook his head.

'Come now,' said Chas, 'the lady will not spurn you for that, in fact, does she not have a cousin well placed in the military who would see it as something in your favour?'

Barstie looked willing to be convinced.

Chas took his silence as consent. 'We will do it,' he said.

'You may expect a visit from Inspector Sharrock very soon,' said Frances. 'And of course, anything you can tell me about the businesses of J. Finn Insurance or Anderson, Walsh and Whibley would be very much appreciated.'

�֍

That afternoon Frances unexpectedly received a short note from Mr Lathwal of the Vegetarian Society, asking if he might have an appointment to see her later that day, on a matter unconnected with the subject of their recent meeting. She replied that he might call upon her at four o'clock.

Sarah had delivered Frances' note to Mrs Finn and after taking tea with Mrs Goswell, brought back a reply. Mrs Finn was, as Frances had anticipated, very grateful to discover that her husband had been consulting an expert in healthful diet. She revealed that she had recently had another conversation with him on the subject of his weight, and to her delight had received an assurance that he was willing to bow to her pleas. In view of the brighter weather, she hoped, if the morning mists should rise and the sun appear, that she would take a stroll in Hyde Park with the children after church the next day, and she would be very happy to see and speak to Frances then.

Mr Lathwal arrived promptly at four and sat across the table facing Frances with a mournful expression and fretful manner, his eyelids swollen with lack of sleep. 'Miss Doughty, I am not sure if you can assist me, but your advice would be most welcome,' he exclaimed. 'I have already spoken to a solicitor and I am even considering the police, but then I have nothing to show them. All I have is my worry and my suspicion.'

'Please explain,' said Frances.

'As you know,' he began earnestly, 'the cause of vegetarianism means a great deal to me. It is so much more than a diet which is the most healthy and natural one for mankind. It is a principle which benefits the spirit. We live in a busy world full of care and only by abstaining from killing and eating our fellow creatures can we attain a measure of peace. Of course it is a hard thing to persuade others of the wisdom of this path, something I have always endeavoured to do, and I intend to make it my life's work, but with my poor resources progress is very slow.'

Frances hoped he was not about to try and recruit her to the cause of vegetarianism, which she felt might not suit her, but she let him go on. This was evidently a very troubled young man.

'You can imagine, therefore, how happy I was to meet Mr Outram, a fine gentleman who became converted to the vegetarian principle while living in India. He often declared himself to be very satisfied with the work I was doing for the cause, and assured me many times that he would leave a substantial property to the Vegetarian Society to use in perpetuity as a centre for the dissemination of information, and also a sum for the purchase of an annuity to be employed in the promotion of vegetarianism. It was to be a very generous bequest.'

'I see,' said Frances, who now saw where the matter lay. 'And from your distress I assume that he did not do so?'

'Oh, but I am sure that he did,' exclaimed Mr Lathwal fervently. 'About a year ago he showed me a draft copy of his will and said that he was due to sign it and have it witnessed the very next day. I have no reason at all to doubt that he did as he had promised. But his executors have searched high and low, and it cannot be found.'

'Who is his solicitor?' asked Frances. 'Does he not have a copy of the will?'

'I am not sure if Mr Outram employed one, or at least none has come forward. The only will that can be found is one he made thirty years ago in which he left small sums to various charities and all the rest of his fortune to his wife.'

'Do you recall who the executors were for the will that he intended making?'

'He asked me if I would be willing to act, and of course I said yes. If there was another I don't recall his name.'

'This draft you saw,' said Frances, 'was it in Mr Outram's own handwriting or another's?'

'It was in Mr Outram's hand. I am familiar with his writing as we corresponded often.'

'So it might not have been the final document, but only something he had written out for the guidance of the professional man who would draw up the will for him,' said Frances, seeing Mr Lathwal's hopes slipping away.

'I suppose so,' said Lathwal, reluctantly admitting the force of her comment. 'But I cannot believe that Mr Outram would have gone against his promise to me. We had such a wonderful funeral breakfast to honour him. I paid for it all myself,' he added plaintively.

'Did Mr Outram mention anyone at all, any person whose advice he might have sought, or who he might have been considering asking to be another executor? Was anything to be left to another organisation such as the Pure Food Movement?'

Lathwal gave this some thought and shook his head. 'No, I don't believe so.'

'Do you know the source of Mr Outram's wealth?'

'Land, I believe. Good farmland that has been in his family for many years. He didn't farm it himself, but rented it.'

'So he would have had a land agent, and possibly also a professional gentleman he went to for financial advice?'

'Yes, he did, and I thought to consult him but the gentleman died very recently.'

Frances had an unpleasant feeling that she knew the identity of Mr Outram's late advisor. 'Not Mr Thomas Whibley?'

'I am afraid so. I went to the office and spoke to another gentleman but he was very curt with me and said he knew nothing of any will.'

Frances did not need to ask the name of the curt gentleman. 'Mr Lathwal, you mentioned your worry and your suspicion. Tell me, what do you think happened about the will?'

Mr Lathwal looked very uncomfortable. 'I do not wish to make accusations, especially where I have no proof,' he said.

'In that case,' Frances assured him, 'you are something of a rarity. But I do not believe that you have come here to consult me without sharing your thoughts. I promise I will not think badly of you for harbouring suspicions, and neither will I repeat anything that could be construed as slander.'

'That is very kind and understanding of you,' Lathwal said gratefully. 'Very well, I will speak freely. I think that Mr Outram did have the will made, and since it was not found amongst Mr Whibley's papers, he must have kept it at his home. Mrs Outram is not, by inclination, a vegetarian. I know for a fact that while Mr Outram did not permit meat or fish to enter his house, his wife dined on both items when from home. In fact, I am sorry to say that she was wholly opposed to the vegetarian principle.'

'I see,' said Frances. 'You think that after her husband's death Mrs Outram found the new will and destroyed it?'

'Yes,' said Lathwal, almost in a whisper, 'I do.'

'You are right to be so hesitant, that is a very serious allega-tion,' said Frances. She thought for a moment. 'Now supposing that the document you saw was not a will, it was merely a plan to make a will. I happen to know that Mr Whibley was something of an expert in wills. It might have been he who drew it up; he might even have witnessed it, but there would have been another witness.'

'No one has come forward,' said Lathwal. 'It might have been some junior employee who was not even permitted to see the terms of the document and would therefore not be a witness of any value. I have thought about it again and again, and I cannot see that there is anything I can do!'

'I am sorry,' said Frances, 'but I must agree that you are in some difficulty. You yourself did not see a valid will so there is no proof that it was ever drawn up, let alone signed, witnessed and subsequently destroyed.'

'I thought as much,' said Mr Lathwal, miserably.

'Have you spoken to Mrs Outram?'

'Yes. She said she knew nothing of another will and asked me to take away her husband's library of books on the subject of vegetarianism. When I called upon her —' he shuddered, 'I could smell roast beef.'

Frances allowed him a few moments to compose himself, and eventually he thanked her and prepared to leave. 'How much do I owe you for the consultation?' he asked, apprehensively.

She smiled. 'Nothing, since I am unable to act for you. I still have the booklets you supplied on the subject of vegetarianism — do you wish them returned to you?'

'No, please keep them with my compliments. I fear that you are not —?'

'I am not.'

'You would not consider adopting the vegetarian way?' he asked hopefully.

'I think it unlikely, although I applaud your efforts to bring peace to the world,' she said.

'Ah,' he said, disappointed, 'but if you ever consider it, the doors of our society are ever open.'

Sunday promised to be fine, and the morning sun soon burned away any troublesome mist. After church Frances, Sarah, and those inhabitants of Bayswater eager to take the air and enjoy the improved weather, descended upon Hyde Park, still far from spring-like, but holding in its flower beds and the smooth bare branches of its shrubs the promise of a fine colourful display before too long.

Mrs Finn was walking in the company of Mary Ann, the nursemaid, who was pushing a handsome twin perambulator of the modern four-wheel design, in which the youthful Finns, aged perhaps two and four, sat swaddled against the elements and distracted with dolls. It was of course a necessary fiction that Mrs Finn and Frances had never met, so it was up to Sarah to greet Mary Ann as if they had met there by chance. A conversation ensued in which Sarah, who had never been noted for a fondness for children, expressed her intense admiration for the two little Finns, and asked so many questions as to their feeding and clothes that the nursemaid, glancing at Sarah's bulky form, seemed from her expression to have made an incorrect conclusion as to the reason for her interest. The distraction did, however, enable Mrs Finn and Frances to move aside and engage in a private conversation.

'Miss Doughty, I am so very grateful to you for setting my mind at rest,' said Mrs Finn. 'I hope you will not be offended but it seems as though I will not be requiring your services any further.'

'I am not at all offended,' Frances reassured her. 'All my commissions must reach a conclusion and I am happy that you are satisfied. I will arrange for Sarah to bring you a note stating the fees due.'

'Of course, and I promise that they will be settled without delay.'

'I hope that your husband is well? I was passing his office yesterday when I was notified of the attempted burglary. Since I have been making enquiries about Mr Sweetman, I went in to see what was amiss, and I observed that Mr Finn seemed very weary.'

'It was a terrible ordeal for him and he was very shaken by it,' said the anxious wife. 'Once the police had gone, he came straight home to rest, but the outcome was that at last we had a long and very frank talk on the question of his health, and he has finally admitted to me that he is far from well and in constant pain from his back. He has now agreed to go to Bath very soon to take the waters, and expects to be there for a month. Mr Yeldon will go with him so he will be in good care. Perhaps when he is away you could call and take tea. I would like that so much!'

'That would be delightful,' said Frances, and it was agreed that an appointment would be made very soon.

Sarah and the maid were busy making cooing noises over the children, and playing a game in which a doll was made to dance to amuse them. As it capered prettily, Mary Ann provided it with a voice, so it seemed that the doll was singing for the children. 'I am a farmer's daughter, and a milkmaid I would be,' she trilled, 'but I don't know how to milk a cow, oh please take pity on me!' There were cheerful giggles from the perambulator.

Frances hoped that her reaction as she suddenly froze in place was not immediately obvious. She glanced at Mrs Finn, whose attention at that moment was fortunately taken by the sight of her children being amused. 'What a curious little song,' said Frances. 'I don't believe I have heard it before.'

'Oh, there are a dozen like it that Mary Ann sings to the children,' said Alice Finn, innocently. 'I believe they are well known.' Frances, however, remembered Edward Curtis telling her about his cousin Mary Sweetman singing for the family and his impression that she had made up the songs herself. But was his recollection correct? He had, after all, been only a child himself at the time and might have misunderstood what he was told. Had Mary really composed the songs or had she simply claimed to have done so?

It was not, thought Frances, the best time to question the nursemaid about the song, which she might have heard from a relative or a friend or anyone in the Finn household. That should be done at a subtle and private interview.

Neither should she question Mrs Finn about the maid and her antecedents, which would at once arouse suspicion and perhaps unfairly lose the young woman her place. Frances walked over to the perambulator supposedly to admire the children, who, she saw sadly, would if they were too much indulged grow to resemble their father more closely than their mother, but in actuality, her object was to take a closer look at the maid. There was nothing remarkable about the appearance of the young woman, who was perhaps about twenty-five, and the usual height for a female. She had a round pleasing face with a pretty smile as she looked at the children, and light brown hair gathered smoothly into her bonnet. Mary Sweetman, it had been rumoured, had gone into service. Could this be she? Judging by her age and appearance it was certainly possible.

Once home, Frances stared again at the photograph of the Sweetman children, but Mary's face was too unremarkable for a certain identification. There was, all the same, something about the expression; an intelligent, watchful look, that she had seen somewhere before.

❧

On Monday morning promptly at ten, Frances arrived at Providence Hall, Church Street, to attend the resumed inquest on Susan Sweetman, with Dr Hardwicke, that wise and experienced coroner for Central Middlesex, presiding.

Dr Collin, Frances' own medical man, was there to give evidence, exuding the urbane and satisfied air of a respected practitioner who was kindly to all and never made a mistake, in both of which latter opinions, Frances knew, he was unjustified.

The little court was crowded with the usual pressmen with their notepads and pencils, including Mr Gillan, who took care to sit beside Frances, as if to announce to the others that she was his own very special informant and should not be questioned by anyone else. The other men, from their hard glances, were more than a little jealous. Inspector Sharrock was there, as was Edward Curtis.

The circumstances of Mrs Sweetman's death were now very clear. It appeared that she had entertained a visitor, since there were two glasses on the table, both of which had contained brandy. Mrs Sweetman's stomach also showed that while she had eaten bread and jam and tea for her last meal, this had been followed about an hour or so later by a significant amount of brandy, the absorption of which had not proceeded for very long before her death. Dr Collin was of the opinion that Mrs Sweetman had been tipsy, but not incapable, when attacked. She had been struck on the right side of the head, in all probability by the brandy bottle, which had been found on the floor where it had rolled behind a chair. The blow, which might have come from either the front or the back, would have rendered her dazed, even unconscious, but not killed her. The attacker had then knelt on the unfortunate woman's chest, and strangled her. There were deep dark bruises on her throat from the imprint of two powerful thumbs. When he had been brought to see the body, it was actually frozen and it was therefore impossible to say how long she had been dead.

Inspector Sharrock gave evidence about the scene of the crime, which furnished no clues as to the identity of the attacker apart from the newspaper with Mr Sweetman's advertisement circled. He had made enquiries about the brandy bottle which it was thought had been brought by the murderer, but it was a very common type, on sale all over London. One of the jurors asked if it was known whether Mr Sweetman had purchased a bottle of brandy between leaving prison and the date on which his wife's body had been found, and Inspector Sharrock was obliged to admit that there was no evidence to suggest he had.

Mr Curtis was allowed to give evidence but said that he had not seen his aunt for many years and knew nothing of her associates. He said that his uncle was a kind and gentle man who had never been known to be violent and he did not believe him ever to have committed a crime. He added that he did have brandy in both his home and his surgery for medicinal purposes, but it was not the same kind of brandy as the bottle found at the scene of his aunt's death. His uncle never drank brandy; indeed, he had never seen him under the influence of alcohol.

The inquest jury had no difficulty in delivering a verdict of murder by some person or persons unknown.

'Of course I had heard rumours of how my aunt was found,' said Mr Curtis, dolefully, when Frances spoke to him afterwards, 'but to hear it in that detail, discussed so calmly … Naturally, in my profession one hears stories of all sorts of medical disasters, although fortunately I have not yet had any patient suffer injury through an anaesthetic, but when it is one's own aunt who is being spoken of, it is hard to listen to, very hard indeed. Do you have any clue as yet to who the murderer might be?'

'I am afraid not,' said Frances, 'although I feel sure that the police are not convinced that your uncle was responsible, so there is good hope for him. I have made progress in other areas, however, which might well lift the cloud of suspicion from him in the matter of the burglary.'

'If this lady can't solve the mystery no one can!' declared Mr Gillan, enthusiastically. 'And now, Mr Curtis, might I trouble you for an interview? I know the readers of the *Chronicle* would be very interested to hear about what a kind, sober and gentle soul your uncle is.'

'Oh, yes, by all means!' said Curtis, and Gillan grinned at his rivals before ushering Mr Curtis away. Frances only hoped that her meeting with Mr Matthew Gibson that afternoon would clear some of the dense mystery that surrounded Mrs Sweetman's latter years.

❦

Over a simple luncheon, Sarah told Frances that she had called again to see the Finn family servants, and had asked in a careful way about the songs sung to the children. It transpired that both Mary Ann and Mrs Finn like to sing, although Mrs Goswell professed to have no voice that anyone might care to hear. Teased into singing, Mrs Goswell amply demonstrated that she had no talent for the art, and there was much amusement. While they talked, Mary Ann came down to the kitchen to fetch a pudding for the children, and there was some light and pleasant talk about nursery songs.

'I think either Mary Ann learned the song off Mrs Finn or Mrs Finn learned it off Mary Ann,' said Sarah, 'but I didn't want to push it too much because if they suspected what I wanted to know they might have took fright.'

'What I am not sure of,' said Frances, 'since this is not an entertainment I am familiar with, is whether the song is well known, which would make it a matter of coincidence that Mary Ann sang it to the Finns' children, or whether it appeared only rarely, or if Mr Curtis was right and the only person ever to sing it was Mary Sweetman.'

'One of my brothers likes the music hall, at least I think he likes the girls and their costumes and doesn't take too much notice of what they do, but he doesn't know the song,' said Sarah. 'He said if it was sung all those years ago and didn't catch on then no one would remember it.'

'Someone did,' said Frances, 'but who?'

CHAPTER NINETEEN

Mr Matthew Gibson, who was a gentleman of modest but sufficient means, was staying at a small hotel just off Bayswater Road, where a faded though clean dining room served a simple tea. Frances asked to be shown to Mr Gibson's table, and found that she was expected and tea had already been ordered. The attendant, while assuming a practised expressionless demeanour, nevertheless allowed himself a sideways glance of frank curiosity, and Frances hoped that he had not assumed that she was there for a quite different kind of appointment. The room was mainly occupied by elderly ladies, either alone or in pairs, and one rather younger couple who sat in a corner facing away from the door as if they did not wish to be observed. A single gentleman who appeared to be above eighty years of age, rose from a table to greet her. His hair was perfectly white and rather long, as was his beard, and he was dressed in a suit of clothing that had long passed out of fashion, which made him look like a portrait of a great personage that should hang in a museum. This, Frances thought, must be his London attire, as he did not look at ease in it. Doubtless, when in Shoreham, he would dress as he pleased for comfort. He moved very slowly with the aid of a stick, but showing a game determination not to allow weak legs and stiff knees to impede him in anything he wished or was obliged to do.

'Miss Doughty,' he said, 'I am much obliged to you for agreeing to see me. Please be seated and we will have our tea, and I will tell you everything I can.'

London, he said, as the sandwiches and cakes arrived, was a necessity he preferred to endure as infrequently as possible. It was too noisy and the traffic too dense and the people impolite. He had a little property, however, not far from

Paddington Station, and it fetched a good rent, so he was obliged to keep it on. He sighed at the cruelty of a world that valued houses in uncongenial places.

'Tell me about your brother,' said Frances, once the tea was poured and the waiter had departed. 'Of course I never met him, but everyone who did has spoken very highly of him.'

'Yes, he had worked for Finn's for many years and was a model of diligence and reliability. It was so very like him to stay on late to ensure that his work was complete.' Mr Gibson raised his cup with a shaky but firm hand and sipped the near boiling liquid without blinking. 'After that terrible attack he was never the same man. He was forgetful, and sometimes flew into rages for no reason. His decline was terrible to watch. I took him to live with me and cared for him as best I could, but he died less than a year after the robbery. The only mercy was that he had no memory of the terrible thing that had happened to him.'

'And you believe that his attacker was Mr Sweetman?'

'I do, yes. Who else could it have been?'

'I have read the report of the trial, and when your brother gave evidence he said that the last thing he could recall that night was looking at his watch at half past eight and noting that his work would be complete in half an hour. Was there no other detail, however small, that he was able to remember later?'

Mr Gibson attempted a scone, which was unusually tough, and gave up. 'No, nothing else. There was something he kept trying to remember, but I don't know what it was; he kept saying that he had something of great importance to tell Mr Browne. But when I asked him what it was he couldn't say.'

'Mr Browne? The same man who said he had passed by the office that night? Were they very friendly?'

'Not especially.'

'And Mrs Sweetman visited your brother?'

'Yes, poor woman. It was as much a shock to her as anyone. I was so very sorry for her. The man she had loved and trusted with her happiness, the father of her children, had betrayed her most terribly. She could not even bear to see him. And of course, if Arthur had died then her husband would undoubtedly have hanged.'

'And she never for one moment thought he might be innocent?'

'Only in the first moments after hearing of his arrest. The police had come to the office and taken him away, and the managers, out of kindness, went to see her to tell her what had happened, rather than have the police come to her door. At first she had wanted to defend his good name, as a wife should, she even offered to give him an alibi for the time of the robbery, in case his sister was not believed, although she knew that he had been away from home that night. But then they told her about other things he had done.' Gibson spooned jam onto a slice of sponge cake and manoeuvred it past his beard. 'She wouldn't tell me all the details. She said the company had suffered enough without more scandal.'

Frances examined a scone, which appeared to be a day old, and resisted the temptation to test it by tapping it on the plate. At least the tea was fresh and hot. 'Who were these "managers"?' she queried.

'She didn't tell me their names. Mr Finn must have been one of them, I suppose. She felt sorry for him, as he was a very good-mannered and considerate gentleman.'

'Was it ever suggested,' Frances ventured, 'that Mr Sweetman had been taking money from the company?'

'Not only suggested, but proved beyond doubt,' asserted Gibson. 'They found the proof after his arrest, but it had to be kept secret or the company's reputation would suffer. It was bad enough that they had harboured a criminal, they did not want to be seen as negligent. Did you know of Sweetman's financial hardships? After his arrest some evil individual began plaguing his unfortunate wife for payment of debts the size of which she had never suspected.'

'Yes, he was in need of money, he has freely admitted that to me, for his sister's care and his nephew's education, and he had unwisely borrowed from a moneylender,' said Frances. 'The police assumed that he stole the money to repay his debts, but if the lender continued to apply to Mrs Sweetman then this cannot have been the case. But I am not at all sure that it was Mr Sweetman who stole money from the company.'

'It was his business alone to write in the books, and he had the key to the safe,' said Mr Gibson, as if that put the matter beyond doubt. Frances saw that she was unlikely to sway him from his well-entrenched opinion of her client.

'The thing that I wish to know is why Mrs Sweetman refused to see her husband again,' said Frances. 'She thought him a robber, and a desperate man who had committed violence to escape detection, but many wives will forgive anything up to and including murder.'

Gibson stirred his tea thoughtfully. 'If it had been only that, she might have found it in her heart to forgive him,' he said, 'but, as you have guessed, there was more. Much more. As you have correctly deduced, Mr Sweetman did not steal to pay his debts. Neither did he steal to help his sister or his nephew. No, he had formed a wicked plan to abandon his family, his wife and his children, and leave them all to starve; he needed the money to make his escape and start a new life.'

'I can scarcely credit that,' said Frances, wondering if they were even talking about the same man.

'Neither could his poor wife at first. But it was true.'

'You are sure the lady you spoke to was Mrs Sweetman? You had met her before?'

'Yes, once before the robbery, in the company of her husband.'

'But how did she learn of this plan?'

'After his arrest a friend told her all the story.'

'What friend was this?'

'She wouldn't tell me the name.'

'Surely,' said Frances, 'however much she trusted the friend, she would still have gone to her husband and confronted him with such a terrible accusation?'

'Yes, that was her intention, but then –' he glanced at her, studied her.

'I know I am young, but I have seen a great deal. You must tell me everything.'

He dropped, almost threw, his teaspoon in the saucer with a clatter. It was a gesture of disgust. 'There was a young woman. A pretty young thing, barely twenty, and soon to become a mother. She went to see Mrs Sweetman and there was an interview of a most painful nature. She said that on some of the evenings when Sweetman was supposed to have been at the bedside of his sister he had been in her company instead, and her situation was the result of their connection. He had professed himself to be in love with her, said that he could not be happy with any other. He wanted to go away with her so they could live together as husband and wife, but, without funds, it was impossible. He said he had a plan to obtain the money. He actually told her that he no longer cared for his wife or what became of her and the children. That is not an address to which any honest woman should have listened. And her story was not only words, she brought proof, letters in Sweetman's own hand, blotted with his tears. Now you see the kind of man you are trying to help. But he is cunning and can put on the face of innocence.' Gibson pushed his cup and plate away. He had no more appetite.

'What was the name of this woman?' asked Frances.

'I'm afraid I don't know.'

'Did you see Mrs Sweetman after her husband's trial? Did you ever discover how she lived and where?'

'I only saw her once more, a few weeks after the trial and she was in a bad way. She said her children had found employment, and she was no longer being troubled for her husband's debts, but she could barely support herself. A gentleman had offered to be her protector, and she thought … well, I suppose there was no other course for her. She wanted to stay in London to be near the children. I was unable to do anything for her; I had my brother to care for. We must all look to our own first. That is what Mr Sweetman should have done.'

Mr Gibson's repugnance and Mrs Sweetman's sense of betrayal were all too apparent, but Frances knew better than to equate the strength with which a belief was held with the probability of its being correct. Neither did she think that she had unequivocally established her client's innocence, and it might still transpire that it was she who was the dupe. Although she believed that an act of fraud had been committed and Sweetman made the scapegoat and removed from the scene when it looked as though it was about to be discovered, there was not one shred of proof for this theory. All the accusations, deductions and insinuations in the world would not help her.

❧

Frances decided to do what Mrs Sweetman ought to have done; call on Mr Sweetman and confront him with the accusation of infidelity. She was saddened to see by his expression when she came to his cell door that he anticipated that she had arrived bearing good news. Instead, she was obliged to tell him the outcome of her meeting with Matthew Gibson. His reaction was utter bewilderment, and he made her repeat the story more than once as he seemed unable to grasp it the first time.

'Is there any foundation at all in this allegation?' asked Frances.

'None whatsoever. Are you sure that I was not being confused with another person?'

'I don't believe so.'

'The only thing I can think of is that the young woman who went to see Susan must have been suffering from a delusion.'

'Can you suggest who she might have been? Was there at the time someone of your acquaintance who meets that description? Young, pretty and about to become a mother?'

He shook his head. 'No, I can think of no one. But why would a stranger come to Susan and say such a thing of me?'

'She was said to have brought proof – letters.'

'Letters? I wrote no private letters to any woman other than my sister. Oh my poor dear Susan, she was such a simple trusting soul! What pain she must have felt!'

'Mr Sweetman, I believe that you were accused of the robbery because you were about to uncover evidence that another man had embezzled money from the company. Mr Matthew Gibson told me that your wife was considering giving you an alibi if you needed one, and was only dissuaded when she was led to believe that you had betrayed her with another.'

'But – I don't understand – who could be so cruel?'

'I think it was the late Mr Whibley. He had the skill and the knowledge to do it. The young woman might have been a relative of his or a mistress.'

'But he was a friend of mine! He told the police he thought I was innocent! He told me he suspected Minster of the robbery!' Sweetman put his head in his hands and groaned. 'But if this is true how can any of it be proved? I am a dead man, Miss Doughty, or I might as well be.' He sat up and a strange calm settled over him. 'The magistrates will consider my case next week, and I will be at the Old Bailey this spring, and then they will hang me and that will be an end to my troubles. Then at least I can see Susan again and tell her that I never stopped loving her and was never untrue.' He gave a sudden smile. 'So perhaps I may be content at last.'

CHAPTER TWENTY

That evening Frances was to appear at Westbourne Hall in the Grove to address the ladies of the Bayswater Women's Suffrage Society. The subject she had selected was how every woman could be her own detective in the home. Ladies had already learned how to be nurses and doctors and teachers and cooks and accountants and needlewomen and musicians and just about everything else in the home, so the only profession that seemed to remain unconquered on the domestic hearth was that of detective. Frances often wondered why women, supposedly the weaker sex, were expected to be several things at once while men were only ever directed towards a single profession. The subject might appear be a difficult one on which to give useful instruction, although fortunately she knew that most of her audience would only be there to sit in the warm and enjoy tea and bread and butter and cake, and not in order to learn how to be a detective.

Many of the ladies in the society were concerned about dishonest servants, but Frances was well aware that some of her audience were of the servant class themselves, and would take offence at the assumption that they were not to be trusted and should be under close observation. She decided therefore to talk about vigilance in general. Most puzzles, Frances knew, were of a mundane and everyday nature, but the secret was to be alert to the possibilities of what might occur before it did. This was not only in regard to actual criminal behaviour, such as theft of valuables or household supplies, but vigilance on all matters relevant to the good management of the home; the possibility of waste, and signs of approaching illness or of unspoken discontent. Detection, Frances told her audience, was not only about finding thieves, but about living a better and more useful life.

Miss Gilbert and Miss John naturally applauded Frances with great energy and enthusiasm, and the rest of the audience followed suit, some of them having to be elbowed into wakefulness to do so. The talking over, there was a noisy outbreak of conversation, and tea flowed in abundance, a near magical fluid without which Frances was sure she could not think as clearly as she did. It was good, too, she thought, to see that some of her listeners were men, who, as long as they were sincere supporters of the society and its principles, were welcome to attend provided they behaved themselves decently. Not all the women members approved of permitting men at the meetings, and some, Frances felt sure, had every reason to want to avoid the company of men altogether, but Miss Gilbert had pointed out that since men currently wielded legislative power it was only by convincing them of the cause of female emancipation that victory might be won.

Sarah was as usual attending to the business of ensuring order, and casting a suspicious eye on anyone – male or female – who looked as though they had come not to listen but disrupt the meeting. Many women did not want the vote and some had actually spoken out deriding their strident sisters, but Frances had observed that those ladies who lacked the determination to fight for the right to have some say over their own lives were the ones least likely to do anything adventurous to prevent others from doing so. That evening there were two men in particular who Sarah thought should be closely observed. Both were strangers, and there was something in their demeanour which suggested that they were there on some business of their own and not in order to listen to the speakers, none of whom they applauded. They spent the entire meeting lurking at the back of the hall, occasionally indulging in whispered conversation.

'I don't like the look of them two,' said Sarah, 'not that they've caused any trouble, but they need watching.'

'Press, perhaps?' suggested Frances. The two individuals, both in their twenties, were clad in rough greatcoats and boots, with hats that sat rather too low over their eyes. One was a thin lanky figure with a soiled scarf twisted round a scrawny neck, and a tangle of long yellow hair, the other shorter and broader, exhibiting a bristly black unkempt moustache.

'They didn't write anything down or draw any pictures. Looking for something to steal more like,' said Sarah.

Despite the temptation of ladies' reticules and pockets, however, the men did nothing but look about them, and eventually they left the hall together.

The night was warm under a blanket of cloud that did not threaten rain, and the sharp breeze had dropped, so Frances and Sarah walked home arm-in-arm like sisters and talked about what the world would be like when women had the vote. Sarah thought an experiment should be tried where things were turned about and only women should be able to vote and be in parliament, and then the men would find out what it was like to have no say in things. Frances thought that this might not be entirely fair although it would be amusing to try it out for a while.

They were walking along the narrow passage that linked Newton Road with Kildare Gardens, a quiet and respectable location, when they heard footsteps behind them. This was not entirely unexpected, as the way was very much used, but both women felt that the steps were hurrying a little more than was normal. They glanced at each other, stopped, turned around and found themselves facing the two suspicious-looking loiterers they had observed at the meeting. Had the men been going about some honest business they would have tipped their hats and continued on their way, but instead, they too stopped. The lane was not well lit, and a distant gas lamp provided only a sickly glow, but it was enough to see that their expressions were neither friendly nor respectful.

'What is it you want, gentlemen?' asked Frances.

'You were at Westbourne Hall just now,' said Moustache.

'I was, yes, but if you wish to discuss my lecture this is not the best time and place.'

He smiled. 'No, I just had something for you, that's all.' One hand had been behind his back, and he now brought it forward with something white clutched in it. For a moment, Frances thought it was a paper, then she saw that it was a handkerchief and before she could ask what he was about, he suddenly darted towards her and pressed it over her face.

She at once recognised the sweet, pungent, stinging smell of chloroform. She coughed and held her breath, turning her head to one side, reaching up and grasping his wrist with both hands, backing away and pulling the cloth as far from her face as she could. This was not the reaction he had expected and there was something of a struggle. He grunted hard, grasped her shoulder with his other hand, and used his weight and strength to push her against a wall, all the time trying to force the cloth over her nose, but with her head turned away he was in some difficulty. He was panting hard and there was the reek of bad teeth and tobacco from his open mouth.

Frances used the last of her breath to give a loud scream for help, then kicked her attacker's shins as hard as her skirts would allow. She tried to wriggle away from him, but he grabbed a handful of her hair, put his legs one on either side of her, slammed her back violently against the wall and tried to pull her head around. The solidity of his body and the pressure of his thighs appalled and disgusted her. Frances held her breath, hung determinedly onto his wrist – digging her fingers hard into his flesh – and tried to push her elbows into his chest. He cursed in frustration. How long the tussle might have lasted had she been alone it was impossible to say, how long her strength would have held out against his she did not know, but the loathsome weight of his body against her was suddenly released as he was seized from behind and dragged away by Sarah.

Frances gasped for breath, shaking at the brutality of the attack and fury at the insult. No man had ever touched her like that before, and while she knew that most were far stronger than she, it was frightening to realise that even a man not as tall as herself was endowed with a muscular power far superior to her own. Had he chosen to do so he might easily have struck her with his fists and dazed her into submission.

The force of being wrenched aside had caused Moustache to trip over his own feet, and he went sprawling onto the ground, but quickly scrambled up again. He looked around quickly for his companion, and saw the lanky man stretched out on the path groaning, with blood streaming from his nose.

Astonished at the two women's apparent immunity to chloroform, and with the uncomfortable knowledge that the odds had suddenly turned to his disadvantage, Moustache, with rather less confidence than before, held out the cloth towards Sarah's face. She balled her fists. 'Try it and you're a dead man!' she roared. He then did the first sensible thing he had done that evening, which was to turn on his heels and run away.

Sarah at once went to Frances' side. 'He's not hurt you, has he, 'cause if he has, I'll find him and I'll break him.'

'I am unhurt,' Frances quickly reassured her, 'which is more than one can say for this other fellow.' Sarah watched Frances carefully as her breathing slowed to something approaching normal, concerned that she was about to collapse with fright and waiting to catch her if she did. Frances took out a clean handkerchief and wiped her face in case any of the chloroform should have touched her skin, and found that her hands were still trembling. She attempted an encouraging smile.

Lanky was choking on his own blood and trying to sit up. He rolled over and got onto his hands and knees, moaning, then tried to stand, but Sarah went over to him and casually kicked him on the rear of his anatomy and he made a strange gurgling sound and fell forward.

'Who are they?' asked Sarah. 'I've never seen 'em at the Hall before.'

'Nor I,' said Frances, who was beginning to recover her calm, 'but whoever they are I can say two things about them for certain, they are not supporters of women's suffrage, and have clearly never read Dr John Snow's excellent volume *On Chloroform and Other Anaesthetics*.'

Ever since the introduction of chloroform as a surgical anaesthetic, the newspapers had published stories concerning supposedly respectable gentlemen, who had been discovered in infamous houses in a state of undress and in the company of women to whom they were not married, and their explanation was always that they had been chloroformed and carried there against their will. These stories were invariably exposed as nonsense by doctors, but despite this, the public as a whole had somehow acquired the wholly erroneous impression that it was possible to render an unwilling victim unconscious with a chloroformed pad in a matter of seconds instead of the substantially longer time actually required. Dr Snow, who had administered chloroform to Queen Victoria during the birth of her two youngest children, and was the pre-eminent expert on the subject, had recounted several stories of attempts to chloroform victims for the purpose of robbery or worse offences, which had failed because of that misunderstanding and resulted instead in the apprehension of the criminal.

There was the sound of running footsteps coming towards them and they looked up quickly in case this was the warning of a new threat, but the dim glow soon revealed the shape of a uniformed policeman, and as he came closer they recognised the shiny face of Constable Mayberry. 'Why, it's Miss Doughty and Miss Smith!' he exclaimed. 'I was on point and heard you call, so I came as soon as I could. Can I be of assistance?'

'You certainly can,' said Frances. 'We have been violently attacked by this man.' She pointed to the miserable object lying face down on the pathway in a pool of his own blood.

'Oh my word!' said Mayberry.

'And also his associate who has now run away. We must take the miscreant to Paddington Green at once.'

'Certainly, Miss,' said Mayberry. 'In fact,' he added, 'Inspector Sharrock says I'm to do what you say at all times.'

'Inspector Sharrock is learning,' said Frances.

'He says it's for your own safety,' he added, pulling the lanky fellow to his feet. 'Now then sir, you're to come with me!'

'If he tries to get away he won't go far,' said Sarah, grabbing the prisoner's other arm.

A small sponge lay on the path, which Frances deduced was the item with which Lanky had tried to attack Sarah. She picked it up and followed Sarah and Mayberry as they marched their captive, who showed no resistance and was somewhat shaky on his legs, to a better-populated street. A cab was procured and they all boarded it.

Frances knew that after they reached the police station she might have no opportunity to question the man, and determined to do so before he was bundled away into a cell. 'Now then,' she said, 'what do you mean by trying to kill us?'

'We weren't trying to kill you,' he spluttered. 'We was told not to hurt you.'

'No? Well you've a very strange way of going about not hurting us.'

'No hitting; we weren't to leave any marks, those were the orders, just the chloroform, that's all. So you'd go to sleep.'

'And who told you to do this?' she demanded.

'I don't know. It was a man, and we didn't see his face. He paid us and gave us the bottle.' He dug in his pocket and produced a bottle of chloroform. Mayberry took it into his possession, and Frances handed him the sponge.

'So your mission was to make us sleep and then what were you to do?' Frances was suddenly struck with a greater horror, and shuddered. 'Oh how vile!'

'No, no, really,' Lanky protested, 'we weren't to do any violence to you, not of any kind, we just had to carry you somewhere – a house – where there were other women – and they were to adjust your dress, and then we had to make sure that you were found there by a press-man.'

Frances understood. 'So this was not an attempt either on my life or my virtue. The object was to destroy my reputation.'

'I can punch him again,' said Sarah. 'The constable can always look the other way.'

Mayberry looked alarmed. 'No, leave him,' said Frances, 'or he'll never be able to tell his story to the Inspector.'

They reached Paddington Green with their cowed prisoner showing no inclination to attempt an escape, and Mayberry and Sarah between them brought him to the front desk where the sergeant looked up from his record book. 'Well, what have we got here?'

'He tried to chloroform me and send me for a hoor!' said Sarah, bluntly.

'I'll notify the asylum at once,' said the sergeant. 'Bring him through.'

Inspector Sharrock was out on another case, so they waited for his return, and Sarah told Mayberry to bring a cup of water.

'It's a nasty shock when a man lays hold of you like that for the first time,' said Sarah, as Frances gratefully gulped the water. 'You never ever want it to happen again.' She patted Frances' hand.

'I am getting close to the truth,' said Frances, 'that much is clear, though I am not yet sure what it is. The man who set those creatures onto us may have known nothing about the proper use of anaesthetics, but he was otherwise clever and subtle. He knew that if he had murdered us that would have told the police that my suspicions should be pursued with vigour. By taking away my reputation, however, no accusation I make will ever be regarded seriously.'

When Sharrock arrived, he stopped and rolled his eyes despairingly when he saw the two women waiting for him, then, after a brief word with the sergeant and a glance at the new prisoner in the cells, he called Frances and Sarah in to his office. 'Do you know that fellow?' he asked.

'No, I think he is just a hireling,' said Frances. 'I do not know who my real enemy is.'

'You see, Miss Doughty,' said Sharrock, heavily, 'this is the very thing I have been warning you about. You could have made a dozen enemies or more, what with all your goings-on, and they might try it again. Chloroform, nasty stuff,' he said, looking at the bottle and sponge on his desk. 'You don't seem to be marked by it, are you sure that's what it was?'

'It was unmistakable,' said Frances. 'Try it for yourself. I think there may still be the scent of it on the sponge.'

'Well *I've* no intention of sniffing it,' said Sharrock, with a short laugh.

'Such a small trace will do you no harm,' she reassured him.

'Hmmm,' said Sharrock, dubiously, 'but if it was chloroform, why didn't it work?'

'Our attackers had assumed incorrectly that we would fall unconscious in moments, so they took no steps to prevent us resisting them. And the remainder of their unsavoury plot could never have succeeded. They no doubt imagined that we would be soundly asleep for as long as it took to remove us to some low establishment, but the effects of chloroform last for only a minute or two if not re-applied.'

'Now I know that can't be right,' said Sharrock. 'There was a jeweller's shop robbed only the other day and the assistant said he was chloroformed almost before he knew it and didn't wake up for an hour.'

'Then he is lying,' said Frances. 'I suggest you interview him again as he is obviously in league with the robbers.'

'Oh!' exclaimed Sharrock, taken aback. 'Well, perhaps I better had. In the meantime, I suppose it is too much to hope that you might give up this kind of life? There are lady clerks nowadays; that kind of work might suit you. You might meet a nice gentleman clerk.'

'The profession of clerk is not without its dangers, as Mr Gibson learned,' Frances pointed out to the Inspector, 'and I sometimes think that the role of wife is the hardest and most dangerous of all.'

🌺

Frances and Sarah took a cab home, Sarah with an expression more than usually grim. 'Now then,' she said, 'I'll not hear you say no, because you've had a bad shock – you're to have hot cocoa with a double dose of brandy and then straight to bed. No detective work, no letters, no newspapers, no reading about Miss Dauntless. And a big plateful of fried ham and eggs for breakfast tomorrow.'

'It sounds wonderful,' said Frances.

Tom was waiting for them in the hallway. 'It's late,' snapped Sarah, 'can't this wait?'

'Oh it can wait all right,' said Tom, 'but only if you don't mind not knowing straight away who Mr Sanitas is.'

'Come up,' said Frances. 'Sarah is making cocoa.'

Sarah stamped off resignedly to the kitchen, and Frances and Tom went up to the apartment where Frances compared the original of the Sanitas letter with a scribbled note with an enquiry to a grocer about the availability of best dried peaches. 'You're right, Tom! We have our man!' she exclaimed.

'An' it's a gent you already know,' said Tom with a grin.

CHAPTER TWENTY-ONE

The following morning, after receiving a report from Tom that Mr Finn had departed for his office, and Mrs Finn and Mary Ann were out strolling with the children, Frances called at Hereford Road and asked to see Mr Yeldon.

'Is he expecting you, Miss?' asked the housemaid, who was the identical young person Alice Finn had entrusted to carry her private messages.

'He is not,' said Frances, presenting her card, 'but he will know my name. Please give him this and tell him it is a matter of considerable importance.'

'Please come in and wait in the parlour and I will tell him that you are here.'

Frances, after hearing Sarah's favourable reports, was interested to see the interior of the house, and saw that it was a home decorated and furnished in good taste, neither ostentatious nor austere, and meant for the comfort and ease of its occupants. It was a minute or two before the maid returned alone and with a troubled expression. She was still holding the card.

'I am very sorry Miss Doughty,' she said hesitantly, 'but I was mistaken just now in believing that Mr Yeldon was here. I am afraid he is not at home.'

'Did he tell you that himself?' asked Frances who knew very well that Yeldon was in the house.

'He said –' the maid went a little pink about the face.

'Very well,' said Frances, gently, 'I am not blaming you. Please go and speak to him again, and tell him that I am being very difficult; that I am refusing to go away and insisting that he is here.'

The maid hurried away and returned rather more slowly. 'Mr Yeldon still says that he is not here, and that he might be out all day, and even if he does come back today he will be too busy to see anyone, and after that he will be going away.'

'Ah yes,' said Frances, 'the trip to Bath for Mr Finn to take the waters. When will they be going?'

'Next Monday.' She paused. 'So Mr Yeldon says.'

'But in actuality?' asked Frances.

'*I* think they're really going on Friday afternoon.' They exchanged conspiratorial smiles. Frances sensed that the maid did not care a great deal for Mr Yeldon.

'Wonderful,' said Frances. 'Such strenuous efforts to avoid speaking to me. Where is he now?'

'He is not in the house at all, Miss, and most especially he is not in master's dressing room,' added the girl, mischievously.

'I understand,' said Frances. 'And you have been a good girl not to reveal any information to me. I will go up at once.'

She mounted the stairs and arrived on the landing in time to see Mr Yeldon emerge into the upper hallway. He was clearly startled, and glared at her angrily. He might have been dyeing his beard, since its curled margins were an even more unnatural red than before. 'What are you doing here?' he demanded. 'Has that girl let you in?'

'It is entirely my fault,' said Frances. 'I am a detective as you know, and therefore an ill-mannered person. It is my profession to enter places where I am not wanted.'

'You will leave this house at once!' he exclaimed.

'I will not do so until I have spoken to you, Mr Yeldon,' said Frances. 'Or should I perhaps be addressing you by another name?'

'I don't know what you mean!' he said but his eyes flashed with sudden shock; she knew that her words had found their mark.

'I will not argue with you, since I have proof,' she replied.

'What proof is this?' he retorted. 'You are lying, I do not believe there is any!'

'The letter you wrote to the *Chronicle* under the name of Sanitas; I have the original and also a sample of your handwriting. I have compared them and they are the same.'

He was silent for a time, making a determined effort to calm himself, while lost in thought. 'Very well,' he said at last, 'we will discuss this if you must, but I consider it to be a trivial matter. Let us go down to the parlour, it would not do at all to be talking here.'

'Or we might meet in Mr Finn's study?' suggested Frances.

'Out of the question,' said Yeldon, rather too abruptly, and ushered her downstairs.

Mr Yeldon showed none of the politeness Frances might have expected, not even suggesting she take a seat, which would have been usual for a lady visitor but not, Frances supposed, for someone who he regarded as an intruder. She could easily manage without courtesy if by so doing it brought her closer to the truth. They stood facing each other, he with arms folded close to his body.

'Do you admit that you wrote the Sanitas letter?' asked Frances.

'Very well, what if I did?' he said defiantly.

'You should know that I am acting in the interests of Dr Adair who is a believer in the Banting diet, Mr Rustrum of the Pure Food Society and Mr Lathwal of the Bayswater Vegetarian Society. These three gentlemen have been put to some trouble and distress over your letter. Many people have been whispering that it is Dr Adair himself who is the author, and I must point out that there are sentiments expressed in it which both Mr Rustrum and Mr Lathwal were very offended by and which could, were they so inclined, form the basis of an action for libel.'

'I only said what I thought and what I believe to be true!' Yeldon protested. 'That cannot be libel.'

'It can if it is untrue and damaging,' Frances told him. 'However, the gentlemen are prepared to avoid any legal action on the strict understanding that you will not write such letters again. May I give them that assurance?'

'Is that all you require?' he said, with evident relief. 'You may tell them that I have no intention of addressing the question again. In any case, the newspapers have dropped the subject and moved on to other matters.'

'My clients have been kind enough not to ask for an open letter of apology for publication in the newspapers, and I think that that is as well, as it would only bring the dispute before the public eye once more.'

'I was not about to offer such a thing,' said Yeldon, testily, 'and I stand by what I wrote.'

'You are not a medical man and your opinion on such issues can have little importance,' said Frances, 'but by signing yourself with a pseudonym you left it open to speculation that you were in fact a doctor of medicine. Many people who followed a perfectly safe dietary regime were made unnecessarily anxious and upset.'

He looked unrepentant and Frances sensed that he was about to dismiss her, so she spoke again before he had the opportunity. 'I assume,' she said, 'that your motive in writing the letter was to support the contention of Mr Finn that his weight is not deleterious to his health and offer some reasons to dissuade him from what might be considered dangerous diets.'

'My motives are my own and I need not comment on them,' said Yeldon, stiffly. 'And now I think our interview is over.'

'I showed the letter to Mr Finn and he claimed not to recognise the hand,' said Frances.

'I am his valet and not his secretary,' said Yeldon. 'There is no reason for him to know my hand.'

'But you ought to know that he disassociated himself from the harsher expressions in the letter.'

Yeldon had half turned away and been about to make for the door, but he stopped, and faced her again. 'Yes, I recall him reading it in the newspapers and he commented as much at the time.' An expression of concern crossed his face. 'Miss Doughty, is it your intention to reveal to your clients that I am the author of the letter?'

'I think it would be best for everyone if I did not,' said Frances. 'If I simply advise them that you regret writing it and will not write another that should be sufficient.'

He nodded. 'Feel free to say so if that will put an end to the matter.'

There was nothing more to be said and they made a frosty parting.

The case closed, Frances decided to pay a visit to Mr Rustrum to impart the news. She might have done so by letter, but she was curious to question him on what advice he had been giving Mr Finn. On calling at his home, however, she found that he had just departed on another lecture tour and was not expected back for a month. She left a note for him and returned home, where she wrote to Dr Adair and Mr Lathwal to advise them of her success and her final fee. She had just completed this when she received an unexpected visitor, Mrs Minster, her garments still reeking of the tobacco and beer and bad pies that were the permanent fragrance of the Cooper's Arms.

Mrs Minster was a coarse-featured woman who might have been any age between thirty and forty. If she had ever been fresh and beautiful, and that was by no means an impossibility, it was no longer apparent. Time and Mr Minster and the Cooper's Arms had seen to that. She sat across the little table, and clasped her thick-fingered hands.

'I suppose when you saw my husband he showed you my grandfather's will?' she said.

'Yes, he did,' said Frances.

Mrs Minster gave a short, mirthless laugh. 'He shows everyone that if they ask him where he got the money from. And people believe it. But then people do. Tell them things, and they believe you. Only look angry or sad, and make them feel something, that's all it needs. Show them a paper, and of course, if it's written down then it has to be true, gospel if it's signed. And if the news is very good or very bad, then so much the better, they'll believe it all the more. People are such fools. Even you, Miss Doughty.'

'What are you saying, Mrs Minster?' asked Frances, evenly.

'Only that there wasn't any will,' she sneered. 'There was never a will. It was all a job, and I don't know how he fixed it but he did. My grandfather didn't make a will because he had nothing to leave except a few sticks of furniture that weren't worth anything and some unpaid rent.'

'Where did your husband get the money to go into his new business?' asked Frances. 'It was two hundred pounds – two years' salary. Did he rob the office of J. Finn Insurance?'

She shrugged. 'I don't know. He goes where he wants and does what he wants. He doesn't tell me anything and I don't take much mind of what he gets up to. The less I see of him the better.'

'What you appear to be saying,' said Frances, 'is that the will your husband showed me is a forgery designed to divert suspicion from the fact that he might have got the money by some dishonest means. Do you want me to report this to the police?'

'Do what you like,' she said sullenly.

'If I did, they would want to speak to you about it, and they would ask, as I am doing now, why you have said nothing before.'

'Well, it's obvious, isn't it?' she said, aggressively. 'What else could I do except stay quiet? It was that or the streets. I could have done *that* once, but I never had the courage. And every time I thought to leave him, I got in the family way. I had five and they all died.'

'But why are you telling me this now?'

She uttered a long, miserable sigh. 'Because *I* was a fool, too. A stupid trusting fool! He said that if I told on him and he went to prison then the government would come and take away everything we had worked for, and I'd starve. Well I knew it was true because when Mr Sweetman went to prison all his things were taken away, so I believed it.'

'That was the law once, but it was changed long ago,' said Frances.

'I know that *now*. I read something in the paper that made me think and I asked people, and that was how I found out.'

'The thing is,' said Frances, thoughtfully, 'it will be simple enough to prove that your grandfather never left a will, that can be checked, which will mean of course that the document in your husband's possession must be a forgery. But it is a will in your name, not his. Although anything you inherited before 1870 became your husband's property there is no way of proving that he had any hand in the forgery. He might claim to know nothing of it and blame it all on you.'

Frances recalled Mr Minster's comments on Whibley's expertise with wills. 'And if the forger was the late Mr Whibley, which seems very probable, he can say nothing about who employed his services or why. Do you have any more information which might help me?'

Mrs Minster thought for a moment and shook her head.

Frances felt as though she was being confronted with an enormous jigsaw puzzle. There were hundreds of pieces, and she was sure they would fit together to make a picture, but as yet she did not know how they fitted, or what the final picture might be. The one thing of which she felt sure was that a great many pieces were still missing. 'When your husband told the police that he had been walking down Westbourne Grove on the night of the robbery and saw a light on in the office at half past nine, was he telling the truth?'

'I don't know.'

'Do you remember what he was doing that night?'

'That was years ago, of course I don't!'

'Mrs Minster, I believe what you have just told me is very helpful, nevertheless, if I was to pursue it without any other proof than your claim that your husband is to blame it might have serious repercussions on you. All I can do at present is to gather further information to make a good case.'

Mrs Minster considered this and then nodded. 'All right. I've said what I had to say and you can do what you like with it.' She departed in very ill-humour.

❧

Frances spent the remainder of the afternoon in an appointment with three new clients, who arrived together. None of them, thankfully, wished to engage her in cases of murder, libel, faithless lovers or missing pets. All were members of the Bayswater Ladies' Suffrage Society and all said they were being followed by a man. He had neither approached nor spoken to them and seemed to offer no threat, but what had been a vaguely uncomfort- able feeling had, since Frances' admonitions on the subject of vigilance, become a sense of alarm that was quickly amounting to terror. The ladies had exchanged information on the subject and they were now all convinced that they were being followed by the same man and not three different ones. Frances received the impression that they would have preferred to have had one follower each, rather than a nuisance who diluted his attentions in a way that was almost insulting.

As she finalised her arrangements to deal with the matter there were two more visitors who were wholly unexpected – Mr Edward Curtis and his uncle Hubert Sweetman, who had just been released from the cells without charge.

Mr Sweetman looked tired and relieved and Mr Curtis thanked Frances rather more warmly than she felt she deserved. There was much shaking of hands, and Mr Curtis even shed a happy tear, a display for which his uncle seemed to have insufficient energy.

There was so much emotion in the air that Frances sent Sarah to make some tea. Mr Curtis had brought a box of dainty cakes and even a posy of flowers, which made the table with its plain cloth look very pretty. They settled to an impromptu party that Frances thought was quite deliberately not taking place at Mr Curtis' home, probably because of the disapproval of Mrs Curtis.

'We are so very grateful to you, Miss Doughty,' said Mr Sweetman. 'I know that the murderer has yet to be apprehended, and of course that may not even be possible given the fact that no one saw him go to Susan's home or come away, but at least the law has now taken the view that there is really no case against me.'

'That has been my contention from the start,' said Frances, 'not only from the lack of any evidence but also from my observation of your character. I do not believe you are a violent man, Mr Sweetman.'

'Inspector Sharrock had to do his duty of course,' said Curtis, 'we do understand that, but I noticed that once the courts had decided not to proceed he showed no sign of resentment or frustration — no indication that he disagreed with their conclusion. And I believe, Miss Doughty, that it was you who influenced him in that direction.'

'Oh you are far too kind,' she replied modestly.

'He mentioned you most particularly, not perhaps in the most gentlemanly manner, but his implications were clear to me.' He beamed at Frances, and Sarah poured more tea as if the pot was a weapon. 'I ask only one thing. Please tell no one for the present that my uncle has been released. I appreciate that the press will hear of it soon enough, but if he can have just a few quiet days of rest before they do, it would be a blessing. He will not be going back to his old lodgings of course, I have found other suitable accommodation, but you may always write to him at my address.'

'I entirely understand,' said Frances, 'and will not communicate the news until you give your approval. But I must ask, in view of this favourable outcome, what you now require me to do. When we first spoke at Paddington Green you asked me to help, and I agreed to try to discover your aunt's murderer. Of course, at the time our most pressing concern was the accusation against Mr Sweetman. Now that this is resolved, can you both advise me how you wish me to proceed? I have already uncovered some material that suggests that the conviction in 1866 was unsound. I have also been following clues that I hope may eventually lead me to discovering Benjamin and Mary. If I do, they might have information about Mrs Sweetman's more recent associates. It will not, I fear, be an easy task or one that can be accomplished quickly, but I will pursue it if requested.'

Sweetman gave a weak smile. 'It seems like an age since I first sat here and asked you to find my family,' he said. 'Please do go on, I miss my children so very much. Why they did not appear at Susan's inquest and funeral, I don't know. I fear, I very much fear, that if they are still alive they may be in some terrible situation, a prison or worse. I can understand that they might not want to see me, and there is nothing I can do about that, but that is no reason why they should have failed to pay their respects to their own mother. If you find them, please tell them that I shall always care for them, no matter what they may have done or the circumstances of their lives.'

'I promise I shall,' said Frances.

'I think if you could make that your first concern,' said Mr Curtis. 'Now that my uncle is no longer suspected of murder the police will, I hope, be making their own enquiries into that terrible business. And the Inspector did tell me that he was worried that your involvement had placed you in some danger. I would not want to see any harm befall you.'

'And as to the robbery,' said Sweetman with a sigh, 'even if you were to exonerate me, how would that give me back my lost years?'

'If Benjamin and Mary were to find that you were innocent after all, it might bring them back to you,' said Frances. 'You mentioned that Mr Whibley thought that Mr Minster might have been the robber. Did he have any evidence, or was this merely supposition?'

'No, there was no evidence, or at least none that he mentioned to me. I think it was only because Minster seemed like the type to do such a thing. Whibley asked me if Minster had ever borrowed my keys and I said he hadn't, and we both agreed that none of us three keyholders had ever let them out of our sight. Minster had never been to my house.'

'Who, out of the people who worked at J. Finn Insurance, had ever been to your house?' asked Frances, wondering if a seemingly innocuous call had provided someone with the opportunity to make an impression of Mr Sweetman's keys.

'Well, Mr Gibson was there about a week before the robbery. That's when I think he may have dropped his pocket book. I never did discover how it came to be in the drawer.'

'Yes, I had forgotten about the pocket book,' said Frances. 'What about after the robbery and before your arrest? Were there any callers then?'

'Only that one visit from Whibley, when we talked about Minster.'

'Ah,' said Frances. 'I had been under the impression that the discussion you have just described, the one about Mr Minster, took place at the office.'

'No, it was at the house. The day after the robbery.'

'Did any of your other colleagues call on you during that week?'

'No, he was the only one.'

Whibley, Frances recalled, had been the first man on the premises the next morning and discovered the injured Arthur Gibson. How easy it would have been for him to take the book from the unconscious man's pocket, and later hide it in Mr Sweetman's house. But if Whibley had been implicated in the crime in some way, why had he given the alarm and then done everything he could to help Gibson? Why leave the possibility of the man surviving and remembering everything that had happened and revealing the identity of the robber?

In the end, thought Frances, everything came back to Mr Whibley: the fine fellow whom everyone liked; the man who had been kindness itself to his mistresses and children; who had generously supported a worthy charity; the man who was so clever with wills and ledgers; the man who had in all probability embezzled money from his employer and had another man's life destroyed to cover his tracks; the man who, as his heart failed him and he felt the hand of death on his shoulder, and was asked to present his final set of accounts, realised that on the balance sheet of good and evil the business of his life was bankrupt and that nothing he could do would fool the great Auditor.

CHAPTER TWENTY-TWO

Thomas Whibley, thought Frances. What kind of man had he been? He was undoubtedly clever with law and finance though what other skills he might have had were a mystery. Was he kind, sociable or witty? Did his manner inspire trust? Was his generosity merely outward show to acquire a reputation in the eyes of the world, or was it a product of genuine feeling? Importantly, did he have a conscience? If he had embezzled funds from J. Finn Insurance, and then, in order to avoid discovery, removed Mr Sweetman by masterminding the robbery, probably with the connivance of the unsavoury Mr Minster, it looked as though he had done so with an easy mind. He had lived on, seemingly untroubled by remorse, for fourteen years, until Hubert Sweetman was released from prison, and came to him, not with any question about the robbery, but simply to discover the whereabouts of his family. What was it about this apparently innocuous enquiry that had so disturbed Mr Whibley? Why did he feel a sudden rush of guilt? Or was it not guilt at all, but fright? Was there something Sweetman had said which suggested to Whibley that retribution was on its way? Had Mr Sweetman unknowingly aroused memories of other crimes that Whibley had committed that Frances did not as yet know about?

Frances reviewed the career of Mr Whibley once more. The obituaries stated that he came from humble antecedents and when he first came to work for J. Finn Insurance in 1860, it was with only modest expectations. Later, he determined to better himself by study, undertaken in his own time, with the ambition of qualifying as an accountant. In 1866, Mr Whibley finally and successfully completed his studies, left J. Finn Insurance and went to work for Anderson and Walsh in a junior capacity. The books of that company, too, thought Frances, might well be found to require a close examination. Whibley, at thirty-five, was rising in the world, a man who had worked hard to achieve his position, worked harder to maintain it, and did not stint himself on amusements. The more she read about him and his career the more a picture emerged of a man who spent long hours at his desk, and whose achievements and standing were a product of toil and determination rather than innate brilliance. There were no tributes to him as a sociable man, he seemed to buy his pleasures rather than earn them. There were occasional mentions of his charitable interests, the foundling home to which he made regular donations, and a plan to establish a hospital for the aged poor that had not yet come to fruition. Were these genuinely selfless schemes, or were they also commercial transactions – the purchase of popularity, social acceptance and a place in heaven? He had not initially, thought Frances, been destined for great wealth, since his opportunities for extracting large sums from both firms were limited. The substantial and unexpected turnaround in his fortunes had happened on that fateful train ride.

Frances returned to the offices of the *Chronicle* to see if there was anything further she might learn about the chance that had made Mr Whibley a wealthy man. The *Chronicle* had lengthy reports on the accident, the inquest and official enquiry that had followed, but Frances was unable to learn a great deal more than she already knew. She wondered if there was a newspaper for Keymer or Brighton that might give more detailed information.

The section of the Brighton line where the collision had occurred was well known to suffer misty weather at all seasons of the year. The train had been approaching the station known as Keymer Junction, where the line passed over a steep embankment, when it ran into a patch of mist, and slowed down to five miles an hour. The stationmaster had sent warning messages by telegraph and the signalman had attempted to alert an approaching express, but neither he nor the signals were visible until it was too late. The driver of the express had seen the danger and made desperate attempts to throw the train into reverse to avoid an accident, but without success. The express was still going at some forty-five miles an hour when it plunged into the rear carriage of the slow train, which was badly crushed, left the rails, and toppled half way down the embankment. The engine of the express was thrown across the line and several of its carriages were smashed while others slid down the embankment. In all, four people were killed and twenty injured. As the shattered carriages came to rest, shocked passengers began to crawl from the debris and help free those who were trapped. The injured were carried to the station waiting rooms, where a clergyman offered comfort to the victims and ladies volunteered to act as nurses. The most extraordinary escape was that of Mr Draper, the conductor of the express, who, immediately before the impact, had just come out onto the platform of the front carriage. Draper was thrown bodily down the embankment, rolled down to the bottom and picked himself up, shaken but uninjured apart from a bruised forehead. He had at once given assistance to those in the rear carriage of the slow train, where a heavy fall of wood from the collapsing roof had caused serious injuries, and was praised for both his courage and quick thinking.

Company officials later brought up a special train from Brighton to take the injured, most of whom had suffered fractures, to a Sussex hospital.

As Frances wrote in her notebook, Mr Gillan appeared, always keen to see what she was about. 'Ah, the Brighton excursion accident,' he said. 'Nothing suspicious about that, though … or since you are reading about it, perhaps there was?'

'I don't think so,' said Frances, 'but the gentleman I would really like to speak to is Mr Draper, who must surely have a story to tell. Do I have to travel to Sussex to learn more, or are you able to enlighten me?'

'We do keep cuttings from other papers where they have Bayswater interest,' said Gillan. 'But come now, share and share alike, why are you so concerned with this?'

'I am trying to learn all I can about the late Mr Whibley, who was injured in the accident,' said Frances. 'Whether it would benefit either myself or my client I am not sure, but I have a feeling that he might be guilty of some of the crimes laid at Mr Sweetman's door.'

'Oho, now that sounds interesting!' cried Gillan. He hurried away and returned very soon with a folder of cuttings from *The Times*, the *Illustrated Police News* and the Sussex newspapers. 'Have you found Sweetman's son and daughter yet?' he asked.

'I am continuing my enquiries,' said Frances, carefully. She opened the folder and extracted the papers.

'Ah, so the answer is yes,' he declared triumphantly.

'I have said no such thing!' she retorted.

'But I can see that you have found something out. It will be a touching story I am sure.' He grinned.

'I can give you nothing for publication. Not, I suppose, that that will stop you from making it all up. May I ask you not to print anything on the subject?'

'Now, you know that's not your decision or even mine, but the editor.'

'The editor may only print what he is given,' said Frances. 'And an incautiously worded item in the newspapers now may harm my efforts, and then you will have no story at all. Oh!' she exclaimed, picking up a sheet of paper from the file. A few names were scribbled on it but this was not what had drawn her attention. Plain as it was, she knew it well. It was cheap paper used for rough notes, sold to offices by weight, and it was identical to the paper used for both the Bainiardus letter and the anonymous accusation against Mr Thorpe that Frances had received.

'Mr Gillan,' she said, 'do you happen to be acquainted with a Mr Alfred Thorpe of the West London Bank?'

Mr Gillan looked undeniably alarmed. 'Why do you ask?' he said sharply. 'What has he been saying?'

'Mr Thorpe, as you are obviously clearly aware, has had reason to complain about anonymous letters accusing him of unnamed irregularities. Some of these letters were sent to the police and one was sent to me. It was on paper identical to this sheet.'

'But that kind of cheap paper is all over London,' he protested.

'Not all have this uneven edge where the batch was imperfectly cut. What do you have to say?'

Mr Gillan capitulated. 'I should have known there is no fooling you,' he said ruefully. He glanced over his shoulder, pulled up a chair and sat down beside Frances. 'I'll tell you all about it, but you must promise it is not to go any further.'

'Really?' asked Frances. 'You surprise me. It sounds like a promising story. Will you not be publishing it in the *Chronicle*?'

Gillan sighed. 'You have me there.'

'I shall require a reciprocal promise.'

'Oh very well,' he said grudgingly. 'I promise to write nothing about the Sweetman boy and girl until you tell me. Yes, this is paper bought in bulk for our office use some years ago, and I took some of it home. My sister uses it for shopping lists and such like. Well, she's thirty now and single, and I suppose she felt that time was passing her by on the romance front, and whenever she spoke to Mr Thorpe at the bank he was nice and polite and she thought he was in love with her, but then she found out that he loved another. I didn't find out until too late that she had been sending those foolish letters. Anyhow, I was able to smooth it over, and she has since met a deliveryman who seems like a decent sort of fellow, so she has another interest now. I made sure that all the letters I could find had been destroyed, but I didn't know you had had one, too. There, that is all the story.'

'Not all,' said Frances. 'There is another letter I am interested in, signed Bainiardus. It uses the same paper and is in the same hand. Your sister's hand, but not, I think, her sentiments. I think *you* composed it and sent it here for publication. Of course in the *Chronicle* office your handwriting would be recognised, so you had to employ your sister as secretary.'

'Ah,' he said, 'what sharp eyes you do have, Miss Doughty. I can see there would be little point in my denying it. Well, you must admit it was a good story and it led to some very interesting correspondence.'

'And it terrified perfectly healthy people who rushed to see their doctors and wasted a great deal of time and expense,' said Frances sternly.

He shrugged. 'No real harm was done.'

Frances was not so sure of that.

When Mr Gillan had gone away to further enlighten the news-hungry population of Bayswater, Frances studied the folder of newspaper cuttings and read all about Mr Draper of Brighton, who was being touted as the hero of the hour. There was even an engraving from the *Illustrated Police News*, which loved to champion the achievements of the common man, showing Mr Draper rolling down the embankment, then leaping up energetically to rescue the injured from the crushed carriage. Mr Draper had made the most of his brief fame, describing in some detail what he had found. The rear coach of the train had been crushed to splinters, and the first thing he had seen when he looked in at what had once been a window was a very distressed and rather attractive young lady, trying vainly to move a portly gentleman who had been thrown on top of another, who she said was her husband. The portly gentleman was bleeding from a head wound and his leg was badly broken. He appeared to be unconscious. An elderly gentleman was also at the window calling out for assistance, saying that he was unhurt and begging that his sister, a lady of similar age, who was in a bad way, should be rescued quickly. The roof had come down in a great cascade of broken wood, and a younger man was on the other side of the carriage, out of immediate reach, trapped under its weight, his arm badly crushed and bleeding. He was groaning in pain and trying unsuccessfully to free himself. The elderly lady who sat opposite was buried under a heap of wood. She was clutching her chest and seemed dazed and confused. Draper saw at once that the whole structure was unstable and a further collapse was imminent. He managed to draw out the young woman who was sobbing but unhurt, and laid her to one side so she was out of danger. He then returned and at some risk to himself rescued the elderly lady. Another gentleman who had been in the next carriage then came to help, and the portly gentleman was brought out with considerable difficulty, but as they tried to reach the other occupants, a further shift in the unstable material brought down more shards of wood. Work had gone on for some time clearing the debris, and it was found that the elderly man, who had been unhurt by the initial impact, had died in the aftermath.

Draper, for all the acclaim that came his way, said he felt unhappy that he had not been able to save all the victims.

He thought that had he helped the elderly man out of the carriage before his sister, he might have saved them both, and this troubled him so much that his head had ached ever since the accident. Three days later, Draper suffered a fit, collapsed and died.

The inquest and detailed inquiry that followed concluded that the weather was at fault. All the railway officials had acted as they ought to have done, and no one was to blame. The cause of Mr Anderson's death was suffocation, to which the diseased state of his lungs had undoubtedly contributed. Mr Walsh had died after a splinter of wood had entered his throat. Whether Mr Anderson had gasped his last before or after Mr Walsh shed his last drops of blood, was impossible to determine.

Frances was now able, from the newspaper accounts, to establish where everyone had been seated in the fatal carriage. On the side nearest the rescuers, at the window seats, Mr Walsh had sat facing Mrs Anderson. Mr Anderson had sat beside his wife, facing Mr Whibley. The two occupants who had been most badly injured by the falling wood, Miss Walsh and Mr Elliott, had both sat on the far side, which had suffered the greatest damage.

There could be no doubt that the accident was unplanned and unforeseen, but Frances could not help wondering who, apart from Mr Whibley, had gained from the two deaths on that day, and in particular the fact that Mr Walsh was deemed to have died first? Was it possible that someone might have seized the chance of eliminating Mr Walsh?

Mrs Anderson financially had neither gained nor lost. She had been widowed possibly only a matter of months earlier than she might have been, given her husband's poor state of health, and had been left only those things that she already enjoyed.

Mr Elliott had gained a wealthy wife, but then again, only a few months earlier than he might otherwise have done.

Miss Walsh, Mr Walsh's elderly sister, had been badly injured. She had inherited an annuity from her brother's estate, but was no more comfortable after his death than she had been before.

As far as Frances could see, it was only Thomas Whibley who had truly gained by the accident, and gained very substantially in a way that he would never have done without it. When Mr Walsh had last been seen alive the only other occupants of the carriage were Whibley and Anderson, who were both unconscious, and Elliott, who had been trapped immobile under debris on the side furthest from Walsh. The other two people present who were uninjured were the railwayman Mr Draper, who could scarcely be considered a suspect, and the gentleman who had assisted him.

Inevitably, the newspaper listed only the names of the dead and injured and some of the railwaymen, but if as Draper had said the unnamed gentleman had come from the next carriage, there were really only two people he could have been, the close-mouthed chief clerk, Mr Richardson, and the son for whom he harboured ambitions. Frances had been thinking that the only person in the carriage who had any motive to hurry Mr Walsh to his end, and who knew about the reciprocal wills of Mr Anderson and Mr Walsh was Mr Whibley, who had not been able to take any action. She now perceived that one other person who might very well have known about the wills was the trusted chief clerk Mr Richardson, and he had an excellent motive for the business not to go to Mr Walsh's relatives. Frances resolved to interview him once more.

There was also, she reflected, one other living person who had been in the fatal carriage and whom she had not yet interviewed, and that was Emily Anderson, the future Mrs Elliott. It seemed unlikely that she had been in a position to observe what occurred since the heroic Mr Draper had removed her from the carriage soon after the accident, and while Mr Walsh was still alive, but all the same, Frances made a note to pay her a visit.

Her one final mission in the *Chronicle* offices that day was to examine everything the newspaper had published about the Bijou Theatre during the period when young Benjamin Sweetman had been working there. Since he had occupied such a minor position, and only the managers and performers were ever mentioned, it seemed unlikely that she would find any reference to him, however, she persevered, studying every notice advertising future performances and every review. In 1873, when Benjamin would have been twenty-one, she found that a play had been performed, the story, which was of no consequence, being about a lonely village in which there was an inn which was reputedly haunted. The piece was apparently comedic in nature, and involved various persons coming to the inn and being frightened away by pieces of white cloth being waved about on the end of broomsticks. The account in the *Chronicle* had been kind, since the performance was for charity and the actors all amateurs. Without actually saying whether the play was a good one or not, which rather suggested that it was not, the reviewer made generous remarks about the energy and enthusiasm of the players, one of whom represented a whistling post boy. Neither the character nor the actor, who, it was said, 'whistled very tunefully', were named, however the title of the play was *The Yeldon Mystery*.

Frances stared at this. It was probably not long afterwards that Benjamin had left his employment. Had he started a new life with better prospects under a new name? Was Mr Yeldon actually Benjamin Sweetman? Was that why he had grown such a large beard and coloured it red? There was also the milkmaid song, sung by the Finns' nursemaid Mary Ann, which was another connection with the Sweetmans and their time at the Bijou.

Frances recalled that when she had confronted Mr Yeldon about the Sanitas letter she had suggested she should call him by another name and he had been very alarmed. She had thought nothing of it at the time, but now she felt sure that when she had mentioned the name Sanitas, he had appeared to be almost relieved that it was the letter she wanted to discuss with him and not something else. Was that because he had feared she had caught him out in a far greater deception? If Mr Yeldon was indeed Benjamin Sweetman, however, Frances was unsure as to how she might prove it.

And then there was Mary. Mr Curtis had spoken of how devoted his cousins were to each other, and how sure he was that if one of them was found then that one would know where the other was. During the time that Mr Yeldon had been followed to see if he was purchasing foodstuffs for Mr Finn, he had not visited any young women or indeed any women at all. There were, thought Frances, four possibilities. The first was that he had not communicated with his sister during the time he was being followed. The second was that he had not visited her but had communicated with her by letter. The third was that she worked at one of the shops on the Grove, or for Dr Collin, whom he had visited. The fourth was that she was one of the women in the Finn household. The housemaid was too young, but Mrs Goswell, the cook, Mary Ann, the nursemaid, and Mrs Finn herself were all about the right age.

It was a delicate issue, and Frances was sensitive to the fact that the Sweetman children, if they were living under other names, must want to conceal their identities, so as not to be associated with a convicted felon. She must make it plain that she did not wish to expose them, only to beg them to see their father.

When Frances had completed her reading, she wrote a short note to Mr Yeldon saying that she understood that he had once been employed in an administrative capacity by the Bijou Theatre and she wished to speak to him in connection with this. The note delivered, she hastened at once to the offices of Anderson, Walsh and Whibley, only to discover that it was no longer trading under that name. A new and very highly polished brass plate announced that the business was now to be called Richardson & Son.

CHAPTER TWENTY-THREE

Frances walked in, her step brisk, her manner dignified. She brushed aside the enquiries of an obviously very junior person, who was so startled by her effrontery that it was several moments before he followed her. She knew her way and pushed open the door of what had once been Mr Whibley's office but was now, judging by the crisp new sign, the office of Mr F. Richardson. She was unsurprised to find that the occupant was Mr Richardson senior; in fact, she had already deduced that his son played as yet only a minor role in the business.

Richardson was at his desk, pen in hand, attending closely to a well-ordered pile of papers, but on hearing the door, he raised his head sharply and regarded Frances with the eyes of a very annoyed tortoise. 'There is clearly some mistake, Miss Doughty,' he declared. 'You have no appointment with me.'

'Thank you, but I need none,' she said, and sat down. The clerk she had earlier ignored now hovered in the doorway, unsure of how to deal with the intruder.

'I am a busy man. I have a great deal of business on hand and cannot see you now,' said Richardson, gesturing to the clerk. 'Please escort Miss Doughty from the building.'

Frances did not move. 'I am a busy woman and I have a murder to investigate – several in fact,' she said.

'Really, Miss Doughty,' said Richardson, more in dry scorn than irritation, 'I hope you have not come here to accuse me of murder.'

'Not at all, however, if you are offering to make a confession I will listen with interest.'

He put his pen down. 'Extraordinary!' he said.

'When we last spoke,' said Frances, 'you referred to the railway accident in which Mr Whibley was injured. There were details which you omitted from your description of the incident. In fact, virtually all of the details.'

'That was not, as I recall, the main topic of our conversation,' he said reasonably.

'Details that could be vital to my investigation and which I suspect you did not want me to know.'

Richardson hesitated, his expression moving from displeasure to hostility.

'Sir?' asked the clerk.

'Leave us,' said Richardson. The clerk vanished.

'Interesting,' said Frances. 'I take you to be a man who, given a choice, would prefer there to be a witness to the kind of conversation we are about to have, yet you choose not to.'

Richardson gave her a cold stare. 'I have nothing to hide,' he said sharply, 'but some things should remain private.'

'In the last few days,' said Frances, 'I have found some very full descriptions of the accident and accounts of the subsequent inquest and inquiry in the newspapers. I also questioned Mr Elliott, who has been quite forthcoming. In addition, I learned about the reciprocal wills of Mr Anderson and Mr Walsh. I am sure that a man in your position would have been well aware of the existence of those wills and the consequences should Mr Walsh predecease Mr Anderson.'

'Of course I was,' said Richardson, 'but the accident was simply that, an accident that no one could have predicted. I really can't imagine why you attach any significance to it.'

'I understand that you and your lady wife were travelling in the carriage that was immediately in front of the one that took the greatest impact. Can you confirm who was sharing the carriage with you?'

Richardson looked as if he was about to protest at being questioned, but then replied in a tone that suggested he was only doing so in order to draw the interview to a close as speedily as possible. 'My son, Roland. He was just fifteen at the time. And there were two ladies who were travelling together. We were shaken and bruised but fortunately none of us suffered serious consequences.'

'Did any of you get out and try to help the people in the carriage that had rolled down the embankment? The carriage with your associates in it?'

'The ladies did not, of course, climb down to the other carriage, but they offered to tend the injured. I told Roland to stay with his mother and went to see what I could do.'

'There was a conductor, a Mr Draper, who had been on the express and was thrown clear. He was first at the scene and he helped Mrs Anderson and Miss Walsh from the broken carriage. He said that after he had done this a gentleman came and helped him. I believe that gentleman was you.'

'Yes,' mused Richardson, as a scene that he would have preferred to forget was conjured up afresh before his eyes. 'I remember the railwayman who rescued the ladies.'

'What happened next?'

'We did what we could, but we had no tools, only our hands, and could not cut through the fallen wood. We tried to move Whibley first because he was lying on top of Mr Anderson. It was hard work, made more difficult as we could see how badly his leg was injured and we naturally did not want to exacerbate matters, but we succeeded at last, and brought him out and laid him down on the ground, then we went back for the others. Of course, by then it was too late.'

'When you lifted Mr Whibley out of the carriage was Mr Walsh still alive?'

'Yes, he was, in fact he tried to help us move Mr Whibley. He was almost seventy-five but very strong and active for his age.'

'So,' said Frances, trying to think about the timing of events, 'you and Mr Draper together brought Mr Whibley out, and then carried him a short distance away. How long did that take? How long was it before you were able to return to the carriage?'

'It's hard to say; it wasn't an easy task. At least a minute or perhaps two.'

'And what did you find when you looked in the carriage again?'

There was a short silence. Richardson rose, and went to a small side table where he poured a glass of water from a carafe. He offered some to Frances but she declined. He returned to the desk and stared into the glass, then took a small sip. 'This is not a pleasant subject, Miss Doughty,' he said. 'It is not one I choose to dwell on; rather I have tried to expunge it from my mind. Mr Walsh was a man for whom I had enormous admiration, and Mr Anderson was also someone for whom I entertained considerable respect. On that terrible day, I saw that both those excellent gentlemen were beyond our help. Please do not ask me to describe how I knew this! Mr Elliott, however, was calling out for assistance, so we did our best to move the wood that was trapping him and got him out.'

'Mr Anderson is said to have died from being crushed by Mr Whibley's weight, but according to both Mr Draper and yourself, Mr Walsh was unhurt by the accident. In fact he must have died in that brief space of time between your rescuing Mr Whibley and returning to the carriage.'

'Do you really imagine I don't know that?' said Richardson, and for the briefest of moments his torment and self-reproach were very apparent. He took a large gulp of water. 'Have you interviewed Draper?'

'Unfortunately that has not been possible,' said Frances. 'Mr Draper died suddenly a few days after the accident.'

'That is regrettable, but not entirely surprising,' said Richardson. 'I saw that he had suffered a serious blow to the head and I said he should get it tended to as soon as possible, but he laughed it off and said it was nothing.'

'Mr Draper thought it was a movement of the crushed carriage that brought more splinters down and killed Mr Walsh.'

'That was, I am sorry to say, a consequence of our removing Mr Whibley, but what else could we have done? We hoped that by doing so we might save Mr Anderson, and until Whibley was out we could not reach Elliott at all.'

'Mr Draper believed that had he pulled Mr Walsh out earlier he would have lived.'

'I can only agree.'

'Then why didn't you? He was seated right by the window; you could easily have reached him.'

'Yes, but Walsh wouldn't permit it, he was adamant that the injured should be taken out first.'

'What did he say?'

'After the ladies were brought out, Draper offered to help Mr Walsh next but he said something like "no, you must take this poor fellow first, his weight is on another man and will surely crush him to death." So I helped Draper pull Whibley out of the carriage while Mr Walsh somehow got behind him and pushed. As we carried Whibley away there was a terrible creaking noise and part of the roof fell down. That must have been when it happened. The next time I saw Walsh he was, sad to say, beyond help.'

Mr Draper, Frances mused, would, had he lived, have been the ideal independent observer, however, while the former Mrs Anderson could say nothing about what had happened inside the carriage after she left it, she had been within sight of it during the rescue of Mr Whibley and Mr Elliott, and might at least be able to confirm whether Mr Richardson's account of his actions was true or false. She determined to interview Mrs Elliott before asking Richardson any further questions about the accident.

'I assume that I may now return to my work?' he said, interpreting her thoughtful silence to mean that the interview was over.

'If I might ask you about another matter,' said Frances. 'Can you advise me whether Mr Whibley ever acted in a professional capacity for the late Mr Outram?'

Richardson gave her a look of extreme distaste. 'Is this regarding the peculiar and may I say unsupported assertions made by Mr Lathwal?'

'If you could just answer the question …'

'Oh very well,' he said, his manner brittle with ill-grace. 'Yes, Mr Whibley did deal with Mr Outram's property accounts. There is nothing very remarkable about that.'

'And his will?'

'I cannot assist you with any information on that point.'

'Did Mr Whibley ever advise his clients about wills?'

'It was a subject about which he was knowledgeable.'

'So he might have advised Mr Outram?'

'It is possible, of course, but I cannot say whether he did or not. I saw no such document, and I have already advised Mr Lathwal of this.'

'You were executor of Mr Whibley's will, though.'

'Yes, why should that be of importance?'

'I have been trying to discover what matters Mr Whibley had on his mind immediately before his death, shortly after his interview with Mr Sweetman. He was about to make some changes in his will, was he not?'

Richardson stared at her. 'What do you know about that?' he said suspiciously.

'Mr Elliott told me about Mr Whibley's intentions when I interviewed him.'

'I see.'

'Nothing was settled, and Mr Elliott went away to make some enquiries but when he returned he found that Mr Whibley had died. Do you know what Mr Whibley had in mind?'

'Well, he only hinted about it to me, but that was some time before he saw Sweetman.'

'Oh,' said Frances, surprised. 'He was thinking of changing his will *before* he had the meeting with Mr Sweetman?'

'Yes, about a week or so before. But nothing could be done until the other parties were consulted.'

'Other parties?' Frances enquired.

Richardson paused. 'It seems to me, Miss Doughty, that you do not know as much as I had supposed and I have already said too much. What did Mr Elliott tell you?'

'That Mr Whibley was thinking of establishing a charitable foundation that would bear his name. He was feeling very ill, and it may be that he sensed he did not have long to live. He was hoping to find a suitable property, and naturally consulted Mr Elliott.'

'Ah, that is a quite different circumstance,' said Richardson. 'Not, of course, incompatible with the matters which were previously on his mind, if he subsequently fell ill.'

'What was previously on his mind?' asked Frances.

'I am not sure if it would be advisable to mention it.'

'Why, was it something to the detriment of his reputation?'

'Not at all,' said Richardson hastily. 'No, it was a private rather than a business matter.'

'Another child about to be born out of wedlock, perhaps?' queried Frances.

'No, far from it, in fact – well I suppose it cannot harm him to say so – Mr Whibley was considering marriage.'

'Marriage?' exclaimed Frances. 'This is the first I knew of it. Was it a general desire to marry or was there a lady in mind?'

'I believe there was a very specific lady who was the object of his admiration, but he did not reveal her identity. I only know that they could not marry at once, as there was an obstacle of some kind, he did not say what. Given Mr Whibley's tastes,' he gave a regretful shake of the head, 'I rather suspected he was waiting for her to reach the age of majority so her parents could not intervene.'

❧

On her return home, Frances found a note from Mr Yeldon. That gentleman denied having ever worked at the Bijou Theatre and said he would not call on her, as there was no purpose in his so doing. Frances realised she had no alternative but to confront Yeldon face to face, and she would have to do so soon, as he was very shortly to depart with Mr Finn for a month's stay in Bath. She did not reply to the note, but composed another to Mrs Elliott, asking if she might call and speak to her. She thought she would have a better chance of obtaining an interview with the lady if she did not reveal her intention to revive the memory of the rail accident that had claimed her first husband's life.

❧

The next morning, at an hour when Frances knew that Mr Finn would be at his office, she appeared once again at the front door of the neat house in Hereford Road. The young maid opened the door, and when she saw and recognised Frances there was no doubt that the visit was unwelcome.

'I am here to see Mr Yeldon again,' said Frances, firmly. 'It is a matter of some importance.'

The maid looked unhappy and uncomfortable. 'Miss Doughty, I am very sorry, but Mr Yeldon has given strict orders that he is not at home to you. If I let you in I will lose my place.'

'Of course I would never put you in such a position,' said Frances. 'You are only doing your duty.' She bid the girl goodbye and turned away, having decided to walk around to the rear of the house and try the servants' entrance. It would not be the first time she had undertaken such a subterfuge.

The maid must have guessed what was in her mind, for she added, 'I am afraid all the servants have been told the same. You're not to be let in.'

Frances looked back at her. 'But he is in the house?'

'Not to you, Miss. But yes, he is here.'

What, thought Frances, would the daring Miss Dauntless have done in such a situation? Would she have donned a pair of alpinist's breeches, climbed up to the roof, knotted a length of rope around a chimney pot and swung herself in through a window? She glanced up and a curtain twitched. She was sure that the face behind it had a red beard.

'Perhaps you might take him a message from me,' she said.

'I don't know about that, Miss,' said the maid, cautiously.

'Have you been told to take him no messages?'

'No, he never mentioned that.'

'Well, then.' Frances drew out her notebook and pencil, and was just thinking what to write when she heard the sound of laughter. Mrs Finn and the nursemaid came down the stairs with the children, the nurse with the older child by the hand and Mrs Finn carrying the younger. She paused when she saw the maid at the door and, recognising Frances, came forward with a welcoming smile, handing the child to the nurse.

'Why Miss Doughty, how pleasant to see you again after our little meeting in Hyde Park. Do come in!'

The maid looked understandably alarmed.

'My business is actually with Mr Yeldon,' Frances explained, 'but he has declined to see me on account of being so very busy.'

'Oh, yes he is packing for the excursion to Bath. They are to go after luncheon tomorrow. But no matter, come in and see me. I shall be in need of company when my husband is away.'

Frances stepped into the hall and the maid started to scurry towards the stairs, no doubt with the intention of warning Mr Yeldon of what had occurred.

'I don't suppose,' said Frances, very quickly, 'I could trouble you for a glass of water?'

'Oh, that is no trouble at all,' said Mrs Finn. 'Lizzie, would you fetch a glass for Miss Doughty? Bring it to the parlour.'

The maid stopped mid-scurry, turned and went down to the kitchen with a glance at Frances, a little smile of admiration.

'I hope you don't mind,' said Frances, 'but I do need just a moment of conversation with Mr Yeldon, and since he is going away tomorrow this might be my last opportunity for some time.'

'I hope it is not something very shocking,' said Mrs Finn, with a worried expression.

'There is nothing affecting his honesty or reputation, it is just a private matter,' Frances reassured her.

Mrs Finn nodded. 'Mary Ann, could you take the children upstairs and ask Mr Yeldon to come to the parlour?'

'I had thought,' said Mrs Finn when they were settled, and Frances was sipping her water, 'that you had come to see me about the payment due.'

'I do not demand settlement quite so soon,' said Frances. 'But tell me, how is your husband's health? I have observed that he makes use of digestive mixtures and Apollinaris Water, which I know has a good reputation as a stomachic.'

'Oh yes, there are times when he looks quite ill and then he declares that nothing else will do,' said Mrs Finn. 'He says the bubbles settle his digestion. But I am so relieved and happy that he is taking my advice at last.'

Mr Yeldon appeared at the door, outwardly polite but with a face that did not conceal his fury.

'Miss Doughty says she has a business matter to discuss, so I will leave you,' said Mrs Finn, rising from her seat.

'It will take but a minute to conclude our business,' said Yeldon, coldly.

Mrs Finn, who either did not appreciate the valet's annoyance, or cared nothing about it, maintained an amiable countenance and left the room.

'How dare you come here!' said Yeldon, when the door had closed. 'I have nothing to say to you and suggest you leave at once.'

'Mr Yeldon, you really have nothing to fear,' said Frances, soothingly. 'I have no wish to expose your true identity. I know that you have your own reasons for secrecy and I am here for only one purpose, to ask you in the name of charity either to go and see your father, or at least to send him a message reassuring him that you and your sister are well and happy. It would mean so much to him.'

'This is ridiculous! A delusion!'

Frances hesitated. When she came to think about it, she actually had very little proof. 'So you were born with the surname Yeldon?'

'Of course I was!' he insisted.

'Then all you need to do is show me your birth certificate and I will admit my error and depart,' said Frances.

'I need prove nothing to you.'

'Humour me, Mr Yeldon. Only provide the certificate and I will trouble you no further.'

Frances well knew the look of someone deliberately creating delay, and Yeldon was showing all the signs. 'I cannot lay my hand on it at once,' he said.

'You surprise me,' said Frances. 'Do you keep your papers in such disorder?'

'Of course not, only –' he appeared to be casting about for a story.

'Oh please do not insult me by saying it has been mislaid or destroyed by accident,' Frances interjected. 'I have no patience with such crude attempts at evasion. Certificates are readily available at Somerset House and if you could confirm your full name and the year of your birth, it would take very little time for me to see whether or not you are listed in the registers. I could have that information today.'

He looked angry, as any man might be who had been caught out in a lie.

'You once worked at the Bijou Theatre, where for several years you were employed as a seller of tickets and distributor of notices. Before you left, you took the surname Yeldon after the title of a play that was performed there,' said Frances. 'I have recently spoken to a lady who appeared in amateur performances at the Bijou and she remembers you well.'

Yeldon said nothing.

'She also recalled you and your sister appearing in a variety programme in October 1866. Your performance consisted of whistling, and Mary sang a song about a girl who wanted to be a milkmaid, one that I believe she composed herself, a song that I have heard nowhere else except that Mrs Finn's nursemaid sings it to the children.'

He remained silent.

'You are Benjamin Sweetman,' said Frances.

'I admit nothing,' he said.

'But you do not deny it,' said Frances. 'I have been engaged by your father to find Benjamin and Mary, to bring him some comfort in the knowledge that his children are well and happy. I believe that he is innocent both of the crime for which he has served fourteen years in prison, and the murder of your mother. Can you not find it in your heart to see him? If you can, tell me and I will arrange a meeting.'

'Regarding Mr Sweetman,' said Yeldon, coldly, 'I have nothing in my heart. I will not see him or send him any message and I do not want you to mention me to him.'

'I promise I will not mention you by name,' said Frances. 'And your sister, Mary? Is she alive and well?'

He hesitated. 'I cannot speak of her.'

'But she is alive?'

He opened his mouth to speak but closed it again.

'Can your father expect a message from her?'

'No.'

'I have also been engaged by your cousin Mr Edward Curtis to enquire into the murder of your mother. It may be that the real culprit is someone she did not meet until after your father's conviction. If you have any information that could help me in that regard, I would be most grateful.'

'I can tell you nothing about that,' said Yeldon.

Alice Finn returned to the room and sensed at once that the interview had not been an amicable one. Yeldon said nothing to her, but turned on his heel and walked out.

'I hope you did not bring him bad news,' said Alice.

'I am not at all sure what I did bring him,' said Frances.

Mrs Finn handed her an envelope. 'Your payment,' she said. 'And I do hope that now business is done we can be friends. Please come for tea next week. Would Tuesday at three be convenient? We may walk in the park if the weather is fine.'

Frances said she would be delighted to take tea with Mrs Finn. Once home she wrote to Mr Sweetman by way of his nephew to inform him that his son was well and engaged in a respectable occupation, but did not wish to enter into any communication.

CHAPTER TWENTY-FOUR

Frances spent the afternoon dealing with correspondence and speaking to a young man brought to her by Sarah, after Tom spotted him following one of the ladies of the Bayswater Women's Suffrage Society. It emerged that the culprit was a newspaper correspondent who had been engaged not by the *Chronicle* but by their rival, who were a far less respectable organ of the press. He was to keep a close watch on the ladies in the hope of discovering any scandal that might arise from their behaviour. Had he observed them in a situation that might interest the readership, such as sitting on the lap of a bishop, or patronising a low beer-house, he was instructed to make a sketch of the event, which could be turned into an illustration for the moral instruction of those who amused themselves with such things. Despite his efforts, he had seen the ladies doing nothing more disgraceful than shopping, selling pamphlets and distributing handbills.

'If you make up stories I shall know who was responsible,' Frances advised him severely. 'Your editor will be in court, the paper will collapse and you will find yourself without an occupation. Don't imagine for a moment that I do not have the power to bring this about.'

The man, who looked hardly more than twenty and had already been admonished by Sarah, looked frightened enough to believe her. Before he left, he asked Frances if he could have an introduction to one of the ladies he had been following, who he thought was very pretty. Frances had Sarah throw him out.

A note arrived for Frances in the elegant script of Mr Elliott informing her that his wife was indisposed and unable to receive visitors, however, he promised that an interview would be arranged as soon as she was once more in good health. Frances was disappointed, but replied wishing the lady a speedy recovery.

The London edition of the *Chronicle* was freshly printed and, as usual, Frances examined it with care. The press had somehow learned of Mr Sweetman's release and had printed it as a 'stop-press' announcement, although fortunately it did not give his address. She was sure, however, that Mr Curtis' connection with Mr Sweetman was well known and that the young dentist might well find himself deluged with enquiries, to the great displeasure of his wife.

🌺

The following morning at ten, a cab drew up outside the apartments and Frances, peering out of the window, saw a now familiar and ungainly figure descend with some difficulty. Mr Finn, swaying with more effort than was usual even for him, laboured up the steps to the front door and was admitted. He was breathing hard as he reached the landing, and it was not entirely from the strain of his ascent. When Frances opened the door, she saw that his face was set and angry, and he appeared to be restraining his emotions only with some difficulty. She invited him in and offered him, not the straight-backed chair at the table, but an easy chair with a firm cushion at his back. This little consideration did not soften his mood.

She drew up a chair to face him and sat down. 'How may I help you?' she asked.

'Miss Doughty,' he said, with no trace of his previous ease and affability, 'I have been told some very upsetting news by my valet, and as a result I have also been obliged to ask some questions of my wife. I must inform you that my dear Alice, who has never previously kept any secrets from me, has just made a full confession of her transactions with you. I cannot find it in my heart to blame her as she did all with my welfare in mind, but I find it hard to credit that a supposedly respectable woman such as you claim to be, actually countenanced such a scheme and had the effrontery to charge a fee to carry it out. I have found that both my valet and I have been followed about the streets by your spies. You have even trailed me to the home of my friend and medical advisor, Mr Rustrum.' He took a large handkerchief from his pocket and drew it across his brow, which was bright red and glistening with sweat. 'May I take it that you have not as yet interrogated Mr Rustrum about my consultations with him?'

'I have not,' said Frances, omitting to mention that she had only been prevented from doing so because of that gentleman's absence from home.

He looked relieved. 'I also find that you entered my house, uninvited, while neither Alice nor I were present, somehow confusing my unfortunate housemaid into believing that you had permission to do so, which you did not, for the sole purpose of questioning my valet on the subject of a letter he wrote to the newspaper. During this questioning you had the audacity to accuse him of criminal libel.'

'That issue is now closed and there will be no charges,' said Frances. She was curious to know what Mr Finn thought about the fact that Mr Yeldon had made unpleasant insinuations against Mr Rustrum, but felt that, on balance, this was a question best left unaired.

'Not only that,' added Mr Finn, 'but I discover that you have committed the offence a second time and questioned Mr Yeldon again, this time about his family connections, which are no business of yours.'

'This is relevant to a private enquiry of mine,' said Frances, wondering what Mr Finn would have thought if she had arrived in the manner of Miss Dauntless by climbing through a window. 'I should reassure you that Mr Yeldon is not suspected of any crime or indeed any dishonourable act. I regret that I was obliged to interview him at your home, but I required a private location in which to do so, and he refused to come to me.'

'I am about to go away for a month, to Bath,' said Mr Finn, 'although since you are so well informed of my affairs I expect that you already know this.'

'I do,' said Frances, unashamedly.

'In my absence I wish you to have no contact of any kind, either by word or in writing, with any member of my family, not my wife or my children or my servants. You are not to come to my house, or see them in the street or in any public place, neither are you to enter my place of business, or speak to any of my employees or clients. In fact, you are not to discuss my affairs, either personal or business, with anyone. Is that clear?'

'Very clear,' said Frances.

'You are not the only private detective in London, and I have already made arrangements to safeguard both myself and my interests from your unwanted attentions while I am out of the capital. Any attempt by you to interfere further will be met with the full force of the law.' A brief spasm of discomfort crossed his face and he applied the handkerchief to his forehead once more.

'Are you unwell, Mr Finn?' asked Frances. 'May I offer you some refreshment – a cup of water, or tea, or a glass of sherry?'

He shook his head, thrust the handkerchief back into his pocket, and rubbed his considerable stomach. 'No, no, nothing. Now our business is done and I believe we understand each other. You are a very intelligent and interesting young woman, Miss Doughty, and I am only sorry that under the circumstances it is impossible for us to be friends, or indeed ever to see each other again.'

'I am sorry for that, too,' said Frances, 'but you have my good wishes for your health and that of your family.'

He nodded, and suddenly winced. Frances realised to her alarm that this was the expression of someone experiencing not some trivial discomfort, but concealing actual pain.

'Are you sure there is no assistance I can give you?' asked Frances.

He threw his head back and uttered some deep gasping breaths. 'Only – if I might sit here a minute or two longer before I depart.'

'Yes, of course. Do you wish me to send for your wife, or Mr Yeldon?'

'No,' he gave a dismissive wave of the hand, '– it is merely a recurrence of my old digestive trouble which I know will be cured when I take the mineral waters. I will rest quietly for a while until it eases and then I will return home.'

'You are leaving this afternoon, I believe?'

'Yes, immediately after luncheon.' Mr Finn did not look like a man about to enjoy luncheon. Frances watched him carefully, and during the next few minutes was relieved to see his obvious distress gradually abate.

Sarah returned from an errand and was understandably surprised to see Mr Finn in the parlour. He chuckled ruefully when he saw her. 'Ah, the strong pair of hands that Alice said was needed about our house. Your agents are everywhere, Miss Doughty, you will have spies in every house in Bayswater, eyes on every street corner. No one will be safe from you. Well, I am ready to depart, now, if you would be so kind as to order a cab.' He made to rise from the chair, but gave a sharp cry of pain and sat down again.

Frances leaped to her feet. 'Mr Finn, you are clearly unwell and I shall summon a doctor.'

'No!' he gasped, with a look of dreadful apprehension on his face. 'No, I beg you! I do not wish to see a doctor!'

'Then I will arrange for you to be conveyed straight home where your wife will no doubt know what is best to be done.'

He shook his head very emphatically. 'No, please,' he begged, 'I must not go home.' He was quite clearly undergoing more than the usual pain that might have been accounted for by indigestion and sweat was once again breaking out on his brow.

'Mr Finn,' said Frances sharply, 'you must know that I am the daughter of a chemist. I worked as his assistant for several years and made some study of medical books. I do not pretend to diagnose what is wrong with you, but you are in such great pain that I suspect it is a disorder of the bowels and not mere indigestion. You must see a doctor without delay.'

'Just let me rest and I will be better soon,' he insisted, panting with renewed agony.

Frances thought of all the things that could be ailing him: strangulated hernia; an obstruction of the intestines; an inflammation that might be serious enough to lead to peritonitis and death; even poison. 'Have you had these symptoms before?' she demanded.

'Yes, I have, and they passed with time, and I was well again. Just bring me a drink of water.'

Sarah gave Mr Finn a hard look, as if well used to men who refused to admit to any weakness and never saw their doctors when they should. She went to get the water, and he sipped it thirstily. Without asking permission, Sarah loosened Mr Finn's collar to ease his breathing, and since his face was the colour of a cooked lobster, dipped a cloth into cold water and bathed his forehead.

'I will send for Mrs Finn,' said Frances.

He shook his head. 'No, I cannot permit it; I do not want Alice to be alarmed.'

'Then what must I do? Shall I fetch Mr Yeldon? Is he at your house?'

'No, he is not; he is out purchasing some items needed for the – for the journey.' He laughed; a strange mirthless laugh that ended in a groan of pain.

'Do you know where he might be? What is he purchasing?'

'I don't know; I can't say.'

He was clearly unwilling rather than unable to tell Frances the nature of Mr Yeldon's errand, but despite her suspicions, this was not the moment to interrogate him further. 'Perhaps the eyes and ears I have everywhere will discover him,' she said dryly. 'Sarah, can you put Tom on the case? We'll need all his available men.'

Sarah nodded and hurried away.

Frances, left alone with the suffering Mr Finn, could do no more than continue to offer him sips of cold water and bathe his brow, which he found very refreshing, and gradually, his pain eased. 'I can't remain here long,' he said, 'I must travel to Bath this afternoon. Yeldon will take me there. I will have a note delivered to my home so that when he returns he will bring the luggage here in a cab.'

'Mr Finn, you are in no state to undertake a train journey to Bath or anywhere else,' said Frances. 'But I do not have charge of you, and I suppose I must leave that decision to Mr Yeldon and your own conscience. But I warn you, men have died from such foolishness as this.'

'Oh,' said Finn, with a strange smile, 'I can assure you, no man has ever died from what ails me.'

Sarah returned to say that Tom and his men were all over Bayswater trying to find Mr Yeldon. She looked at Mr Finn, who had lapsed into a state of exhaustion, but then had another sudden paroxysm. 'Where does it hurt?' she said.

'In my very soul!' he panted. Finn suddenly cried out, not in pain, but horror, and clutched at his lap. Rapidly spreading stains on his nether clothing showed that he had abruptly, and copiously, lost control of his bladder. 'Please, bring me a napkin,' he begged, 'anything!' Sarah went to get some towels, and the unfortunate man, almost in tears over his embarrassment, quickly covered his loins. 'I am so sorry, so very sorry,' he cried miserably. Frances could have nothing but compassion for him, and hoped that Mr Yeldon would be found soon and take charge of his master.

Suddenly Sarah snatched away one of the towels and examined the stains closely.

'What is it?' asked Frances. The towel was white, and she saw not the yellow moisture she might have expected but something more nearly pale pink, and odourless. Sarah's eyes narrowed suspiciously, and she abruptly leaned forward and put both her hands palm down on Mr Finn's belly. He flinched and tried to push her away but she ordered him to remain still and deftly moved her hands around, firmly but gently pressing all over. As she did so, she stared deep into Mr Finn's eyes and he quailed under her gaze, but could not look away. Sarah handed back the towel, and he took it from her and quickly thrust it between his legs. 'I'll take charge of this,' she said. 'Come with me.' He made no protest as she helped him to his feet, indeed, it seemed to Frances that he was clinging to Sarah for support, as if she was the only person that could save him.

'Is there anything I can do?' asked Frances.

'Yes, bring more towels and more sheets, and plenty of water,' said Sarah. 'So,' she said to Finn, 'how long have you had the pains?'

'All morning,' he groaned, 'I thought it was just indigestion.'

'Well, it'll get worse before it gets better,' said Sarah.

With the stricken man shuffling, they slowly proceeded to the little dressing room that was Sarah's bedroom.

'Sarah, do you know what is the matter with Mr Finn?' asked Frances.

'Yes,' said Sarah, bluntly, 'she's pregnant.'

She then disappeared into the room with her charge, and closed the door.

Frances dashed about, finding towels and sheets and pillows and anything she could think of, understanding that she had at last discovered the cause of Mr Finn's inability to reduce his weight.

By the time she appeared at the door of Sarah's room, Sarah had rolled up her sleeves and got her patient undressed and into bed. 'Don't you worry,' she said, 'I've seen it all before. I've helped nieces and nephews into the world and this won't be any different.'

The figure on the bed moaned in pain and stretched out a hand to Sarah, who took it in a rare moment of gentleness. 'It won't be long now,' she said.

The commotion inevitably brought the landlady, Mrs Embleton, to the door asking if anyone had been taken ill, and Frances was obliged to explain that she had received a visitor, a lady who was expecting to become a mother in the next week or two, and whose situation had become unexpectedly advanced. 'I know it is your rule that there are to be no children in the house,' she said, 'but I cannot move them without danger to either mother or child.'

Mrs Embleton was a sensible and sympathetic lady. The cries from the apartment told their own story and on the arrival of Mr Yeldon she assumed that the gentleman in a hurry was either a medical man or the father of the child. 'Of course I would not dream of asking a lady to leave in that circumstance,' she said, 'however, I do have the peace and quiet of my other tenants to consider.' She gave Frances a meaningful glance as if to say that she had already overstepped that mark quite some time ago.

'I will make arrangements for other accommodation as soon as possible,' Frances promised her. This was not the time for questions, but practical action. By the time Mr Finn, who she now understood to be Mary Sweetman, was cradling her new daughter in her arms, Frances had already secured the promise of clean lodgings, engaged a nursemaid, sent a note to Alice Finn explaining that her husband and his valet had departed for their journey a little earlier than planned, and secured their luggage, which she had correctly guessed included all the requirements for a lying in.

Mr Yeldon, pale but relieved, sat in the parlour clutching a medicinal glassful of brandy in trembling fingers. 'I am grateful,' he said, 'and I speak for my sister too I am sure, for all that you have done. But now we are both understandably afraid that you will reveal our secret to the world.'

'I assume that Mrs Finn does not know the truth?' asked Frances, who thought it very unlikely that the artless wife could have been a knowing confederate in the deception.

'No, she does not.'

'Were they married in church?'

'Yes, they were,' Yeldon admitted.

'It hardly needs me to advise you that your sister has contracted a marriage which is both illegal and invalid. However, I am not about to take steps to destroy Mrs Finn's happiness. I venture to say that many another woman has a worse husband. You know the situation and what you decide to do next I leave to your conscience.'

He gave a great exhalation of relief. 'I thank you for that.'

'I believe,' hinted Frances, 'that I am at least due an explanation of the events of the last fourteen years.'

He smiled wryly. 'Yes, I suppose we owe you that. After our father's betrayal – you know, I expect that he was about to abandon us to poverty and committed the robbery so he could escape abroad with a young woman who was his mistress – Mary and I knew that we must make our own way in the world. We had some silly childish dream of appearing on stage, which lasted just the one night, but as a result, I was offered employment as a useful boy to run errands. Mary was always the clever one, but saw that as a girl with too little education she might be reduced to domestic drudgery, so she put on my clothes, called herself John Johnson, and secured employment in an office. There she flourished. As time passed and her feminine form became more apparent, she found that by gaining flesh she could conceal her sex. In due course, she changed her name by legal means, using my birth certificate. She became old Mr Finn's trusted assistant, and was taken into his confidence. He had no male heir, only Alice, his great niece, and it was hinted the two should marry, adopting the family surname. Alice –' he paused. 'This is a delicate subject.'

'I am used to delicate subjects,' said Frances. 'Please be frank.'

'Alice was very gently brought up. The deception as to the nature of the relations between husband and wife was not difficult. And you have seen for yourself, they are very fond of each other. Alice is a kind, good-tempered young woman, and Mary has a genuine regard for her, as she would a sister. Once Mary was in a position to employ me, I joined her as a valet and have always sought to protect her identity.'

'And the children?' asked Frances.

'Ah, yes, the children,' said Yeldon. He took another sip of brandy. 'Mary, for all that she lives as a man, is a true woman in every regard. Sometimes she likes to attire herself in her feminine form. On occasions, she will even go out as a woman, usually escorted by me. Great secrecy is, of course, required. Everything necessary is kept in the study, which is locked at all times. A large cloak will conceal all until we are far from our usual haunts. Some years ago —' he paused. 'I believe and have always believed that Mary was most unwise — she went out alone as a female and encountered a man. They started an innocent conversation on the subject of healthful diet, on which he offered advice.'

'Mr Rustrum?' said Frances.

'The same. I do not pretend to understand how or why matters progressed as they did, but Mary found herself in a very unusual position. Alice had become concerned about her "husband's" excess weight, and Mary as Mr Finn had already told her that a doctor had said he could never be a father. So Mary appeared to yield to Alice's entreaties to take a cure, and went away to have the child, returning as you can imagine somewhat lighter, leaving the child with a nurse. In time, it was suggested that they adopt a child, Mary claiming that she was helping a cousin in hard circumstances and thus her own child was restored to its rightful family. I had hoped that Mary would be content with that, but the association with Mr Rustrum continued, much against my wishes, with a second result.'

'Mr Rustrum is seventy-four,' said Frances.

'Is he? I had thought him much younger. There might be something to the Pure Food diet after all. I cannot say that I like the man, but he has always done his duty by Mary and the children. In fact, I will need to write to him. He is waiting for us in Bath.'

'The letter you wrote under the name of Sanitas?' asked Frances. 'Please explain.'

'The idea of the letter was Mary's. Alice was always with the best of intentions suggesting that Mary should reduce her weight, but Mary was afraid that if she did, her female shape would become more apparent. She wanted to be able to comment to Alice with some authority on how her weight was not, as Alice insisted, dangerous. The first part of the letter was written at Mary's dictation, but I regret that an excess of emotion caused me to add the latter part. Mary had not long before revealed to me that she was once again in a condition inappropriate to her mode of life. I am afraid she was very annoyed with me when she read what was in the newspapers.'

'She has a beard,' Frances pointed out, 'and it appears to be genuine.'

'Yes, an excess of hair on her face appeared as her girth increased, and what another woman might have plucked out or concealed she decided to cultivate.'

'You must both have been very anxious when I commenced my enquiries,' said Frances.

'Oh, we were, very. We knew your reputation. When you had that first interview with Mary at the office, I came by quite deliberately on the pretext of delivering some invoices so I could look at you and be sure of recognising you in case you decided to follow us or intrude into the house.'

'There was a very unpleasant attack on Sarah and myself,' observed Frances, giving him a searching look.

'Attack?' he looked astounded. 'What attack was this?'

'With chloroform.'

'You don't think we were responsible, do you?' he exclaimed, horrified.

'You had the motive. Did you hire two men to try and silence us?'

'No!' he protested. 'I promise you!'

Frances was not entirely convinced, but reflected that if the Sweetmans had arranged the attack they now had no further motive for a second attempt.

'There is something I need to tell you,' said Frances. 'It is my belief that your father is a much maligned man. I do not think he committed the crime in 1866 and he denies absolutely that he was about to run away with another woman.'

'There *was* another woman,' said Yeldon, 'I know it because my mother met her and she told her all her story. She had letters in my father's handwriting.'

'Supposing I can prove what I say,' said Frances. 'Would you be willing to see him again?'

Yeldon thought for a while. 'I don't know,' he said.

'When did you last see your mother? Did she know of Mary's situation? What do you know of her associates in the last years of her life? I fear that someone she knew in that time was her murderer.'

'I told mother that Mary had gone into service with a lady and had accompanied her abroad. Mother suffered terrible poverty, and we could hardly support ourselves at first, let alone assist her, although we did what little we could. Then she told me that she was about to go into a workhouse and was thinking about visiting father in prison before she did, just to show him what he had brought her to, but in the end she didn't because her fortunes changed.'

'There was a man?' asked Frances.

'I believe so. Mother was ashamed of the connection; she didn't like to admit it as she was of course still married to father. She knew it was wrong, and in her own eyes she saw herself as little more than an unfortunate and unfit for decent society. When I told her that I was to go as valet to a gentleman, she understood of course that she could not come to the house. We did meet occasionally in the street or the park, but then that all ended. I saw her in the street once, and she looked very ashamed and hurried away. She didn't want to ruin my prospects by the association.'

'Did you ever learn the name of the man?' asked Frances, hopefully.

He shook his head. 'No. But I think he treated her brutally.'

CHAPTER TWENTY-FIVE

The next morning, Mary Sweetman, her brother Benjamin, baby daughter and a nursemaid were safely and discreetly conveyed to new lodgings in Bayswater. Mother and child were in robust good health, and it was strongly hinted that the girl would be christened Frances Sarah Finn, and that godparents would be wanted shortly.

Frances had received a message from Chas and Barstie to say that their examination of the books of J. Finn Insurance had produced some interesting results, and she called round to see them. In the short time since their return from the more desolate regions of Essex, the improvement in their situation had become still further apparent. Chas wore a sparkling ring on one plump finger and there was a pile of gold sovereigns on the desk, which Barstie was checking with his teeth before dropping them into a cash tin and making a note in a ledger.

'Well,' said Chas, patting the J. Finn Insurance account books approvingly, 'this is a clever individual and no mistake. I take my hat off to him. In fact, if I knew who he was I would offer him employment. Lawful employment, of course,' he added quickly. 'There is, as you know, an artistry in accounts, a beauty in books, a symmetry that inspires delight.' His recent prosperity had, Frances noticed, resulted in an expansion of his form, especially at the waistline, and he was chewing at a thick slice of roast ham, a repast wholly innocent of bread and potatoes. She wondered if he was banting.

'The only delight I have experienced in such things is the knowledge that the books balance to the farthing,' said Frances.

'As indeed, they should,' said Barstie very solemnly, closing the tin firmly and locking it.

'But sometimes,' Chas went on, 'in fact, all too often, they do not. Usually this is the error of a careless man, and can be found with a little work and a sharp eye. One can paper over such errors and make everything right and no harm done.'

'I take it this is not such a case?' asked Frances.

Chas stuffed the rest of the ham into his mouth and wiped his hands on a napkin. 'No, indeed, and I can see why Mr Sweetman was unable to find where the difficulty lay. First of all, he attributed the failure of the books to balance to simple mistakes, and secondly he assumed, incorrectly, that it was he who had made them.'

'Embezzlement,' said Barstie, darkly. 'Going back a year or more.'

'Do we know by whom?' asked Frances.

'No, but there are only two candidates, are there not?' said Chas. 'As you have told us, only two men other than Mr Sweetman had the skill to do it, old Mr Finn and Mr Whibley. All the writing done before Sweetman's arrest is his, and all that afterwards is Mr Finn's, but −' he opened the ledger at a page where a paper slip had been inserted, and prodded an entry, 'a great deal may be done with a razor blade and a delicate touch. Here and there, numbers have been changed, and done so carefully that all still appears to be in Sweetman's hand, but it is not. See for yourself.'

Frances peered at the writing, but at first could see nothing wrong. Barstie handed her a magnifying lens, and she looked again. Only then did it become clear that there had been some scraping away of ink and another figure substituted for the original.

'So subtle,' she said, 'and so insidious. There is no clue here as to who did this, and the changes having been made in a single digit I assume it is impossible to identify the writing.'

'Not necessarily so,' said Barstie. 'The one thing we can say is that having examples before us of the figure work of both Mr Sweetman and Mr Finn senior, it is neither of those gentlemen. Only supply us with examples of other hands to compare and we may achieve a result.'

Frances looked through the books, examining all the pages where paper slips had been inserted to show where the amendments had been made. 'Was the amount missing as I suggested?'

'It was,' said Chas, 'and very helpful, too, to know to the penny what we were looking for. Mr Sweetman knows his business.'

'Were you able to discover anything about J. Finn Insurance and Anderson, Walsh and Whibley that could have some bearing on this?'

'Only that J. Finn Insurance was less profitable in the last three years before the robbery than it ought to have been. That might have been due to Mr Whibley's activities once he got some knowledge of books, but it'll be hard to prove,' said Chas.

'And what about his uncle's firm? He was a partner and a qualified man by then, so he must have had a still better chance to extract funds.'

'I don't think so,' said Barstie. 'Old Mr Walsh was known for keeping a very close control of his affairs. If anything, admitting a new partner made the business more profitable still.'

'Are you suggesting that Mr Whibley abandoned his life of crime when he went to work for his uncle?' asked Frances.

'Men have been known to reform,' intimated Chas, with a smile. 'But if you ask me, he didn't. Impossible to estimate how much he spent on pleasure, but he strikes me as a man with a taste for the luxuries of life, and men like that don't give it up easily. He might not have been able to filch money from under the eyes of Mr Walsh, but he was well placed to inspire more confidence and enter into his own schemes outside the business.'

'We have been making a few enquiries amongst our associates,' said Barstie, 'and there have been some suggestions that if certain financial services were required, services that Mr Walsh might have frowned upon, the man to go to was Mr Whibley, who would undertake them privately for a fee.'

'What kind of services?' asked Frances.

'Oh, changing bad money into good, and he was said to have had a way with wills.'

'What stories he might have told me if he had lived,' said Frances. She wondered if there was anyone connected with the company she might have missed, any employee of J. Finn Insurance who was alive and not yet interviewed, and able to tell her more.

She turned through the pages and found a list of all the staff in 1866: John Finn, proprietor, Hubert Sweetman, manager,

Thomas Whibley, accounts clerk, Robert Browne, salesman, James Elliott and Frederick Minster, copy clerks, and one other name. Frances stabbed her finger at the page. 'The messenger boy,' she said. 'Timothy Wheelock.'

She had never heard or sought to know the first name of her solicitor's unpleasant clerk, but the coincidence of surname and age was too much. Thanking Chas and Barstie, she took the short walk to the office of Mr Rawsthorne.

A smart young junior clerk, his scrubbed cheeks as yet unacquainted with a razor, greeted Frances politely and assuming that she had come to see Mr Rawsthorne informed her that he was busy in a meeting. 'Thank you,' said Frances, 'but it is not Mr Rawsthorne I wish to see but Mr Wheelock.'

The clerk raised his eyebrows in surprise. Apparently no one ever came in there actually asking to see Mr Wheelock, which, thought Frances, was wholly understandable. In the last year, Mr Wheelock had made substantial progress in the business. He had once been confined to a small desk in the main office, which he had ringed about with as many cabinets as he could cram into the space, thus creating a domain into which few dared to intrude. He now had a room of his own, although admittedly, judging by the size of corner in which it lurked, a poky one that was hardly more than a cupboard. It did, however, have a sign on the door saying T. Wheelock. The clerk, after taking a moment or two to brace himself, went in, and soon emerged with a slightly pinker face than before, saying that Frances might enter.

Mr Wheelock inhabited his room like a predatory animal that liked to drag the carcasses of its prey into a hidden lair, where they were left to rot or mummify. The tiny space was lined with shelves, not an inch of which was wasted, those nearest the ceiling already acquiring thick veils of grey cobwebs, and there were cupboards with multitudes of drawers, some of which were stuffed so full of loose leaves and notebooks that they could not be closed. Everywhere was heaped with books, folders, and thick mounds of paper, and there were rusted iron weights holding down crumbling documents and unidentifiable things wrapped about with rags, some of them stabbed into wood with long pins. On the desk were battered pots crammed with pens and pencils, jars of ink, blotters and several knives. The room smelt of dust, ink, decaying paper, old parchment and unwashed clothing. Wheelock, who clearly neither expected nor wanted visitors, sat behind his desk on the only chair in the room. He snatched up a blackened knife and began to pick his teeth, staring at her suspiciously. 'What do you want with me?'

'Is your first name Timothy?' asked Frances

'No, it's Torquemada!' he sneered. 'What of it?'

'Did you once work as a messenger boy for J. Finn Insurance?'

He stuck the knife into the desktop and wiped his mouth with the back of an inky hand. 'Who wants to know? Who's been asking?'

'The only person who has been asking is me,' said Frances. 'I am looking into the robbery that took place in 1866, and speaking to everyone I can find who worked for J. Finn Insurance at the time, and can remember what happened.'

'Well, it wasn't me robbed the safe!' he snapped. 'And I don't know who did.'

'I'm quite sure you had no hand in it. You were only about nine and I doubt you were strong enough to hurt Mr Gibson.'

His eyes flickered back and forth, the sandy lashes crusted with dirt.

'*Is* your name Timothy? I could ask Mr Rawsthorne if you like …'

'You don't need to trouble him!' he growled.

'So it *was* you who worked at J. Finn Insurance in 1866? Your name is in the ledger.'

'Oh well, that proves it, doesn't it? Ledgers always tell the truth, we all know that!' He picked up a pencil and licked the end with an ink-stained tongue. 'I took messages, that was all, I didn't do anything else.'

Frances looked around the little room and suddenly realised that it was not so much a lair as a store. The miscellaneous nature of the material around her, the variety of age and type, some of it appearing to be no more than the kind of abandoned scrap that could not even be cleaned and re-used and anywhere else would have been considered as mere kindling, this was what Mr Wheelock had surrounded himself with, little pieces of the past, tucked away like old memories. He found, and quite probably even hunted, and retrieved things that others threw away, things that might, many years later, have value and significance. This, Frances realised, was the reason Mr Rawsthorne employed him. He was a man whose very nature it was to pick up and hoard information.

'But how well placed you were to know everything that happened in that office. Maybe things that even old Mr Finn didn't know.'

Wheelock gave a derisive laugh. 'Old Finn! He didn't know anything! You could have stolen his purse from under his nose and he wouldn't have seen it. He trusted people! Can you imagine that? A man in insurance and he *trusted* people. Hah! He was never going to be a rich man and he never was.'

'I have just had the books of the business examined, the ones for 1866 and just before, and there is evidence that someone was extracting money and making changes to cover it up. Mr Sweetman noticed that there was something amiss and was looking into it, but before he could discover where the fault lay he was arrested and charged with the robbery. Can you tell me anything about that?'

Wheelock dipped the pencil into a pot of thick dark ink and stirred it slowly, letting his nostrils hover over the liquid, sniffing it as a connoisseur would have appreciated a glass of good wine. 'Why would I tell you even if I knew?'

'I don't know,' said Frances, honestly. 'I don't know why you would tell me anything.'

'There's reasons not to say things, good reasons.'

'Well, you can hardly be afraid of Mr Whibley now can you? I'm fairly sure he was the man behind what happened.'

'Oh he was the *brainbox* all right.' He sucked his teeth noisily.

Frances wished she could sit down to think, but there was nothing in the room that might have been offered her in the way of comfort. Wheelock's tone had strongly suggested that while Whibley was the guiding intelligence, he had not worked alone. There must have been another man, more daring and more active, a man of violence. She walked around, gazing up at the shelves and their cascade of greasy papers. Messages, she thought, little messages between Whibley and the other man who wanted to keep the association secret and could not, therefore, be seen in conversation, all carried by a nine-year-old boy that no one saw as a danger, all thought to have been destroyed long ago.

'Mr Whibley had a confederate, didn't he?' she said. 'Someone you *are* afraid of. Someone cruel and ruthless. Here's what *I* think happened. Mr Whibley saw Sweetman worrying over the ledgers and realised that he was on the track of his crimes. So he decided to get him out of the way by having him arrested for robbery, and of course get a nice profit himself from the theft. So he established an alibi by going out to dine with the unimpeachable Mr Finn senior, but before he went out, he lent his keys to Mr Minster, a man very keen to get hold of money so he could realise his ambition of opening a public house. Mr Minster carried out the robbery. He expected to find the office empty, but instead he found Mr Gibson working late and silenced him. Then, as arranged, he went to the police and told them he had seen the office lights on at half past nine, so proving that the robbery had happened when Mr Whibley was out dining. Of course he wasn't to know that Mr Browne would really be there at a quarter past nine.'

Wheelock laughed. 'Oh you think you're very clever!' he said.

'But I'm right, you *are* afraid.'

He leaned back in his chair, licking ink from his fingers. 'Look, all I know is about the messages that I took back and forth. I didn't see what was in them, well, not if they were sealed up, I didn't.'

'And when the messages were thrown away? Put into a pile of kindling? Did you collect them up and read them then?'

He shrugged. 'Anyone might read anything.'

'But these messages – they were between Mr Whibley and Mr Minster?'

'Some – a few. But Whibley didn't trust Minster, hated him, said he was a roughhouse brute and a coward and good for nothing, and wanted rid of him, so he paid him off. You see, Whibley was clever with numbers, but that was *all* he was clever with. And Minster wasn't clever with anything. Anyhow, it can't have been Minster who did the robbery. Mr Browne saw the robber and he was sure it wasn't him.'

'But Mr Browne must have been mistaken. It was dark and he felt unwell. He thought at first he had seen Mr Gibson, which can't have been right either. A man doesn't take a blow like that to the head and then go walking about.' Frances stopped and suddenly recalled the unfortunate Mr Draper of the Brighton railway who had walked about with what proved after three days to be a fatal injury. 'Oh, but he does – he can!' she exclaimed. What had Matthew Gibson said – that his stricken brother had believed there was something of importance he wanted to say to Mr Browne? Supposing, thought Frances, that Mr Gibson, left lying on the floor after the savage attack, had got up, wandered about in a daze, seen Browne looking in and tried to speak to him, but in his confusion couldn't recall what it was he wanted to say, so turned, went back in and collapsed where he was found. Browne, she realised, had been right from the very beginning – he *had* seen Mr Gibson that night.

'Did the police never suspect Minster of the robbery?' asked Frances.

'Yes, until it turned out he was in a beer house till after nine.'

'Was he?'

'Any number of witnesses saw him there.'

'Then I'm not sure I understand.'

'That's because you don't know what I know,' said Wheelock with an inky grin.

'Then you had better tell me,' she demanded.

'I'm telling you nothing. And if you are half as clever as you think you are you should be able to work it out for yourself.'

Frances thought. She wished right that moment for nothing more than a big pot of tea, as it always seemed to help. 'You just said that Mr Whibley was clever with numbers and Mr Minster wasn't clever with anything. So … if Mr Whibley had a close confederate it must have been someone who was also clever, but with something that *he* wasn't good at. So who could it have been? Old Mr Finn and Sweetman were skilled in accounts. Mr Browne was a salesman but he had an alibi … oh, but there is another man who is also good at sales and dealing with people.'

She thought of Mr Elliott's manner with old Mrs Outram, a manner less of the professional advisor than a fawning suitor. Was he the smiling face that invited custom, the mask that concealed criminality, with Whibley as the man who manipulated the figures? 'Did Mr Elliott have an alibi for the robbery?'

'He had a good one for half past nine, that's for sure. The time when Minster said he saw the lights on. But he didn't have one for earlier.'

'But he and Whibley hardly knew each other.'

Wheelock pointed up at a shelf. 'There's a bundle of paper scraps up there that says different.'

'So it was Whibley and Elliott you ran the messages for?'

'That's all I can prove and it doesn't prove anything else. I know they were planning to set up a business together. Elliott as the charmer and Whibley as the brains.'

'So Minster wasn't anything more than a hired man?'

'That's all he was good for. Of course, he wouldn't have been so helpful, even for the money, if he'd known the rest of what was going on.'

'The rest?'

'Mrs Minster. You wouldn't think it now, but in those days she was pretty as a picture.' He leered.

❦

Frances went home, brewed enough tea for several people and drank it all. She could see it now, Whibley the financial man and Elliott with good looks and manners uniting their very different talents in a variety of moneymaking schemes. When Whibley had gone to work for his uncle, he had recommended Elliott for the first available vacancy. With his new skills and status, Whibley was set fair to make the fortune he had then spent on good living. Was it really Elliott who had broken into the office and battered Mr Gibson? If so, he was a very dangerous man. Had he also murdered Mr Walsh? If Whibley knew the importance of the reciprocal wills, then Elliott, his partner, would have known it also. Frances had deduced that Elliott, who had suffered a crushing injury of the left arm and been immobile, had been trapped in the railway carriage on the side farthest from where Mr Walsh was seated. Draper had said he saw Elliott trying to free himself, so the other arm had been free and uninjured, but even so, if Mr Walsh had stayed in his seat Elliott would not have been able to reach him. But Walsh had not stayed in his seat, he had moved about, helping to rescue his sister, and then, according to Richardson, getting behind Whibley to push, which would have placed him on the far side of the carriage from the rescuers, Elliott's side, where dagger-like splinters of wood were within reach. That must have been when the murderer took his chance.

She thought again of Mr Elliott's office, how pleasant and uncluttered it was, the lack of application and energy which she would have expected to see on the premises of any successful commercial firm. Was that because the day-to-day property work was only a shield for other illegal business? But Wheelock had been right, what could she prove? Scribbled notes did not make a conspiracy, and suppositions did not make a case.

Frances was thinking about making a second pot of tea when Sarah, who had been out helping Professor Pounder with the final arrangements for the ladies' calisthenics nights, returned and they discussed the new information and speculations.

'What about Mrs Elliott?' said Sarah. 'Did she not see anything?'

'Almost certainly not, since she was taken out of the carriage while Mr Walsh was still alive,' said Frances.

'But when they got married he might have told her all his secrets,' said Sarah, 'and she might not mind if he was rich.'

'I have never met the lady,' said Frances, 'so I am not sure what she minds. All I really know about her is that she is a devotee of Mr Rustrum's Pure Food Society. Dr Jilks told me that after the Sanitas letter was published several of his patients came to him very anxious, and Mr Elliott was one of them, worried about his wife's health. I was hoping to interview her but Mr Elliott wrote to me saying that she was unwell.' It was a moment or two before the implications of what Frances had said sank in.

'Perhaps we ought to call on Mrs Elliott,' said Sarah.

'Yes,' said Frances. 'I am not as confident about the state of her health as Dr Jilks was. Mr Elliott will be at the office still. Let us go and see his wife.'

CHAPTER TWENTY-SIX

The cab was not long in taking them to Mr Elliott's home in Westbourne Terrace, but even that short journey seemed too slow for Frances, whose anxiety and impatience grew with every passing moment. She could only hope and pray that her suspicions were unfounded and that she would find the lady to be in no danger. She mounted the front steps at a pace that would have startled any passer-by, and rang the bell. The door was answered by a competent looking maid of about twenty.

Frances presented her card. 'I regret that I do not have an appointment,' she said, 'but I am on an errand of great importance and must therefore appear to be impolite.'

The maid glanced at the card and returned it. 'Mr Elliott is at his office,' she said. 'You will have to call there, or leave a message.'

'It is not Mr Elliott I wish to see,' said Frances, 'but Mrs Elliott. I would not intrude upon her unless it was a matter that cannot possibly wait.'

The maid shook her head. 'I'm sorry, but Mrs Elliott is unwell and does not receive visitors. Master has ordered that she is to be kept very quiet. Good day.' She made to shut the door, but Sarah moved forward and it was suddenly impossible to do so.

'I am sorry to hear it,' said Frances. 'Please advise me how long Mrs Elliott has been unwell.'

'About three weeks,' replied the maid, struggling with the door. 'Please, I must ask you to leave. If you wish to visit in future you will need to write to Mr Elliott for an appointment.'

'Three weeks?' said Frances. 'You surprise me. Less than a fortnight ago I was assured that your mistress was in good health. Is Dr Jilks the family physician?'

'He is,' said the maid reluctantly.

'And has he called on Mrs Elliott?'

The girl hesitated and glanced up and down the street. 'I am not sure, Miss, that I ought to be talking to you about this.'

'We will talk either on the doorstep or in the hallway,' said Frances. 'Which would you prefer?'

The maid was clearly unsettled by both these options.

'*Has* Dr Jilks called in the last three weeks?'

The girl lowered her eyes and bit her lip. 'No, Miss.'

'What is the nature of Mrs Elliot's illness?'

'I am sure I don't know.'

'Perhaps Mr Elliott called in another more eminent man for a second opinion,' said Frances. 'Please let me know who has attended your mistress.'

There was a worried pause. 'All I know is that Mr Elliott went to see Dr Jilks for advice, and he said that Mistress is not to be moved.' She tried to close the door again, without success. Sarah wore an increasingly thunderous expression, and the girl began to look frightened.

'I want to see her,' said Frances.

'I really can't allow that, it's Master's express orders. He said any excitement might put her in danger.'

'I think that Mrs Elliott may already be in danger and I insist on seeing her,' said Frances.

The girl was trembling, but she found a shred of courage and drew herself up straight. 'And I have to insist you leave.'

'What will happen if I refuse?' asked Frances. 'Will you summon the police?'

'I –'

Frances narrowed her eyes. 'Oh I rather wish you would.'

The maid's only response was another attempt at closing the door, but Sarah stepped forward and shouldered her way in. Frances followed her into the hallway.

'Where is she?' Frances demanded.

The maid backed against the wall looking about her for help, but there was none in sight. She shook her head.

'Take me to her *now*.'

'I can't!' said the girl with a terrified sob in her voice. 'She's very bad, and she might die, and Master said he knew best what was to be done and I wasn't to interfere.'

Sarah took her firmly by the arm. 'Where is she?'

'Upstairs. Only it's kept locked, so she isn't disturbed. Master said if she was to be upset then it would kill her, and I'd be to blame!'

Sarah mounted the stairs, dragging the maid up with her. The girl stumbled up the steps, barely keeping her feet and wriggling ineffectually in the clasp of Sarah's substantial fist. There was a corridor on the upper landing with a series of doors. 'Which room?'

'The last one, but you can't go in!'

'We'll see about that.' Sarah marched up to the door, still with the maid in tow, and tried the handle. 'Who has the key?'

'Master has the key.'

'No one else?' A shake of the head. Sarah released the girl. 'Stand back,' she said. The maid hurried to the head of the stairs, but she was by now so thoroughly frightened that on encountering Frances she cowered away and made no attempt to escape. Sarah eyed the door as if it had done her a personal injury, then backed to the furthest width of the landing, and charged. It was a stout door, but not one designed for such an assault, and it burst open with a loud crash. The maid screamed.

From downstairs, there came the sound of distant exclamations as other servants heard the noise. 'We don't have long,' said Frances as she followed Sarah into the bedroom. Inside was dark and smelled foul; worse, far worse than the cells at Paddington Green. Frances crossed the room and drew back the curtains. There was a figure in the bed, a woman both young and old; young because she was probably little more than thirty but old because she had become shrunken and shrivelled. Her hair lay carelessly about, her face and hands were unwashed, and her lips were cracked and parched. At first, she seemed to be no more than a corpse, but then very slowly and with a great effort, the skull-like head turned towards Frances and she extended a thin hand, as if it was all she could do just to lift it off the counterpane.

It was not a sickroom, thought Frances. A sickroom has comforts, and medicines and water, and fragrances, and clean linen. This had none of those things. This was a prison, a torture chamber, a tomb.

There were footsteps on the stairs and a woman in house-keeper's attire with a bunch of keys at her waist appeared in the doorway. When she saw what lay within, she reeled back in horror, her hand clasped over her mouth. 'Who are you!' she gasped.

'I am Frances Doughty, private detective, and this is my associate Miss Smith. We have come to save Mrs Elliott,' said Frances. 'Do not attempt to stop us.'

'We should get a doctor,' said Sarah.

'No,' decided Frances. 'We need to remove her from the house.'

'You have no authority to do that!' said the housekeeper.

'But nevertheless we will,' said Frances.

Sarah began to wrap the sick woman in blankets as gently as she could, and lifted her off the bed.

'Bring us some water,' Frances ordered the maid, who immediately ran to comply.

The housekeeper folded her arms and stood stoutly in Sarah's way, then caught the look in her eye and stepped aside. 'Where are you taking Mrs Elliott?'

'Somewhere where her life may be saved,' said Frances. 'If she stays here she will die.'

The maid had returned with a water carafe and glass, and Frances took them. 'Come with us,' she said.

'But I never —'

'Listen to me,' said Frances, 'you have connived at an attempt to murder this lady, and if you try to deny it or run away things will go very badly for you. But if you come with me and explain that all you did was at the command of your master, which I am sure it was, then you may escape any penalty. Which is it to be?'

'If you go, you needn't come back!' said the housekeeper.

There was a soft moan from the figure being borne down the stairs. 'I'll come,' said the maid, who looked grateful to leave the house, 'but where are we going?'

'You'll see soon enough,' said Frances. She pulled the bedroom door shut and turned to the housekeeper. 'Any attempt to disturb what is in that room will be a serious crime,' she said.

The housekeeper bridled at this statement, but realising that she could not prevent what was happening, ran down the stairs and out of the front door, presumably to summon a policeman or a messenger. Frances had no doubt that Mr Elliott would receive the news in a matter of minutes and she hurried after Sarah. A surprised-looking woman wearing an apron and with flour on her arms, had arrived in the hallway and was staring about and wondering what was going on. 'Nothing to see,' growled Sarah, as she swept past.

Frances hailed a cab and Sarah carried her fragile burden inside, followed by Frances and the maid. 'I can't think when this poor lady last had a drink,' said Frances, offering the water. 'Be careful with her, not too much at first, just moisten her lips.'

'Where to?' said Sarah. 'Dr Jilks?'

'No, her husband might guess that we have taken her to her own doctor, and I want her safe from him. For the same reason we should not take her to Dr Collin as he might guess she is with my medical man, or to any physician nearby.' Frances thought for a moment, then she looked in her notebook for an address. 'Yes, I have it!' Quickly she gave the cabman orders to drive to the surgery of Dr Adair. 'Once she is safe we will go on. What is your name?' she asked the maid.

'Agnes.'

'Agnes, I mean to go next to Paddington Green police station where I hope you will be brave enough to tell Inspector Sharrock what has occurred.'

The maid began to tremble. 'Oh Miss, I don't want to talk to the police!'

'Don't worry,' Frances reassured her, 'you may leave most of the talking to me, but if you are questioned, you must tell the truth.'

On the way, Sarah tended to the feeble woman, a victim of the cruellest neglect, dropping careful trickles of reviving water into the dry mouth. At Dr Adair's house, Sarah carried the patient inside. Frances, while thinking it probable that Agnes would not run away if left alone, decided not to take the chance and remained with her, uttering encouraging words to strengthen and sustain the frightened girl and enable her to tell what she knew. A few minutes later Sarah emerged to confirm that the doctor was at home and was attending to Mrs Elliott as a matter of the direst emergency.

'Excellent,' said Frances. 'Please ask him to compose a letter reporting on her condition and when you have it, join us at Paddington Green.'

*

At the police station, Frances was expecting the desk sergeant to make some comment as she and Agnes approached, but instead he simply ordered them to wait and sent a constable to get Inspector Sharrock, who quickly came striding out of his office.

'Miss Doughty, I was about to send for you and your friend, and you have saved me half my trouble. Where is Miss Smith?'

'She will be here shortly,' said Frances.

'Then you have saved me all my trouble – come with me.' Sharrock waved to a constable. 'More chairs for the ladies!'

When they entered Sharrock's office Agnes gave a little gasp of terror and backed away, for Mr Elliott was seated there, his normally pleasant disposition notably absent. He leaped to his feet when he saw them and pointed at Frances. 'That is the person, Inspector! Miss Doughty! As I have told you, and as my servants will testify, she and her associate entered my house, broke down a door doing criminal damage, and kidnapped my wife, who is a very sick woman! And it seems that she has kidnapped my housemaid, too, or else she is a confederate in this.'

'Agnes is not my confederate, she has accompanied me at my express wish,' said Frances. 'I entered your house because I became suspicious that you were plotting your wife's death. Had I been able to see her and reassure myself that she was well, I would have departed. But your maid, acting under your strict instructions, informed me that Mrs Elliott was unable to receive any visitors. When I discovered that the unfortunate woman was being held under lock and key, I was sure enough of my suspicions to take action and ordered my assistant to break down the door. There we found Mrs Elliott in a state of the most appalling neglect and close to death. We removed her at once to a place where she will receive medical attention.'

'Where is my wife!' Elliott demanded, with a dangerous look.

'Where you cannot find her,' said Frances.

He turned to the cowering maid and shook a fist in front of her face. 'Agnes! Tell me where my wife is to be found! If you do not, you will be dismissed at once without a character!'

Agnes burst into tears. 'It was a doctor's house but I didn't take any note of the address!'

'His name?'

'I don't know!'

'She is a sick woman and should not have been moved,' said Elliott. 'If she dies it will be as a result of your disobedience and Miss Doughty's actions.'

'Who is Mrs Elliott's medical man?' asked Inspector Sharrock.

'Dr Jilks, but –'

'Then we can soon settle the matter by consulting him and determining the true nature of your wife's condition,' said Sharrock reasonably.

Elliott hesitated and Sharrock raised his eyebrows. 'Is there some difficulty about that?' said the Inspector.

'I do not believe that Dr Jilks or indeed any medical man has examined Mrs Elliott until now,' said Frances.

'Is that true?' said Sharrock. 'I find that hard to believe.'

'It was a very delicate matter,' said Elliott, defensively. 'I called on Dr Jilks to ask his advice and then I supervised the care of my wife. But this foolish action by Miss Doughty, and her damage to my home, is the reason I am here and I insist that you place her under arrest, and make her tell me where she has taken my wife.'

'Hmm,' said Inspector Sharrock, rubbing at the coarse bristles on his chin. 'What do you have to say, Miss Doughty?'

'Only two things,' said Frances. 'First of all, we should await the report of the doctor who currently has the care of Mrs Elliott, a report which my associate Miss Smith will bring us very shortly. Also, I suggest that you go to Mr Elliott's home and examine the room in which his wife was kept and you will then see clear evidence of the conditions in which she was allowed to remain.'

Sharrock nodded. 'That seems very sensible to me,' he said.

For a moment, Frances feared that Elliott had already gone back to his home and given orders that all evidence of his wife's cruel treatment be removed, but his expression showed that he had not. He had been so confident of his authority to have Frances arrested and so panicked by her actions that he had come straight to the police.

Elliott took a deep breath. 'Inspector,' he said, with forced calm, bravely attempting one of his charming smiles. 'Perhaps after all this has simply been a misunderstanding. I am sorry to have become so angry, but my servant sent me a message to say that Miss Doughty and her friend had entered my house, broken down a door and kidnapped my wife, so you can understand my feelings. I see now that I may have acted too hastily. You will appreciate that my sole concern is for the health of my wife, who sadly became a disciple of the Pure Food Society, which, as far as I can see, advocates eating nothing at all. I have done my best for her, but it is a very difficult case. My maid has been acting as nurse, but you can scarcely expect her to understand the true situation. I can see why the circumstances have aroused Miss Doughty's suspicions, but she is mistaken.' He smiled again. 'I realise now that foolish as her actions were, she did so with the best of intentions, but she was – confused. You are a married man, I assume, Inspector?'

'I am,' said Sharrock.

'Then you will know from your experience of the world how muddle-headed ladies who read sensational novels can sometimes over-excite themselves, and will often make mistakes. Really, Inspector,' he managed a chuckle, 'which one of us will you believe?'

'I have known Miss Doughty for quite a while now,' said Sharrock, with a perfectly straight face, 'and I am well aware of just how muddle-headed she can be.'

'Well, there you are,' said Elliott, his smile easing and broadening with relief. 'Under the circumstances, I am prepared to withdraw any charges I have made against Miss Doughty. I am even prepared to overlook the damage,' he added generously. 'I am being more than fair. Only return my dear wife to my care and we will close the matter and say all is done.'

'What do you say to that, Miss Doughty?' asked Sharrock.

'I must apologise for my muddle-headedness,' said Frances, 'and I would like to take this opportunity to clarify the situation so that I understand everything fully.'

'There really is no need –' Elliott objected.

'On the contrary,' interrupted Sharrock, 'I would like to hear what the lady has to say.'

'Well, if you insist,' said Elliott, trying to conceal his discomfiture.

They all seated themselves as comfortably as was possible in the cluttered office, Agnes still looking as if she would have liked to bolt, and carefully avoiding her employer's gaze.

'Mr Elliott,' said Frances, in her friendliest tone, 'I believe I am correct in saying that when you and the late Mr Whibley both worked for J. Finn Insurance, you conspired on a number of illegal financial schemes, including embezzling money from the company.'

'What?' he exclaimed, half rising from his seat. 'Inspector, this is slander! Whibley and I hardly knew each other at the time.'

'You exchanged many notes via a messenger boy called Timmy,' said Frances.

'A thoroughly dishonest child, no doubt in prison long ago.'

'He is now clerk to a solicitor,' said Frances, 'and he kept all your notes, even the ones you thought you had destroyed. He has them still. The thing is that when I realised that you and Mr Whibley worked as a partnership, and that what he knew you also knew and what benefitted one also benefitted the other, then a number of things which were previously mysterious became clear.'

'Inspector, are you going to listen to this nonsense?' demanded Elliott.

'Oh yes,' said Sharrock, settling back in his chair and stretching out his legs under the desk, a look of pleasurable anticipation on his face, 'and you will, too.'

'But Mr Sweetman started to notice that something was amiss with the account books,' Frances continued. 'He didn't suspect wrongdoing, in fact he thought he had made some errors and was trying to trace them and put them to rights. He told no one, but I think his agitated manner gave him away, so you and Whibley conspired to have him removed and disgraced before he could discover what you had both done. You planned a robbery for which Mr Sweetman would be blamed. I think Mr Whibley paid Mr Minster to say he had seen the lights on at half past nine, a time when he and Mr Finn senior were dining at a club. That is why you left the gas burning when you left the office after the burglary, to support Mr Minster's story. You, too, conveniently established an alibi for that hour. You could not have anticipated that Mr Browne would be passing the office a quarter of an hour earlier. However, the two reports were near enough that they were not incompatible. It wasn't until later, when some of Mr Gibson's memory returned, that the time of the robbery was established as even earlier, before nine o'clock, a time for which Mr Minster and Mr Whibley both had alibis, but you did not. But by then the case had already been made against Mr Sweetman, strengthened by the finding of Mr Gibson's pocket book at his house. You were, I understand, the only employee of J. Finn Insurance not to visit the stricken Mr Gibson. You dared not, in case it jogged his memory and he recalled that you were his attacker.'

'Miss Doughty, you may not be aware that the burglar entered the building and opened the safe with company keys,' protested Elliott. 'I did not have a set, Sweetman did.'

'We only have Mr Whibley's word that he had his keys on his person that night,' said Frances. 'How simple just to lend them to you. The next morning he was first in the office and found Mr Gibson. Mr Whibley was not by nature a violent man. He was very shocked by what he saw and did his best to help an injured colleague. But he had the presence of mind to take Mr Gibson's pocket book. He went to see Mr Sweetman the next day at his home, ostensibly for a private conversation about the crime, but actually to leave the pocket book there.'

'These are just words, Inspector,' said Elliott, 'the unsubstantiated accusations of an hysterical female. I do not believe there is one fragment of actual proof.'

'The expert gentlemen who have examined the books of J. Finn Insurance have uncovered evidence of tampering,' said Frances. 'They have not as yet identified the hand that made the changes to the figures, except they are sure that it was neither Mr Sweetman nor Mr Finn senior, but if they were to be supplied with examples of suspects' handwriting they could do so.'

The expression of alarm on Elliott's face told Frances all that she needed to know.

'I believe they will find that while the financial acumen behind the scheme was in all probability Mr Whibley's, the beautifully neat, almost imperceptible amendments were carried out by the skilled hand of Mr Elliott. It is also my belief that the attempt to recover and presumably destroy the old books of J. Finn Insurance was made either by Mr Elliott or his confederates, prompted by my asking questions.'

At that moment, Sarah appeared at the door of the office, and gave Elliott a look that might have shrivelled a man with a less hardened carapace. 'Doctor says she'll live, but it wasn't a moment too soon,' she said. 'The lady has started to talk and she has an interesting story to tell.' She handed Sharrock a letter.

'My wife is extremely ill and easily confused,' said Elliott. 'Her mind wanders and she imagines things. It is a sad case.'

Sharrock said nothing and read the letter. 'I have here a report from the doctor who currently has her under his care. A reliable man in his profession, and not I think prone to strange imaginings.'

Elliott darted forward and made to snatch the letter, but Sharrock held it out of his reach.

'I have a right to see it!' exclaimed Elliott.

'You will, all in good time,' said Sharrock. He rose, went to the door, and summoned a constable. 'Miss Doughty,' he said, 'you have made some very interesting allegations against Mr Elliott, with regard to the burglaries and the fraud, but as matters currently stand we have no real proof that what you say is true.'

'There you are! What did I say?' said Elliott triumphantly.

'That situation may of course change as we make our enquiries. In the meantime, James Elliott I am placing you under arrest on suspicion of the attempted murder of your wife.'

Elliott gasped. 'This is outrageous! I demand to see my solicitor at once.'

'Take him away,' said Sharrock.

Once Mr Elliott, protesting loudly, had been removed to the cells and a constable had been dispatched to examine the supposed sickroom, Sharrock sat down and faced Frances,

Sarah and Agnes. 'You may well be right, Miss Doughty, and he strikes me as a very nasty piece of work, but I'm sorry to say we have a very poor case,' he said. 'I doubt we'll make the burglary charge stick, and even his handwriting on the books may not be enough. He can always claim he was acting under the instructions of another more knowledgeable man and didn't know the nature of what he was asked to do. We can interview Mr Minster, of course, but will he confess to aiding and abetting? I don't think so. As to that business with the wife, he'll claim she doesn't know what she's saying and bring any number of experts to agree with him. He could well wriggle out of that one as well.'

Frances thought to mention the forged will, but decided not to, as strictly it was only evidence against Mrs and not Mr Minster. She wondered how much Mrs Minster knew, and recalled Mr Wheelock's revelation that the lady had once been considered a beauty and had been in an intimate association with one of the conspirators. Had she been Elliott's and not Whibley's paramour? It was hard to tell how old Mrs Minster was, but it was very possible that at the time of the robbery she had been about twenty. Could she have been the woman who had gone to Mrs Sweetman claiming to be her husband's mistress, spinning her a false tale of infidelity and a planned flight, with the object of dissuading her from supporting her husband with an alibi?

'Now then, young lady,' said Sharrock to Agnes. 'What do you have to say for yourself?'

Agnes dabbed her eyes. 'I only did what I was told to do,' she said.

'Of course you did, and who shall blame you for obeying your master?' said Sharrock, robustly.

'And the room was kept dark, so I never really saw how bad she was. Master always said that what he was doing was for the best. He said she shouldn't have too much food as it made her ill and upset her. In the last day she never had any water either.'

'And no medicine of any kind?'

'No. Only the chloroform.'

'Chloroform?' exclaimed Sharrock.

'Yes, he got me to buy it for him. The chemist wasn't sure if he should sell it to me, but I said it was to get grease spots off clothes, so he let me have an ounce.'

'And did Mr Elliott actually use it on her or did you?'

'I never saw him use it, and I know I didn't. He said it was just there in case she got agitated. Maybe he changed his mind and threw it away, because the next time I looked the bottle had gone.'

Sharrock pulled open a drawer of his desk and after a quick rummage, removed the chloroform bottle that Frances had delivered to him after the attack and placed it on the desk. 'Was this it?'

Agnes blinked in surprise, as if he had been a conjuror producing a dove from a hat. She peered at the bottle. 'I can't be sure, but it does look very like it.'

'Would you be able to show me the shop where it was purchased and the assistant who sold it to you?'

'Yes, I would.'

'Because the chloroform in this very bottle was used in a serious attack on Miss Doughty and Miss Smith. We traced it to a chemists shop. It was an unusual purchase and the assistant remembers it was sold to a young woman.'

'I didn't know what he wanted it for, I swear it!' said Agnes, looking as if she was about to cry again.

'Of course you didn't,' said Sharrock, with what he hoped was an encouraging smile.

'Have you found the man who ran away?' asked Frances.

'Oh yes, his friend gave him up, and we have them both in the cells now, but neither of them seem able to identify who hired them.'

'They might be more forthcoming if they see that Mr Elliott has been arrested,' said Frances. 'He may have hired the same two desperate characters to burgle the offices of J. Finn Insurance. It is only a shame that we have no firm evidence against him for the murders he has undoubtedly committed.'

'Murders?' gasped Agnes.

'That's a new one on me,' said Sharrock.

'I believe, although I cannot prove it, that Mr Elliott killed Mr Walsh of Anderson, Walsh and Whibley about eight years ago.

It was a death that seemed only to benefit Mr Whibley, who thereby inherited all the business, but now I know that he and Elliott were working in association, I can see that the legacy gave the pair of them free access to some rich opportunities. And if Mr Elliott is guilty of the burglary committed in 1866, then he is also guilty of the murder of the clerk Mr Gibson, who died of his injuries less than a year after the crime. He may even have strangled Mrs Sweetman to keep her quiet.'

'But why would he want to murder own his wife, where's the motive for that?' asked Sharrock.

'To supplant her with another,' said Frances. 'A newly widowed and wealthy lady advanced in years. A lady very susceptible to the flattery of a younger man. A lady whose death soon after the wedding would not arouse suspicion in view of her age.'

'And that lady would be?'

'Mrs Outram. Her husband, who was a dedicated vegetarian and man of property, died very recently aged ninety-two. I think Mr Whibley also had his eye on that prize, but whether she had her eye on him may be another matter. He did reveal not long before his death that he was considering marriage. And Mr Whibley would never have married for youth and beauty. Youth and beauty were things he could buy. I think he connived with Mrs Outram to conceal the fact that her husband had recently made a new will leaving a substantial part of his fortune to the cause of vegetarianism, and hoped that the lady would be grateful enough to marry him.'

'Mr Whibley seems to have had his fingers in a great many underhand things,' said Sharrock. 'Once you put it all together, it's surprising he didn't leave a bigger fortune. He couldn't have spent it all on good living.'

'He was a shrewd man, thinking he would enjoy a longer life than he did,' said Frances. 'Somewhere there is a private bank account that only he could draw upon, in the name of a charity, perhaps, a phantom establishment.' She thought for a moment. 'He was said to have been establishing a new scheme, a hospital for the aged poor. If that can be found then the money will go to the genuine charity that was his residuary legatee.'

CHAPTER TWENTY-SEVEN

rances later learned that the two would-be kidnappers, on being told that Elliott was behind bars and likely to remain so, miraculously regained their memory of the fact that it was he who had hired them to carry out the chloroform attack, and burgle the offices of J. Finn Insurance.

Monday, 14 February brought something that made Sarah laugh, although Frances was unable to see the humour in it: a new edition of the Miss Dauntless stories, *A Mystery for Miss Dauntless*. It appeared that the intrepid lady detective had been faced with a puzzle she was unable to solve, the identity of an admirer who had sent her a greetings card on St Valentine's Day.

That afternoon, Inspector Sharrock sent for Frances. Although he did not reveal the purpose of the request, she complied at once, not without some apprehension that this might be a clumsy attempt at matchmaking. This worry was not relieved when she found a young gentleman sitting in Sharrock's office, who looked about as pleased to see her as she was to see him. 'Allow me to introduce you,' said the Inspector with a grin, 'Miss Frances Doughty, the bane of the criminal classes of Bayswater, and Mr Jacob Pennyforth, former valet to the late Mr Whibley.'

Mr Pennyforth, who was clutching a hat rather more tightly than seemed advisable, jumped to his feet and made an awkward little bow. 'Miss Doughty, I am very pleased to make your acquaintance, and must apologise to you most humbly for my failure to respond to your many enquiries. I can assure you that I had the best of reasons, but all the same it must have seemed terribly impolite.'

'Well, since you are here now, I am content to put that difficulty behind us,' said Frances.

'Mr Pennyforth came to see me this morning with a very interesting tale,' said Sharrock.

'And I owe it to you to tell you all,' said the valet, perching on his chair once more. Pennyforth told Frances that he recalled very well the last occasion on which Mr Elliott had spoken to Mr Whibley; it was on the afternoon of Tuesday, 11 January. Mr Whibley had departed for the office as usual that morning but had unexpectedly returned early. He had not looked ill, but was clearly very anxious and sent a note to Mr Elliott saying he wanted to see him at once. Elliott had arrived soon afterwards. Since Pennyforth was not in the room to hear it, he knew nothing of the subject of their meeting, but he was sure from the tone of the voices that had filtered through the door that it could not have been an amicable discussion on the subject of finding a suitable property for a deserving charity. The exchange had become heated on both sides, and after Elliott left, Whibley had been visibly distraught.

Later that day, Whibley called Pennyforth into his study and a most unusual conversation had ensued. Whibley confessed to Pennyforth that he had not been a good man all of his life, but there were some things that he would not countenance, and now he found that those very things had been done by another man for his advantage, and that for some years he had, without knowing it, been living on money tainted by blood. Whibley gave Pennyforth a key to a drawer in his desk, saying that in the event of his death, Pennyforth was to unlock the drawer in which he would find a packet. He should remove the packet and deliver it unopened to the person whose name was written on it. On no account and on no pretext should he return to the house or have anything to do with Mr Elliott, who was a very dangerous man.

Immediately after Whibley's death, Pennyforth had opened the safe as directed, and found the packet, which bore the name Hubert Sweetman. He did not have Mr Sweetman's address, but took the packet into his charge, determining to make enquiries. He had then left the house and gone to live with his sister, who was the landlady of an inn outside London. The terrible weather that had descended shortly afterwards, cutting off London from outlying towns had prevented Pennyforth from making any enquiries, and by the time it was possible for him to carry out

Mr Whibley's instructions, he learned that Mr Sweetman had been arrested for the murder of his wife. Under the circumstances, he had thought it prudent to wait and see how that situation was resolved. He had recently read in the newspapers that Mr Sweetman had been released, but still did not know where he was residing, or indeed whether he was in danger of re-arrest. Unsure of what to do, he had eventually decided to approach the police. He had, he said, only dared to come forward because he had learned that Mr Elliott was under arrest.

That morning, Mr Sweetman and Mr Pennyforth had met at the home of Mr Curtis in the presence of Inspector Sharrock, and the packet was delivered and opened. It was found to contain banknotes to the value of two thousand pounds and a letter.

'Mr Sweetman, it has to be said to his eternal credit,' said Sharrock, 'was horrified by the sight of the money. He felt sure it was the proceeds of crime and categorically refused to accept it. Whether it is even his is in some doubt, since it ought by rights to be a part of Mr Whibley's estate and go to charity. When I mentioned this to Mr Sweetman he seemed perfectly content with that arrangement.'

'And the letter?' asked Frances. 'Did Mr Whibley explain his actions?'

Sharrock handed the document to Frances. 'I don't know how you do it, Miss Doughty, I really don't,' he said. 'Anyhow, I think you deserve to see this for yourself.'

Mr Whibley's letter was a full confession to masterminding the burglary at J. Finn Insurance, although he revealed that the actual crime was carried out by Mr Elliott. He was adamant that at the time Elliott had convinced him that Mr Gibson's injuries had been accidental, although Frances felt it was very much a matter of Whibley choosing to believe what was best for his conscience. She sensed a certain relish in Whibley's revelation that Mr Minster had been paid to give them an alibi and keep his mouth shut, and that a will had been forged in the name of Mrs Minster in case anyone should wonder how her husband acquired a large sum of money so shortly after a robbery. Whibley had felt no qualms about implicating Sweetman in the robbery since Elliott had told him that Sweetman was a villain who ill-treated his wife

– a lady who Whibley admitted admiring – and deserved all that came to him. After Sweetman's arrest, Whibley volunteered to examine the company books, and told Mr Finn senior that small sums were missing and had probably been stolen by Sweetman, but advised him that for the sake of the company's reputation no further action should be taken.

Whibley had thought very little about Sweetman's fate in the intervening years and was unaware that he had been released early until he arrived at the office asking about his family. Worried that Sweetman might press for his conviction to be re-examined, and that he might inflict further cruelties on his wife, Whibley arranged to meet Elliott to discuss the potential problem. To his astonishment, Elliott had suggested they remove Sweetman in a more permanent way than previously and when Whibley objected, simply laughed and commented that he had not been so squeamish about Gibson and Walsh. It was only then, Whibley claimed, that the full horror of what had been done in his name became apparent. He demanded to know if Sweetman really had been the villainous creature Elliott had represented him to be and found that Elliott could not even recall having made that statement.

Mr Pennyforth squirmed in his seat. 'I – er – I believe I heard the names Sweetman, Gibson and Walsh spoken during their conversation. They were talking very loudly at that point.'

'Why do you think Mr Elliott killed Mrs Sweetman?' asked Frances. 'Was she trying to have her husband exonerated?'

'Oh, Elliott didn't kill Mrs Sweetman,' said Sharrock. 'Quite impossible. The marks on her neck showed an even pressure with two thumbs. His left arm is all but useless. However, we'll get him for Gibson now at least. As you see, Mr Whibley was very careful to start his letter by saying that he believed himself to be dying, and had it witnessed by two servants, though I doubt very much that they were allowed to see the contents. Minster will have some questions to answer, although he might get lenient treatment if he comes clean about his being an accessory to Elliott.'

'I think if you offered the same leniency to Mrs Minster she might have a tale to tell,' said Frances, seeing that Whibley's letter had removed any suspicion against that lady in respect of the forged will.

'She might, but she can't give evidence against her husband,' said Sharrock.

'No, but she can give evidence against Mr Elliott,' said Frances.

Next morning Frances was once again called to Paddington Green, where Mrs Minster was sitting in the Inspector's office stubbornly refusing to make a statement. 'She says the only person she will speak to is you,' said Sharrock resignedly. 'I'm starting to think lady police might be a good idea after all — just to interview women and children of course.'

'Leave us alone together for a few minutes and then bring Mr Elliott in; the sight of him might concentrate her mind,' said Frances.

Mrs Minster, twisting a ragged kerchief in her hands, was red-faced and angry. 'What will I do?' she said. 'They've told Fred he won't go to prison if he talks, so what good would it do me to say anything?'

'It's Mr Elliott they really want, not either of you,' said Frances. 'You were his mistress, weren't you, at the time of the robbery?'

She gave a sour grin. 'He has a way with him; he still does. Good-looking, and that smile would melt the most faithful heart. I was young and I'd not been married long, but I knew it was a mistake. Minster was never any good to me.'

'And he asked you to go to Mrs Sweetman and pretend to be her husband's mistress. Why did you do that?'

She looked amazed. 'How do you know about that?'

'I know,' said Frances, although of course it had just been a good guess.

'He said that he could help get me free of Fred. He said that Sweetman was the robber and had half-killed Mr Gibson, but his wife was standing by him and was going to give him a false alibi so he was going to get away with it, and I had to tell her I was his mistress so she would see him for what he was. He had a letter in Sweetman's writing, something ordinary from the office, but he blotted out some of the words and changed others so it could read like something different. I was to show it to her as proof. In the end the poor woman was so upset she hardly read the letter, but she saw it was in his hand.'

'But he didn't help free you of your husband,' said Frances.

'No, well I had the children soon after, twin boys, and he wasn't happy about that. They died a year later, and I thought it would all be all right then, but when I asked him, he said he was moving up in the world and couldn't get involved in anything like that. Then I saw him with Mrs Sweetman. He tried to tell me there was nothing to suspect, but I knew what was going on.'

'Would you be prepared to tell all that to the Inspector?' asked Frances. 'Mr Elliott is an evil and heartless man. He deserves prison at the very least.'

'Oh, you don't know the half of it!' she burst out.

'I don't?'

Mrs Minster shook her head. 'Everything he says is a lie, every promise he makes he never means to keep! He made me think he cared something for me but the only person he cares about is himself!' So strong was her emotion that her twisting of the kerchief ripped the fabric apart.

The door opened and Sharrock entered bringing with him Elliott, who was in handcuffs. The prisoner was understandably startled to see the two women in the room, and it was unclear which of them he was less pleased to see. 'Mrs Minster, I understand you might have something to say to this gentleman,' said Sharrock.

'Annie —' said Elliott, making a good recovery and adopting one of his practised smiles.

'Don't you "Annie" me!' cried Mrs Minster, jumping up to face him. 'Not after what you've done; and what you made me do! You told me your wife was going to die! You told me you would see to my divorcing Fred! You told me we could be married at last! I should have killed you before I believed a word you said!' She flew at him, and he did his best to defend himself, but it took all of Sharrock's strength to drag her away, though not before she had left two neat thumbprints on Elliott's throat.

❧

'Well,' said Sharrock, after everyone was calmer and he had taken Mrs Minster's statement and charged her with the murder of Mrs Sweetman, 'we have concluded our case. It seems that Mrs Minster was sent by Mr Elliott to see Mrs Sweetman to discover her intentions following the release of her husband, where she found the lady to be in a forgiving mood. She had had some hard years, and considered that as Mr Sweetman had served his time, she was willing to put the past behind her and see if they could be reconciled. Mrs Minster told her that she had already got back with Mr Sweetman and they were going to make a life together, but Mrs Sweetman was not as gullible as she had once been, and said that she would only believe it if she heard it from her husband's own lips. That was when things turned bad. They argued and Mrs Minster thinks that in the heat of the moment she let something slip that told Mrs Sweetman she had been duped all along. And I think Mrs Minster saw that she, too, was a fool and a dupe. She claims she can't remember what happened, but the next thing she knew Mrs Sweetman was dead.'

'I hope she will not hang,' said Frances.

'Not if she helps us hang Elliott, I shall do my best about that,' said Sharrock.

❦

It was not very often that Frances had nothing but good news to tell, but that afternoon she wrote to Edward Curtis to advise him that the murderer of Mrs Sweetman had been unmasked, and it was only a matter of time before charges were made regarding the 1866 robbery and attack on Mr Gibson. His uncle had been entirely exonerated. She also wrote to Benjamin and Mary Sweetman, who were still in their lodgings and caring for a thriving child, telling them that their father had been proven innocent of all charges, and it would also be shown that the accusation that he had had a mistress had been a lie. In both letters she suggested that if a reconciliation was to take place she would be happy to act as an intermediary. How the family might resolve the question of the unusual ménage of Mr and Mrs Finn was an issue she did not address and about which she had no intention of enquiring. She received letters of gratitude from all parties, with the news that Mr Curtis would make the arrangements for the family to be reunited.

Two weeks later, Mr Curtis paid her a visit, and while he still looked strained, the pressing anxiety was gone. 'Miss Doughty, I must thank you from the bottom of my heart for all you have done for my uncle. He is now far happier than he could ever have anticipated! Not only is he a free man with no stain on his character, but he and my cousins have now met and a more touching scene could not be imagined.'

'I hope they are well and prospering,' said Frances.

'Oh, they have been doing very well indeed,' said Curtis. 'It seems that Benjamin has for a number of years been personal valet to a business gentleman, and Mary is nursemaid to the three beautiful children of a young widowed lady. However, the widow has decided to settle abroad and it is all arranged that Benjamin, Mary and my uncle will form part of her household there. I think it is for the best, as there will always be those who, while it can be proven that the name of Sweetman is without blame, will not choose to believe it.'

'I think that is a very wise course of action and I wish them all every good fortune,' said Frances.

Mr Curtis sighed. 'Would that we were all as happy in life!' he exclaimed, suddenly.

'Indeed,' said Frances. There was a silence. 'Is there something I can assist you with?' she asked.

'Well, yes,' he admitted, 'although …' he added cautiously, 'it is a very delicate matter and one requiring the utmost secrecy and discretion.'

'I am often called upon to deal with matters of that nature,' said Frances. 'If you wish to engage my services please let me know what you require. Your secrets will be quite safe.'

He smiled with relief. 'I had hoped you would say that,' he said. 'You know of course that my wife, Ethel, is very much my senior and has two children of her own.'

'So I understand.' Frances waited while he hesitated, trying to choose the best way of expressing what was clearly causing him some embarrassment.

'We are not well-matched and in fact we spend very little time in each other's company. Before we were married, she had for many years been a patient and a friend of Mr Cowan, who, as you recall, left the practice to me. He did so on the condition that I married Ethel, and gave a home to the children. As far as society is aware, Ethel was a widow when we married, but, in fact, she was not; she was a spinster.'

'Ah,' said Frances. 'I think I understand. Mr Cowan was providing for his own natural offspring. But I do not see what it is that you would like me to do. Do you suspect your wife of infidelity?'

'Oh no! Not at all!' he exclaimed. 'You have never seen Ethel and she is not exactly – er – and in any case she has no interest at all in – in –'

'I see.'

'Whereas of course I am still a young man.' He blushed.

'Are you saying that you have taken a mistress? Is that the difficulty?'

'No, no,' he said, alarmed at the suggestion. 'You will appreciate, Miss Doughty, that in my profession reputation and respectability are everything. After all, I administer nitrous oxide gas to ladies in my surgery and they must be able to regard me with complete trust.'

'Of course.'

'And it would be wrong of me to have any association with women of a certain class; the consequences to my position in respectable society would be appalling.'

'I agree. That is very wise of you,' said Frances approvingly.

'What I was thinking, Miss Doughty,' he explained, 'is that what I really require is occasional intimate conversation with a lady, a young lady of impeccable character, who knows how to keep secrets, and can be discreet.'

Frances stared at him. He seemed to take her silence as encouragement for he gave an unnaturally bright smile, and slid his hand across the table until his fingertips were within an inch of hers. 'There are hotels,' he continued, 'not in Bayswater of course, but very comfortable, elegant hotels, where –'

Frances rose to her feet. 'Not another word, Mr Curtis; not one more word. Yes, I can keep secrets and be discreet. I will, therefore, not reveal to any of your friends or patients what has transpired here. In fact, I will do my best to forget that you have ever spoken to me in this way. Go home. Treat your wife with respect. Never come back here again.'

He nodded. Nothing more was said and he made a hasty exit.

Frances found that her heart was thudding with fury. She made tea, and it calmed her. What would Miss Dauntless have done she wondered? That indomitable lady would surely have taken a horsewhip to a man who insulted her in such a fashion. As she sipped her tea, she read again the story of Miss Dauntless and the Valentine's card. The author did not reveal what Miss Dauntless thought about the card, whether she was pleased or discomfited by its arrival, only that she was curious as to the identity of the sender, wondering if it was a gentleman she already knew, but who had not yet made his intentions known, or an as yet unsuspected admirer. Frances wondered whether the sender felt genuine love for Miss Dauntless or had other, baser motives. Given the lady's unusual mode of life, she thought the latter to be more likely. Was this the lot of the lady detective? Miss Dauntless undoubtedly had many loyal friends, but would she ever know the warmth of manly affection?

On an impulse, Frances went to her father's desk and took out the packet of family papers, which included the marriage certificate of her parents; the mother who had deserted her when she was three and the father who had neglected her thereafter. Frances had known the close and fond attachment of her late brother Frederick, the sincere kindness of her Uncle Cornelius, and the fierce unswerving devotion of Sarah, but not, she reflected, that elusive and indescribable thing, true love. She re-read the certificate, which showed that Rosetta Ann Martin married William Henry Doughty on 10 January 1855, both being of full age. Her mother's father was James Cornelius Martin, bookseller, deceased, and her father's father was Henry Doughty, apothecary. She had previously neglected to pay any attention to the witnesses at the wedding and now saw that they were Miss Maude Doughty, her father's sister, and one other, a Miss Louise Salter. Frances had never met this lady or even heard her name. Was she a friend, relative or neighbour? If she could be found, might she know something about Frances' mother? Frances folded the papers and put them away. Her uncle must have attended the wedding, and she could ask him about Miss Salter, but she did not yet feel ready to do so.

Frances was pleased that the Sweetman family had resolved their peculiar situation. In the next few weeks, as February and its snows disappeared to be replaced by a showery but warmer March, she learned that the business of J. Finn Insurance was being sold, and the house in Hereford Road offered for rent at a good price. The classes conducted by Sarah at Professor Pounder's establishment to enable Bayswater ladies to take healthful exercise had proved to be a success, while the Professor was busy training the police on how best to apprehend and immobilise criminals. One evening he held a demonstration of his talents at Westbourne Hall, to which Frances was invited. Sarah distributed handbills and Inspector Sharrock and as many constables as he could spare, as well as the Kilburn police, were in attendance.

'Stout fellow,' said Sharrock, approvingly. 'Are those two making it a match?'

'I don't believe so,' said Frances.

'*You* could do a lot worse,' he hinted.

'Inspector, please stop trying to find me a husband.'

'Hmph! Well, all right then,' he said reluctantly, 'I suppose when you *do* get wed the crime rate in these parts will go up, so it wouldn't really be in my interests would it?'

'There are less law-abiding parts of London than Bayswater,' Frances pointed out, 'so you have little to complain of.'

'Oh no? Well it doesn't matter to those up top how many criminals I put away, there's always crimes that don't ever get solved and they want to know why.'

Frances had often wondered about other detectives and their unsolved cases, but of course, she thought, the police must also feel frustrated in a similar way. 'Do you remember the murder of Mr Sidebottom the moneylender?' she said, recalling that Miss Gilbert and Miss John had suggested she might try to solve it when she had a moment to spare. 'I believe there were altogether too many people who would have profited by his removal. Did you ever find the person responsible?'

'No, never, and it's too late now, even for you. Mind, whoever killed him was a benefactor. It would have been a pity to stretch a desperate man's neck for it.'

'Could it not have been Mr Hatfield, the man who stole money from the Bijou?' asked Frances. 'I was talking to a lady who performed there and she said he must have owed Sidebottom money because they were seen talking – although she did think that he couldn't have done it because he was short and Mr Sidebottom tall.'

'He couldn't have done it because he had an alibi,' said Sharrock. 'Sidebottom was still alive when he was found, so we knew when he was stabbed almost to the minute. As to how tall or short the killer was that doesn't matter – Sidebottom was knifed in the throat but he could easily have been bending down to talk to someone shorter. He was lured into that mews, I'm sure of it, probably by someone offering to pay off a debt. I thought it was one of the dairymen who worked round where the murder was done. We talked to all of them but we didn't get anywhere.'

'Why a dairyman?' asked Frances.

'The constable who was called to the scene heard Sidebottom's last words before he pegged out. He said "dairyman" or some such; the constable swore it sounded more like "dairymaid" but that can't have been right because there weren't any maids working there.'

Frances thought of a brother and sister trying to protect their distraught mother, the girl in the costume of a dairymaid offering – what? – money she did not have, or even her virtue, to pay the debt; arranging an assignation, the man leaning down perhaps for a kiss, and not seeing the knife in the darkness.

A brother and sister who had had more than one reason to protect their true identities thereafter. Which one had wielded the knife – the girl alone, or her brother creeping out of the shadows? 'As you say,' agreed Frances, 'that is a mystery I will never solve.'

✽ END ✽

Author's Note

Daniel Lambert (1770–1809) weighed over fifty-two stone at the time of his death, when he held the record of heaviest man in the world.

Bainiardus was an abbot who held lands with springs of water in the area now known as Bayswater and after whom it is named.

The character of Mr Lathwal is inspired by, but in no way intended to represent, Mohandas K. Gandhi, who started the Bayswater branch of the Vegetarian Society in 1891.

William Banting's *Letter on Corpulence Addressed to the Public* was first published in 1863. He died at the age of eighty-one in 1878.

The mid-January frost of 1881 was widely reported in the newspapers. Fifteen degrees Fahrenheit is -9.55 Celsius.

The idea of the affinity of fat with water and the treatment of obesity by drinking less, as well as the experiment of feeding doves on butter, is in *Obesity or Excessive Corpulence* from the French of Dancel translated by M.A. Barrett (Toronto, W.C. Chewett, 1864) available at www.archive.org.

The Bijou Theatre was at No. 21 Archer Street (now No. 291 Westbourne Grove) and was hired out to amateur companies for charitable performances. The variety nights are the author's invention. It closed down in the 1870s and efforts to turn it into a skating rink were abandoned. It was later refurbished and renamed the Twentieth-Century Theatre, and remains open today.

The Car of Juggernaut was a Hindu temple car. The expression was used colloquially to mean an unstoppable force.

The Photographic Society regularly exhibited their latest innovations at the gallery of the Watercolour Society in Pall Mall. On 4 January 1881, *The Times* reported on the ability of the new art to capture a sharp image of a train travelling at sixty miles per hour.

On Chloroform and Other Anaesthetics by Dr John Snow was published in 1858. For more information about the action of chloroform read the author's *Chloroform: The Quest for Oblivion*.

The Forfeiture Act of 1870 abolished the rule whereby the property of a convicted felon was forfeit to the Crown.

The accident described in Chapter Twenty-Two was based on an actual disaster that happened on the Brighton line on 23 December 1899. A Mr Draper was one of the victims.

Until the Married Women's Property Act of 1870 property inherited by a married woman became the property of her husband.

ABOUT THE AUTHOR

Linda Stratmann is a former chemist's dispenser and civil servant who now writes full-time. She lives in Walthamstow, London.

ALSO BY THE AUTHOR

Chloroform: The Quest for Oblivion
Cruel Deeds and Dreadful Calamities: The Illustrated Police News
1864–1938
Essex Murders
Gloucestershire Murders
Greater London Murders: 33 True Stories of
Revenge, Jealousy, Greed & Lust
Kent Murders
Middlesex Murders
More Essex Murders
Notorious Blasted Rascal: Colonel Charteris and the Servant
Girl's Revenge
The Crooks Who Conned Millions: True Stories of Fraudsters
and Charlatans
Whiteley's Folly: The Life and Death of a Salesman
The Marquess of Queensberry: Wilde's Nemesis

In the Frances Doughty Mystery Series

The Poisonous Seed: A Frances Doughty Mystery
The Daughters of Gentlemen: A Frances Doughty Mystery
A Case of Doubtful Death: A Frances Doughty Mystery

Visit our website and discover thousands of
other History Press books.

www.thehistorypress.co.uk